D1644805

About the Author

Marian Murphy lives in Wicklow with her husband and two young sons. She works as a social worker in Dublin and has been writing for the past three years.

Her first novel, *Take 2*, was published by Poolbeg last year, and she is currently working on her third.

Also by Marian Murphy

Take 2

MILLIONS!

MARIAN MURPHY

POOLBEG

Published 2001
by Poolbeg Press Ltd
123 Grange Hill, Baldoyle,
Dublin 13, Ireland
E-mail: poolbeg@poolbeg.com
www.poolbeg.com

© Marian Murphy 2001

Typesetting, layout, design © Poolbeg Group Services Ltd.

The moral right of the author has been asserted.

3 5 7 9 10 8 6 4 2

A catalogue record for this book is available from the British Library.

ISBN 1 84223 036 0

Typeset by Patricia Hope in Palatino 10/14

Printed and bound by
Omnia Books Ltd, Glasgow

Acknowledgements

I'll keep it brief.

I've had such great support from family and friends since the publication of my first novel, *Take 2*, that I'm almost afraid to thank anyone by name lest I leave out someone who really should be mentioned – but here goes!

Liam first, of course, and our boys, Luke and Michael, who didn't complain much (wonder why?) when I locked myself in the study for extended periods . . .

Dad, who did the catering for the launch of *Take 2*, and The Winding Stair Bookshop on Ormond Quay, who generously provided the great venue . . .

Those who attended the launch, helping to make it a brilliant night . . .

My friends and colleagues in SJH who gave me such a warm welcome back. Special mention for Sinéad (she won't want it!) who read both manuscripts . . .

Eileen Casey and my friends in the writing group . . .

Irene, Mary and Eilis, and Bernadette, my "special advisor" (!) . . .

The other Mary, whose rose grows on my wall, reminding me . . .

And of course all in Poolbeg, particularly Gaye Shortland, my editor.

Many thanks, everyone!

And, having said I'll keep it brief, I can't finish without thanking all of you who let me know that you enjoyed *Take 2*. Hope you like *Millions!*

Marian

For Liam, Luke and Michael

Chapter One

"It's just not worth it!" Colette said as she came flying into the office just after ten. She sat down quickly at her desk, threw her bag into the drawer and reached for the in-tray, glancing over her shoulder.

"You're safe," Maeve said from her desk across the room. "She's in a meeting."

Colette sighed. "Just as well," she said. "Bad enough being late without having to explain it to Her Grace."

Maeve gave a sympathetic smile as she reached for the phone.

Colette opened a file, gave a quick look towards the door and caught Lorraine's eye. The younger woman sat opposite her at a neat, tidy desk and her expression said it all. If she could be on time when she had two young children, then certainly Colette could. Everything about Lorraine was neat, from her short, dark hair to her petite frame to her perfect house and two perfect little children.

1

"We're not all perfect. Only you," Colette thought with the merest trace of malice as the door opened and Suzanne walked in.

Suzanne very nearly *was* perfect. Even Lorraine couldn't find fault with her, much as she tried. Tall, with long blonde hair, blue eyes and a figure Colette would happily die for, Suzanne seemed to have everything going for her. Best of all, you had to like her, Colette thought. She had a warm, engaging manner and an easy-going approach to life. It was obvious she wasn't one bit bothered about being late. Even if Her Grace had been here, Suzanne would have talked her way out of trouble.

It was clear to all of them, including Her Grace, that Suzanne didn't see the General Appropriations Section – or any other section of the Department, for that matter – playing a large part in her future. Nevertheless she worked efficiently when she was actually there, and was already well into her first phone-call of the day when Olive Grace returned to her desk.

Olive Grace was just the sort of boss you wouldn't want. Grey hair, grey eyes, sensible grey cardigans and a steely manner that made it impossible to feel comfortable with her.

"That one is sharp enough to cut herself!" Colette had said more than once to Maeve, who generally laughed it off and advised her to see it as part of her purgatory.

"Put up with it. The money's good, and the work's a doddle," Maeve was inclined to remind her. "And God knows where they'd send us if we applied for a transfer – you could get a lot worse than her!"

That was true enough. So Colette put up with it and, almost before she realised, she'd been in that particular backwater of the Civil Service for eight years – almost as long as Maeve, and a good bit longer than Suzanne and Lorraine. And while she could take or leave Lorraine, she had become good friends with Maeve, and it would be impossible not to get on with Suzanne. If it wasn't for Olive Grace, the job might even be enjoyable.

Colette returned Olive's cool "Good morning" and tried to concentrate on the file in front of her. Not easy, when she was still caught up in this morning's row with her teenage son. Who ever said kids got easier as they got older? Probably no-one, she thought – you just hung in there and hoped it might be true. And it obviously wasn't, at least not in her house. Roll on the tea break, when she could have a bit of a rant with Maeve and maybe calm down a bit.

They had barely sat down in the staff canteen when Lorraine joined them. "Lottery money," she said brightly, notebook in hand. Colette reached for her purse, counted out her £12 contribution for the next four weeks, then caught sight of Maeve's expression. She was looking apologetically at Lorraine.

"I'm afraid I haven't got it –" she began.

"I have it here," Colette interrupted quickly, anxious to save her embarrassment. But Maeve was shaking her head.

"Thanks, Colette, but I'll have to give it a miss. It's a bit steep, £12 every four weeks. You know what the kids are like, it's money every second day. I'll have to drop out of the syndicate."

"You can't!" They said it together.

"I mean, it would be a shame – unless you really have to," Colette added. "What if we won, and you weren't in on it?"

"Some chance," Maeve said with a rueful smile. "The way my luck's been going, you're probably better off without me!"

"No, we're not!" Lorraine said. She looked exasperated. "We all agreed on this. You signed the contract. If you back out now we have to stop doing your lines, or we'll all have to pay more. It would be . . ." – she started doing some quick calculations in her notebook – "£15 for each of us, instead of £12. You'll have to stay in, Maeve. It's not fair otherwise."

Typical, Colette thought. Lorraine watched every penny, though from the sound of things she didn't have to. She thought nothing of lavishing money on her home and her children, but seemed to begrudge every penny she had to spend otherwise. Careful, Colette's mother would have called her. Dirt mean was what Colette and Maeve thought privately. Still, that was her own business.

Except that right now she was leaning hard on Maeve, not taking "no" for an answer.

"Look at it this way," Maeve tried again, with a little

laugh. "You'll get more in the share-out when the numbers come up!"

"Did I hear the magic words?" Suzanne asked, smiling as she sat down. "You're talking about our big moment?"

"Not mine, I'm afraid," Maeve answered, turning towards her. "I'm pulling out of the syndicate."

"But why? If –"

"And it means the rest of us have to stump up more!" Lorraine interrupted.

"Oh, sod that, Lorraine! Hang on a minute! Maeve, if you need –"

Maeve shook her head. "Thanks, Colette's already offered. But I just can't afford it any more."

"Shouldn't let that stop you doing anything," Suzanne said. "Get yourself a friendly local bank manager, like mine! He nearly believes me now when I tell him we'll win any day!"

Colette and Maeve laughed.

"Wish it was that easy," Maeve said. "But I've come to the end of the line – I'm having to watch every penny now. Orla's determined to go on this blessed school trip in the Christmas holidays and it's costing nearly £400."

Suzanne looked surprised. "But that's over ten weeks away! Surely –"

"If you're going to say I can save it by then, forget it." Maeve said. She was laughing, and Colette wondered if the others really understood how tight things had been for her since Larry left.

5

"Actually, I was going to suggest a bank loan again!" Suzanne continued. "I'd never manage without them myself!"

"I don't think the bank would even look at me at this stage!" Maeve said. "No, I'll be throwing myself on my sister's mercy again. But I really do need to watch what I'm spending."

"So do the rest of us." Lorraine's voice was cool. "We'll have to meet and decide what to do, whether to drop your lines or pay extra to keep them. And we'll have to draw up a new contract."

Colette suppressed a groan. Lorraine loved "meetings". She'd have one at the drop of a hat, and it was all the same to her what it was about, as long as she had a platform for her views. She was the most opinionated person Colette had ever come across. Twenty-six years old and she knew everything, and didn't hesitate to let everyone else know it. She had even been known to correct Olive Grace, a dangerous move since Lorraine was the most junior person in the office. Give her ten years, Colette thought, and she'll be running the place.

"So, two o'clock," Lorraine was saying now. "In our office. I'll tell Olive." And she left the table, taking it for granted that they would come to her meeting.

The three of them looked from one to the other and let out a collective sigh of relief.

"That would be the best thing about winning the lottery," Suzanne said with a grin. "Imagine never having to lay eyes on *her* again!"

Maeve laughed. "I might be glad of her, if I was left doing all the work on my own with Malone, while you lot were living it up in the Bahamas!"

"You're sure you're going to drop out?" Colette asked later. They were sitting in the park eating their sandwiches, enjoying the mid-September sun.

"No choice," Maeve said. "I really don't." The jokey tone of earlier had disappeared. With Colette she was free to tell the truth. "Larry's been hassling me again. You know what we agreed, that I'd keep the house and he could have the shares and most of the money?"

Colette nodded.

"Well, it seems he got through it quicker than he expected. So he's come back looking for the only thing left. He wants me to sell the house."

"He can't do that!"

Maeve was staring into the distance, her dark eyes on the mountains to the south of them. Her half-eaten sandwich was still in her hand and she was huddled into the bench, her shoulders hunched slightly and her brown, curly hair lifting in the slight breeze.

"I don't know what he can do," she answered quietly. "You know we're not divorced?"

"You were thinking about it, weren't you? I wasn't sure if you went through with it."

Maeve shook her head, still not looking at Colette.

"Thinking about it – that's as far as it went. The kids were upset enough as things were, so I left it for a while.

And then – well, I suppose I just left it, there seemed to be no real need. I wish to God now that I'd done it. Before he tries to drain me dry."

"You'll need to get some good legal advice," Colette said. "I'm sure he can't make you sell the house while you and the kids are living there, can he? Especially after all you put into it –"

She stopped abruptly, mentally kicking herself as she saw the tears in Maeve's eyes.

"Sorry," she said quietly. Maeve didn't need to be reminded of the time and effort, not to mention the money, she had put into doing up the house she had inherited from her mother.

Maeve shook her head, rubbed at her eyes.

"Not your fault," she said. "Forget it. Maybe it won't happen. But it's what I needed to make me sort things out once and for all. No way is Larry Redmond getting his hands on my house."

She stood up, bundling the remains of the sandwich into its wrapping and tossing it into a nearby bin. As Colette did the same she noticed how pale Maeve looked. The strain she was under was finally beginning to show, Colette thought, as they started walking back up the hill towards the park gate.

"It's a gorgeous day," Maeve said as they left the park, "and I resent like mad having to go back early for that one and her meeting. Though I suppose it's really my fault."

"Rubbish. There was no need for any meeting – it's

just Lorraine looking for an excuse to take centre stage again."

They walked along in silence for a minute or two.

"Maeve?"

"Hmm?"

"Are you sure about this? I'd be happy to put in your share until you get things sorted out . . ."

Maeve stopped walking and turned to face her. She touched Colette's arm.

"I'm positive. Thanks a million, but I've made my mind up. I'm out of it. I need every penny I've got and I might as well be flinging it to the wind as putting it into the lottery. And in the long run," she said, making a wry face as she began walking again and Colette fell into step beside her, "what else is it but gambling? So I'm no different from Larry when it comes down to it. And look at the damage *he's* done. No, I really am finished with it, Colette. But thanks for the offer."

"But – what if we win? Think how you'd feel if the rest of us won and you weren't in it!"

Maeve smiled.

"I'd live with it. D'you really believe you'll win?"

"No, not really. Though I suppose there's a part of me that keeps hoping. Like most people, probably. Otherwise no-one would bother doing it." She laughed. "Well, Suzanne would, because she's not just hoping – she's convinced she'll win."

Maeve laughed. "And people like Lorraine would keep playing anyway, whatever their chances, because they couldn't bear the thought of not being part of a big win. Can you imagine Lorraine leaving the syndicate? She'd never live with herself if they won and she wasn't in on it!"

"You're sure you wouldn't regret it?" Colette asked quietly, her voice serious again. "I mean, just suppose –"

They were almost at their building, and Maeve paused again.

"I wouldn't *let* myself regret it," she said firmly. "I lived for too long with someone who was certain that the next bet was a sure thing, and that if he didn't place it – even if it meant bankrupting us – he'd always regret it. I lost count of the number of times he said 'just once more'. He was convinced, he really was, that we'd live like kings on what he'd make from the Spring Double, or a 40/1 outsider in the Grand National. It was always the next time, just one more bet. So when it hit me the other night that, in a way, I'm doing the very same, I'd no choice but to pull out, even if I could afford it. Which I can't. And look on the bright side –" she smiled as she began walking again – "at least this way I'm not paying into a gambling fund for Larry. If we ever did manage to win, he'd be at the door like a bat out of hell, looking for his share, and he wouldn't be happy until I hadn't a penny left."

"He couldn't do that, once you sort things out."

"You're right," Maeve said, looking serious again. "I'll ring my solicitor as soon as I get a minute."

The others were waiting for them when they got back to the office.

"We've started," Lorraine said, with a very obvious glance at the clock. It was barely past two. "We all agree that we'll keep all the lines – we've been doing them for over two years, so it would be a shame to drop them now. But that means we'll each have to pay an extra £3 every four weeks." She glared at Maeve before turning to Colette. "That's if you agree, Colette. The rest of us do."

Colette nodded. They must have reached agreement in ten seconds flat. She wished some of the other meetings she had to attend in this office could be as focused.

"Now, I've typed up new contracts." Lorraine was in her element, loving every minute of it. Except, maybe, for the extra £3 she'd have to spend each month. "And a Termination of Agreement document dissolving the existing syndicate."

God Almighty, Colette thought. Where did she learn to talk like that? Maybe she'd be running the office in *five* years instead of ten.

"Do we need all that?" she asked. "I mean, can't we just agree among ourselves?"

"Not where money is concerned," Lorraine said firmly. "We need to be clear about everything before I buy the ticket tomorrow. Just in case . . ." She left the rest of the sentence hanging in the air.

Suzanne laughed. "Well, if we win tomorrow I've no objection to sharing with the whole Department. Imagine, £6.5 million!"

Lorraine was not amused. "That's exactly why we need to be clear about it – to make sure everyone takes it seriously."

"Okay, then," Suzanne responded. "And this time I'm serious. I think it would be very hard on someone who'd just left the syndicate, if we *did* win. So what about a clause saying that any member who left would be entitled to buy back in if we won in, say, the next four draws? That should keep everyone happy."

Lorraine looked fit to kill. "You mean, we should pay extra for someone else and then share our winnings with them? I certainly don't agree with that!"

"Well, I do," Colette said. "I think it's a very good idea." She glanced around the group, waiting to see if Olive Grace would make a comment, not really expecting it. The older woman rarely spoke about anything that wasn't strictly work-related. It was a wonder she bothered to take part in the syndicate at all. Sourpuss, Colette thought. She wouldn't know what to do with a million pounds if it fell into her lap.

"It clearly states in the contract –" Lorraine began, just as Maeve spoke.

"I don't agree."

Four heads turned towards her.

"But –" Colette started.

Maeve shook her head. "No, Lorraine's right. If you're not in, you can't win. That's what they say, isn't it? And I'm opting out. So, fair's fair – if you win, I can't expect to be part of it." She turned to smile at Suzanne.

"Thanks, anyway. I'll be the first to congratulate you if it happens."

"*When* it happens," Suzanne answered, her expression more serious than usual. "I wish you'd think about it, Maeve, because we *will* win. I'm sure of it. Seems a pity to pull out now, after so long. Especially when this Wednesday's the big jackpot. Could you not give it another while?"

"I've given it too long already. I could've paid for Orla's holiday with what I've spent. And we've only ever got a couple of quid back."

"£22 each," Lorraine said, consulting her notebook. "And we've each paid out £324 in the past two years. Two years and one month, actually. So we're down a total of £302 each."

"You're keeping count?" Suzanne looked appalled.

"Of course. How else would I know how much it's costing me?"

"Come on, Lorraine! It's meant to be a bit of fun! How can you enjoy it if you're keeping tabs on every penny?"

"That's the part she enjoys." It was out before Colette could stop herself. She glanced away to avoid the filthy look Lorraine shot her.

"It's as well some of us around here are disciplined enough to keep to a budget. And anyway," – she looked around to include all of them – "I'll be reviewing it myself at the end of the year. I've decided that winning wouldn't really make that much difference to me."

Colette, Maeve and Suzanne laughed. Olive, who had been looking out the window, glanced at Lorraine but otherwise showed no reaction.

Suzanne was the first to speak. "Come on, Lorraine! It would have to make a difference!"

"Why would it?" Lorraine's expression was challenging. "I have everything I want – a lovely home, a husband and two beautiful, healthy children. What more could I ask for?"

To be a bit nicer than you are, Colette thought. Maybe a lot nicer.

"So why do you bother doing it?" Suzanne asked. "I know why *I* do it – as soon as we win I'll be on the next flight out of here!"

"And good luck to you!" Maeve said, laughing.

"Well, I wouldn't," Lorraine said. "I have no intention of going anywhere else. I'm perfectly happy the way I am, and winning the lottery wouldn't change me."

But it would.

It would change all of them.

Chapter Two

Colette hated Wednesdays.

Mondays were bad enough – she always felt exhausted after working flat-out at the weekend, catching up on housework. And Thursdays weren't great either. She hated supermarket shopping, and usually ended up doing it all on her own.

But Wednesdays – they were definitely the worst. Wednesdays were when her mother-in-law visited them.

After nearly twenty years Colette still called her Mrs Comerford. And that just about said it all.

She finished peeling the potatoes and put them on to cook, leaving the sliced carrots and chops ready, and sat down to chat to five-year-old Emer who was busy at the kitchen table with her colouring book. Bears, of course. Emer was mad about bears.

"Did you have a good day, love?" Colette asked as

15

she brushed the little girl's silky blonde hair back from her cheek.

"Fine, Mammy," she answered, but Colette knew it wasn't really true. Much as Emer loved Sheila, her minder, she preferred being at home with Colette. They'd had a great time last week, just before school started again. Colette took a few days off and they baked, and went for walks, and made some puppets – all the things she loved doing with Emer but never had time for. It was lovely having nothing to do but concentrate on her little daughter and enjoy being with her.

She chatted with Emer for another few minutes, then stood up and crossed to the cooker again. She put on the pot of carrots, placed the chops on the grill pan and put them under a low heat. They'd be done to death by the time Martin and his mother arrived, but that was how Mrs Comerford liked them – and it was easier, most of the time, to go along with what Mrs Comerford wanted. If Colette had learned nothing else in the past twenty years, she had learned that.

Sighing, she went through to the utility room to sort the washing and empty the dryer. She wanted to give her mother-in-law as little cause for complaint as possible, and a dryer full of clothes 'on a lovely fine day like this' would be enough to set her off. As if Colette had the luxury of waiting for fine days to put the clothes out. It wasn't as if she didn't *enjoy* washing, Colette thought crossly. She loved the look and the smell of clean sheets flapping in the breeze, but she wouldn't be there to take them in if it lashed rain. And she'd had enough of arriving home to saturated washing. Life was too short and she was just too busy.

It shouldn't be like this, she thought, annoyed. Herself and Martin had been married almost twenty years and their mortgage was nearly paid off. She had hoped that, by now, she'd be able to take time off to stay at home with Emer. But it just wasn't possible. Every spare penny they had seemed to go on fixing up Martin's mother's house, when their own was falling down around them. And Colette would kill for a new suite of furniture, but the couple of hundred quid she had saved towards it had gone instead on a special orthopaedic chair for Mrs Comerford.

Colette hadn't the heart or the energy to refuse when Martin suggested it, but she wished he hadn't asked. Sometimes it seemed that nothing mattered to him but the sports results, and his mother, and his work, in roughly that order. Colette felt as if she herself was becoming part of the wallpaper – the peeling-off, needed-redoing-last-year, wrong-colour-in-the-first place wallpaper that covered their hall. It was the one bit of decorating Martin had got round to, several years ago, in between rewiring and painting and re-plumbing his mother's house. She supposed she should be grateful. Or learn to do it herself. If she could ever find the time.

She sighed again as she switched on the washing-machine and carried the basket of dry clothes back to the kitchen, setting it down for a minute while she turned the chops and lowered the heat under the bubbling pot of potatoes.

She checked the clock. Martin and his mother would be here in precisely ten minutes. Colette had given up wondering how he managed it now that traffic was so bad, but manage it he did. He was always bang on time when he brought his mother home for dinner. Her delicate digestive system would apparently go into spasm if she had to eat a minute later than six-thirty. Or anything other than a familiar combination of meat and vegetables. So Martin would be here on time. That was him. Dependable. And – she finally admitted it – boring as hell.

There. She had said it. At least to herself. Her good, kind, easy-going husband was slowly driving her mad. His answer to nearly everything was "Don't worry about it, love. It'll be fine".

And it *was* fine, for him. He was the one who sailed through life while she lay awake at night worrying about money, and work, and the kids. Mainly the kids. Sometimes she felt she might as well be on her own, because she was the one who had to make all the decisions, and try to keep tabs on Declan and Ciara – something that was getting harder to do each week.

This is your life, Colette Comerford, she thought glumly as she began setting the table, working around Emer and her crayons. Make the most of it.

She blinked back the tears, afraid Emer would see

them. This wasn't what she had signed up for, she thought. Or anything like it. She remembered for a moment how she had felt at eighteen, persuading her parents to let her get married, believing that Martin was all she'd ever want in life.

She glanced at the wedding photograph in its simple frame, the centrepiece of a cluster of photos on the wall near the kitchen table. She looked at her young face framed by light brown hair, her slim figure, the shining eyes – hers and Martin's – full of hope, and she felt sad.

So much for hopes and dreams, she thought. She and Martin seemed nothing like that young couple now. She had gained weight with each pregnancy – not much, but enough to feel uncomfortable; her hair looked lifeless now and could best be described as mousy. And as for Martin . . .

He had fared better than her physically, growing into his height, losing the gawkiness of youth – but the boy who had been going to take on the world had become the man who spent his days in an insurance company and his evenings in front of the TV.

She was checking the potatoes and turning the chops again when the song came on the radio, the sultry American voice seeming to mock her with images of Paris and sports cars and the warm wind streaming though her hair . . .

I used to love that song, she thought. When I was young, and just married, and had long shining hair that I'd *want* the wind to stream through. When the world was mine and I still thought I could do whatever I wanted with my life.

What she wanted now, more than anything, was to sit down in the middle of the kitchen floor and cry her eyes out.

She was saved by the sound of the front door opening and a bag being dropped in the hall.

"Mam! I'm home!" Peter's voice.

She smiled as her tall, fair-haired son came into the kitchen, crossed the room to tickle Emer and, while she was still giggling, turned to hug Colette. He never did that when Declan and Ciara were around. The teasing wouldn't be worth it to him.

"No sign of them yet?" He made a face as he asked. He knew by this stage that his mother and grandmother didn't see eye to eye. And who was mainly to blame.

She looked at the clock again. "Another two minutes."

"And what about the others?"

"Don't ask, " she said. "Did you hear Declan leaving this morning? He nearly took the door off the hinges."

"I heard him." Peter's voice was tight. It had been a long time since he got on with his brother. "I heard Ciara, too. She shouldn't talk to you like that. Where is she, anyway?"

"Over at Maeve's, doing her homework with Orla. At least that's where she said she was going. They probably told Maeve they were here."

"You'll have to do something about her, Mam. Get Dad to talk to her."

They looked at each other, knowing how useless that would be. Martin doted on her, he couldn't say a cross word to her if he tried. Or to any of the others. In fairness, he was a good, loving father – if you didn't expect anything from him in the way of discipline.

Colette gave a little laugh as she reached to turn off the grill. "Look on the bright side. At least if she's not here, your grandmother won't see the nose-ring."

"Pity. I'd like to see her face." Peter was smiling as he swung up the laundry basket and headed for the kitchen door.

Colette had hit the roof when Ciara came home with it last Saturday, but Martin just laughed and told his daughter that her nose would probably fall off when she got older. His mother would probably say the same but mean it. Colette could do without the hassle. As she could do without Mrs Comerford tonight.

What she really wanted was a chance to sit down with Martin, just the two of them, and talk about how isolated she felt. How her life was running away from her, with a husband who didn't talk any more about the things that really mattered, and two teenage children who looked at her as if she was trying to poison them.

Forget it, she told herself as she switched off the cooker, put the chops into a dish under the still-warm grill, and strained the potatoes and carrots. Even if I could drag him away from the television, he wouldn't understand what I'm talking about. Ten years ago he would have. But not now.

She helped Emer to tidy away her crayons and was putting the dishes of food on the table just as Martin's car pulled into the drive.

She braced herself as the front door opened again, and Martin and his mother walked in.

Alice Comerford was a tall woman with black, grey-flecked hair and a forbidding manner. Colette wished yet again that she could warm to the woman, but it just wasn't possible.

"I see I've caught you in the middle of tidying up," she said, with a pointed glance at Peter's bag, still resting where he had flung it at the bottom of the stairs.

"Not at all, I don't see much point in tidying the hall when the paper is falling off the walls," said Colette in a cool tone, ignoring Martin's look of alarm. She wondered what had got into her as she led the way back into the kitchen. Not for the first time she wished she had a dining-room she could use, all set up to impress the hell out of Alice Comerford, but she'd long since had to sacrifice it when it got to the stage where Ciara simply refused to share a bedroom with Emer.

They sat down just as Peter came to join them, greeting his father and bending to kiss his grandmother's proffered cheek. Peter did his best, but they all knew that she doted on Declan and refused to see any fault at all in him. She was quick to express her disappointment now at not seeing him.

"He's over with a friend, studying," Colette lied

quickly, ignoring the suspicious glance Mrs Comerford gave to the chop on her plate.

I hope she chokes on it, Colette thought as she half-listened to her mother-in-law's lecture on the importance of studying, and the greater importance of seeing one's grandmother on a regular basis. Not that she'd say a word of reproof if he turned up, any more than Martin would.

The meal went smoothly enough, mainly thanks to Peter who worked hard to keep the conversation going.

"Leave the washing-up, Mam. I'll be down later to do it," he said. He was never as eager to get on with his studying as on the nights his grandmother was there.

"No need, love. It won't take long. Thanks." She began clearing dishes, glad of the excuse to escape further conversation for a while, as Martin and his mother went into the living-room. She had just begun the washing-up when the doorbell rang and she heard Martin going to answer it. Voices filtered in from the hall. Ciara. Plus nose-ring, no doubt.

She didn't come into the kitchen, opting instead to go in to her grandmother. Colette didn't know whether to be glad or sorry – Ciara was becoming a real handful, but could turn on the charm with the best of them when she wanted to. She usually wanted to when her grandmother was there, and it usually worked.

As it seemed to have done this time – in spite of the nose-ring – because there were smiles all round when Colette joined them twenty minutes or so later.

"Ciara was just telling me about her latest school project," Mrs Comerford said. She looked like the cat that got the cream.

"Oh, was she?" Colette asked. News to her that there was a "latest school project" – unless it involved getting to know the 3rd year lads better. Boys were the main topic of interest to Ciara these days. Colette preferred not to think what sort of "studying" herself and Orla were up to this evening. Maybe she'd better have a chat with Maeve.

"My history project. I was telling you last night, but you were busy," Ciara said accusingly.

Mrs Comerford was the picture of disapproval.

"Of course, I told Ciara I'd be very happy to help her," she said. "After all, it's up to everyone to stay involved with young people these days."

But I do, Colette wanted to scream. I try. Even when half the young people I live with look at me like I'm the Wicked Witch of the West.

That wasn't how Ciara was acting now. She was sweetness itself as she assured her grandmother that of *course* she wasn't really old enough to be interviewed for the history project, it was just that she was the most interesting person Ciara knew, and was bound to have some good stories.

Maybe she can become a politician, Colette thought. Or an actor. She wondered if they needed better exam results than Ciara was ever likely to get.

They chatted for a short while, mainly about the

new tiles Martin had put up in his mother's kitchen, and the need now for some new vinyl for the floor, if she could manage to afford it . . .

Colette was almost at breaking-point when Martin went to get his mother's coat and Ciara said she was going with them "to see Dad's hard work".

I don't know how much more of this I can take, Colette thought as she got Emer ready for bed. Twenty years of being polite and pleasant to that one is enough for anyone. I'm just afraid that if I open my mouth to her, I won't know when to stop.

She was in the kitchen, doing a final clean-up, when Peter came back down.

"All quiet?" he asked.

"For the time being. You're very good with her, you know."

"Ah, she's not the worst. Not all the time, anyway," he added quickly as he saw Colette's expression. He hastened to change the subject. "D'you want the lottery numbers?" He reached to switch on the small TV in the corner. "God, imagine winning tonight. Six and a half million quid. Imagine what you could do with that!"

"Some chance!" Colette said, glancing at the screen which was still showing advertisements.

"You know what they say," Peter said, opening the dresser drawer and pulling out the sheet of lottery numbers. *"It could be you!"* He was grinning at her as he settled down in a chair, biro and list in hand, to watch the screen.

Colette came to stand beside him, allowing herself to think for a minute, as the music came on, what she'd do with so much money. That song came into her head again. Paris, in a sports car. At the age of thirty-seven. Her age. She could just imagine it . . .

She was still thinking about it as the numbered balls were released into the drum and the first number was drawn.

Seven.

She was vaguely aware of Peter marking the sheet.

Forget Paris, she told herself. With her luck they'd get as far as Wexford, like every other year. Martin would never agree to go abroad. He preferred familiar surroundings and "decent" food.

Two more balls had been drawn. The numbers were up on the screen, *fourteen* and *twenty-three.*

Not that there was anything wrong with Wexford. They'd had some great holidays there when the kids were younger. But Paris . . .

"And the fourth number tonight is . . . thirty-one."

She glanced over Peter's shoulder. He had four numbers marked, all on one line.

"Great," she said. "We'll get a few quid anyway."

"Shh," Peter said, as the fifth number came out of the drum.

Thirty-seven . . .

He marked the page. They looked at each other. They didn't know they were holding their breath.

Chapter Three

Suzanne kicked off her shoes and stretched out on the sofa. Still tingling from her session in the gym, she debated having an early night since Finn was out of town. She had a quick glance at the TV guide, hit the button on the answering machine to check calls. It only took a moment to decide against Gilly's suggestion of going to a film.

She rang back arranging to meet instead at the weekend.

Then she reached for the remote control.

Tonight was a night for relaxing in front of the television.

And for thinking.

Mainly about Finn.

And how she could convince him that, this time, it was finally over.

Not easy, when he'd never listened before and she

caved in so easily. Thing was, she really loved him, in a way. But more like a brother. Certainly nothing that would warrant the way they'd been behaving.

She smiled, remembering last month in Amsterdam, the little hotel near Leidseplein where they'd spent the weekend. It had been great fun. Wonderful. But . . .

She stood up, yawned, thought about having an early night. Much *too* early for that, though. She must be losing it. It wasn't like her to think about bed any time before midnight. At least, not if Finn wasn't around.

Finn.

She made a quick, impatient sound, got down on the floor and began doing some stretching exercises.

I need to decide, she told herself. I need to sort out where I'm going. Soon.

Where Suzanne was going was usually somewhere interesting, far away, preferably off the beaten track. She'd managed, in the couple of years that she'd been with Finn, to get to Morocco, Bali, Singapore, as well as New York and Amsterdam. She loved travelling, lived for it. And so did Finn. They were two of a kind, in a way. In lots of ways. But somehow . . .

She grunted as she stretched to touch her toes, feeling the pull along the back of her thighs. She was getting back into shape at last. The girls at work had laughed, asking where exactly she was hiding the extra half stone she was worried about. But she just didn't feel right carrying even a few extra pounds. It made her feel flabby, unfit. Out of control.

Not that Finn was complaining.

"It's landed in all the right places," he'd said on their last night in New York, where they'd gone to celebrate Independence Day. "How did you manage it?"

"By eating like a prize pig," she answered, a bit more sharply than she'd intended. "Too many meals out. Too many dinners in. Not enough exercise."

"Oh, we can fix that," he'd murmured into her hair. "I know some moves."

He certainly did. And she couldn't deny she'd had a great time. Same in Amsterdam. But . . .

It was there again, that *but*, she thought, as she turned on her side and began some leg raises.

It just wasn't working for her any more. She enjoyed being with him, loved all the weeks and weekends away, but it wasn't enough.

What she wanted was some sense of getting somewhere, some kind of purpose. Something to plan towards that wasn't just the next holiday.

And marriage definitely wasn't what she had in mind.

She still didn't know for sure whether Finn had been joking when he suggested it, just before they booked the holiday in Bali.

"Why not?" he'd asked. "Come on. It'd be mad!"

"Certifiable," she'd agreed, laughing, and he'd dropped the subject straight away.

And hadn't mentioned it again, to her relief.

Because there was no way it would work. She just

knew it. Looking at her married friends did nothing for her opinion of wedded bliss. Especially once kids came along. That seemed to finish off any chance of having a life of your own.

She finished the series of exercises and swung around gently to sit lotus-fashion, her back to the wall. She took a deep breath, held it, relaxed. Tried to imagine what it would be like doing this with toddlers crawling all over you. Or, heaven forbid, some loutish teenager demanding money and a front-door key.

Poor Colette, she thought. The worst of both worlds.

No, marriage definitely wasn't on the cards. Even without kids. And certainly not with Finn.

She had come to the end of that particular road. Unfortunately, she had no idea where she was going next.

Back to the bank for another loan would be a good idea. If she could manage to talk them into it. You couldn't do anything without money.

You'd think the banks, of all people, would realise that. But banks were strange. You'd expect them to be happy that she was such a good customer, borrowing all that money, paying back huge amounts in interest. But, no. They'd been very pleasant about it last time, and finally said yes, but, God, the questions! Was she sure she needed a holiday while she was still paying off the loan from the first one? And was she sure she couldn't make it cost – well, a little bit less?

Of course she was sure. That's why she was there in

the middle of the lunch hour, when she could have been out doing some more shopping. She wanted to go to Singapore and she wanted to do it in style. No point in going, otherwise. She didn't want to go all the way to Singapore and then find she had to watch the pennies. That would be no fun at all.

She'd put on her most hopeful expression and smiled at the manager. He smiled too, looking at the stack of Brown Thomas bags at her feet – the holiday shopping had started early – and gave in gracefully.

It mightn't be so easy this time, especially if she didn't have a clear idea of what she wanted the money for. But one thing was certain – it would be her escape route from the office.

The girls were great, but the job was going nowhere and she was bored out of her mind. It was time to get out. She was only there by chance in the first place because she hadn't been able to decide what else to do. It had seemed as good a place as any while she made up her mind. But to be still there, ten years on – that was never in her plans . . .

Which was exactly the trouble, she told herself as she stood up and went to the fridge to get some juice. She didn't have any plans and was beginning to feel the need for them. At thirty-two she would have expected to have her own apartment, at least, but here she was, still renting a place that wasn't particularly great, and paying through the nose for it.

So what she needed, she decided as she sat down

and pulled a pen and sheet of paper towards her, was a place of her own and work that would interest her while keeping the bank happy and paying for the kind of lifestyle she enjoyed.

Enjoy! That was the word, she thought, as she doodled on the sheet. She wanted to *enjoy* her life, not just by going on holidays, but by finding something to do that would stimulate and challenge her. As well as pay the bills. And there were lots of bills.

Something in the fashion world? She loved clothes, had wardrobes bulging with them and drawers full of accessories. She knew what worked for her. And for other people. Maybe she could be some kind of fashion consultant . . .

Or interior design? Vaguely she wondered if there was any money in that as she glanced round the small living-room. She knew about colours and fabrics, knew how to make even a little place like this look its best.

Yes, definitely something in fashion, or interiors. Her own little shop, painted in gold and red. Lovely, rich colours. Gold for a luxurious look. And red. For overdrafts.

She laughed, put the pen and paper away. Might as well dream here as in bed, she thought.

It wasn't anywhere near bedtime, but an early night still seemed like a good idea. She'd change into her dressinggown, watch the lottery draw and see if there was a movie on.

As she was coming from the bedroom the doorbell

rang. Probably Val from next door. Really, she didn't feel like answering, but Val would hear the TV and know she was in. She opened the door.

"I see you're expecting me!" Finn said, grinning as he saw the dressinggown.

"How could I be, when you're in London? Well, meant to be."

"Conference finished early. Aren't you going to invite me in?"

He noticed the slight hesitation.

"You're not?" The tone was light but she saw the hurt on his face.

"Of course. I'm just surprised to see you – and a bit tired." She moved back to let him in. "I was thinking of going to bed early."

"Suits me."

"On my own."

"Ah."

"Finn, I've been thinking."

"Again?" He smiled, but he knew what was coming. They'd been there before.

They were still standing in the hallway. "Let's go in and sit down."

He pulled a face. "Let's not. I'd prefer not to get too comfortable if you're about to throw me out."

"Come on, Finn! It's not like that!"

"Isn't it? So what *is* it like? I'm getting just a bit tired of this, Suzy. Either you want me in your life, or you don't."

He studied her expression for a moment, then his gaze flickered away. "I see."

He moved towards the door. She put her hand on his arm. "Finn, wait!"

He looked at her, said nothing.

"I don't want you to go. I just don't want to end up in bed again. I want –"

"I know, you want to be *friends*." The word came out hard and cold. "Well, forget it, Suzanne. That's not what's on offer."

"Finn –"

But he was gone.

She had tears in her eyes as she wandered back into the living-room. The lotto draw was just finishing. There were five numbers up on the screen.

Barely glancing at it, she crossed the room and switched off the television before going to bed.

Chapter Four

Olive dreaded the moment when she put her key in the door each evening. She barely had time to get into the hallway before her mother's querulous voice reached her.

"What kept you?"

Suppressing a sigh, Olive opened the living-room door. Her mother was, as she had expected, sitting comfortably by the fire, the remote control on the arm of her chair. A tray with a teapot and china cup sat on the table near her. Vera, her home help, had obviously been in that afternoon.

"Traffic was appalling," Olive said as she set down her briefcase and went to pick up the tray. "How was today?"

Her mother snorted. "I'm sure you're worried how my day was. It's not easy, you know, having to be on my own for so long."

"Mother –"

"If you're going to say you've no choice about going out to work, save your breath. Nuala Cassidy's daughter is after taking early retirement to look after her. You could do the same if you wanted to."

"It's not that easy," Olive answered as she went into the hallway and down the corridor to the dark kitchen. And anyway it was the last thing she wanted, though she could never admit that to her mother. But to be stuck all day in the big, dark old house, with only her mother for company, would be more than she could bear.

"You could do it, you know," her mother continued as Olive came back into the living-room and put some more coal on the fire. "You must have a good bit put away by now and the pension would be all right, wouldn't it? Nuala's daughter got a lump sum that she was able to invest. Vincent would be able to give you good advice."

I'm sure he would, Olive thought. And for a nice fat commission, too.

There was no love lost between herself and her brother, three years younger than her. Neither he nor Raymond, a year younger again, could do any wrong in their mother's eyes. And Olive could do no right.

I could stand on my head singing opera, Olive thought, and she still wouldn't be impressed.

No, the only thing Bridget Grace was impressed by was money. And, of course, her two sons.

Bridget sat looking at her, waiting for a response.

"I'm not quite old enough," Olive said. "I don't think they would consider me unless I were fifty-five. Maybe I can see about it then."

"That's two years. I could be dead by then. And it's not fair, you know it isn't, leaving me in the house on my own all day."

"Now, Mother, you know we've been through this before."

They had, several times, and Olive found it very upsetting. She couldn't agree to staying at home. Her mother was an extremely difficult woman – and Olive found it almost impossible to stand up to her. No, she really couldn't bear the idea of being with her all day.

"It's a very hard thing to live with, knowing your own daughter doesn't want to be with you. The boys would have me with them if they could, if they didn't live so far away. You've no idea how much I miss them."

"Well, you'll see them for your birthday on Sunday, don't forget." Olive forced a smile. "That's something to look forward to, isn't it?"

Her mother was still grumbling to herself as Olive went upstairs to take a shower.

Twenty minutes' peace, Olive thought, and then I'll be able for her again.

She stood under the warm stream of water, feeling as if it were breathing life back into her. She shampooed her hair, feeling the knots of tension in her shoulders begin to ease as the water flowed over her and the floral

scent of the soap enveloped her. Not her choice of soap –
her mother's – but no matter. These few minutes each
day were bliss. They were her own.

She dried and dressed quickly, towelling her hair
and brushing it into shape. Not bad, she thought. Thick,
straight, in good condition. But the colour . . .

Once, and once only, she had considered putting a
rinse in to give a lift to the steely-grey. Her mother had
been quick to dismiss that idea and Olive had given in.
Really, it was easier just to agree with her. It wasn't as if
it mattered all that much.

Briefly, as she came back downstairs, Olive considered
going out for the evening. She was sure the choir still
met on Wednesdays, though it had been months since
she had managed to be there. And she wouldn't get out
for her usual walk on Sunday – she could hardly go out
on her mother's birthday, especially since there would
be dinner to prepare for her brothers and their wives.
So maybe . . .

"I'd like an omelette for my tea," Mrs Grace said as
Olive came into the room. "Make it nice and fluffy, not
like last time."

"I'll do that." Olive paused, one hand on the living-
room door. "I was thinking of going out to the choir
tonight. I thought perhaps you might like to come?"

Her mother's eyes were gleaming daggers.

"And how do you expect me to go, in my condition?
You know well what the doctor said. But you go on.
Don't mind me. You go ahead and enjoy yourself!"

"The doctor said it would do you good to get out, that he realises the arthritis can be painful, but if you're careful not to exert yourself too much, the change could be very beneficial."

"That's not what he said to me. He said I needed to mind myself and I needed to be looked after. So don't expect me to go traipsing along to the choir just because you want to get out. Though why it's not enough for you to be out all day, I don't know. Go on off and enjoy yourself. And never mind the omelette. Don't bother about me. If I get hungry I'll ring Vera."

"You know you can't do that, Mother." Olive struggled to keep the note of alarm from her voice. If they lost this home help, heaven knows where they would find another. "Vera has her own family to look after."

"She said she'd never see me wanting and that she knows what it's like for me stuck here on my own all day. She said any time I need her I'm to ring and she'll come straight over. She never lets me down."

Olive kept her voice carefully under control as she saw the guilty expression in her mother's eyes. "Do you ring her often?"

"Only now and then. When I need something or when I feel a bit lonely. Not often," she added quickly.

"You know she's only supposed to come twice a day, Mother. And certainly not in the evenings."

"That's only because I'm not supposed to be on my own in the evenings. I'll only ring her if I need her, if I have no choice."

The hard look was back in Bridget's eyes.

Defeated, Olive went to the kitchen to make the omelette. She resigned herself to yet another night spent in front of the television. At least tonight there was a film on that she'd like to see. Set in Paris. Olive loved anything to do with Paris. She had never managed to go there – her mother preferred holidays in Ireland. But her father had been there once, when he was young, and one of Olive's strongest memories from her childhood was of sitting beside him in the evenings, looking through his scrapbook and watching the faraway expression in his eyes as he talked about Paris.

Her mother had never had any patience for listening to him. Paris had been a waste of time and money, as far as she was concerned, even though he had gone there before they met. Not for the first time, Olive wondered what had ever drawn two such very different people together.

Her mother had changed to RTE 1 when Olive came back with the omelette. "The lottery is on next," her mother said. "You might as well take down the numbers. Though I don't know why you bother doing it." She glared first at Olive and then at the omelette which was beginning to collapse on the plate. "It's only a waste of money."

That much was true, Olive thought as she sat down. And even if she won it, no amount of money would allow her to escape from her mother. It was her very last promise to her father, that she would stay with Bridget and take care of her. Nothing so far had stood between her and her sense of duty. Winning the lottery would make no difference at all, and she only joined in the syndicate because she already felt so isolated from all the other women in the office.

Idly she watched as the numbers came out of the drum.

Seven . . . Fourteen . . . Twenty-three . . . Thirty-one . . . Thirty-seven . . .

Chapter Five

Lorraine Kearns was delighted with herself. She was smiling as she left her mother's house with her two young children in the back of the car. As she drove along Templeogue Road she congratulated herself on how well she had handled the situation. Her mother had agreed to keep on minding Gavin and Amber, at least until Christmas.

It should never have come up, really. Joan Hickey knew how much Lorraine depended on her. She couldn't have the children going to a crèche – you'd never know what habits they'd pick up, never mind anything else. Not to mention the cost.

"Eighty-five pounds each?" Lorraine had said, hardly able to talk with the shock, when her mother had told her about the "lovely" new crèche, just at the end of the road, which still had a few vacancies. She didn't seem to realise that Lorraine didn't have that kind of money – and that, even if she had, there were better things to spend it on than crèches.

She'd love a new suite of furniture – the one they had was nearly two years old and beginning to show its age.

Patiently, she had explained to her mother that if she was paying that amount of money every week, it would hardly be worth her while working at all. No, things were fine just as they were. Especially as her mother was doing it for nothing – and had agreed to continue doing it.

It had been easy to persuade her. Lorraine had simply reminded her that if the children were in a crèche all day they'd hardly see their Nan at all. They'd be too tired to call in on the way home, and weekends were out of the question because they usually went to see David's parents.

And, of course, if childcare was costing so much she might be better to give up work altogether and move to a house with a smaller mortgage. Probably on the far side of the city, over near David's parents. Which would be fine. Though, living so far away, the children wouldn't get to see Joan very often . . .

It worked.

Joan gave in and agreed that she would mind them until Christmas anyway, and forget about the extra-mural course she had planned to do.

Lorraine smiled and nodded, telling her mother that spring was a much better time for evening classes anyway. Who wanted to go out in the cold and the rain when you could be sitting at home by the fire?

She chatted away happily, knowing Joan probably wouldn't raise the subject of childminding again for a long time – and if she did, it would be easy to persuade her to keep going. Just until the children were old enough to start school. After all, it was lovely for them, as well as for her, that they could spend so much time together . . .

Still smiling, Lorraine pulled into her drive and sat for a moment admiring the house. She had no intention in the world of selling it, in spite of what she'd said to Joan. This house was exactly what Lorraine wanted and exactly where she wanted it. It would take something very big indeed to make her move from here.

The children were cranky as she took them from the car and into the house. Lorraine hated that. She had so much to do before their bedtime in an hour, and the last thing she needed was to have to spend time settling them down.

They couldn't be hungry. Joan would have fed them less than an hour ago. Lorraine normally only had to give them milk, some fruit and a yoghurt before putting them to bed at 7.30.

She left them in the playroom and went to answer the phone. David, saying he'd be late home. That suited Lorraine. She never bothered cooking if there was just herself. It was a waste, really. Of time as well as money. And Lorraine hated waste.

She prided herself on using everything that came into the house to the best possible advantage. Leftover food was never thrown away, even if there was only a little bit left. It would always do for lunch next day. She went to the fridge, took out some yoghurts, brought some fruit to the table and went to get the children.

She never liked this time of the evening. David seemed to have it much more under control, and would sometimes bring the children out to play in the garden before giving them a bath. But Lorraine had no intention of dealing with dirty clothes and mud trailed in on the floor tonight. She had plans for the evening. With David out, it was the ideal time for going through their budget closely to see how long it would take to afford that Italian leather suite she'd seen in Arnott's. She could imagine it in their living-room already . . .

She finished her fruit and yoghurt and began hurrying the children with theirs. She needed to have them in bed in ten minutes so she could get organised for the morning and then have a clear run at examining the budget.

"Now, hurry up, Amber," she said in her sweetest tones.

"Don't want to," the child responded, looking at her sulkily. Lorraine felt like hitting her. Not that she ever would, of course. But at three, Amber was surely old enough to do what she was told. She should be setting a good example to Gavin, who was nearly two. He copied her in everything.

"Don't want to," he said now, setting down his messy spoon.

"That's okay," Lorraine said, speaking slowly, ignoring the mess the strawberry yoghurt was making on the table. "Let's just go and get our jammies on, and then I'll read you a story."

"Want Daddy to." Amber's bottom lip was trembling.

Gavin joined in, right on cue. "Want Daddy to." His little blue eyes had a piercing quality Lorraine had never noticed before. As had the scream he let loose.

Amber took one look at him and started sobbing.

That was it. Lorraine had had enough. She scooped Gavin up and told Amber, in a not-so-sweet voice this time, to follow her. With two children bawling and Lorraine herself close to tears of sheer frustration, they made their way upstairs to the bedroom with its cot and small bed. She got them changed and into bed quickly, taking no nonsense.

They were still crying quietly so a story was out of the question. She reached up to the shelf where she kept the soothers in their little plastic container. She really hated these things and would never admit to using them. But David thought they were a good idea, and she supposed, as long as they were kept clean, that they were all right. As long as they didn't ruin their teeth. And as long as nobody saw them.

They were working now. The children lay in their beds, sucking on the soothers, and already Gavin was beginning to close his eyes. Amber, her teddy clutched in her arm, glared at Lorraine before very deliberately turning her back on her.

Never mind, Lorraine told herself as she switched off the light and drew the door out, leaving it slightly open so the light from the landing would flow in.

But she *did* mind. It wasn't fair that her mother and David were able to manage the children so well, while she found it nearly impossible sometimes.

It wasn't as if she didn't love them. Last thing at night, every night, she would look in on the two little blond heads, the rosy cheeks and chubby little hands, and think how lucky she was. And when she had them dressed up they always looked beautiful. Everyone said so.

She just needed to be a little bit firmer so they would get used to doing what she told them instead of looking for David all the time.

She tidied the kitchen quickly and went to get her accounts book. She thought about making some tea but decided against it – David would be home in an hour or so and there was no point boiling the kettle twice. It paid to be careful about these things. She had already reduced the electricity bill by five per cent over the past year.

Tonight she would look at their food bill.

And the cost of presents.

That had been astronomical last year, even with her Christmas plan. Maybe this year they would be better off not getting presents for anybody at all. It was all such a waste of money.

Lorraine was careful about presents. Any she got

which didn't suit her were brought to a very good swap-shop she knew, or else put away in tissue paper until she needed a gift for someone. She kept a catalogue of who had given her what so that she never had the embarrassment of giving the same gift back to the person who had given it in the first place.

Most of the ornaments she got were recycled in this way, unless they were ones she really had to keep. Or something good, like Aynsley or Lladro. She had several pieces of these displayed on high shelves where the children couldn't reach.

But normally she couldn't bear ornaments around the house. They cluttered up the place and gathered dust. And people hardly ever got it right, in spite of her hints about what she liked and what she definitely did *not* like. If they wanted to give her something she'd much rather have the money and be free to choose for herself.

She had finally got the message across to her mother-in-law last Christmas, though David hadn't seemed too happy about it. But Lorraine knew it made sense and, though it took a little while, Margaret Kearns had finally agreed with her.

Lorraine had explained that they wouldn't be giving Christmas presents themselves, because with the family so much bigger now – David's two sisters had both had babies during the year – it would cost a fortune to buy for everyone. They were usually things people didn't want anyway. So she and David had decided instead to put their money towards the new bathroom suite they wanted.

Of course, if anyone *really* wanted to give them a present they might like to contribute to the cost of the bathroom. And she was sure people would want to give the children presents anyway. That was what Christmas was for, when you thought about it. Presents for the children.

Lorraine had been surprised at how generous Margaret and James had been, giving an amount that was far more than what they usually spent. And the children loved the toys their grandparents brought them.

David had been annoyed, saying that she had backed people into a corner. His parents had been embarrassed into giving more than they could afford. Her own mother, he pointed out, hadn't given them half the amount that his parents had.

Lorraine had countered by reminding him of the big cheque her four brothers and sisters – all of them older than her and very generous – had given.

She didn't say a word about his sisters, who had given absolutely nothing except for small little toys for Gavin and Amber. And they were sour about it, into the bargain. Mean skinflints.

Well, this year she'd show them. This year she would give them nothing, even for the children. They would be getting plenty of things anyway. So it would be a waste.

She could always put away one or two small things, suitable for anyone, as she usually did, with "Happy Christmas from David and Lorraine" on the gift-tags.

That way she was prepared if anyone brought an unexpected gift and she really had to give something back. But otherwise she would do no Christmas shopping at all. Absolutely none. Because this year she had other plans.

If she could cut down the household expenses a bit more, and didn't have to buy any presents at all, except for Gavin and Amber . . .

Her Christmas present to herself this year would be that lovely, expensive leather suite from Arnott's.

She spent a very satisfying hour curled up on the nearly perfect two-year-old sofa, going through the accounts. Before finishing she had a list of measures drawn up to show David. He mightn't like the one about not renewing his gym membership, but after all he loved running and football – he could go back to those to keep fit and they'd cost nearly nothing.

She left the list on the table and switched on the television for the lotto draw while she waited for him to come home.

She heard his car pulling into the drive as the lottery music came on.

She didn't hear his greeting as he came to the living-room door – she was too engrossed in watching the lottery.

They had five numbers.

Five numbers in a draw for six and a half million pounds!

She watched, electrified, as the sixth number came out of the drum.

Chapter Six

Maeve Redmond was livid.

She had just spent the last hour with Robert Shaw, her solicitor – and so far it had not been an easy meeting.

"What do you mean, he could still have a claim on the house?" she asked, horrified, as he sat across the desk from her in his wood-panelled office. He looked calm, professional. As well he might, she thought. He had thirty years' experience at this sort of thing – and it wasn't *his* world that was falling apart.

Maeve was trying very hard not to scream.

"You're not formally separated," Robert explained again, patiently. "The agreement you came to, that he would have your jointly-held shares and most of what was in your savings account, while you would keep the house, was an arrangement between yourselves. If you file for divorce, it could all be open for re-negotiation."

"You're saying I might have to sell the house!" She was fighting to control the panic.

"I'm not saying that for certain. These things never *are* certain. It would depend on so many things. I'm simply saying —"

"But it was my mother's house! He can't have it. He never put a penny into it! Even when I got the mortgage to pay my sisters' share, he never paid a penny!"

"I know, Maeve."

Robert had been her mother's solicitor as well. He had known Maeve since she was a teenager, knew how much she loved the big old house, how hard she had worked to look after it. And he had long suspected that Larry Redmond was no addition to her — as well as being a man who wouldn't give up easily.

"And, really, I don't wish to see you upset about this," he continued. "But his name is on the deeds, Maeve. Joint names, you remember?" he said quietly.

"But that's not fair! He never paid a penny —"

"Fair or not, I'm afraid it's how it works. We won't know how it's likely to turn out until we go to court."

"So should I just leave it? Not follow up on the divorce?"

"I wouldn't advise that. You said he's already putting pressure on you. That's likely to increase as he runs into more debt — as he undoubtedly will. It could be better in the longer term if you begin to sort matters out now. You might have more peace of mind, knowing where you stand financially."

"But I could lose the house."

"It's a risk," he said gently. "But no court is likely to order that a family home be sold, at least until the youngest child is independent. And your children are now – ?"

"Orla's fifteen, Senan is nearly thirteen. Fergus is just gone eight."

"So you should be safe for the next ten years at least. It could be longer if, for instance, your youngest opts for third-level education. That might allow you several years more. But . . ." He spread his hands wide on the oak desk, palms down. His gaze was direct as he took a deep breath. "I should warn you of one other possibility."

"What is it?" She was almost afraid to ask.

"What I have outlined is the situation as it normally occurs – that is, that the house remains the family home while the children are growing up. However, in your case" – he paused for a moment – "there is one other consideration. The value of the property."

"Why would –"

"You must know that it is worth a great deal of money, Maeve. Given its location and condition, as well as the current state of the housing market. The Court might well rule that it should be sold in any case and the proceeds divided – though not necessarily in two equal parts. Both you and Larry would be in a position to buy more modest homes in the same locality. The children could continue at their present schools, so there would be no disruption there. The court could well regard that as a fair and reasonable outcome."

"Well, I don't think it's one bit fair!" Before she could stop herself she burst out crying. She was scrabbling through her pockets in search of a tissue when he reached beneath the desk-top and passed her one from an unseen drawer.

He waited patiently as she brought the tears under control.

"Sorry," she said after a few minutes as she crumpled the tissue up and put it into her pocket. "I just don't want to lose the house. I really don't."

"I know that, Maeve." His eyes were compassionate as he sat looking at her. "And I'll do my very best. I can promise you that. But I'm afraid there are no guarantees – none at all. We'll just have to go ahead and see how it turns out."

She still had tears in her eyes as she left his office. She hoped she didn't look too much as if she had been crying.

She got into her car, which was parked just outside, and checked her face in the mirror. Not great. With luck she might have time for the short detour home to wash her face and put on some more make-up before collecting the boys from her sister's house nearby, just off the Howth Road.

Life was tough enough but without her sisters it would be impossible. The eldest, Maura, collected the boys from school every day along with her own two and kept them until Maeve was able to pick them up on the way home from work. Orla, at fifteen, could make her own way home from the nearby secondary school.

Maeve would prefer if she'd go to Maura's instead of home to an empty house, but she had given up that particular battle last year. There were too many others to be fought with Orla these days.

"That bad?" Maura asked sympathetically as she opened the door and saw Maeve's face.

Maeve nodded.

"Want to come in and talk about it?"

"Not in front of the kids. And I need to get home to Orla. I'll ring later, okay?"

The boys came out and she was home with them in ten minutes. There was, as she expected, no sign of Orla, just a note saying she was going to Ciara's to study. Maeve thought that Ciara was turning into a cheeky young one these days, and she didn't think she was a great influence on Orla. But there was nothing she could do about it. Apart from the awkwardness with Colette if she refused to let them see each other, she wasn't sure Orla would listen to her anyway.

In fact, she was sure she wouldn't. Orla didn't seem to listen to anything she said these days.

She began cooking chips and chicken nuggets for the boys, her mind miles away. She didn't know what she'd do if she lost the house. It should never have come to this. She'd kill Larry, really she would. Well, she would if she thought it would do any good.

She could hear the boys playing a video game in the next room. They were great kids and made things easier for her, but she was under no illusions about how hard it was for them, as well as for Orla. They all idolised Larry. And he loved them, she had no doubt about that.

But not enough to stop gambling away the money we needed, she thought bitterly as she called the boys for their tea. She would never forgive him for the time he lost the fifty pounds she had put aside for Senan's ninth birthday. He'd had his heart set on some football strip and it was left to her to tell him he'd have to wait a bit longer. She could still see the disappointment on his face. The fact that he took it so well, his little chin up and only a trace of tears in his eyes, made it ten times worse.

She had wanted to rant and rave and tell her son exactly why he wasn't getting his present – but she couldn't do that to him. Instead she watched his slow realisation, over the years, that what Larry promised very often didn't happen.

Orla had realised that long ago. Maeve just hadn't realised soon enough.

And still the children loved him. They lived for the Sundays he came to take them out, made excuses for him on the days when he "forgot" and they finally had to accept, sometime in the very late afternoon, that he wasn't coming.

He didn't know how lucky he was. And how stupid, to throw it all away on the roll of a dice or on a horse race.

She had made her own excuses for him over the years, telling herself it was an illness, that the Larry she loved was still there and needed her, that he would control the addiction if he could. And she watched as, gradually, it grew beyond any control he was willing or able to exert, and their lives descended into chaos.

At least, that's how it felt to Maeve. As for her husband, she began to feel that the expression "happy as Larry" was coined just for him. Nothing bad seemed to touch him, even when he lost substantial amounts over a weekend and she only knew when she got the final demands for the telephone or electricity bill – and once, terrifyingly, for the mortgage – exactly where the money was going.

The final straw had been when those two men came to the door and Fergus answered and came running to look for her.

The suits had done nothing to disguise their muscular build, the smiles didn't quite reach their eyes. The voices were soft but the threat was clear as they told her that Larry hadn't kept his part of the bargain about a "business deal" and he should now come up with the £2,000 he owed them.

They didn't say "or else". They didn't need to.

After they left she had sat down and thought long and hard, deciding that for her sake as well as the children's she couldn't go on like this.

That had been over three years ago. Larry had left quietly enough, promising to send her money – which, to his credit, he still did occasionally. He was better at keeping his promise about staying in touch with the children, but it had still been impossibly hard for all of them.

And now, just as she was beginning to feel on solid ground again, he was back looking for the only thing they had left that was of any value.

She glanced across at her sons, busy finishing their tea while she cleaned up around the kitchen. She couldn't, she simply couldn't believe that Larry would do something like this to them. It would take away whatever sense of security they still had.

She gave the worktop a final wipe, rinsed her hands and went to join them at the table.

"Are you not eating, Mam?" Senan asked quietly. He missed nothing. She sometimes felt he'd had to grow up too quickly. He seemed to see himself as the man of the house after Larry went, and though she tried not to depend on him too much, it was great to have an ally. She sometimes felt she could drop down dead in front of Orla and her daughter wouldn't notice.

"I'm not hungry," she answered him. "I might have something later, when Orla gets in. Did you get your homework finished?"

"We both did. Fergus didn't have much, but I helped him. Didn't I, Goose?"

"Stop calling me that," Fergus yelled, as they had expected. But he was grinning. Senan could call him whatever he wanted and he wouldn't care. Senan had been a doting big brother from the time Fergus was born, and the age gap between them – nearly five years – still didn't make a difference. They were as close as ever, and Maeve loved to see it. She was very close to her own three sisters and had hoped for the same kind of relationship with her daughter.

Some hope, she thought, as she continued chatting to the boys. Orla didn't even try to hide her boredom when Maeve spoke to her. And mostly, if she answered, it was to challenge what Maeve said. She was even worse since she started hanging around with Ciara. Maeve suspected they were pushing the boundaries further than they might otherwise go, just to impress each other.

As if on cue she heard the key in the door and Orla's footsteps going upstairs. It would be nice, just for once, if she bothered to come and say hello. Little Madam, Maeve thought. She and I are headed for a serious talk. Not that it will do much good – but I have to do *something* to try and get through to her.

She got Fergus settled into bed and was watching TV with Senan when Orla came downstairs. Maeve heard her in the kitchen, presumably helping herself from the fridge. For the past year or so she had refused point-blank to eat the dinners Maeve prepared, saying they made her feel ill. So instead Maeve made sure to leave plenty of good food available, in the hope that Orla would eat sensibly. It seemed to be working. She hadn't lost weight and was never unwell.

She came into the room now, carrying two coffee cups – two! – and a cup of hot chocolate for Senan.

Wait for it, Maeve told herself. She's looking for something.

Orla set down the tray, passed over the coffee and hot chocolate and perched on the arm of the sofa.

"Mam," she began.

Definitely looking for something, Maeve thought. She rarely called her that. These days it was Maeve, or Mother. Or, more often, nothing at all.

"Jenny Costello told me she's getting £500 from her mother, for the school trip – for new gear and stuff. So I was wondering –" She saw Maeve's face and rushed to continue. "I *know* we don't have that kind of money. I'm not *that* stupid." She stopped, watching Maeve's reaction. "I thought I could get a job. Just a few evenings a week. The money's good."

Maeve sighed. They'd been through this before. She really didn't want Orla working until at least after her Junior Cert exams. But she didn't kill herself studying, from what Maeve could see, and she *would* need some extra cash . . .

"Have you talked to Paddy Quinn?" He was the manager of the local supermarket.

"Not the supermarket."

"But where else – I *don't* want you working in a pub at your age!"

"I don't *want* to work in a pub." Maeve saw the slight flush creep into Orla's cheeks. "Johnny Griffin's father will give me a job. He owns Ace Racing. He knows Dad –"

"Orla! For God's sake, you don't expect me to let you work in a bookie's!"

"Dad would let me."

"He probably would – if he was here."

Orla stood up, banging the coffee cup down on the table. "We all know whose fault it is that he's not!"

Senan looked from one to the other, his face tense. "The lottery's coming on," he said, his voice pleading. "Let's watch it, Orl. Come on. Sit down."

"For all the good it'll do," Orla said. But her voice was quieter and she sat down beside him. She had a soft spot for Senan. The family peacemaker, he could usually get round her.

Maeve opened her mouth to tell them she had left the syndicate, but Senan was already taking the numbers from the coffee-table drawer, and she decided to say nothing. No harm in letting them watch one more draw. Let them have the pleasure of dreaming, just for this few minutes. She'd tell them before next Saturday's draw that she was out of it.

There was silence in the room as the numbers came out of the drum and Senan began marking them off one by one with Orla watching over his shoulder.

One after the other they came out. She knew them off by heart.

"Seven . . . Fourteen . . . Twenty-three . . . Thirty-one . . . Thirty-seven . . .

And the final number out of the drum is . . . Forty-two!"

All of them. Dear God, all of them.

Senan and Orla jumped up, shouting, hugging each other.

She couldn't look at them, couldn't meet their eyes.

Instead she watched as the cup she had dropped rolled over against the fireplace, its contents spreading in a dark-brown stain all over the faded carpet.

Chapter Seven

Colette hadn't slept a wink all night.

She had lain there, tossing and turning beside Martin who was sound asleep. She hadn't said a word to him and had sworn Peter to secrecy. Because it couldn't be true. She didn't have that kind of luck. It just couldn't possibly be true.

But if it was!

Peter had been jubilant. He had the list. The numbers were there in front of him.

"Ring one of the others, Mam," he had said, more than once. "Go on, ring them. Find out for sure."

"They would have rung me if we had it." But Colette couldn't be certain of that. She picked up the phone, put it back down. Because who could she ring? Suzanne was bound to be out, she usually was. And even if she had phone numbers for Olive and Lorraine she really didn't want to ring them.

She wanted to ring Maeve.

And she couldn't.

All the joy she was feeling, all the heady *"what if it's really true?"* exhilaration vanished every time she thought of Maeve.

They would just have to change that stupid contract. No matter what anyone said. They couldn't leave her out of something as big as this.

When Colette arrived at the office Lorraine was the only one there. She was already at her computer, looking like the cat that got the cream. She removed a document from the printer and waved it in the air.

"My letter of resignation!" she said triumphantly. "Want me to do one for you?"

"So it's true?" Colette managed to ask. She was stunned. Lorraine had never before, as far as she knew, offered to do anything for anyone. It *must* be true.

"Did you not check your list?" Lorraine looked at her as if she was slightly mad.

"Well, yes – but I thought it might be wrong, or something. Are you sure?"

"I typed it myself." Her voice was cold now, back to her usual self. Colette remembered what Lorraine had said, about a win not changing her. Too right, it would take a miracle. Except this *was* a miracle.

Colette sat at her desk, still looking at Lorraine.

"I know. I didn't mean it like that, Lorraine. It's hard to believe it, that's all. It's just not sinking in."

"Well, believe it. Because as soon as the others get here we're going straight to the lottery office to pick up the cheques. There was only one winning ticket. So we each won £1,631,780." She called the amount out slowly, taking great pleasure in it.

"How did you work it out?" Colette asked. Her head was spinning. She couldn't begin to imagine so much money. What it would look like. What she could do with it . . .

Lorraine made an exasperated sound. "How do you think I worked it out? I divided the total of £6,527,120 by four. Which makes £1,631,780 each."

£1,631,780. More money than any of them had ever expected to see in their lives. Well, except Suzanne, maybe. She had told them again and again that she was certain they would win, that it was only a matter of time. But surely even she couldn't have imagined this much money.

A fortune.

No matter how you divided it.

"Lorraine." Colette spoke slowly. It was still hard to take it in. "What would the six million be, divided by five?"

Lorraine stared at her. Her tone was pure ice. "Why would you want to know that?"

"I was just wondering – it's a lot of money . . ."

Lorraine waited. Her expression didn't invite any further comment. It was clear that she wouldn't be open to a suggestion of sharing with Maeve.

I still need to try it, Colette thought. Maeve will

never agree to take it unless we're all behind the idea. Probably not even then.

She held her breath as the door opened, but it was Suzanne.

She looked as if she hadn't slept much either. In fact, she didn't look well. There was none of her usual bounce and she barely smiled when she greeted them. That wasn't a bit like her.

"Exhausted from celebrating?" Lorraine asked.

Suzanne just looked at her.

"Well, you could answer me!"

"Sorry, Lorraine," Suzanne said in a tired voice. "I was trying to think of an answer."

"Well, were you or weren't you?"

"Was I or wasn't I what?"

Lorraine looked from one to the other as if they were lacking something essential. Brains, maybe. She raised her eyes to Heaven.

"Thank God I'm getting out of here!"

"You're leaving?" Suzanne asked.

"Of course I'm leaving. Aren't you?"

The penny dropped for Colette as she listened to them. "You don't know, do you?"

"Know what?" Suzanne asked, perplexed.

'£1,631,780, that's what!" Lorraine's exasperation vanished as she broke the news, looking more animated than Colette had ever seen her before. "We won! We won the lottery! Don't tell me you didn't watch it last night?"

Suzanne looked from one to the other of them, a smile spreading across her face. "Get away!"

"It's true," Colette said. "Really, it's true!"

Suzanne burst out laughing. Suddenly she ran across the room, kissed Lorraine, hugged Colette, shrieking with excitement, and they were all laughing and talking at once when the door opened again and Maeve walked in.

The bubble burst. They stood looking at her, nobody quite sure what to say.

"Maeve," Colette began.

Maeve's smile was strained, but her voice was warm. "I know. Isn't it great? And didn't I say I'd be the first to congratulate you all?"

"We have to talk about this, Maeve."

Maeve sat down at her desk, still looking at Colette. "Nothing to talk about. Except how I'll manage when you're all gone." This time the smile wavered.

"Oh, don't be ridiculous, Maeve." Suzanne said. She was radiating warmth and energy and sheer exuberance now, the earlier tiredness gone without trace. "Of course we have to talk. It's not as if you're gone ages from the syndicate. It gets split five ways. No question."

"What do you mean, no question?" Lorraine asked sharply. "I'd have plenty of questions if you tried to split it in five when there are only *four* of us in the syndicate. No, thank you very much! I'm keeping to what we agreed. What we *all* agreed." She was looking pointedly at Maeve.

"There *is* another way." Olive Grace stood just inside the door. None of them had heard her come in. Colette glanced at the clock. 9.10. The win had definitely changed *her*. She had never come in after nine as long as Colette had known her.

She came further into the room as she spoke. "You take your share, Lorraine. I presume you've worked out exactly what it is?"

"£1,631,780."

"So we'll have one cheque made out for that amount," Olive continued, looking around at them. "And we'll divide the balance four ways. That way, everyone is happy, and we'll still have a great deal of money each. And you, Lorraine, will have the full amount to which you feel entitled."

"I *am* entitled to it! The rest of you can do what you like with your share, but I'm sticking to the agreement we made. After all, if it was the other way around you'd expect me to keep to it."

"You do have a point," Olive said. "But this needn't concern you. We'll work out the amounts now – that's if everyone else agrees with me?" She looked from Colette to Suzanne, both of whom nodded. "Good. Then I suggest we ring the Lottery people once we've done our calculations." Her glance swept round to include all of them, stopping when she came to Maeve, who hadn't said a word.

"I can't do it," she said now. All eyes were on her as she spoke. "Thanks a million" – she gave a little laugh –

"For once, I really mean that. But you know I can't take the money. Like Lorraine said, we had an agreement. Or at least, all of you had."

"Come on, Maeve. You're only delaying us," Suzanne said, smiling. "Just take the money and run! Enough of this rubbish about agreements. We're making a new one right here and now." She gave a scathing glance at Lorraine. "The four of us."

Maeve was shaking her head.

Colette stood up. "Come on," she said to her. "Excuse us for a few minutes," she said to the others as she steered Maeve out into the corridor.

"Are you mad?" she hissed, keeping her voice low. "Have you completely lost it? Whether you take the money or not, we'll all still be millionaires! Come on, Maeve! Just do it!"

Maeve was standing against the wall, arms folded. She glanced at the floor, shook her head. "No, Colette. Thanks, but I can't. Really, I can't. I made a decision, and I'm sticking with it."

"Think of the kids, Maeve!"

Maeve hesitated for a moment. There was a sharp pain in her stomach as she remembered last night, Orla's incredulous rage and Senan's struggle to hide his disappointment as he hugged her and told her it didn't matter.

Of course it mattered – and it would be so easy, in a way, to accept their generosity, take her share.

Only it wasn't her share. She had opted out, so she

was out. Her pride wouldn't let her do anything else.

She shook her head without saying a word, took a deep breath and walked back into the room. She stood near the filing cabinets for a moment, composing herself. Then she looked around the room, from one to the other of them, avoiding Lorraine's unpleasant stare.

"You have no idea how much I appreciate this. You couldn't. But I can't take the money. And that's my final word – except to wish you all luck and happiness with it – and to say I'll miss you when you go." Well, not Lorraine, she thought – but then, she wasn't actually addressing her.

"Why should you think we're going?" Olive asked gently. "I certainly have no intention of leaving here."

"You haven't?" It was a chorus of disbelief.

"No, I haven't. To be truthful, I enjoy being here. It's been my life now for a very long time."

Lorraine's expression said it all. Pathetic.

Still, it wasn't her problem.

"Well, I'm certainly leaving," she said. "I've written my letter of resignation, giving a month's notice."

"A month's notice?" Suzanne's face was a picture. "You mean, we have to stay here for another month?" She made it sound like a life sentence.

Olive smiled as Suzanne looked questioningly at her.

"I don't see how they can actually force you to stay." She smiled. "I've heard Italy's wonderful in September."

"Forget Italy. There's a whole wide world out there!

Wonder what Blake's Travel have on Africa?" She was reaching for the phone. "I'd better ring my mother, and Finn –" She broke off abruptly, her hand dropping away from the phone.

Uh-oh, Colette thought. She knew what *that* meant.

They all busied themselves, covering up Suzanne's sudden silence.

Olive went to tell Mr Malone, the Assistant Principal, that half the section was leaving – preferably right now.

Colette sat with a sheet of paper in front of her, doodling figures on it.

Lorraine was singing as she reached to answer the telephone.

And Maeve took out her in-tray and tried to get down to work.

She had never, in her entire life, felt more unlucky.

Or more alone.

Chapter Eight

Olive still hadn't broken the news to her mother. She hadn't really had the opportunity. On Wednesday, when the lottery draw took place, she had made a mental note of the numbers but said nothing to her mother when she thought she recognised five of them. Better to wait and be certain before raising her hopes.

She had checked the sheet after she helped her mother to bed. Checked it again, marked off the numbers. Six of them! Six!

She had watched the late news, heard the announcer say that there was one winner of the midweek lotto jackpot of £6,527,120.

Quickly she had done her calculations, dividing the amount by five. Of course Maeve would be part of it – to think otherwise was ridiculous.

Over £1.3 million each! What on earth would she do

with that amount of money? She could give up work and –

And stay at home with her mother?

Reality came crashing in as she realised that, no matter how much money she had won, it would make no significant difference. Not when she had her mother to care for. She could see the years stretching ahead, interminable, totally without promise.

Several times on Thursday she began to tell her mother, but was interrupted each time. Bridget Grace simply wasn't in the habit of listening to her daughter.

Maybe it was just as well, Olive told herself on Friday evening when her mother had gone to bed. This way, she could wait and announce it on Sunday when her brothers were here for Bridget's 78th birthday. They had planned a low-key celebration but perhaps they could do something different – maybe even go out to lunch. They had never done that as a family. She had hardly ever done it herself, being in the habit of bringing sandwiches to work each day and going for a brisk walk afterwards. But yesterday had been such a wonderful experience. She really would like to do it again.

It had been Suzanne's idea, of course. She had persuaded them all, Maeve included, to go for lunch in Peacock Alley – and Olive had enjoyed herself more than she could have imagined. She would never have dreamed of going there before. And she couldn't wait to do it again.

Lunch had been a leisurely affair with all of them talking at once, making plans for the money, taking care, at the same time, that Maeve wouldn't feel too left out. To her credit she had joined in the celebrations, giving in gracefully when Suzanne had dismissed her attempt to pay for her share of the meal.

There had been only one difficult moment. Well, two. And both of them, not surprisingly, concerned Lorraine.

It had happened towards the end of the meal, and Lorraine had probably drunk more wine than she should have. She told them in great detail, for what was possibly the third time, how she intended spending the money, before turning to Maeve.

"I suppose it's only fair, really, the way it's worked out."

"What do you mean?" Maeve had asked, cautiously.

"Well, you know. That lovely big house of yours. It must be worth a fortune. None of the rest of us has ever had anything like that – so now things have balanced out."

All eyes were on her. Olive was the first to speak.

"You surely can't mean that, Lorraine!"

"Why not? It's true, isn't it?"

Olive had always known Lorraine was mean with money, but such absolute meanness of spirit was incredible. As she struggled to think of a reply she allowed herself, for the first time, to recognise how thoroughly she disliked the woman.

Lorraine continued speaking, oblivious to the reaction of the others.

"What goes round comes round, isn't that what they say? So now it's my turn."

Maeve looked steadily at her. "That's what they say, all right, Lorraine. It would be interesting to see how things turn out by this time next year."

"Ooh!" Lorraine feigned surprise. "The knives are out! Well, you needn't –"

"Quiet a minute, Lorraine!" Suzanne had jumped in, eager to restore the semblance of harmony. "That's a great idea! Suppose we were to meet here again in – a year's too long – say nine months –" She was whipping out her diary as she spoke. "The twentieth of June, okay? We'll all meet here for lunch on the twentieth of June and see how things have gone for us!"

"You must be mad!" was Lorraine's answer as she stood up from the table. "Why should I want to see any of you again when I don't have to? You do whatever you want – but don't expect me to be here!"

"In that case, I might just come," Maeve had said.

Lorraine was right, Olive had thought privately as they walked the short distance back to the office. The knives were indeed out.

She had tried not to let the atmosphere in the office affect her. They would all be together at least until the following Friday, which would be Suzanne's last day.

Colette and Lorraine were staying on for a further four weeks: Colette, because she didn't want to leave Maeve on her own just yet, and Lorraine – they could hardly believe it – because she was unwilling to forego a month's salary by not working the required notice period.

Olive herself had no clear idea of what she intended to do, beyond telling the family on Sunday. She would continue working as usual, she assumed. There was no reason to do otherwise.

By Sunday morning she felt exhausted, as much by the effort of keeping the secret as by the preparations for her mother's birthday.

Bridget had refused Olive's tentative suggestion – as Olive had known in her heart that she would – of going out for lunch.

"Waste of money," she had said. "And anyway I prefer to be in my own house with my children around me."

Which was all very well, Olive had thought, except that, as usual, it fell to her to make all the preparations before her brothers and their wives arrived. Fortunately Raymond was bringing only three of his children – the two older ones were away for the weekend – which meant nine to cook for instead of the expected eleven.

"You'd think they'd find time to come for their grandmother's birthday," Bridget had complained. "And after all I've done . . ."

For once Olive didn't jump to their defence. Let Raymond make excuses for them this time, she thought. She was tired of doing it for him.

He wasn't the worst, she mused as she prepared the

meal. At least he and Della offered to stay with Bridget occasionally, now that their children were getting older. Which was more than Vincent had ever done.

Not that it made any difference, of course. Bridget had refused point-blank to let them stay. She had put it in terms of concern, saying it wasn't fair to "the boys" to have to come so far – Raymond lived all of ten miles away – and to disrupt their routine. It wasn't as if Olive had plans for going anywhere, was it?

And Olive gave in every time. What was that expression she had heard her niece use – a wimp? Well, that was her, she thought as she scraped savagely at the potatoes. A wimp. She couldn't remember ever – not once – disagreeing openly with her mother on anything that really mattered. Any more than she had ever spent a single night away from her.

Too late to start now, she told herself as she continued with the lunch preparations. But surely winning the money must make *some* difference?

She wondered what their reaction would be. Predictable enough, probably. Raymond would wish her well, Vincent would offer her financial advice – as if he knew anything about money apart from spending it – and her mother . . .

Her mother would act as if it were hers and try to take control of it.

Olive had long suspected that the money Bridget took from her to "put away for a rainy day" was going to her sons, or at least to Vincent. He and Norma had extravagant tastes, and Olive had no idea whether his "financial consultancy" brought in sufficient income to support his lifestyle. Norma, of course, didn't work – she was too busy with the tennis club and her various committees.

She always went into elaborate detail about these on the rare occasions when she and Vincent came to visit. Olive's capacity for politeness was always stretched to the limit at such times. She considered her sister-in-law a silly, vain woman with nothing much to talk about but herself. More than once Olive had thought it would do her the world of good to have to go out and earn a living. She wondered what it would be like, not to have to go to work, to be able to please yourself . . .

She stopped, almost in shock.

It had been like that since Wednesday evening, the sudden surge of remembering, the disbelief, the joy bubbling up every now and then –

Followed by the realisation that, really, it didn't make any difference. She was in no hurry to give up work, couldn't think of what else she might do that wouldn't involve staying at home to look after her mother.

Who really didn't need looking after at all, when it came to it. Certainly, she had arthritis, and it was more difficult for her to get around now. But far from impossible. Olive's main function was to keep her company, look after the house and pay the bills.

Just as her father had done.

Olive felt silly that, even after all these years, the very thought of him brought a sharp stab of pain. But there it was. She had never stopped missing him, not once in the thirty-nine years since he had died. She remembered clearly the day he finally gave in. Even then, his concerns were for her and her mother.

She had never forgotten his words –

"They're here!" Her mother's voice, as excited as a young girl's, interrupted Olive's thoughts and she glanced through the side window of the kitchen to see Vincent's car – a gleaming, brand-new one – pulling into the drive.

Bridget was beside herself in her eagerness to get to the door. She moved down the hallway with surprising speed, calling out to him that she was coming before he had even rung the doorbell.

A wonder she didn't kill the fatted calf, Olive thought acidly as she heard the door opening and the voices in the hallway. Loud, confident voices of people very sure of their place in the world.

Bridget led them into the living-room, talking non-stop about what a great pleasure it was to see them and how good it was of them to come all this way. Vincent and Norma lived in Cork but Olive doubted very much that they had travelled all that way for Bridget's birthday. More likely, they had managed to combine the event with a social function or two in Dublin.

"You'll never guess," Norma said as Olive came into the living-room to greet them. "Vincent had to see some business associates in Dublin, so he suggested an afternoon meeting in their Dublin offices on Friday, followed by a round of golf at their club yesterday. We had dinner with them on Friday evening. Dreadfully boring, really, but important for business – you know. Wasn't he clever to think of seeing them, when he would have been here anyway for your birthday?"

"That's my Vincent!" Bridget was beaming.

That's our Vincent, all right, Olive thought as she stood by the doorway, her smile firmly in place. And no doubt he wrote the whole journey off for tax purposes.

She excused herself, glad to escape back to the kitchen. She checked the food and went through to the dining-room where she was putting the final touches to the table when Raymond arrived.

"Just in time," she said as she opened the front door. "Do you want to go in and say hello, then come on through to the dining-room?"

Raymond nodded as he stood back to leave Della go in, followed by three of their children. They greeted Olive warmly, then made their way through the narrow hallway to the living-room. Raymond hung back for a second as he closed the front door behind him.

"How are you?" he asked Olive quietly, smiling down at her. Like Vincent he was tall, but he had none of his elder brother's panache. He looked worn out, Olive thought. Exhausted.

"I'm –" She started to answer, hesitated. Didn't really want to spoil the surprise by telling him here. "– very

well," she continued, "very well indeed. I have news –"
a big smile broke through, "but you'll have to wait."

"Go on, tell me." He was laughing, enjoying her good
humour.

"Later. Shhh! Now go and bring them into the dining-
room for me!"

Lunch was more pleasant than Olive had anticipated.
Bridget was in great good humour, as well she might be
with everybody dancing attendance on her. Let her
enjoy it, Olive thought generously. Not everyone gets as
far as their 78th birthday in good health.

For once, Raymond's children entered into the spirit
of the occasion, managing to hold their own in spite of
Norma's attempts at dominating the conversation.

The two girls, eighteen-year-old Naomi and sixteen-
year-old Rachel, were making an effort to be pleasant to
their grandmother, and even Matthew – fifteen, and much
happier on a rugby field than anywhere else – was on
best behaviour. Della, as usual, helped with the serving
and with clearing away the dishes. She never said very
much when Norma was around. Olive suspected she
found Norma daunting and was much happier helping
out in the kitchen than trying to make conversation
with her.

"We'll bring in the cake now," Olive said as they
cleared off the last of the dinner plates. "Do you think
the children will sing 'Happy Birthday' – or have they
gone past that stage?"

"Oh, they'll sing it all right," Della said grimly.

The two women looked at each other and laughed. Della had obviously warned them to behave. Olive found herself warming to her sister-in-law, not for the first time. There was no harm in Della. Her life revolved around her children, and usually she could talk of little else, which Olive found trying since they seemed forever to be going through 'a difficult stage'. But recently things seemed to be on a more even keel, and Della was certainly looking more relaxed than she normally did.

It would be good if they became closer, Olive thought. She badly missed having a sister, someone to share the burden of her concerns about Bridget. Maybe, even, someone to go out with occasionally.

She put the cake on the plate and Della lit the candles she had brought. Children's candles, a big 7 and an 8. A nice touch, Olive felt. She hadn't thought of getting candles herself.

Bridget was delighted with the fuss of blowing out the candles and 'Happy Birthday' being sung, and the children producing little gifts for her. Raymond's present of a china vase was admired, then put carefully aside in favour of Vincent's large, brightly-wrapped package.

He had excelled himself. He helped Bridget as she tore off the wrapping to reveal a framed newspaper page.

"From the day you were born," he explained.

Olive knew that her mother hated such things. "Waste of money," she had remarked when Olive had suggested getting one to mark her 70th birthday. "Who wants to be reminded of things that happened that long ago?"

She did, obviously, because now she *oohed* and *aahed* over Vincent's present as if it was the one and only thing she had ever wanted.

She *didn't* want the cardigan Olive had carefully chosen some weeks ago.

"You know I never liked that colour. I don't know what possessed you to buy it."

Only your telling me you *would* love a mauve cardigan, Olive thought.

She bit back the hurt as she looked around the table. The children were staring at their grandmother while Della moved slightly in the chair, looking uncomfortable. Raymond glanced across at Olive and gave a slight wink. Vincent and Norma were, of course, oblivious, still delighted with their cleverness in finding the perfect gift.

"I'm sorry you don't like the cardigan, Mother, but if you tell me what you *would* like, I'll be happy to get it for you."

Bridget barely glanced at her. "No point in that now, is there? My birthday is today. Besides, I have the presents I want. And it's not as if you've money to waste on rubbish that no-one needs."

That cardigan cost £48 and was hardly rubbish, Olive thought. She took a deep breath. It was now or never.

"Actually, I *do* have money. Not that I want to waste it – but I have money, a great deal of it."

She had their attention.

"I wanted to keep it as a birthday surprise, Mother," she said quickly. Bridget wouldn't thank her for not telling her straight away. "You know I'm in the lottery syndicate at work – well, we won, last Wednesday –"

"How much?" Bridget interrupted quickly.

"You're joking!" Vincent said loudly. "That jackpot was over six million pounds –" his expression changed as he realised she meant it.

Olive nodded. "Over £1.6 million each," she said, feeling the warm surge of delight again, watching their faces as they registered what she was saying.

And suddenly they were all talking at once and her mother was beaming at her.

"Well, aren't *you* the clever girl?" Norma said, coming to put her hand on Olive's shoulder and kiss the air beside her cheek, a habit Olive detested. Do it or don't do it, she wanted to say, but don't *pretend* to do it.

"Cleverness didn't actually come into it. It was pure luck."

"Whatever. It's wonderful news – and marvellous timing."

"I don't –"

"Vincent is just about to expand his business, aren't you, darling? So it's a perfect opportunity for you to get in at the right time, Olive. Imagine – you and Vincent, partners!"

Olive took a deep breath and held her nerve. She tried to pretend she was at a meeting in work. She never had any difficulty there in dealing with people.

"Actually, Norma, it's good of you to offer – but I'd rather have time to think about what I should do with the money."

Bridget's expression changed instantly. "Don't be ridiculous!" she said sharply. "How much did you say it is – over one million six hundred thousand pounds? What would you expect to do with that much money? The obvious thing is to share it out among your family."

"Of course I'll look after everyone," Olive said. "I just need a little while to get used to it, that's all . . ."

"Well, don't be too long about it, because your brother needs that money. The fairest thing is to divide it four ways – and then you can take all the time you want to decide what you'll do with your share."

Norma was nodding encouragingly, Vincent was rummaging in the drinks cabinet, saying something about a toast "to our good fortune". Raymond was looking steadily at Olive while Della concentrated on the pattern of the tablecloth. The children were already discussing, loudly, what they would do with "their share".

She had to get out of there.

She stood up suddenly. "I could do with some fresh air."

After a slight pause Raymond said, "I'll come with you."

"I'm only going to the garden."

"I'll follow you down in a minute or so."

As she went through the back door she could hear

the voices getting louder and Vincent's roar of laughter eclipsing all of them.

She *had* to get away. The garden was narrow but very long, with a little wooden summerhouse at the far end. She made her way towards it, pausing now and then to deadhead some roses that had reached the end of their summer. Her father had planted them, as he had everything in the garden. It had been his oasis. She felt close to him here.

It was years since she had been in the summerhouse and she was dismayed at the state of it. She brushed aside some spider-webs at the doorway and cleared a space on the old wooden bench inside. This was where she used to come when she was young, in the long difficult days after her father died. When she had felt quite alone in the world. When she had needed space, and time, to think.

She sat quietly, watching as a spider spun its web in the corner.

Her thoughts drifted, coming back again and again to the money. She didn't want it. She didn't need it. Certainly not so much of it. And of course she had intended sharing it with them.

So why did she feel resentful at her mother trying to take control of it? Heaven knows, at this point of her life she was used to her mother exerting control.

She was still trying to puzzle it out when she heard footsteps and Raymond appeared in the doorway.

"Private party?"

She moved over a bit on the bench. "Not really. But

you'll get filthy." She paused. "You didn't like the other party?"

He gave a dry laugh as he sat down. "Vincent and Norma's one, you mean? They think all their Christmases have come together."

"They have."

"Ollie." She looked at him in the dim light. He hadn't called her that for years. Decades. "What are you going to do with the money?"

"You know I'll share it."

Raymond shifted on the narrow seat. He sat, absently rubbing his arm with one hand, looking through the open doorway into the bright garden.

"That's not what I mean. I mean – for yourself."

"I'm not sure yet. There's very little I need."

"You wouldn't think of buying a house, investing the rest?"

He sounded uncomfortable. Olive sat up straighter, turning to look at him.

"But why would I buy another house?"

"For security." He still wasn't looking at her.

"I don't need that kind of security," she said. "I really don't want the bother of buying a house only to rent it out – I'd prefer to invest in savings bonds or something like that to give me a nice, reliable income."

"Have you never thought of buying a house for yourself? To live there, not to rent out?"

"No. Well, once, maybe – but that was a long time ago . . ."

"You could still do it."

"Of course I couldn't. What would happen to Mother?"

He took a deep breath. "Have you ever thought about what would happen to *you,* when she's gone?" It came out in a rush, startling her. Raymond wasn't usually so blunt.

She hesitated. "Not really. I suppose I just thought I'd live my days out here, going in and out to work. That's if I thought about it at all."

"Olive."

He was looking directly at her now. Suddenly she felt afraid.

"You wouldn't have the house, Olive. The house would be gone."

"No, Mother said the house would be mine. Because I've lived here all these years and put so much money into it. As far as I know she has insurance policies and money put away for you and Vincent, in lieu of your share."

There was a long pause as Raymond gazed out into the garden again.

"Is that what she told you?"

"Yes, some years ago." She saw his expression. "What's wrong? Did you think –?"

"It's not hers any more, Ollie. She signed it over about five years ago, to myself and Vincent."

She sprang up. "She couldn't have!"

Oh, yes, she could. The thought came immediately. Slowly she sat down again.

"But why didn't you say something?" she asked when he continued to sit in silence, not looking at her.

He sighed, shook his head. "I should have. Of course I should have. But she swore me to secrecy. And, well . . ."

He didn't need to continue. Raymond was no match for the alliance of Vincent and Bridget.

"And what was to become of me?" Olive asked in a tight voice.

"I would have looked after you. I always meant to split my half with you, when she's – and I assumed you'd have some money put by."

"Little enough. I didn't realise how much I needed it."

"More than you know. Vincent managed to get a loan on the strength of his share – and they're calling it in."

"The house would have had to be sold?" She was shocked as he nodded.

"He was looking for part of my share, as well. He's in over his head. But he has the devil's own luck – you came to the rescue just in time." He smiled at her finally. "You'll think about what I said?"

She looked at him. "Oh, yes. Yes, I'll think about it. You go on in. They'll wonder what's keeping you. I'll be in soon."

He stood up, hesitated a moment and left.

She lost track of time as she sat there, watching the spider weaving its web in the dark corner. She couldn't get the image of her mother out of her mind.

She trapped me, Olive thought. Just as surely as that spider will trap the next poor foolish fly that comes along. And my father helped her to do it, without ever meaning to. When I promised to take care of her, he didn't mean it to cost me my whole life.

It had cost her enough already, she realised. She had been heading for disaster without even knowing it, as surely as that unsuspecting fly.

The difference was that now she knew. Now she could do something about it.

She stood up slowly, still watching the spider as a sense of exhilaration filled her. She had done her best and it hadn't been enough. Well, now she would stop trying and let the others take their turn.

It had begun, she thought, as she left the summerhouse and walked back up the path. Lorraine had been right – winning the lottery wouldn't change her life.

But she could change it herself.

And now she had the means to do it.

Chapter Nine

"I'd give it all back if I could – right this minute!" The words were out before Colette could stop herself.

"Come off it, Colette!" Maeve said. "You don't mean that."

"Want to bet?" Colette asked grimly. They were sitting in Maeve's kitchen on Saturday morning, almost three weeks after the big win.

"You know I don't make bets," Maeve said sharply. Her tone softened slightly as she continued. "I hope you don't mean it, Colette. Because you'd be a fool not to enjoy this. You must be getting *some* good out of it."

Colette gave a slight laugh. "Well, there's the thought of getting away from Lorraine –"

"Sure," Maeve said. "God, she's been a bitch, hasn't she? But at least I won't have to put up with her either, after next week."

"Do you mind that you'll be on your own?" Colette asked tentatively. "I still feel as if I'm – well . . ."

"Abandoning me?" Maeve finished for her. "Wouldn't let that worry you. I'll be happy enough once we get a few new people in – think how much I'll impress them when I'm the only one around who knows anything!"

"And Malone will give you a big promotion –"

"And I'll be able to afford some decent furniture –" Maeve paused, and an uneasy silence hung between them.

"Maeve – I could –"

"Don't, Colette! Don't even think it!"

Colette sighed. She reached for her bag and stood up.

"I'd better go. I told Martin I'd be back in time to mind Emer. He's going shopping with his mother. Thanks for the coffee."

She began moving towards the kitchen door, then paused with her hand on the door handle. Maeve still hadn't spoken. She just sat there, looking miserable.

"Please, Maeve."

Maeve shook her head firmly, looking at the table.

"Just drop it, Colette, will you? Please? It's not fair to keep on at me."

"I didn't mean to. I just wish you'd –"

"And I wish you'd drop it!" This time she did look up, her eyes blazing.

Colette took a deep breath. "That's what I mean, Maeve. That's why I'd give it all back – because of the way it's changed things for us."

"It's meant to change things. Otherwise nobody would – what d'you mean, for *us*?"

"You know what I mean, Maeve. A month ago we wouldn't have been having this conversation. We've done nothing but snipe at each other ever since I won that bloody money!"

Maeve made an exasperated sound. "Is that what you think we're doing? Sniping?"

Colette nodded. "That's how it feels." Her voice was strained. She turned the knob to open the door.

Maeve stood up, sighed and crossed the room to put her hands lightly on Colette's arms, holding her there. "Come on. Sit down for a minute. We need to sort this out."

"No, I'd better go. Martin is picking his mother up to go shopping."

Maeve looked at her steadily. From the sound of things Martin's mother had gone shopping every single day since the lottery win. It would do her no harm at all to look after Emer for an afternoon instead of going off spending Colette's money.

Colette seemed to reach the same conclusion. "Just a few minutes more, then."

She sat down at the table again, putting her bag on a chair beside her.

"It would kill me to think it made a real difference to us," Maeve said. "We've been friends too long for that."

She waited. Colette didn't answer and couldn't meet her gaze.

"Don't you agree?" Maeve asked.

Finally Colette looked at her, still saying nothing.

Maeve was shaken by the sadness in her expression. "You *don't* agree," she said.

Slowly Colette shook her head.

"Of course it makes a difference." She spoke slowly, as if she was working out every single word. "Don't you see, it has to?"

"I don't –"

"Come on, Maeve! Four weeks ago we were listening to Lorraine going on and on about the new suite of furniture she's getting. We were laughing at her and her notions, and at the same time wishing *we* could manage it. And now –"

"Now you can do it."

Colette nodded. "But you can't," she said softly. "And you won't let me get you anything. Don't you see that makes a difference?"

"No," Maeve said firmly. "To be honest, I don't. I don't care if you buy a dozen suites – I'd be delighted for you!"

"I know, Maeve. But before, I could have been delighted for you, too. It was swings and roundabouts."

"So what's it now?"

"Now I feel like I'm walking on eggshells. I can't even offer to buy you a sandwich without you jumping down my throat!"

Maeve's voice was guarded. "Why would you buy me a sandwich, when I can buy my own? I don't need –"

Colette wanted to scream in frustration. "There, *that's* what I mean! What happened to the way we used to do things? Taking turns? Whoever had money did the buying, and no-one kept tabs. It all worked out in the long run. But now it's 'I owe you 22 pence', and you're counting the bloody pennies out, and I want to *spit*! *That's* the difference it makes! And we can't even talk to each other any more!"

Her voice had risen and Senan poked his nose around the door to see what was going on. He took one look at the two women and withdrew quickly.

Maeve shifted her gaze to look out the window. "Of course we talk to each other. Don't be ridiculous!"

"So why aren't you looking at me? Why aren't we doing what we used to, going round the shops on a Saturday, looking at all the things we'd like to buy! Why aren't we doing that?"

"Nothing to stop you, Colette!"

"It's no fun on my own, Maeve. Come on, why don't we –"

"You could go with Martin."

"And his mother? No thanks."

They looked at each other and laughed, the tension vanishing.

"God, can you imagine it!" Colette said. "Bad enough having to admire the stuff she brings home! If she buys one more thing and gets Martin to pay for it, I'll brain her."

"No, you won't."

Colette grimaced. "You're right, I won't. But I'll wish I could."

"So why don't you?" It was something Maeve had always wondered. "Why don't you tell her to back off? And tell Martin he's married to you, not his mother?"

"Can't you just see me?" Colette said. "Martin wouldn't know what I was talking about. But herself would – and then the whole family would be down on me like a ton of bricks for upsetting their mammy."

"D'you see much of them?"

Maeve didn't add "since the lottery win". She didn't need to.

Colette laughed. "Only every second day. All except Carmel – she's gone off to Florida for a break with her husband and the kids. I'll probably be handed the Visa bill when she gets back."

"And what about your own family – sorry, I shouldn't ask, none of my business."

"Ask what you like – it's a relief to talk about it."

Maeve looked sympathetic. "That bad?"

"Yes and no. My own family's fine. They were thrilled for me and they don't seem to be expecting anything. I'll look after them once I sort things out, but at least I'm not feeling under pressure. It's Martin's crowd are the problem. Not to mention Martin." Her hand went to her mouth. "God, I shouldn't say that!"

"Why not?"

"It doesn't feel right, talking about him behind his back. But he's driving me mad."

"What's the problem?"

"Trying to get him to sit down and make plans, that's the problem. I have investment advice coming out my ears, and still I don't know what to do because he won't help me decide. The money won't last forever, but Martin's acting as if it will – you'd think his chequebook had a 'best before' date on it. And as for his mother –"

"But can't you stop them, Colette? It's *your* money." Maeve reminded her.

Colette gave a rueful laugh. "Try telling them that!"

"Why don't *you* try telling them?" Maeve asked.

"You think they'd listen? I don't mind them having a share of it. It's just that it'll run out in no time, the way they're spending. And I'm fed up with the whole lot of them calling to see us, and humming and hawing, and we all know why they're there, but nobody's saying anything, and we have to sit there and be polite until Martin 'persuades' them to take another cheque. Yesterday it was £10,000 for his sister Anne, for a new kitchen. You know the state of our own kitchen, but he's not interested in that. If he's not at his mother's house, he's over with one of his sisters or brothers, helping them make out more shopping lists!"

She ended with a little laugh that didn't fool either of them.

"You'll have to sit him down and talk to him, Colette. Decide what you want to do, and stick to it."

Colette sighed. "That's part of the problem. I don't know what I want – except to give everyone maybe

£20,000 or so and leave it at that for the time being, until we get our heads around it. But he'd never agree to that. He's acting as if it's bad luck to even *talk* about putting limits on what we spend."

"And it's taking all the fun out of it for you?" Maeve asked as the thought struck her.

"That's it. I feel one of us has to keep on top of things. I think it would be sensible to sit down and make a list. He thinks it would be mean. So I'm kind of in limbo. I haven't spent anything at all except to clear off the mortgage."

"Lucky you." Maeve sounded as if she meant it.

"I know, but –"

"Colette, would you get a grip!" Her voice was sharper than she intended, and she paused as she saw Colette's face. She reached out and touched her hand. "I don't want to hurt your feelings, Colette. But it's high time you stood up for yourself. This is the best chance you'll ever have to grab hold of your life and make what you want of it. And the first thing you need to do is stand up to them and stop being such a wimp."

Colette pulled her hand away.

"Is that the way you see me – a wimp?"

Maeve looked steadily at her. "Maybe that's a bit over the top. But you have to admit you never say no, even when you want to. If you don't stand up to them now, you'll never do it."

Colette laughed uneasily. "Easier said than done. The habits of a lifetime!"

"So change them," Maeve said. "Look at Olive."

Colette gave a sigh, visibly relaxing as the two of them thought about Olive. "I still can't believe it," she said after a moment. "Now, *that's* what I'd love to do!"

Maeve raised her eyebrows in amusement. "Abandon everything and go off to live in Paris?"

They laughed. "Wouldn't it be great?" Colette said. "And can't you just see Martin's face if I told him?"

"Sure," Maeve agreed. "But even if you went he still wouldn't be as surprised as we were about Dragon-lady – God, I'd better stop calling her that."

"Why? Just because she amazed us all by jacking in the job and heading off doesn't mean she's turned into a decent human being!"

Maeve didn't reply.

"You think she has?" Colette asked after a minute, when Maeve still wasn't saying anything. "Come on. She never had a good word to say to anyone!"

"Or a bad word, either," Maeve reminded her. "She was always fair – she just didn't have much to say if it wasn't about work."

"Still, she could've –"

"Colette." Maeve's voice was quiet. "Look, she'd hate if she knew I told you – but she rang me the night before she left, and invited herself over."

"She *did*?"

"She did," Maeve said. "We talked for a long time. And then she offered me money."

"Did –" Colette bit off the rest of the sentence.

Maeve gave a little laugh. "You don't think I'd take it from her and not from you? No, I wouldn't take any. Or from Suzanne, either. She phoned too, before she went off to the States."

"Good old Suzanne," Colette said. "That doesn't surprise me – but Olive!"

"She's changed," Maeve said. "She's a different person. It was like seeing somebody you thought you knew, but didn't."

"Well, good for her!" Colette said. "I hope she likes Paris. It's somewhere I'd love to see."

"Martin?" Maeve asked without much hope.

"No chance. He thinks Wexford is the only place in the world for holidays. No, I'll just have to –" she paused as the thought struck her. "Maeve, why don't you come with me? We'd have a great time –"

She broke off as she saw Maeve's expression.

"I know – there I go again. But this'd be different, Maeve." She reached across the table, putting her hand on Maeve's arm as she spoke urgently. "You'd be doing me a favour. I really want to go, and there's no-one else –"

"What about Therese?" Maeve knew Colette's sister loved travelling. She had a busy job with an advertising agency and seemed to spend half her time abroad.

"I suppose so," Colette said reluctantly. "But you know Therese – it's all old hat to her. She's been in Paris a dozen times. She probably wouldn't be interested. Besides –" she took a deep breath – "it's you I want to go with. I'll shut up about it now – but if you change your mind, let me know."

Maeve smiled, stretching her hand out to cover Colette's.

"I'd love to go. And maybe we will, but not just yet, okay? I've things I need to sort out for myself first. And will you think about what I said? About making the most of all this, and standing up to Martin's crowd if you have to? You're set up for life, Colette. You can do anything you want to do."

Colette laughed. "I wish that was true!"

"It's true," Maeve insisted. "Anything you want. You just have to want it enough."

Colette looked steadily at her. "And what about you, Maeve?" she asked quietly. "What do you want?"

Maeve looked towards the window, concentrating on the question. "To get Larry off my back, that's my number one priority." She paused. "After that, I'm not sure."

She turned back to face Colette "But I know I don't want to stay in the Department. I'm beginning to feel I'm wasting my life in there. I'd much rather be home with the kids. It's the one thing I really envy you about the win. And I never realised until now how bored I am with the work. It'll probably drive me mad when you're gone."

She attempted a smile, but Colette wasn't fooled. They both knew how different it would have been if only Maeve hadn't left the syndicate.

"You'll manage," Colette said, trying to sound cheerful.

"I will," Maeve agreed. "But only for as long as I have to. I'm not trained for anything else, but it's time to have a serious think about what I want from my life. And once I know that I'll go after it." Her voice was firm now, her eyes bright.

"Good for you, Maeve. You could do anything you wanted, if you set your mind to it."

Maeve laughed. "Isn't that exactly what I'm telling you? Figure out what you want, go after it – and get it. That's what I'm going to do."

"And if it takes money –" Colette began.

Maeve gave her a look of fierce determination.

"If it takes money, then I'll get that too."

Chapter Ten

Maeve was putting the finishing touches to the paintwork in the family room when her sister Brenda called in a few nights later.

"Great job," Brenda said, peering in from the hall where she had dumped some bags of shopping. "Let me sort these out, then I'll give you a hand clearing up."

"Thanks, Bren. You're an angel," Maeve said as she smiled across at her elder sister. "Time for a cuppa?"

"Just about," Brenda answered. "John's picking the kids up from swimming and they'll be starving, so I can't stay long."

She stopped at the door of the TV room for a minute to say hello to her niece and nephews before going to the kitchen to put the kettle on. Maeve came in, drying her hands on a towel, as Brenda was making the tea.

"This is the bit I hate about painting," Maeve said, scrubbing with her nail at some of the green paint that was still sticking to the back of her hand. "This stuff's impossible to get off, even with turps. And I'll have to put up with the smell of it for the next week."

"Well worth it," Brenda said, pouring the tea. "It really does look great."

"Sure," Maeve said. "As long as you're not the one doing it!"

Brenda laughed. "That's it. Wouldn't have the inclination, even if I had the time! It's a huge job, and it looked all right the way it was. I'd have lived with it."

"I needed something to get stuck into. Something that would take my mind off things."

She paused to take a sip of tea. Brenda, sitting across from her, looked at her sympathetically.

"It really was rotten timing, wasn't it, Maeve? You'd think they'd have included you in the share-out."

"I told you, Bren, they wanted to and I wouldn't let them. And anyway, everyone except Lorraine has offered me a share."

"And you wouldn't take it? You're stone mad, Maeve. Think what you could do with, say, even £100,000 – not to mention whatever it was they got – well over a million each, wasn't it?"

Maeve nodded. "£100,000 is just about what I need. It might be enough to get Larry off my back for a while. But I couldn't take it, Bren. It wouldn't feel right, especially when I know what Larry would do with it."

"Maeve, come on! You wouldn't give it to him, would you? Even if you had it. He got what he was entitled to, right? That was all done and dusted!"

"Not exactly. We only ever had a verbal agreement, nothing formal. He took the stocks and some of the savings, I kept the house –"

"It was yours anyway!"

"That doesn't seem to count. You remember I went to see Robert Shaw last month about sorting things out, and he said it could be up for grabs if I went for a divorce?"

"It'll never come to that," Brenda said. "It's a family home. Larry can't touch it."

"Seems he's going to give it a damn good try," Maeve said. "I had a letter from him two days ago, saying what he got in the first settlement wasn't enough, that with the price of property going up so much I'm sitting on a goldmine. Which I suppose is true."

"If it's a goldmine, it's your goldmine, not his! When Mam left it to us, you were the one who took out the mortgage to buy us out – and you're still paying it off, aren't you? I bet he hasn't put a penny towards it."

"No, he hasn't," Maeve said. "But that doesn't stop him having a claim on it."

"You're wrong, Maeve. He can't have – he got his share of everything when he left here. And you know how I feel about that – he shouldn't have got a penny after what he put you through!"

Maeve smiled at her. Never mind the house, she thought. The very best thing in her life – apart from the kids – was having sisters like hers.

Maura, the eldest, mothered them all, and the

youngest, Noeleen, had a great job in public relations and was always willing to help her out financially. But it was Brenda, a bare year older than Maeve, who had always been her staunchest ally. Brenda, who had seen through Larry and his too-easy charm from the very first time she met him. Who had tried her best to warn Maeve.

And who had never, not once, said, "I told you so".

"I wish I *was* wrong, Bren. But Robert Shaw says –"

"Shaw could be wrong. Maybe you need someone a bit younger, Maeve – someone a bit more, well, aggressive – if you're going to take Larry on. Robert Shaw's a gentleman. He wouldn't know how to deal with the likes of Larry."

"Don't underestimate him, Bren. He's a good solicitor –"

"And don't you underestimate Larry, Maeve. You know by now what he's capable of."

Maeve's face crumpled and Brenda was over beside her in a moment, her arm around Maeve's shoulders.

"Oh, love, I didn't mean to upset you. I can't stand the thought of him still hassling you, that's all –"

Maeve rubbed at her eyes with the heel of her hands.

"Don't mind me, Bren. I'm just –"

The next moment there were tears streaming down her face and she dug into the pocket of her jeans, hunting for a tissue.

"God, I keep *doing* this! I feel I'm falling to pieces, Bren! Everything's going wrong, and I can't cope with it, I just can't!"

She put the back of her hand against her mouth, trying to stifle the sobs, and Brenda stood just behind her, arms around her and her cheek bent against Maeve's, making soft soothing sounds as she used to when they were children in the darkness of the night.

Back then she could always comfort her little sister when she woke from the terror of a nightmare.

If only it was that easy now, Brenda thought as she stood there holding Maeve, hoping the children wouldn't come in. This particular nightmare had already gone on too long.

Finally the sobbing eased and Maeve looked up at her, blinking away the remaining tears, rubbing at her eyes again.

"Look at me," she said with a shaky laugh. "Thirty-nine years old and still crying like a baby. I thought I'd got over all that."

Brenda moved slowly away, still looking at Maeve, and sat down again at the far side of the table.

"You're not over him at all, are you, dote?"

Maeve bit her lip, almost on the point of tears again. 'Dote' was what their mother used to call them, her special pet-name that was reserved for when they needed a bit of extra love and comforting.

"I thought I was," Maeve said, her voice unsteady. "God knows I should be. But –"

"You still love him, don't you?" Brenda's voice was soft as she asked the question.

"Yes, I still love him. In spite of everything, and

though I'd never live with him again. I had three kids with him, Bren. I remember the look on his face the day Orla was born. You don't ever forget things like that."

Brenda sat quietly, looking at her sister but saying nothing.

"I know what you're thinking," Maeve continued. "We've been through hell and back because of him and now he's doing it again." She paused, a determined look on her face. "But I'll fight him to the bitter end on this one, Bren. He can try taking the house but it'll be over my dead body. He's not going to take any more from us than he already has." She paused, took a deep breath.

"He's not getting this house, Bren. No matter what he tries. Even if he never gambles again as long as he lives. He's not getting my house."

"And you think Shaw can stop him."

"I hope so. He'll do his best, anyway. And, one way or another, we'll figure something out. I'm certain of it."

Her smile was firmly back in place. "Don't mind me, Bren. It just hits me like this every now and then. That money would have made things so easy, and I'm still kicking myself for opting out. But opt out I did, of my own free will, and I'll live with the consequences. It felt like the right thing to do. My reasons were good."

She gave a slight shrug, the smile rueful now. "But you're right, Bren, my timing was lousy. And I'll just have to live with it and move on."

"What was it that really stopped you taking the money? Pride?"

Maeve thought for a moment. "Partly. But I really, really didn't want Larry to get hold of money if I won. I couldn't stand the thought of that. So I suppose the one good thing about this is that it made me think about my legal situation. As well as the financial one. Just as well, since he was obviously thinking along the same lines."

"You gave Shaw a copy of the letter you got?"

"I posted it the same day."

"So what happens next?"

"Next I just wait and see," Maeve said. "I'll leave it in Shaw's hands – I've enough to worry about."

Brenda leaned forward, looking concerned.

"What else –"

"Oh, nothing major. I shouldn't make it sound so dramatic. Just that work is driving me mad – Lorraine is a real bitch. She won't even talk to me now. I'm getting fed up saying good morning to thin air and getting no response. I've never met anyone as ignorant in my life. I'd love to see that one get her comeuppance."

"Everyone does, sooner or later," Brenda said. "At least you won't have to put up with her for much longer. When is she leaving?"

"Three more days." She laughed. "And I'm counting the hours. The only thing is that Colette is going too. I'll really miss her."

"She was mad to stay on at all."

"She wanted to give me a hand training in the new people."

"I suppose Lorraine wasn't much help?"

"You must be joking. She's only staying on to get her last paycheque – imagine! – and she's spending all her time on the phone to shops and estate agents."

"Hope it keeps fine for her," Brenda said. "What are the new ones like?"

"Three girls, one fella. All half my age."

"And you'll be in charge now?"

"I suppose so, though Malone still won't talk about it. He's the moodiest man I ever met – I don't know how Olive Grace put up with him all these years!"

"You do what you have to, I suppose!"

Maeve smiled. Brenda had always been a great believer in getting on with things, and some of her attitude to life had rubbed off on Maeve.

"Chin up, keep going?"

"That's it," Brenda smiled back at her. "Things go in cycles, Maeve. It'll get better – you know that."

"God, I hope so. Right now it feels like they're getting worse. Orla's really getting out of hand."

"What's she doing?"

"Spending all her time with Ciara Comerford. Now Ciara has a lot more money to lash around and I'm afraid they'll buy their way into trouble."

"Can't you have a word with Colette?" Brenda asked.

"It's Martin who's giving Ciara the money."

"But –"

"I don't think Colette even knows. From the sound

of things he's spending her money like there's no tomorrow – himself and the rest of the Comerfords."

"You'll have to say something to her," Brenda said as she stood up to leave. "God, look at the time," she added, glancing at her watch. "They'll be eating the legs off the kitchen table!"

Maeve walked with her to the front door.

"Will I get Shane to have a word with her?" Brenda asked, pausing with her hand on the door. They both knew that if she was likely to listen to anyone it would be her eighteen-year-old cousin.

"Can't hurt," Maeve said. "She'll be raging that I said anything, but someone has to talk to her. And she won't listen to me."

"And Larry –?"

"What do you think?" Maeve asked. "He's supposed to call for her on Sunday, but he'll probably let her down again – the usual story. Anyway, I'd prefer if he didn't know about the win."

"You think he'll give you a hard time for missing out?"

Maeve nodded. "Plus, I'm afraid he'd try to put the squeeze on Colette."

"He wouldn't –" Brenda began, then cut herself short. He would, of course. Larry Redmond would get money wherever he could, from whoever he could, and have no qualms at all about it – whether it meant asking Maeve's friends for a handout, or forcing her to sell the house.

As she closed the door after Brenda, Maeve reached automatically to slide the heavy bolt into place, wishing that locks and bolts were all it would take to keep her house safe from Larry.

She stood there looking around the hall at the intricate cornices and mouldings that she had paid to have restored, and painted herself. Larry, of course, hadn't even noticed and hadn't been one bit interested when she pointed them out.

Her gaze swept around the floorboards polished to a high sheen, the elaborate doors and banisters that she had stripped and varnished with great care, the stained-glass windows that it had taken her months to find.

She loved this house, every single inch of it. Years of her life, and part of her soul, had gone into making it what it was.

And nobody – not Larry, nor anyone else – was going to take it from her.

Chapter Eleven

Olive walked briskly along the Rue de Rivoli, not quite sure where she was going but moving quickly anyway. After a lifetime of rushing it was impossible to slow down and take a more relaxed pace. Beside, the quick strides suited her, gave her a sense of being in control.

She turned down the steps to the Métro, oblivious to the one or two older men whose admiring glances lingered for a moment on the tall, slender woman with the camel-hair coat, intelligent grey eyes and general air of purpose.

Olive would have been astonished to realise that they even noticed her. In a city this size she felt totally invisible. In the immediate neighbourhood of the *Collège des Irlandais* she was used to being greeted by some of the people she had come to recognise – the man in the *bureau de tabac* where she bought her newspapers, the chestnut-vendor on the street corner – and it gave her great pleasure to return their greetings in her rudimentary French.

But once she went beyond the immediate environs of the College she felt a sense of exhilaration at the freedom of it. This wasn't Dublin, where she was Bridget Grace's daughter when she met any of their neighbours in the supermarket or the church or – most annoying of all – in Bewley's, on the rare occasions when she managed to escape to Grafton Street on a Saturday afternoon.

Here, in the centre of Paris, she felt she was nobody at all – which left her free to be whoever she wanted to be. She found she rather liked the feeling.

She turned right in the Métro tunnel, following the Clignoncourt direction, deciding on the spur of the moment to go as far as Rue Varenne and the Rodin Museum. It had quickly become one of her favourite places in Paris, and she had been there several times already. It was a perfect day – unseasonably warm for mid-October – to go and sit among the sculptures in the wonderful old garden and think about what she was going to do.

She couldn't stay in the Irish College forever. It had been a wonderful haven, a refuge of half-familiarity while she tried to get used to being on her own in an unknown city. The Irish accents, the plaques around the little courtyard with their resonant, familiar names of ancient Irish dioceses – Cashel, Clonfert, Ferns, Kilfenora – all of these bade her welcome, grounded her, told her she belonged.

But now it was time to move on, and she must decide where to go next.

She alighted from the Métro, moved quickly to the exit, and walked the short distance around the corner to join seven or eight others queuing outside the gate of the Museum. Once inside she moved quickly through the building, giving just a brief glance in the direction of the sculptures she passed. She never tired of looking at them, would have time for them later. For now, what she wanted most was to sit on a stone bench in the museum garden and begin to make some plans.

It had been a good idea to come here, she thought as she sat on a stone bench in the quiet of the garden a few minutes later. To Paris, and to the Rodin garden. There was a wonderful sense of peace here among the old trees and the sculptures.

There weren't many people about. Some Japanese tourists, an elderly couple, three or four young people in a group, and the artist in her flowing, purple cape.

Olive felt a little burst of pleasure at seeing the woman again. They had only ever exchanged nods, but the woman with the auburn hair was a reassuring presence. She made Olive feel, without ever speaking to her, that she wasn't alone – that there were other middle-aged women in Paris who came and sat by themselves in a garden, and that that somehow made it all right for Olive to do the same.

The woman sat with her sketch-pad, intent on the statue in the near distance as she moved with swift strokes across the pad.

Olive glanced at her from time to time, wondering

about her, before finally taking out her own notebook and pen, and quickly skimming through what she had written the previous day.

Keeping a diary was something she hadn't done for years, but in a strange kind of way it was company for her as she sat there, brow furrowed in concentration, planning what her next move would be.

She was familiar by this stage with many of the inexpensive little hotels around the Latin Quarter and had considered moving to one of them after the first week or so, but she hadn't really had the courage then to leave the security of the Irish College.

Now that she felt she could make the move, she wasn't at all sure that a hotel was what she wanted – even the charming family-run one she had visited yesterday near the Madeleine.

No – what she needed, she thought as she scribbled quickly on a fresh page, was a place of her own.

The thought filled her with exhilaration as well as alarm. She had never lived alone before. She had never even chosen a piece of furniture without consulting her mother. Well, she thought as she continued making rapid notes, that was the first of many things that would change. Indeed, had changed already.

She paused for a moment, remembering her mother's face when she told her she was going to Paris.

"I forbid it!" Bridget Grace had said. "You're not to dream of doing such a thing!"

And when Olive had gone quietly about her packing, and came home on the Monday – the day after she broke the news – to announce calmly that she had gone to the travel agent instead of to work, and would be leaving in two days' time, her mother had gone nearly hysterical.

"What about me?" she had demanded in a shrill voice. "What will happen to me? You know I can't stay here on my own!"

For the first time in over twenty-four hours Olive looked directly at her mother.

"I'm sure your sons will be very happy to look after you," she said quietly. "Particularly as you've looked after *them* so well."

Bridget's temper flared. "If you mean the house, it was the least I could do. Vincent and Raymond have always been good to me."

"Of course," Olive agreed. "And I'm sure they'll continue to be good to you now."

"You can't do this to me!" Bridget was almost screaming by this stage. "It's not fair – you're my daughter. It's your *duty* to stay and take care of me!"

Olive sat down slowly, looking across at her mother in the armchair beside the fire.

"You know, Mother, I never realised just how many rules you have. How many absolutely ridiculous rules. Sons inherit houses. Daughters give up their own lives to look after their mothers. Children do what they're told and never answer back – even when they're adults.

Even when they should have spoken out long ago, instead of spending most of a lifetime dancing to someone else's drum. So many rules, Mother. So many things I should never have believed."

Bridget Grace was speechless – but not for long. She tried changing tack.

"It's all his fault. That father of yours, with his ideas, giving you notions about yourself. Olivia, my eye! I don't know what possessed him, calling you after a film star. Olive Bridget was as good a name as anyone could want. I got my way there and he had no right to go calling you Olivia, down in that summerhouse of his, filling your head with nonsense and talking about all the places he was going to take you to. Do you remember that? Because I do! And look at all the good it's after doing you. You'd better come to your senses, and fast, my girl, and forget all this rubbish about going to Paris!"

Olive was hardly listening. She was remembering those long evenings at the bottom of the garden, the scent of roses wafting in through the open window of the summerhouse and her father dreaming dreams with her, both of them cocooned in a world where, for a short time at least, they could escape Bridget and her constant demands.

He had indeed called her Olivia at those times – their secret, she had thought, not realising until now that her mother must have crept down to listen – and he had promised that her life would be better than this, that she would have adventure and happiness, and that some day he would take her to Paris.

Quickly Olive had blinked back tears, the tears that had come freely the previous evening as she sat alone once her mother had gone to bed, leafing through the pages of her father's scrapbooks filled with photographs and mementoes of his journeys in Europe, lifting his pipe carefully out of its pouch to inhale the familiar scent that was his.

The sense of him in the room had firmed her resolve.

And she must be firm now, she had thought as she sat facing her mother.

"I'm going to Paris, Mother. I'm sure you'll be fine. I'll write to you."

"You don't care about me! You never cared about me!"

Olive looked at her mother for a long moment.

"I cared about you much more than you could ever appreciate. I cared enough to stay all this time, enough to –" She took a deep breath, banishing that painful thought before beginning again. "I only wish you had cared, even a little, for me."

Her mother didn't deny it, didn't protest.

Instead she said coldly, "I assume you've made arrangements with Vincent about the money."

Olive said nothing. She sat, pretending bewilderment.

"You'll have to lodge cheques in our accounts! You know you have to do that before you can go!"

Olive continued to sit silently, looking at her. She

remembered all the money she had put into the house over the years, all the money she had given her mother which had almost certainly gone to Vincent to support his unsuccessful "businesses". If it hadn't been for the lottery she would have had nothing to her name, at fifty-three years of age and after thirty-five years on a good salary, except the clothes in her wardrobe and a few thousand pounds in the bank.

"I need time to think about what to do with my money, Mother. It *is* my money, and it may have to last me a very long time. Until I decide exactly what to do with it, I'm going to keep every penny of it in my own account."

She hadn't, of course. Before leaving for Paris she had gone to see Raymond and Dell, offering them enough to pay off their mortgage and putting plans in train to buy the house that had been her mother's.

"You'll continue to own it jointly, but with me this time," Olive had explained. "In addition, you'll get your half of what I pay for it, as will Vincent, and he can do whatever he likes with the money – that's up to him. I don't intend to give him any more. Mother can continue to live there if that's what she wants, or make other arrangements. But I'll be gone. I should have gone long ago."

"You'll write?" Raymond had asked anxiously, not quite sure how to take this new assertive Olive. They were standing at his front door. She had stayed barely twenty minutes, intent on getting home to finish her packing so she would have time to go and see Maeve.

"Of course I'll write," she had said then, her voice softening as she smiled at him and went on tiptoe to kiss his cheek. "And maybe you'll come to see me, once I'm settled." Her glance had included Dell, standing beside Raymond. "And let me know as soon as you need anything else."

She had left quickly then, brushing away their thanks, wanting to get away before tears betrayed her. She had hardly realised until that moment how close she felt to them, how much she would miss them.

"Excusez-moi, madame. Je pense que c'est votre sac?"

A pleasant voice intruded into her thoughts, bringing her back quickly to her surroundings in the Rodin garden.

She looked up to see the woman in the purple cape standing in front of her holding out Olive's bag which had fallen, unseen, from the bench beside her.

"Votre sac, madame?" the woman repeated, smiling at Olive as she offered her the bag, raising her other hand to brush back the long auburn hair that was lifting in the slight breeze.

Olive returned the smile as she took the bag and thanked the woman in faltering French. She watched as the woman turned to go, regretting that she didn't have sufficiently good French to attempt a conversation. She felt she would like this woman if she got to know her.

She went back to her notebook, listing the thoughts that were skimming through her mind.

I'm all alone here. I don't know a soul. I don't speak French very well. I have nowhere to live, and no clear idea of what to do next –

And I have never been happier in my entire life.

Chapter Twelve

Colette pushed her hair back from her forehead, feeling hot and sweaty as she washed the kitchen floor. There was nobody in the house but herself and Emer, who was in the living-room watching Barney on television. Colette decided that she'd go and keep her company once the floor was finished.

This is my life, she thought as she poured away the dirty water and rinsed out the mop. We have one-and-a-half million pounds in the bank, but someone still has to wash the kitchen floor. And guess who that someone is?

So much for the lottery changing everything.

She made some tea and brought it into the living-room.

At least *some* things had changed, she thought as she sat down on the couch and Emer cuddled in against her. There was this, and she wouldn't give it up for the world, the freedom to collect her little girl from school every day instead of just occasionally, and sit watching television with her all afternoon if that's what Emer wanted.

I really didn't know what I was missing, Colette thought as she put her hand out to caress Emer's hair. I can even put up with watching Barney for the pleasure of being with her instead of at work.

But there's got to be more to it than this.

The thought came unbidden, making Colette feel guilty. The number of times she had wished for nothing more than to stay at home with Emer. How could she want anything more?

But why not?

The voice in her head was as clear as if the words had been spoken aloud. Her own voice, asking the questions that refused to go away since her conversation with Maeve a few weeks ago.

Anything she wanted to do, Maeve had reminded her. She could do anything she wanted to do.

And it had been like a mantra ever since.

The first thing she had wanted was to give up work and stay at home with Emer, and she had managed that, and was happy with it.

But it wasn't enough.

And it was about time she admitted it to herself.

Colette had always thought she would be perfectly happy staying at home looking after her family. And now, when she had the chance to do it, she was finding that it wasn't enough for her. She wanted something more.

She had no idea what – just that what she had wasn't enough.

And it was all to do with that damned money, she thought as Emer's giggle broke in on her thoughts.

"Look, Mammy! Are you watching?" The child's eyes were dancing as she looked at the television, turning her head towards Colette every now and then to see if she was enjoying the programme too.

Colette made appropriate noises, her thoughts wandering again.

Whatever you want to do.

That was the trouble, she was doing what she had always thought she wanted to do, and it wasn't enough for her.

She should have been in paradise. All the time in the world, and what seemed like all the money in the world.

But it wasn't working out as she had expected.

And it was all to do with Martin.

"Whatever makes you happy, love," was his stock response when she tried to interest him in making plans for the house, or a holiday – anything at all that would let her enjoy the sensation of having won all that money.

She didn't want to go out spending it on her own. There was no pleasure in that. She wanted him to enter into the spirit of it, with *her*, not with his family or with the new-found friends his new-found cash had brought him in the local pub.

"You'd want to see the size of the screen they have," he said when he came home one night, slightly the worse for wear. Martin, who usually didn't even bother with a second pint.

"You could have a screen like that here," she had pointed out, "and an extension to put it in." She was only half-joking.

"It wouldn't be the same," he had replied. "And anyway, we don't need the hassle."

Martin was a great believer in avoiding hassle. His favourite phrases were "It'll sort itself out" and "Anything for a quiet life" and "Don't worry about it, love, it'll be all right".

But she did worry. And the less Martin worried, the more she felt she had to. And there was plenty to worry about since they had won the money.

The effect on the kids, for one thing. And the fifty-pound note that had disappeared from her purse, and she wasn't sure whether it was Declan or Ciara who took it, but it had to be one of them. And Martin spending more time than ever with his family, and less and less at home, and talking about giving up work when he was still refusing to sit down and sort out how the money should be invested.

And most of all she worried about how all this money, that should have brought her nothing but happiness, was making her feel cut off from everyone and everything instead.

Martin would never understand it, this sense that people were looking at her differently now. She was imagining things, he'd say.

And maybe he'd be right.

But one way or the other Colette was no longer feeling at ease with the neighbours, or with the acquaintances who were still ringing from work to congratulate her.

Try as she might to feel "normal", she felt a sense of expectation hanging around the edge of every conversation, as if people were leaving deliberate little spaces into which she might drop the offer of a loan or a gift if she felt inclined to do so.

And when the organisers of the local old folks' club came collecting, Colette had nearly died of embarrassment, torn between her natural inclination to be generous, and not wanting to go over the top. In the end she gave them a cheque for £100 and spent the rest of the day agonising about whether they had expected ten times as much.

But Martin would never understand any of that. Martin was even more caught up in his own view of things than he had been before the win, and Colette had to cope on her own with the nagging sense that this wasn't right at all, that things weren't turning out anything like she had hoped and expected.

Her first two weeks off work had been spent happily in dropping Emer off at school and enjoying the luxury of a walk in the park afterwards, or coffee at the new delicatessen nearby, or the odd trip into town on the bus to look at all the things she could now afford.

But, in fact, she had bought very little. It was as if she didn't know where to start, except with one or two new outfits for Emer. Martin had given money to the other three, and none of them would thank her for bringing back something they could now go and pick for themselves. So even that pleasure was gone.

"Barney's over. Mammy! Time to bake!"

The cheerful little voice interrupted her train of thought and Colette suppressed a sigh as she stood up and went towards the kitchen with Emer. She used to think she'd love this, having the time to bake to her heart's content, teaching Emer the skills she had learned from her own mother. But after three weeks of it the pleasure was wearing a bit thin.

More than I can say for myself, she thought ruefully as her jeans pulled tight against her waist when she bent to take the mixer from the bottom shelf.

She had just about squeezed into them this morning. If she didn't watch herself, her tendency to plumpness would become a fully fledged weight problem. She was getting even less exercise now than when she had been at work, and was eating far more than she usually did, out of sheer boredom.

Boredom.

That was it! she thought as she reached into the cupboard for sugar and flour, and bent again to take out the baking tray.

She loved being at home with Emer.

And she didn't mind the endless chores that went with looking after the house, had toyed with the idea of employing a cleaner and then decided she'd still want to do it all herself anyway, and that she'd spend twice as much time trying to make the place look decent before the cleaner came than she ever did cleaning it now.

It wasn't a problem to her, even though Peter was the only one who ever offered to help.

No, the problem was that she had nothing else to do. She was at home all day in a neighbourhood where everyone was out at work. She had never had time before to join any sort of clubs or groups . . .

And she was bored out of her mind.

She was bored with the house.

She was bored with the curtains and the worn carpets and the shabby, untidy look of the place that she had just had to put up with before. She was so bored with it all now that she wished she could just throw everything out and –

She laughed aloud, making Emer pause in her task of cracking eggs to ask what was so funny.

She could just do it. That's what was so funny, that she still forgot how easy it would be to do just that. She could throw out every single thing, extend the poky living-room that had always annoyed her a bit, have a new kitchen put in, build a whole new *house* if she wanted to –

Only she'd never get Martin to go along with her.

She found herself detaching the bowl from the mixer and beating the butter and sugar by hand, savagely almost, as she remembered her efforts over the past few weeks to get him involved in any sort of plans for their future.

"You go ahead, love," was his usual response. "Whatever makes you happy."

But that was the problem.

She wasn't one bit happy.

They were sitting on an absolute fortune, and she wasn't anything *like* happy.

Because Martin, who should have been sharing all of this with her, was having the time of his life with his family instead.

He took care of the chequebook.

She took care of the cleaning, the cooking, their youngest daughter, their eldest son and their middle two, the teenagers from hell.

And all Martin did was tell her not to worry, that it would be all right.

But it wasn't all right.

Her house was falling to bits around her.

Her in-laws were spending her money like there was no tomorrow, and she hadn't the guts to stand up to them.

She still hadn't a notion what she wanted to do with her life.

And the man she had promised to love and cherish, the kindest, most generous, most laid-back man she had ever known, was also, she finally realised, the most boring as well.

Forget the curtains, forget the carpets. It was Martin who was slowly, but very surely, boring her to death.

And there wasn't a thing she could do except put up with it.

Chapter Thirteen

Lorraine was feeling very pleased with herself. November wasn't even halfway through and she had managed to finish every single bit of her Christmas shopping.

She hadn't intended doing any shopping at all, of course, except for toys for the children. Her intention had been to save hard and economise where she could, and not spend money foolishly on things that nobody really needed. Instead her hard-earned money was to be used for the gorgeous Italian leather suite she had seen in Arnott's.

She felt a little glow as she walked down Grafton St in the slight drizzle. The suite was hers now, of course. She hadn't wasted one minute once she had the lottery cheque in her hand, and the suite had been delivered two days later. It now had pride of place in her living-room, where it looked absolutely wonderful. The room itself was a different matter. It –

She hesitated as she passed Bewley's coffee shop. She didn't normally go for coffee in town, seeing it as an extravagance, and besides coffee always tasted better in your own house, she felt. But on the other hand, she deserved a little treat after all the shopping she had done, so maybe just this once . . .

She went into the inviting warmth and joined the queue at the counter, juggling her bags so she could manage the tray. She only had two bags to take care of, because the presents she had found this morning, though perfect, were small. No point in embarrassing everyone with something elaborate, especially since she hadn't intended giving anything at all until the lottery win. And even then . . .

David had been ridiculous about it all, really, she thought as the queue inched forward at the counter. It had taken him quite a while to see her point that the only sensible thing to do was ignore the fact that they had won and continue much the same as before. Otherwise the money would last no time, especially since Lorraine wasn't working now.

He still hadn't been happy with her idea of keeping to their original plan of no presents, so this morning's shopping expedition had been a compromise, really. She had bought something for everyone, searching hard to find pretty little presents that looked more expensive than they were. And she had been very successful, staying well within the stringent budget she had allowed herself.

Maybe she deserved a cake as well as a coffee, she

thought as she passed the confectionery counter full of delicious little cakes. But it would be a waste of money, really, and besides there was her lovely slim figure to think of –

She was still deliberating when a hand reached from behind her into the cabinet and took the very cake she had her eye on. Cheek, Lorraine thought, turning to glare at the person behind her. Her jaw dropped when she realised who it was.

"Colette!"

"Hi, Lorraine. I didn't know it was you in front of me."

They stood awkwardly for a few seconds, half-facing each other, neither of them sure whether to continue the conversation, until a man behind Colette stepped around them with an impatient sound and they realised the queue had moved on.

Lorraine told Colette to go on, she'd be after her in a second. Then she quickly took a slice of cheesecake from the counter and hurried to catch up with Colette, reaching her just as she was paying for her coffee and cake.

Lorraine put her own tray down beside the cash register, watching Colette walk to a nearby table. She wasn't sure if she'd bother to join her or not. On the other hand –

"£3.75, please," the cashier said, and Lorraine began rummaging slowly through her coat pockets, her two shopping bags and finally her handbag with its multitude of zip pockets, ignoring the queue growing impatiently behind her and glancing instead towards Colette in an effort to catch her eye.

It worked.

Colette stood up and came over, reaching into her bag for a £10 note which she handed to the cashier.

"Thanks, Colette," Lorraine said, and followed with her tray as Colette went back to her table. There was no need to ask if Colette minded her joining her – Lorraine knew that she'd be only too happy. She settled herself at the table opposite Colette and then began the rummaging process all over again.

"I'll pay you back now – I have a £20 note in here somewhere."

"Don't bother, Lorraine. There's really no need."

"Well, if you're sure," Lorraine said, smiling as she put her bag down.

Colette would want to watch herself, she thought. The lottery win mustn't be doing her much good – she had a very sour expression on her face and it didn't suit her at all.

"So what have you been doing with yourself?" Lorraine asked as she nibbled daintily at the cheesecake.

"Nothing much," Colette said. "Some Christmas shopping. Isn't it lovely not to have to count the pennies?"

She brightened up as she said that. Silly woman, Lorraine thought, if she's spending more than she would have, just because of the lottery.

"And what about you?" Colette continued, eyeing the

bags. "Have you started your Christmas shopping as well?"

"I finished it all this morning," Lorraine said triumphantly. "I already had the children's toys and my mother's present. Everything else is here. Fourteen presents altogether."

She followed Colette's gaze as she looked at the bags again.

"Fourteen? You must have – oh, I see. You're giving everyone money as well." She stopped as she saw Lorraine's expression. "Or did you get them jewellery – ?" Her voice trailed off uncertainly.

Lorraine waited a long moment. "I presume you're joking," she said finally, her voice cool.

"Well, no, I – sorry, Lorraine, it's none of my business."

"You're right, it isn't," Lorraine said, watching in delight as Colette flushed. Silly cow, it really *wasn't* any of her business.

Collete couldn't leave it be. "I was just wondering, well –" She brushed her mousy hair back with one hand, looking distracted. She really should do something about that now, Lorraine thought. Have a decent cut and colour. She surely couldn't *want* it to look like that.

Colette seemed to make up her mind about something. "Lorraine, don't answer this if you don't want to, but – are you finding that people expect all kinds of things from you now? I mean, relatives and – you know, with all the money, and getting letters from people you never even heard of –"

Lorraine was looking at her as if she was stone mad.

"So what if people expect things?" she said. "It's my money, to spend as I please. Any begging letters I got, I just threw in the bin. Why should I give a penny to people I don't know?"

She made it sound like a reasonable question.

"But what about your family?" Colette persisted. "Did you give them all a share, or –?"

"It really isn't anything to do with you," Lorraine said in what she thought was quite a pleasant voice, considering Colette had no right at all to ask questions like that. She seemed to be under some kind of pressure, Lorraine thought, as if the answer really mattered to her. She actually looked agitated, unhappy even.

Lorraine was intrigued. "Why do you ask?" she said after a moment.

"Well, because –" Colette hesitated and seemed to be considering what to say. Then it all came out in a rush. "Don't you find that people keep coming looking for something? I mean, when you have all this money, and other people in the family don't, they expect you to help out and buy them things, and, well, I mean, you'd want to, of course, but –"

"And why would I want to?"

Colette stopped talking. She looked a bit confused.

"Well, to help out, of course. It's a huge amount of money. People expect –"

"People only expect what you let them expect," Lorraine patiently explained the obvious. "I've made it quite clear that most of the money – all except £20,000 or so – is going towards paying off the mortgage and buying a new house. We're going to rent out the house we have and it'll be there for Gavin and Amber in the future."

Colette looked stunned. "It must be some house you're buying, Lorraine! Even in this day and age, a million and a half pounds will get you –"

"Who said anything about that much?" Lorraine asked.

Colette looked puzzled. "But that's the amount –"

"I have no intention of discussing the amount with anyone," Lorraine said calmly. "It's nobody else's business, and it's up to me how I spend my own money. I certainly don't intend giving people the idea that they can come to me with their hands out. I mean, my sister Audrey came looking for a loan before I even had a chance to lodge the cheque, because they're in a bit of trouble with the mortgage, and I had to explain to her that all the money will be tied up in the new house."

"But you could have managed something, surely? Wasn't it Audrey who bought tickets to Paris for yourself and David, for your anniversary?"

"What's that got to do with anything?" Lorraine asked. Really, she was regretting ever coming in for coffee, or going out of her way to sit and chat with Colette. She was remembering all over again that she couldn't stand the woman when they were working together.

Colette seemed uncertain of what to say. "I suppose I assumed that you'd help people out when they'd been good to you," she began tentatively. "I remember you telling me that your sisters and brothers always looked after you because you were the youngest, buying you stuff when you needed it. So this is your chance to – well, to sort of pay them back, isn't it?"

This conversation was getting worse by the minute, Lorraine thought, deciding to finish up her coffee and go. "I don't see that I have to pay anyone back for anything," she said, making her voice as frosty as she could to prevent any more of these ridiculous questions. "They gave me things because they wanted to, not because I might *owe* them something for it. And besides, I told you I can't afford it."

"Now *that's* ridiculous," Colette said.

She really was very rude, Lorraine thought. "What gives you the right to say that?" she demanded, watching with satisfaction as Colette flushed again. "It's up to me to decide what I can afford," Lorraine continued. "It's my money, and I'll spend it whatever way I want."

She paused to take a sip of coffee, watching as Colette, obviously trying to hide her embarrassment, did the same. She must know she'd been out of line.

"Besides –" Lorraine paused for effect "– you obviously weren't listening when I told you that I never said how much I won. It's nobody's business but mine. And David's, of course. Everyone was very sympathetic when I explained about leaving the syndicate two days before the draw so my share-out was very small under the new agreement we had."

Colette spluttered her coffee all over the place, making a curious choking sound as she tried to get her breath.

My God, the woman had no manners at all, Lorraine thought as she calmly picked up her bags, said goodbye and left her to it.

Some people had a lot of growing up to do, she thought smugly as she made her way briskly through the coffee shop and out the front door to join the mid-afternoon throng in the November drizzle of Grafton St.

If she had bothered glancing back, she would have seen that Colette was still mopping frantically at the table with some paper napkins, an expression of pure disbelief on her face.

But Lorraine didn't believe in looking back. There was far too much to look forward to. She had money in the bank, and from now on she was going to do exactly what she wanted with her life.

She might just treat herself to a taxi home, she decided as she turned left towards Dame St. After all, she had saved £3.75 by letting Colette buy the coffee and cake for her. Yes, she'd definitely get a taxi home.

It was the very least she deserved.

Chapter Fourteen

Suzanne was having the most amazing time.

No surprise. She had always known it would be exactly like this – that the money would give her the freedom to travel wherever she liked, and do exactly what she wanted.

She could still remember her bank manager's face when she told him she wouldn't invest a single penny, except in every air ticket she could buy. He was a nice man, but no imagination. He had tried his best to interest her in stocks, bonds, property – all good bets at the moment, he had told her. It was extremely important to have liquid assets these days . . .

"Oh, but I intend to," Suzanne had promised fervently. "Lots of them. And there's plenty to go round." She had given him a big smile as she left a bottle of Moët et Chandon on his desk and turned to go.

In fairness to him, he had bitten back whatever he might have been about to say, smiling as he thanked her. Maybe there was hope for him yet, she had decided, making her way to the travel agent.

She had become their very best customer since.

New England with her parents had been fantastic – her mother had always wanted to be there as the leaves turned in the Fall. And Thailand was planned and booked for late November. There had just been enough time to squeeze in this little break in Crete before going back home to pack again.

She had been slightly disappointed that she hadn't had any takers for Africa.

"Too many things that eat you," Gilly had pronounced with a look of utter horror when Suzanne had suggested it.

Michelle had been keen, but was put off by images of snakes, plus the fact that Keith, her husband, had been appalled enough at the thought of looking after their four small children for a week, let alone a month. Africa would take a bit of working on him – and in the meantime there were the Greek Islands to enjoy.

Suzanne lay back in the deck chair and adjusted her sunglasses.

"Beats roughing it, girls!"

"I would have come anyway!" Michelle said, reaching for her glass of retsina.

"Me too," Gilly added. "But this is better!"

They all laughed, knowing Gilly's fondness for comfort. It had been the same in their inter-railing days. The three of them had spent two summers together in

Europe, "looking for work" while they were at college. They'd had no definite plan in mind other than to start in Amsterdam, turn right – or was it left? – and keep going until they hit the Mediterranean.

And they had managed, both years, to move on whenever it looked like work might find *them*, and had arrived home with a smattering of French and Greek, glorious tans, empty pockets and an abiding love of travel.

"Only three more days," Michelle said. "Doesn't seem fair."

"You could –" Suzanne began.

"I couldn't," Michelle interrupted regretfully. "Not if I want a husband to go home to."

"And do you?" Gilly asked, with just a trace of a barb in her voice. It was no secret that she had never thought much of Keith.

"Beats frozen dinners for one, Gilly," Michelle said cheerfully, tossing her hair back as she reached for her novel and stretched out on her deck chair.

Gilly sat, mouth open, waiting for inspiration that didn't come.

Whoops, Suzanne thought as she opened one eye and sneaked a look at them. I remember the downside of those summers. It was never any fun being the meat in their sandwich.

"Okay, girls, enough! Three more days – let's make the most of it!"

There was an immediate protest that they *were* making the most of it.

What else could they want, besides sunbathing and swimming and eating delicious food and chatting up delicious waiters –

"I never!" Michelle said to this last comment of Gilly's.

"Maybe you should!" Gilly shot back.

"Forget it, Gills – Shirley Valentine I'm not!" Michelle was laughing as she spoke.

"True. Not nearly attractive enough –"

"Maybe you should drop it, Gilly," Suzanne suggested quickly, in case Michelle took her seriously. "Let's plan what to do for the next three days."

"Chat up waiters?" Gilly said hopefully.

"Lie in the sun and forget the pile of washing at home?"

"Sad," Gilly pronounced as she looked across at Michelle. "Very sad."

Michelle sat up. "I really didn't mean it, you know."

"Sure you did."

"Gilly –"

"Will you shut up, the pair of you," Suzanne said, torn between amusement and exasperation. "You've been at this all day, and I'm here to enjoy myself! We really do have to make plans if we're to get to Knossos and Santorini. There isn't much time left."

"We could do Knossos tomorrow," Michelle suggested. "But Santorini I'm not sure about – you know me and boats!"

"No problem, I checked it out," Suzanne said. "We can go across by helicopter."

"You must be joking!" Gilly said. "I don't think I want –"

"Forget it," Suzanne snapped. She stood up, picked up her towel and bag, and walked back towards the hotel.

She was sitting in the small taverna across the road from the hotel when they joined her half an hour later.

"Sorry," Michelle said as they sat down at her table.

Gilly gave a slight shrug and a smile by way of apology. "We were a bit over the top."

"Doesn't matter," Suzanne said, but they could tell from her face that it did.

"We don't have to do everything together all the time," Gilly said. "We never did in the old days – it was always two of us ganging up trying to persuade the other, or one of us going off on her own, and it didn't matter."

"It doesn't matter now," Suzanne repeated.

"But it does," Michelle said. "Because now –"

It sat there unsaid, hanging in the air between them. Because now Suzanne called the shots. Now Suzanne was paying for everything.

"I don't like the way it makes me feel," Michelle said eventually in a quiet voice.

"The way what makes you feel?"

"You know – well . . ." Michelle's voice trailed off.

Suzanne waited for further explanations but neither of them said anything.

"You mean, that I'm paying for things?" she asked, as the realisation hit her.

149

Michelle and Gilly both nodded.

"But that's ridiculous! What is it but a few hundred pounds? Money hasn't ever mattered before!"

"That's because we never had it before," Gilly said after a moment. "Not much, anyway – and we shared what we had."

"So?" Suzanne said. "That's what we're doing now, isn't it? Sharing what we have?"

"It's different," Gilly said. "Now we're sharing what *you* have."

"I still don't see why it's different," Suzanne said. "You'd share with me, wouldn't you?"

They didn't meet her eyes. Michelle never had much money anyway, Suzanne realised, and Gilly spent whatever she had even faster than Suzanne, so she'd always been on the receiving end.

But it really *hadn't* mattered. They'd shared all sorts of things besides money. One blanket between them in a freezing cold tent, sleeping space on the floors of each other's flats, even their best clothes when the need arose, and about a million laughs –

"It just doesn't feel right, Suzanne," Michelle said finally. "It's all take and no give, and I don't like it. I'll never be able to afford to take you on holiday – no, wait! – so the only thing I can do in return is go along with whatever you want. Even though looking at old ruins isn't my idea of fun. I don't know when I'll see the sun again. I just want to lie on the beach."

"And I don't want to go flying out over the

Aegean," Gilly said. "I keep thinking of that guy in the book you made me read, falling out of the sky and into the ocean, him and his feathers –"

"I did *not* make you read it!" Suzanne's voice was rising now. "Just because I loaned you a book of Greek myths doesn't mean you have to read it, for God's sake! And it's ridiculous if you won't go in a helicopter just because –"

She broke off in exasperation, running her hand back through her hair. "What's going on? I was having a great time! I thought we were *all* having a great time!"

The others looked uncomfortable.

"We were," Michelle said.

"Honestly," Gilly added.

"It's just that –"

Suzanne waited for Michelle to continue.

Michelle took a deep breath, looked at Gilly, who nodded.

"It's just that, well, we're tired of not being Finn."

"What?" Suzanne was stunned as she looked from one to the other.

"It was great of you to ask us, Suzanne –" Gilly was leaning slightly forward, looking at her intently.

"And we really are enjoying it –" Michelle continued.

"It's just that we don't want to do the things you want," Gilly went on. "We want to be beach bums and soak up all the sun we can get before we head back to a cold, miserable winter –"

"But we feel we should do what *you* want, so you'll

enjoy yourself. It's just that all those things you want to do – well, you were never interested in archaeology and stuff before, and we're not now," Michelle said. "And, well –"

"You should really be doing them with Finn," Gilly said, as if stating the obvious.

"Don't go there, Gilly," Suzanne said quietly.

Michelle picked up on the warning note in her voice and flashed a signal at Gilly. Too late.

"Come on, Sooz, you have to admit –"

"I said *don't*, Gilly!" She stood up, reaching for her bag.

Michelle put a hand on Suzanne's arm. "Sit down, Suzanne. Please!"

Her tone was somewhere between request and command, and Suzanne, after the slightest hesitation, sat down again.

She looked sheepishly from one to the other. "Sorry, folks. I'm on edge a bit."

"You're missing him, and you won't admit it," Gilly said, taking a chance.

Suzanne nodded. "Maybe I am. But I'd still rather be here with you two right now – if we could all stop hassling each other. I really *was* having a great time."

She looked close to tears for a moment. "And I thought you were, too. I'm sorry if you feel under a compliment, I never meant it to be like that!"

"It's not really –" Michelle began.

"No?" Suzanne asked. "Then what was all that about?"

Gilly laughed. "Let's be honest. It *is*, really. But it's nothing to do with you, Suzanne. It's us feeling like the poor relations. Tell you what, I promise that when *I* win the lottery I'll bring you wherever you want to go, and feed you on caviar and all the old ruins you can manage. And in exchange, I'll enjoy the rest of this holiday doing exactly what I want. Deal?"

"Deal," Suzanne said, smiling at her. "So what is it you want?"

"To do nothing but sit in the sun and look out at the sea, with a glass of wine in my hand!"

"And you say *I* should play Shirley Valentine?" Michelle murmured.

"Shh, Michelle," Suzanne said. "We're getting places! You could do that on Santorini, Gilly, in that restaurant on the cliff I told you about."

"The one you went to with Finn last time?" Gilly asked.

"That's the one," Suzanne said, looking at her steadily. "Come on, you'd love it." She turned her head slightly so that her gaze took in Michelle. "I'll go to Knossos myself tomorrow, and the day after we'll go to Santorini. How about it? Come on, I promise you'll love it!"

"And the helicopter?" Gilly asked, still not convinced.

"You can close your eyes. Especially when they're lowering you down the cliff in a harness."

"No chance!"

"Okay, I'm joking. But you don't have to come if you

don't want to – I'll go on my own, because I really want to see Santorini again. It's gorgeous, full of little white buildings with blue rooftops. And the restaurant's great – I know you'd love it."

Michelle and Gilly looked at each other.

"We can sunbathe all day tomorrow?" Michelle said.

"Sure. Whatever you want."

"And you'll make sure they have parachutes on the helicopter?" Gilly asked. "I mean, I'm stone mad to even think of going, but –"

"Parachutes. Of course. With feathers on them."

She laughed at the sudden look of alarm on Gilly's face. "Come *on*! Stop worrying. Life's too short! Let's make the most of the next few days!"

And they did, helicopter ride and all, and Gilly only screamed twice.

But the girls were right, Suzanne conceded as they headed for the airport at the end of the week.

It just wasn't the same without Finn.

Chapter Fifteen

Colette seemed to spend a lot of her time the following week thinking about Lorraine. The gall of her! She really was unbelievable – to refuse Maeve a share and then tell the whole world that she had left the syndicate herself.

And the worst of it was –

The worst of it was, Colette realised, she wished she could do the very same herself. At least it would keep her in-laws off her back.

But it was too late now – and she wouldn't have been easy with it anyway.

That was the trouble. She wasn't easy about anything at all since that damned win.

And one way or another something would have to change very soon if she was to get any good at all out of it.

Anything you want. You just have to want it enough.

Maeve's words were there again, as they were most days, like a lifeline that Colette found herself clinging to when things got difficult.

She really missed Maeve. It just wasn't the same without her around, but she didn't feel she could intrude on Maeve's busy evenings and weekends. She'd never realised how much time they'd spent together at work – words snatched here and there in the course of the day, shared coffee breaks, lunch together in the park or, on Fridays, in the pub. A lot of sharing. A lot of laughs. A lot of depending on her.

And now, something they couldn't share, and all the other sharing was suddenly gone.

And besides –

Colette grabbed her jacket and reached for the keys, brushing hastily at her eyes as she made for the front door. This was ridiculous, to be crying like this at her age when she shouldn't have a care in the world.

The trouble was, everything was suddenly getting on top of her. She needed – what was it Maeve had said? – to get a grip. To stop being such a wimp.

Colette had always seen herself as helpful, obliging, willing to put herself out for people. But she was mortified now at the thought that Maeve saw her as a pushover, a jellybean who wouldn't stand up for herself.

And she didn't want to face Maeve again until she'd figured out if that was true and, if it was, what she could do about it.

But, God, she missed her.

She walked briskly down towards Fairview Strand and turned left until she came within sight of the sea at Clontarf.

This was better, she thought as the sea air hit her, lifting her spirits as it always did. No point in staying at home moping when the house was empty and there was nothing to do.

It wasn't like her to let things get her down. It was just that she had no life of her own that she could pick up on, no friends to see while Emer was at school.

She had to find something to do, and soon. But she just didn't know where to start.

She was sure there must be other women in the same position but she certainly hadn't seen them around. Those she saw at the school gates were usually dressed to the nines, looking fit for anything as they headed for their snappy little cars to get them into work where no doubt they did all kinds of interesting things all day.

She felt frumpy and aimless by comparison as she waved Emer off each morning and wondered how to spend the time until she could collect her again.

She had let herself go now that she didn't have to dress up for work herself. And, no question about it, the solitary coffee-and-doughnut sessions were taking their toll. She was definitely gaining weight.

She passed an older woman walking her dog and smiled a greeting as they went by at a brisk pace.

Maybe that's what I need, Colette thought. A dog.

Something to keep me occupied, and I could take him to the park with Emer when I picked her up from school.

Pathetic, the voice in her head proclaimed. *You don't even like dogs that much.*

True, Colette argued with herself. *But I need some kind of company. Sometimes I don't talk to another adult all day unless it's to ask for something in a shop.*

She had thought of voluntary work but didn't think it would suit her. There was so much work on offer everywhere these days that most of the charity shops were finding it hard to get staff and would have welcomed her with open arms, but in the two she visited she felt out of place. It really wasn't what she wanted to do and she contented herself with leaving a large donation instead, telling herself that that would be far more useful to them.

But she would have to find some way of spending her time, she told herself as she headed for a nearby bench and sat looking across the bay. The view was uninspiring – she hated all those oil tankers even if they *were* painted in attractive colours.

She turned to glance back across the road, wondering about the frequency of buses to take her to St Anne's Park or to Howth. For the first time ever she found herself wishing she had a car.

Colette had never learned to drive. It was one of those things she had always meant to do, but marrying young and having children quickly didn't leave her either the money or time that might have made lessons possible. And Martin, of course, had been no help at all.

She'd lost count of the number of times he'd put her off when she asked if he might teach her at least the basics. They couldn't afford a second car, he reminded her, and he needed his to get to work, so what was the point? If they ever got a bit of extra money, maybe then would be the time –

Colette stood up quickly and began walking in the direction of a car showroom which was, she thought, a half-mile or so up on the Howth Road. If a lottery win wasn't a bit of extra money, she didn't know what was.

She walked briskly, energised by the sudden decision. She'd have a look at what they had on offer and discuss it with Martin when he came home this evening –

Or maybe she wouldn't.

She paused in mid-stride, remembering recent efforts to discuss anything at all with Martin.

She had tried. She really had.

Last Sunday, when their three teenagers were out and Emer was with her aunt Therese for the day and none of Martin's family was around – for once – she had sat him down and tried to get through to him how she felt and how unhappy she was.

She hadn't even fully realised it herself until she began talking, and then it was as if the floodgates had opened and there was no stopping her.

He had listened in growing astonishment as she tried to explain how isolated she felt, how she had no-one to share things with when he was caught up with his mother and sisters and brothers, how her own family were keeping a distance in case she might think they were pressurising her – she skipped lightly over this one, afraid that Martin might be hurt if he thought she was making comparisons – and how things hadn't been the same between herself and Maeve since the win and she was worried that they mightn't ever be really close again.

His astonishment had remained just that as she spoke, instead of turning into the understanding she had hoped for. He just couldn't grasp where she was coming from when she tried to tell him that there was no joy in any of it when they didn't plan things together, that winning all that money should make things better, not worse, and that she had never before, in her whole life, felt so lonely or bored.

She had known she was getting nowhere after twenty minutes or so when she caught him glancing at his watch and sneaking a look at the picture on the silent TV screen to see if the game had started.

She had made one last, half-hearted attempt.

"If I get some holiday brochures tomorrow, will you have a look at them with me? I really think it would do us good to get away as a family, ourselves and the kids. Maybe the Canaries or somewhere."

"Whatever you want, love," he had answered vaguely, his eyes never leaving the screen.

She could have sworn he hadn't heard a word since the game started, and suddenly she had known exactly what she wanted. She wanted to march over and unplug the TV set in the corner and strangle him with the flex.

Instead she had gone to the kitchen to put the kettle on, seething inside as she waited for it to boil.

So maybe discussing it with Martin wasn't the best way to go, she told herself as she continued on up the Howth Road. Because he'd tell her to do whatever made her happy, but he wouldn't give her a word of encouragement otherwise. So maybe the thing to do was to choose the car, possibly even *buy* the car, and arrange for lessons at the local motoring school.

There was nothing at all to stop her doing that. And if it didn't work out, she'd just sell the car and find something else she wanted to do.

Anything you want.

It was a good feeling, having something you wanted to do and being able to go for it. A *great* feeling.

And there had to be other things she wanted.

She'd make a list, she decided, excitement coursing through her as she drew near the car showroom.

And top of the list, right after the new car, would be some kind of assertiveness training so she could stand up to those in-laws of hers.

She squared her shoulders as she opened the door of the showroom and glanced around, wondering how long it would take before she had one of these lovely shiny machines out on the road.

And if she could learn to drive in Dublin traffic, she told herself, then she could learn to do anything on God's earth if she put her mind to it.

And that included standing up to the Comerfords.

Chapter Sixteen

Maeve marked off another day on the calendar in the kitchen. November 24th.

Four weeks and three days to Christmas.

And three weeks exactly to the meeting with Larry and his solicitor.

She hadn't expected it to happen so quickly, had been really upset that it was taking place this side of Christmas.

Normally she loved the run-up to Christmas, counting down the days with the children, climbing up into the big attic to bring down treasured decorations they had collected over the years.

Even the prospect of Larry's gambling had never cast a shadow on their celebrations, because every year since she realised the extent of his problem Maeve had managed to put away a few hundred quid in her own post-office account where it was safe from him. And if he was ever puzzled about where the money had come from for turkey and ham and toys and chocolate and all the other trappings of Christmas when he knew their bank account was at rock bottom, he had sense enough not to make an issue of it for that one day of the year.

Keeping me sweet for the Stephen's Day racing, Maeve thought bitterly now as she began sorting out the decorations she and the boys had brought down last night.

It was much too early to put them up, of course, but she wouldn't let that stop her. She wanted to make Christmas last for every possible minute this year, in case –

She wouldn't let herself finish the thought, concentrating instead on taking the glittering ornaments carefully out of their wrappings.

This house was made for Christmas, with the big space in the hall to the right of the stairs where the Christmas tree had stood for as long as she could remember, and the deep window seats in the front room where she and her sisters used to curl up while her mother played carols on the piano.

Everywhere she turned seemed full of Christmas memories.

And she wouldn't let herself think, even for one minute, that this might be their last Christmas here.

And all because of Larry.

Damn him! she thought. Damn him for trying to take this away from my kids, when he's taken everything else!

The phone rang, interrupting her thoughts. She waited a moment to see if one of the boys would pick it up but they were in the playroom, engrossed in Saturday morning TV. Orla, of course, was off somewhere, having sneaked out early to avoid any explanations.

Maeve stood up from the box she was rummaging through and went into the hall to lift the phone.

"Hello?"

"Maeve? Hi, it's me, Suzanne. Do you mind if I call around for a few minutes?"

"Suzanne! No, of course not! You know the address, don't you?"

"Sure. Twelve o'clock okay?"

"Fine. See you then."

Maeve was puzzled as she hung up. She had only heard from Suzanne once since she had left the office, a brief phone-call, just before she left for the States, offering a cheque for £326,356.

"It's really yours, you know." Her voice had been business-like, insistent, warm. "I've worked it out. That's the difference between dividing the winnings by four, and by five. I wouldn't have got it if you'd stayed in, so really it's yours."

"You know it's not, Suzanne." Maeve had been glad they were on the phone so Suzanne couldn't see her holding back tears.

"It's yours if you want it, Maeve. Just say the word."

And Suzanne had brushed aside Maeve's thanks, telling her to get in touch if she changed her mind.

Maeve went back to sorting the ornaments, wondering whether Suzanne intended to offer her the money again, face to face this time.

Over £300,000. Roughly half the value of the house. Enough to pay Larry off.

Forget it, she told herself quickly. Nothing would satisfy him if he was as deep in debt as suspected – he'd take the money and still come looking for "his share" of the house.

And she'd have to find some way to stop him. This house had never meant anything to Larry but it was security for her children's future.

Maeve began shaking out the long strands of decorations, dusting them off, looking with a critical eye to see what would last for another year and what would have to be discarded. The boys would help her to put them up later. And, who knows, she thought, maybe even Orla . . .

She wouldn't hold her breath.

She glanced at the clock, wondering if she had time to do a bit more sorting before Suzanne came. Not really. She paused for just a moment, reaching into the big cardboard box to lift out an old china figure of St Nicholas and place it carefully on the mantelpiece. It had sat there in pride of place every single Christmas since her grandmother had come to this house as a young woman, seventy years ago or more, bringing it with her from her own home.

Maeve fingered the intricate ornament, remembering

her grandmother sitting in that chair there, just by the fireplace, telling stories to four dark-haired little girls in nighties who curled up on the rug in front of the fire, hanging on her every word.

She had wanted exactly that for her own children, had been saddened beyond words that they never knew her mother. Orla, only two when Maeve's mother died, had no memories of her, and the boys had never known her at all.

And that's why I have to keep this house, Maeve thought. My mother's spirit is here. I can sense her in every room. Granny's, too. And Dad, of course. But somehow it was always a woman's house. It has that kind of feel to it, as if every woman who ever lived here left a little bit of herself behind. And I can't let that go, not for anyone.

The doorbell rang and she could hear one of the boys running into the hallway to answer it. She gave a quick glance in the mirror, put a smile on her face and went out to welcome Suzanne.

The welcome was genuine. She had always liked Suzanne, couldn't help but like her. She looked fantastic, Maeve thought, as she saw her standing on the doorstep chatting to Fergus.

"Come in, Suzanne! Fergus, stand back and make room!"

The little boy looked at Maeve doubtfully, then back at Suzanne.

"She's a stranger, Mam."

"Too right, they don't come much stranger!" Suzanne smiled down at him as she waited for him to stand back. He relented after a moment and opened the door a bit further so she could step past him into the large hallway.

"He makes a good butler!" Suzanne laughed as she and Maeve surveyed each other.

"Among other things!" Maeve replied. "Come on, we'll go down to the kitchen."

She led the way through the hall and along the passage into the big, bright room that looked out over the back of the house.

"It's gorgeous, Maeve! You lucky thing!"

"You haven't seen it before?"

"No, I wasn't in here the time we came to your Christmas party. When was that, four or five years ago?"

"Must be," Maeve said, gesturing to Suzanne to sit down. She remembered the party well. Their last happy year, really, before the gambling took over. She brushed the thought away. "You'll have tea? Or coffee?"

"I'd love some tea. I can't stay long, though, I'm packing."

Maeve laughed. "Again?"

"Again," Suzanne said with a big smile. "Thailand this time. Myself and Finn."

Maeve half-turned from the sink where she was filling the kettle. "I thought –?"

She left the question hanging in the air between them.

"You thought he was out of the picture?" Suzanne

was still smiling. "He was. Still is, really, because I don't want the boy-girl bit any more, so that kind of complicates things. But he's agreed to go to Thailand with me."

"Just good friends?" Maeve teased as she sat down across from Suzanne.

"I hope. He wants a bit more, but – we'll see."

"He seems like a lovely guy."

"Don't they all?" Suzanne asked. "Whoops."

"You're right. They all do." Maeve held Suzanne's gaze. "That's why you need to be careful about what you're getting into. None of my business, but if you've already had doubts . . ."

"I trust him," Suzanne said. "I'm just not sure I want to spend the rest of my life with him. But I really don't want to go to Thailand without him."

"And he jumped at the chance," Maeve said as she stood up to make the tea.

Suzanne didn't answer until Maeve was sitting opposite her again, pouring the tea.

"Actually, he didn't," she said, taking the cup Maeve handed her, reaching for the milk jug. "He took a bit of persuading. No surprise, really, since we kind of finished with each other the night of the lottery draw. That's why I didn't know about it until next day, in work."

"Suzanne –"

"Maeve, I'll say this quickly, and only once. Finn absolutely didn't want to come to Thailand. He felt it wasn't fair, spending my money when we'd just broken up, more or less. But he changed his mind eventually, when I reminded him that if *he'd* won the money, I'd go on holidays with him at the drop of a hat. Promise me you'll think about that?"

"Going to Thailand?" Maeve tried to make a joke of it.

Suzanne looked at her steadily. "You know what I mean."

Maeve dropped her gaze, concentrating on adding milk and sugar to her own cup.

"So will you?" Suzanne prompted quietly.

Maeve nodded. She could promise to *think* about taking the money; it didn't mean she had to do it.

"Good," Suzanne said. "Because that makes it easier to ask a favour." She paused to sip the tea. "Feel free to say no, because it's a big one. A friend of mine needs a place to stay for the next four or five weeks. Our landlord is selling the house – he gave me notice to quit when I came back from the States – and Val hasn't had any luck finding somewhere. So I was wondering if she could stay here for a while. I'll help her sort something out when I get back."

Maeve didn't hesitate. "Of course. I've plenty of space, and it might be nice to have someone else around."

"Great. That's what I thought. She'll pay well."

"There's no need –" Maeve began.

"Now, don't be silly. You're doing her a huge favour.

And me. I didn't feel right swanning off to Thailand while she's at her wits' end."

"And what about you? Where will you put your stuff, and what'll you do when you get back?"

Suzanne laughed. "You know me. I'll worry about that when I get back. I'll leave all my stuff at Finn's until I get sorted. At least I'll be able to afford the rent when I find a place!"

"You're not going to rent again, are you? You could afford to buy any number of places now – including the one you're living in."

Suzanne considered it for a moment. "Mmm! Never thought about that. Still, it's not worth the hassle and property ties you down. You start falling in love with a place, and then you're afraid that – what is it, Maeve?" She asked in sudden alarm as she saw tears in Maeve's eyes.

"Nothing," Maeve said, giving a quick wipe at her eyes with the back of her hand.

"It must be *something*. Look, if it doesn't suit you to have Val staying here –"

"No, no, it's nothing like that." Maeve paused. "It's just that when you talked about falling in love with a place . . ." she paused again, took a deep breath. "I've been in love with this place my whole life. And now there's a chance I might lose it. Larry and I are going for a divorce."

"Maeve, no!"

Maeve tried to smile. "To the divorce, or losing the house?"

"The house, of course. You can always get another man – but this house is something special!"

Maeve's smile was a bit easier this time. "Another man is the last thing I want."

"If it's a question of money, Maeve –"

Maeve shook her head. "There'd be no stopping him, if I start giving him money. No, what I need is to get this all sorted out, see how much I'm supposed to pay him. With luck it won't be much, because he did get all the shares – I got those from my aunt – and a lot of our joint savings."

"I assumed everything would have been – well, gone."

"They were special savings accounts that couldn't be accessed for a number of years. He got at them the minute he could."

"So he mightn't have a claim on the house at all?"

"He can try."

"Pity it's not a family business or something. That might make it harder for him."

"It might. And maybe it's time to start thinking about a few ideas I've had – because one way or the other I'm going to hang on to this house."

Chapter Seventeen

Olive was humming to herself as she strolled along the Boulevard Port Royal, stopping as she reached the market stalls. She had discovered this little market on her second week in Paris and loved coming here on Saturdays. The food was incredible, a range of cheese and fruit and fish such as she never saw at home.

The tantalising smell of *choucroute* wafted towards her, reminding her that breakfast had been several hours ago. She had spent a busy morning, and felt that she had earned her lunch. She wandered though the stalls that lined the wide pavement, glancing at the various offerings before finally coming to a stall where the *choucroute* was a veritable feast of bacon and garlic sausage and potatoes, heaped high on a huge frying-pan over a gas burner.

She spoke a few words to the stallkeeper, passed over some money and took a little plastic dish full of delicious-looking food. As she moved back into the shelter of the wall behind the stall to begin her meal, she reflected that she would have been far too self-conscious to eat in the street like this when she first arrived in Paris. So much had changed for her in just seven weeks.

But not enough. She was still staying at the Irish College, reluctant to break the tenuous link with home. But she was fast getting to the point where she must decide what to do, and where to go. If she was to remain in Paris she must begin to carve out some sort of life for herself.

And she would remain. She had no doubt at all about that.

She had spent part of the morning in estate agents' offices collecting details of apartments, trying to decide where she might want to live. Somewhere central, certainly, but quiet, and within walking distance of the river. She loved to walk along by the Seine, even now that the evenings were colder. There was something about the skyline, fast becoming familiar, that reassured her, made her feel safe, as if she belonged here.

Sometimes she felt she had been born to live in this city, that nowhere else could touch her in the same way. *How can I tell?* she would ask herself. It wasn't as if she had experience of anywhere else, apart from Dublin. But, somehow, she *knew*. She wasn't sure what shape the future would take, but she was certain that this was exactly where she was meant to be.

Paris was her father's gift to her.

Every now and then, as she rounded a corner or emerged from the Métro, she would stop in startled recognition of a monument or streetscape she had never seen before yet felt she knew intimately. It was her father's scrapbook come to life, his voice whispering to her as she walked through each *arrondissement*, visited every museum and art gallery and concert she could find, determined to make this city her own.

But it was the people who drew her more than the place itself. She had heard all the stories, that Parisians are arrogant, that they had no time for tourists but were happy to take their money, that they had no patience at all with those who couldn't speak their language perfectly.

It wasn't her experience. She had, of course, come across incredible rudeness from time to time, but that could happen in Dublin as well. For the most part people were pleasant and polite, and one or two – the elderly man at the street stall where she bought her copy of *Le Monde* each morning, the young blonde woman who worked at the Métro station – seemed to make a special effort to exchange a few words with her.

Her French was improving all the time, so it had been easy enough to speak to the estate agents this morning and try to give them some idea of what she was looking for. The problem, she thought as she crossed the pavement again to place the empty plastic dish back on the stall, was that she didn't really know what she was looking for herself. There seemed to be so much choice, and she had never had the luxury of choosing for herself before – certainly not anything as important as this.

As she went into Port Royal Métro station Olive thought briefly again about the suggestion from one of the estate agents this morning that *Madame* could rent instead of buying until she knew exactly what she was looking for. But that wasn't what she wanted, she decided as she reached the platform and boarded the train that was just pulling in. She had lived in someone else's house for quite long enough. This apartment would be hers – and if she didn't like it, she thought in a sudden burst of exhilaration, she could always buy another.

That was the wonderful thing about the money. It opened up all kinds of possibilities. She hardly thought about it on a day-to-day basis, once she had got used to having it. But it was there, and it was hers. She could buy whatever apartment she wanted and still live quite happily on the balance, provided she invested it wisely. Her needs were small after a lifetime of frugal living with her mother. She would manage very well once she got good investment advice.

Which definitely ruled Vincent out, she thought, smiling as she alighted from the Métro at St Michel a short time later. She hadn't heard from Vincent or her mother since leaving Dublin, though Raymond kept in regular contact. She hoped she might persuade himself and Dell to visit once she was settled in her new apartment.

Which meant she really should be thinking of somewhere with two bedrooms. Mentally crossing the one-bedroom apartment on Rue de la Bucherie from her list, she began walking through the crowded, cobbled streets in the direction of a two-bedroom apartment she had details of, with a view of Notre Dame.

She knew the area fairly well by now – it was one of her favourites, along with Montmartre and the quieter streets round the Madeleine – and she found the street she wanted almost immediately. It was mainly lined with restaurants and small souvenir shops, and she walked along slowly, looking for number seventeen.

It sounded promising. The apartment was on the third and fourth floors of a nineteenth-century building, just one street back from the river, with an asking price roughly equal to that of a glorified broom-cupboard in some of the more fashionable parts of Dublin.

Too good to be true, she thought, as she continued along the street, watching the numbers. And it was.

She stood outside the noisy Greek restaurant adjoining the apartment building and looked across at the tall buildings lining the opposite side of the street, blocking any chance of the promised view of Notre Dame. The only possible way to catch a glimpse of it, Olive decided, would be by leaning alarmingly far out the top-floor window, turning her head well to the left and holding on tightly to the inside sill. Preferably with her toes . . .

Smiling at the idea, and only slightly disappointed

since the location was a bit too boisterous for her liking, she began making her way towards Rue de la Harpe and the second apartment on her list. A bit pricier, this one, but in a lovely area in the heart of the Quartier Saint Germain – and if she liked it, she could well afford to buy it.

The quiet excitement of that struck her yet again.

Olive couldn't remember ever having more than two or three thousand pounds to call her own before the lottery win. Now there was well over £1.2 million left after buying her mother's house and clearing Raymond and Dell's mortgage. It was sitting in an account in Dublin like a huge safety-net, giving her all kinds of options. Her own account this time, not like the one "shared" with her mother, into which Olive had deposited most of her earnings and Bridget had withdrawn them just as fast to support Vincent's many ill-founded "business schemes". And the account she had opened in BNP for her living expenses in Paris was still looking healthy. Just for a moment, Olive wished she had some of Suzanne's capacity for splashing out and *enjoying* money. Years of having to answer to Bridget Grace had taken away any pleasure Olive could hope to have in spending on a lavish scale. And yet . . .

This apartment would be something very special. All she had to do was find the right one, in the right area.

But maybe not here. She loved the area around St Michel with its crowded, cobbled streets and lively ambience, but looking with the new eyes of a would-be resident she wondered whether it mightn't be just a bit *too* lively for her liking. Which probably ruled out most of the apartments on her list, including the one at Rue de la Harpe . . .

Uncertain whether to keep going and at least have a look at it, or head back towards the Métro and some of the quieter locations on offer, she came to a stop outside the church of St Séverin and decided to go in for a few moments. She had been to two classical music concerts here already, a lovely experience in the setting of the old church. It would only take a minute or two to see what their schedule was for December.

She entered the church quietly, struck by the air of calm after the bustle outside. She spent a few minutes in a pew near the back, letting her mind wander in a way that she occasionally thought of as prayer. Finding an apartment was only the very beginning, she thought. It was the first big step she had ever taken on her own, apart from coming to Paris in the first place, and she still had to make a life for herself, learn to speak French properly . . .

She could almost hear her mother's mocking voice, dooming her to failure. *Notions, that's all it is, notions, put into your head by that father of yours . . . Olivia, indeed!*

Needing to shake off the negative feeling that was settling over her, Olive stood up and went quickly to the noticeboard on the back wall of the church, so intent now on the concert listings that she didn't see the woman until she had actually bumped into her.

"*Oh, pardon, madame,*" she said, turning – to be met by the half-familiar face of the woman in the purple cape. She was wearing a dark green coat today, but it was unmistakably her – the same unruly reddish-brown hair and hazel eyes, the same warm smile as she addressed Olive quietly in rapid French.

Olive thought she caught the words "*jardin*" and "*hiver*" but she couldn't be certain. Her confusion must have shown in her face, because the woman continued much more slowly, "*Vous n'êtes pas française, madame?*"

This time Olive understood, and replied, "*Non, je suis irlandaise.*"

The woman's smile grew wider and she gestured with her head towards the porch, an unspoken invitation to come outside with her. They stopped just inside the front door of the church, standing back against the vestibule wall.

"You're Irish?" the woman asked. "I've just come back from there, my first time in Dublin." An American accent. "Are you on holiday? I'm Ellie Carpenter, by the way."

"Not a holiday exactly," Olive replied. "I've been here for nearly two months now."

"Great. You like Paris? I've spent almost a year here. It's really wonderful, isn't it? Do you know many people here yet? I've only ever seen you on your own in the Rodin gardens, I almost went and talked to you once or twice since that day I picked up your purse but you always looked so busy with your notebook –"

She continued talking nineteen to the dozen, barely pausing for breath, and Olive, normally cautious with strangers, could feel herself responding to her warmth and openness.

"I assumed you were French," she said when she finally got a word in edgeways. "Were you fluent when you got here?"

"I should hope so," Ellie said, laughing aloud before throwing a quick glance towards the inner door of the church, obviously wondering if the sound had carried. "I'm French-Canadian, from Quebec. I don't suppose we should really talk here. Would you like to go for a coffee?"

Olive hesitated, not sure if she had time to spare but wanting to spend a little more time with this engaging woman.

Ellie took her hesitation for a refusal. "Maybe some other time," she said with a smile and a slight shrug.

"I'd like to," Olive said quickly. "It's just that today doesn't suit because I'm flat-hunting. I only came in to check the concert list."

"Give me a call when you're free and we'll meet," Ellie said, beginning to rummage in her large handbag. "Let's see. I should have my card in here somewhere – we could go to a concert if you'd like – ah, here it is!" she added triumphantly, fishing out the card and handing it to Ellie. "What kind of music do you like usually?"

"I really don't know much about music," Olive said,

slightly flustered. "I've just started going to the concerts here recently . . ."

"Excellent – a very good start!" Ellie said. "And there are all kinds of opportunities here in Paris. It's one of the things I love about it. There are all sorts of concerts to go to, and *soirées*, and –" She paused for breath. "Actually, I'm having one myself tomorrow night, if you'd like to come – I live in Boulevard Port Royal – do you know it? – we'll just have ten or twelve people there, you'd be very welcome –"

And Olive, who wouldn't have dreamed until this moment of taking up an invitation from a stranger, found herself nodding agreement.

Ellie smiled again. "Great! That's really great!" She opened the door and began to go through. "Say about 8.30." She hurried into the street, waving a hand in a brief gesture of farewell, then stopped suddenly and turned back towards Olive who was still framed in the church doorway. "By the way, you didn't tell me your name!"

"No, I didn't," Olive said. She hesitated for the merest fraction of a second and then spoke again. "It's Olivia."

The sound was full and rich on her lips, new and yet totally familiar.

She smiled, repeating it quietly to herself as Ellie nodded and hurried away.

"Olivia. My name is Olivia Grace."

Chapter Eighteen

"Magic, Mam! Way to go!" Peter said when he came home from college to find the new car in the driveway.

"She got it free in a cornflakes packet," Declan said sourly from where he was leaning against the doorway, arms folded. "I mean, would you look at the size of it?"

It was, Colette had to agree, fairly small – but that was exactly what she had wanted. Something manageable, something that wouldn't frighten her out of her wits every time she had to take it out on the road.

Declan hadn't finished. "What did you ask them for, a dinky toy?"

"Put a sock in it, Decko," Peter said. "It's gorgeous, Mam. Have you signed up for lessons?"

She nodded. "This morning, just after I got it. And then I walked back to the showroom and got the man to drive me home."

"You mean two people can fit in it?" Declan asked, as Peter shot him a warning glance.

"I only need one to fit in until I learn to drive," Colette said, "and that might take a while."

"You'll need someone beside you while you're on a provisional licence," Declan reminded her, smiling as he saw the look on her face. Bull's-eye.

"Why should she, when no-one else bothers?" Peter countered quickly. "Besides," he added, putting an affectionate arm around her, "I bet you'll be a whizz. Top of the class!"

"We'll see," Colette said, with the first trace of uncertainty.

She still couldn't believe she had actually done it, and must have run out ten times this afternoon just to check that it was really there and wasn't a figment of her imagination. It was exactly what she wanted – small and red and snazzy.

That's what she had told the salesman when he finally paused for breath after reaming off all kinds of details about turbo-drive and side impact barriers and torque and fuel-injection systems. Just for a second she had wanted to say "a sports car" as the words of that song came into her head again, about Paris, in a sports car . . .

And then she told herself to have sense, that she'd have a hard enough job as it was persuading Martin that she hadn't lost her marbles.

So she banished thoughts of a sports car from her mind and finally got the next best thing – a car that was spanking new, exactly the size she wanted so that she just might learn how to park it – and, most important of all, *hers*.

But God knows how Martin would react, she thought as she followed her sons back into the house. And as for his –

His mother! In her excitement she had completely forgotten that it was Wednesday. And her ladyship would be arriving in exactly – she checked the clock – twelve minutes. She hadn't a hope of getting a meal ready by then. She was going to order pizza for herself and the kids, and reheat the remains of the stew for Martin, but there wasn't enough of it for him *and* his mother . . .

She bent to check the freezer without much hope. There was plenty of meat there, but without a microwave to defrost it – Martin didn't believe in them – it was no good to her. And Declan had finished the last of the beefburgers when he came in from school, so she didn't even have them to try and concoct something out of . . .

It would have to be egg and chips. There wasn't anything else.

She could just see their reaction. Heavy sarcasm from Alice Comerford and a hurt, mortified silence from Martin when he saw what was being served up to his mother.

To hell with them, she thought in sudden defiance. I've spent nearly twenty years dancing attendance on them. Egg and chips won't kill them for once.

Quickly she put the chips on to cook and was setting the table when she heard the front door opening and Emer's excited voice as she ran out into the hallway.

"Daddy, Daddy, did you see Mammy's new car! Isn't it lovely! And she's going to take me for a drive, Daddy, isn't it *gorrr-geous*!"

She was pulling on his arm, mad to get his attention, and he laughed, saying, "Hold on, you'll have me on the ground! Where's your Mam?"

"In the kitchen, and there's chips for tea, and we're having pizza as well. Peter phoned for it. Mammy said he could!"

Colette arrived into the hall in time to see the look of alarm on Martin's face and the sniffing disapproval on his mother's.

"Not for me, I hope. I've never eaten that kind of –" she hesitated for a moment, searching for an adequate description but not finding one " – that kind of *food* in my life and I don't mean to start now!"

"No, of course not, Mam." He helped her off with her coat. "Colette knows that. She'll have something ready for you." He hung up the coat, glancing across at Colette for confirmation. "Isn't that right, love? And whose is the car, anyway? Emer thinks it's yours." He gave a little laugh.

"Actually –" Colette's voice, in spite of her best efforts, came out in a kind of squeak. She changed it into a cough, tried again.

"Actually, the car *is* mine, I bought it today and

that's why I was so busy and didn't have time to get dinner ready." The words tumbled over each other and she held her breath, waiting for the reaction.

Martin was a man with very clear priorities. The little red box sitting in his driveway, blocking his way in, could wait. His dinner couldn't.

"So what are we having?" He spoke slowly, as if that would help her to come up with the right answer.

"There's a choice," she said brightly, trying to avoid looking directly at her mother-in-law. "Egg and chips. Or an omelette. Or some stew – enough for one of you," she added quickly.

Her mother-in-law threw Martin a look that told him how much she pitied him. "You go ahead and have the stew, love," she said to him. "You need *some* bit of nourishment after a day at work. I'm not really hungry – and I can always have a sandwich when I get home. That's what I usually do."

The lying old bitch, Colette thought. She had never in her life left Colette's house hungry. Talk about rubbing it in, making sure she got the message – and making Martin feel even worse into the bargain. So much for the motherly love bit. She'd sicken you if you let her.

And I'm not going to let her, Colette thought, wishing she could do something to take the wretched look off Martin's face. Boring he might be, and too caught up with his family, but he deserved better than this.

"Will I heat the stew for you?" she asked quietly.

"Or –" Inspiration dawned as she turned to her mother in law. "We could go out to eat – it's not too late and Ciara might come with us. She's been dying to try that new place in Clontarf."

"Thank you very much, Colette." Mrs Comerford's tones were pure ice. "But I didn't leave the comfort of my own fireside on a night like this to go traipsing off to a place where they probably serve nothing but –"

"Pizza?" Declan asked, coming into the hall as the doorbell sounded. He would have heard every word from the living-room.

Well done, Declan, Colette thought. I knew I could depend on you to stir it up.

"Pizza," he repeated, all innocence as he opened the door, took the money Colette handed him from her purse on the hall table and paid the delivery man. "I'm with you, Granny," he said over an armload of pizza-filled cardboard boxes. "I'd give anything for a decent dinner – we usually have to put up with this kind of stuff unless it's Wednesday."

Colette opened her mouth but no sound came out. The brat! She'd kill him stone-dead as soon as his grandmother left.

"Now, Declan –" Martin began, but Declan just shrugged, gave a lazy grin and yelled "Come and get it!" up the stairs to Peter and Ciara as he turned to go into the kitchen. "Whoops, looks like you're needed, Mam!" he said casually over his shoulder as he walked in and put the boxes on the kitchen table.

"The pan!" she shrieked, rushing into the kitchen.

Too late. The flames spurting from the chip-pan weren't particularly high yet, but they were spectacular enough to put the heart crossways in her. The fire blanket – where was the –

"Under control, Mam." Peter's voice. He grasped her shoulders from behind, moved her swiftly from between him and the cooker and bent to the cupboard beside it to pull out the fire blanket. Martin, coming suddenly to life, dashed into the utility room to grab the extinguisher and stand next to Peter as back-up.

No need. It was, as he said, under control. He laid the blanket gently across the flames, watched for a few minutes to make sure there was no fire licking around its edges, and finally moved back from the cooker.

"Nobody touch it," he warned, taking the extinguisher from Martin and leaving it within easy reach on the worktop, just in case.

"So chips are off the menu?" Declan enquired of nobody in particular. "Pizza, anyone?" He had been sitting at the kitchen table, tucking into the pizza, pretending not to notice the drama going on less than ten feet away from him. Nothing to do with him. He only lived here.

Ciara and Emer came slowly into the room, Ciara trying to her best to combine her "why did I get you for a mother?" look with the "butter wouldn't melt" expression she reserved for her granny.

Colette ignored her, turning instead to Emer whose bottom lip was trembling.

"Don't worry, poppet," she said as she lifted her up. "It's all over. Everything's fine now."

That wasn't exactly the truth. The tiles at the back of the cooker were blackened from the smoke and she'd have to replace the wallpaper because there were scorch-marks going up the side of the cooker.

"I suppose we should look on the bright side," she said, looking around the circle of faces – Ciara's accusing, Martin's hassled and his mother with her "I told you not to marry her, but would you listen?" expression. "The kitchen needs re-doing anyway, so now we'll *have* to get going on it."

"Before or after tea?" Declan asked through a mouthful of pizza.

"Shut it, Declan," Peter warned quietly. But not quietly enough.

"I suppose that's what you're learning in that college of yours?" his grandmother asked, sniffing.

Peter grinned at her. "That, and a few other things, Granny. Want to hear some of the new words I've learned?"

She didn't even deign to answer him. Instead she turned to Martin. "I think it might be best if you bring me back home, and I'll cook you up a nice bit of fish I have in the fridge. Colette seems to have other things on her mind today, and I wouldn't wish to intrude."

"There's no need –" Colette began, but then stopped herself. There was every need.

She had nothing in the house to feed them with, and

she had had just about enough of her mother-in-law for one evening, dinner or no dinner.

She returned Alice Comerford's curt goodbye and told the kids they could bring the pizza into the TV room – something she didn't usually allow, but she felt she needed to be on her own for a few minutes.

She put on the kettle, put some bread in the toaster and then sighed as she sat down at the kitchen table. Disaster, she thought. She'll never let me live this down.

At least it took their minds off the new car.

At the thought of it she could feel the excitement bubbling up again.

It had been a great day, she reminded herself. A small chip-pan fire that was under control in a few minutes wasn't exactly a major catastrophe, and in any other family they could have shrugged it off and thanked God it wasn't worse, and if it went the rounds of the Comerford family then that was their problem, not hers.

She had done her best all these years, and it still wasn't good enough for Alice and the rest of them. Maybe now was the time to start doing things her way, instead of trying to please them and getting nowhere.

And Peter seemed to think so too, she thought, as he came into the kitchen with some pizza on a plate.

"Try a bit of this, Mam?" he asked.

"Thanks, love, I won't. I've toast made." She began to stand up.

"You stay there," he said, putting a hand on her shoulder. "I'll get it for you."

Quickly he made the tea, buttered the toast and came to sit beside her.

"She was something else, wasn't she?"

Colette nodded in reply as she took a bite of the toast.

"Did you see her face when you answered her back?" she said after a minute.

"I probably shouldn't have –" he began, colouring slightly.

"Indeed you should, and you didn't say half enough. It's about time one of us learned to talk back to her."

"Declan and Ciara don't need to. She's wrapped around their little fingers." He said it as a matter of fact, without a trace of self-pity.

"Do you mind?" she asked. She had often wondered that but hadn't brought it up for fear of hurting him.

"No, I'm used to it," he said cheerfully. "Besides, she might change her tune when I start standing up to her a bit more. Dad'll probably hit the roof, but I've had enough of being Mr Nice Guy. She'll probably show me a lot more respect if I don't take so much bullshit from her."

Colette looked at her eldest son with something approaching amazement.

"Good for you, Peter. It's only now I'm beginning to realise that myself – I wish I'd known it at your age, things might have been different."

"They can be different now."

"They can, and they will," Colette laughed. "That granny of yours won't know what hit her."

Chapter Nineteen

Olive had absolutely no idea what to wear to the *soirée*. She could feel the quiet panic mounting as she went quickly through her limited wardrobe. Her clothes were of good quality – one thing she had always made sure of – but there was nothing remotely resembling what she imagined should be worn to a *soirée*.

The very word conjured up images of elegance and sophistication. Heaven alone knew what she would say to these people, how she could in any possible way be of interest to them. Ellie could only have asked her out of pity, having seen her alone so many times in the Rodin museum.

Maybe it would be better not to go. She always found it difficult meeting new people anyway – she could never manage the small talk that seemed to come so effortlessly to others. She could ring tomorrow morning to convey her apologies. Ellie would surely understand –

And might never again invite her to anything.

And if Olive was certain of only one thing, it was that she wanted to see Ellie Carpenter again. She had reached Olive in a way no other woman had ever managed, her warmth and openness breaking easily through the defences of a lifetime with a domineering mother. Olive would face even the nightmare of small-talk with total strangers if it meant seeing Ellie again.

She examined her outfits once more. There were only three possibilities, and she wasn't sure that any of them would be suitable. A soft tweed skirt that she normally wore with one of two cashmere sweaters, a pleated grey skirt which came to just below her knees – and a flowing, low-cut black dress, bought in a moment of madness, that had met with an appalled reaction from Bridget Grace the only time Olive had tried it on at home.

"No daughter of mine is going out in something like that," Bridget had said vehemently. "You look no better than a tramp. You're to take it right back to where you got it and see that you get your money back, because you're not wearing that – *thing* – while you live in this house."

And Olive never *had* worn it – but in a gesture of quiet defiance she had tucked it, still in its bag, away on the top shelf of her wardrobe. She hadn't even looked at it in the intervening two years – but it was the first thing she packed for coming to Paris.

Her mother was right, Olive decided, as she held the dress up to her and looked at her reflection in the small mirror. No daughter of Bridget Grace's would ever dream of wearing such a dress . . .

But a daughter of Matthew Grace would.

Olivia Grace would wear it, or something very like it.

She would go shopping tomorrow, and get advice, and find out what one wore to a *soirée*. She would get her hair done in a very expensive, wonderful-looking salon. She would arrange to be made-up and perhaps have a manicure. She would go along tomorrow night and make small talk if it killed her – which it almost certainly wouldn't. And she would do her very best to make the most of the evening. She hadn't done that in far, far too long.

She put away the clothes, feeling a wholly new sense of anticipation as she prepared for bed. She'd need to be awake early if she was to have any hope of fitting everything into tomorrow.

* * *

Olivia. My name is Olivia, she reminded herself as she stepped out of the lift to be met by a murmur of voices coming from the open doorway of the nearest apartment.

Taking a deep breath, she drew back her shoulders slightly and moved towards the entrance. There were several people just inside, in animated conversation – English as well as French, to her relief – and they moved aside, smiling, to allow her in. She smiled back as she scanned the room, trying to locate Ellie.

"Olivia, *there* you are. Lovely to see you! Did you have any trouble getting here? Oh, don't you look *wonderful*!" She had grasped Olivia's hand and now held her at arm's length to get the full effect of how she looked – which was, indeed, wonderful. "Come with me. There are so many people I want you to meet! Do you drink? Would you like some wine?" She half-turned to the small table beside her. "Red or white? Oh, Sophie, just a moment, I must introduce you . . ."

And within minutes Olivia found herself, wine-glass in hand, part of a lively group of seven or eight people, most of whom were talking loudly, articulately and all at once. Definitely friends of Ellie's, she thought, amused, as she kept an ear on the conversation while stealing glances round the apartment.

She had never seen anything like it before. The room they were in was enormous, with high ceilings and an elaborate fireplace with a welcoming fire in the grate. In the corner to the right of it was a grand piano with several music stands grouped around it and a dozen or so ornate, comfortable-looking chairs ranged in a semicircle a little distance from it. The room was lit by several exquisite chandeliers which sparkled in the reflected firelight.

Ellie was obviously a woman of considerable means as well as good taste, Olivia decided. She must –

"I don't think I've seen you here before, have I?" the man to her left asked, and she found herself drawn into conversation with an ease that was completely new to her. She had never before had this experience in a group of strangers, the sense of being relaxed and welcome and wanting to be part of it instead of somewhere, anywhere, else.

It didn't really surprise her. It was just another part of the transformation that she could hardly believe had taken place in a single day.

Everything had fallen smoothly into place once she had found her dress. It had taken most of the morning, but the result was well worth the effort. The dress was exactly right – simple, black and mid-length, in a soft fabric that skimmed gracefully over her tall figure.

Madame, looking delightedly at Olivia's reflection as she made some minor adjustments to the dress for her, had been pleased to recommend the *salon* where they took care of her own beautifully cut hair, and had phoned immediately, managing against the odds to get an appointment for her.

And Olivia, though she resisted the stylist's suggestions of – as far as she could make out – something that would give her *"une bonne couleur"*, was very pleased with the final result. Her hair, still a shining steel-grey but now swept up softly into a different and very feminine style, had never looked more attractive.

She had hesitated only for a moment before going into the upmarket jeweller's she passed on the way back to the Irish College, and had emerged after a very short time with a gold necklace and earrings – a world apart from the simple studs she usually wore – and with her BNP account the poorer by close on a thousand pounds.

And it was worth every penny of the frighteningly huge sum her afternoon had cost her. She did indeed, as Ellie had said, look wonderful. And she was enjoying that sensation more than she ever would have believed possible.

Ellie approached the little group Olivia was in just as three men and a woman moved to the corner by the piano and began tuning their instruments.

"Would you like to sit down? The music's about to start and almost everybody's here – Max –" she turned to a dark-haired man who was holding a violin. "– I don't think we should wait any longer for Thierry, do you? He must have been delayed –"

As if on cue a tall man in his mid-fifties who was dressed entirely in black appeared in the doorway. His silver-grey hair, sweeping down past the collar of his black jacket, framed a youthful-looking face from which intense blue eyes swept the room, lighting up when he saw Ellie.

He was, without question, the most attractive man Olivia had ever seen.

* * *

Tonight would be her first time at the Paris Opéra.

Olivia had often wanted to go but had felt uncomfortable about going alone. Now, as one of Ellie's party, it was a pleasure she had been looking forward to for the past week, since Ellie had invited her on the night of the *soirée*.

198

"A spare ticket," Ellie had said just as Olivia was leaving. "*Orpheus*, have you seen it? I'm told it's absolutely magical! Ring me in a day or two. Let me know if you can make it. Even better, we might get to meet for that coffee!" She turned for a moment to say goodbye to some of the other guests who were leaving just then. "*Solange, Philippe, à la prochaine fois! Portez-vous bien, chéries!* – You *will* ring me?" she said over her shoulder to Olivia who had moved slightly towards the door.

Olivia nodded, mouthing a final "thank you" as another couple came towards Ellie and began kissing her goodbye in the elaborate French style – one, two, three, four, on alternate cheeks – that Olivia used to think was overdone. *A time and a place*, her mother would have said. Well, her mother wasn't here now. And if ever there was a time and place for such open affection, it was surely in the company of someone as warm and gregarious as Ellie.

She had never met anyone quite like her, Olivia had thought as she made her way to the nearby Métro station. Ellie had obviously taken her under her wing, with a generosity of spirit that was touching. She would have to be careful not to be swamped. For the time being she had had more than enough of claustrophobic, one-to-one relationships. But nothing about Ellie was in the least bit stifling – and it would be very good indeed to have a friend.

Over coffee two days later Olivia had commented on the wonderful apartment, saying that she was still searching for somewhere but wouldn't know how to *begin* to furnish it like that even if she found such a place. Good manners prevented her from asking what she would love to know – how Ellie had managed to find it and how on earth she could afford it. But, Ellie being Ellie, she didn't need to ask.

"I know. Isn't it really something?" she had said. "I don't know how I'll ever settle back into my own ordinary little home when I get back to Montreal!"

"It's not yours?"

Ellie had laughed. "On an associate college professor's salary? I wish! No, it's my brother's – he's the business mind of the family. He does something amazing and very lucrative in the stockbroking world. I don't understand a word of it myself but I'm happy to enjoy the fruits of his labour and he's happy to have me house-sit while he's back home for six months. Where exactly are you looking for an apartment?"

And to Olivia's delight Ellie had known "just the place". It had, indeed, been exactly as she described it, a charming two-bedroom apartment with an open fireplace – something Olivia had decided she couldn't live without – that was just about to be vacated by a friend of Ellie's. And Olivia was due to move in tomorrow, 1st December, with an option to buy if she still liked it after three months.

She had almost been tempted to stay at home this evening and savour the quiet anticipation of finally moving into a home of her own. Almost, but not quite.

An evening at the Opéra was far too good an opportunity to miss.

She knew she would enjoy Ellie's company. She might, or might not, enjoy the opera itself, but she was more than willing to give it a try. She was looking forward to meeting Ellie's friends who were joining them –

And she wanted to see Thierry again.

She didn't know what it was about the man that had attracted her, but there was something about his presence, his energy, the very way he had walked into the room on the night of the *soirée*, that Olivia found compelling. To her dismay he had left, quickly and quietly, immediately after the string quartet had finished playing.

Her reaction had astonished her. She hadn't ever felt so drawn to a man before. Well, once, but that was different, and a long time ago.

She had wanted to ask Ellie about him when they met for coffee, just as she wanted to ask now.

"The others should be here in just a few minutes," Ellie said.

They were standing in the Grand Foyer of the Opéra. Olivia was almost overwhelmed by the size and splendour of it. As they stood at the foot of the enormous central staircase her eyes were drawn upwards towards the two statues which were holding a marble pillar aloft over the doorway to the amphitheatre.

There were statues everywhere, she noticed, most holding sconces which, together with the huge central chandeliers, cast a warm glow over the crowds of people gathered beneath.

"Ellie, there you are!"

The voice, English, male, came from Olivia's right and she turned as Ellie began a flurry of introductions. Two men – neither of them Thierry – and a woman Olivia recognised from the *soirée*.

"Shall we go on up?" Ellie was asking. "Thierry will join us if he can – he knows the number of our box."

She continued talking as they made their way up the central staircase and followed the smaller one curving to the left.

"Box 38, let's see, it should be just about – here!" she finished triumphantly, leading them through the open door and into the box with its ornate pillars, walls covered with red damask and half-a-dozen comfortable chairs waiting for them.

As Olivia moved towards a seat at the front of the box in response to a gesture from Ellie, she caught her first glimpse of the magnificent *chambre de spectacle*.

It was breathtakingly opulent. Red and gold everywhere – red seats with elaborate gilt carvings, red and gold on the front of the boxes which, like their own, were ranged in tiers to either side of the stage. She had never seen anything like it.

And then there was a sound at the open doorway behind her and she turned to see Thierry de Rochemont standing there. And it was as if everything else had disappeared and nothing existed but him.

Chapter Twenty

She would make a list, Colette decided. That was always a good place to start.

Potatoes, broccoli, butter, firelighters, toothpaste, tomato ketchup.

More Christmas cards, some crackers, clothes for the Baby Born doll that Emer was getting from Santa . . .

And a makeover, a week in that fancy health farm in Wicklow, a holiday in the Bahamas and a brand new house for herself. . .

If only!

Laughing, she looked back through the lists spread out around her on the kitchen table.

As Ciara was fond of saying, time to get real.

The first two lists she could manage. The third –

Well, why not? she asked herself. Why not make a *serious* list of things she'd like to do, things she had always wanted to do – or had never in her life thought of doing, but maybe now was the time to give them a try?

She wasn't getting any younger – she'd be thirty-eight on the 23rd April, less than five months away.

There it was again, that blessed song about Paris going through her head. A reminder that she'd blown it. Just how many other things were there that she wanted to do and never would?

Maybe not that many, she decided. But there had to be some.

And if she was ever to do them then now was the time.

Look at all the money still sitting there, in spite of Martin and his family. Maeve was dead right – she'd be a fool not to enjoy it.

She'd been thrilled when Colette phoned her on the Wednesday evening to tell her about the car. Good job somebody was, Colette thought. Martin had come home from his mother's with a face like stone, telling Colette how disappointed he was in her.

Disappointed!

She would have laughed, but she was still stunned that he'd said anything at all. On the rare occasions when he was sufficiently upset about something, he usually went into a sulk, putting the onus on her – and the kids, if they were involved – to try and coax him out of it.

And he was *disappointed*. How in God's name did he *dare* to be disappointed? He had taken it for granted all these years that she would run around looking after his mother every Wednesday evening after a day's work, and do the shopping on her own on Thursdays while he was doing his mother's, and put up with excuses every time she wanted something done in the house and he was "needed" instead at his brothers' or sisters' houses, or was "busy" watching a football or hurling or rugby match –

And *he* was disappointed?

If anyone had a right to be disappointed, Colette thought, it wasn't Martin Comerford.

Martin Comerford should think he was in Heaven, with a mother who thought the sun shone out of him, a wife who ran their home without making any demands on him at all, and a fortune at his disposal in the bank.

And if that didn't satisfy him, maybe it was time for Colette to take another look at what she was getting out of it all.

An expression of Maeve's came back to her out of nowhere.

"If you keep doing what you're doing, you keep getting what you're getting."

She drew a fresh sheet of paper towards her.

WHAT I WANT, she wrote on the top in bold capitals.

She sat for a moment or two chewing on the end of the pen, looking out through the kitchen window at the wintry garden.

What *do* I want? she asked herself – then suddenly

she was scribbling furiously as ideas came thick and fast.

1. A car, and driving lessons.

She put those at the top of the list, with a tick in a little box beside them, and immediately she felt better.

2. A whole new image.

She wouldn't dare! Would she? She was comfortable the way she was –

Sure. Nearly two stone overweight, her hair straggly and in need of colouring, and nothing in her wardrobe that was less than two years old. And she was *comfortable* with that?

She underlined the words *"A whole new image"* and moved on to number 3.

3. Join a health club.

She had never even been inside the door of one before, imagining they were all full of svelte supermodels in to-die-for clothes. And maybe they were, but what the hell – she had nothing to lose but her dignity. And two stone, she reminded herself. And wouldn't it be better if she could do it all in the one go, in time for Christmas? She'd need a miracle – which was exactly what that new health farm promised, wasn't it? She wrote it down.

4. A week in a health farm.

And afterwards, when she was sleek and toned and wonderful – a week in Paris . . .

She stood up quickly and crossed to the telephone before she could talk herself out of it. Her sister answered on the third ring.

"Eileen? What would you think about a week on a health farm?"

Eileen burst out laughing. "Listen, you, just because I was forty last month!"

"And you look great – for forty!" Colette teased. "But I look about ten years older than you. I need to do something about myself. If I go, would you come with me? I'd never do it on my own. I need the moral support!"

Eileen hesitated at the other end. "Well, there's the kids," she said. "What would I do about them? Joe is keeping what's left of his holidays for Christmas. And – well – don't those places cost a fortune?"

Colette laughed. "Maybe they do, but who cares? My treat, to cheer you up for being forty! Come on, Eileen, say 'yes'!"

"Are we allowed to bring the kids?"

"What do you think, are we allowed to bring the kids? Of course we're not allowed to bring the kids – are you cracked?"

"I am!" Eileen said. "I'm driven demented here with the lot of them. If I can't bring them then I'll definitely go! Joe's mother might look after them. When were you thinking of going?"

"As soon as I can. I need to get in shape for Christmas!"

Eileen laughed. "Some hope! Don't be insulted, I'm the same. I've been stuffing myself since we moved down to Mullingar – I'm the size of a house!"

"So you'll definitely come?" Colette asked.

"Definitely," Eileen promised. "Only not this side of Christmas. I'm up to my eyes trying to get organised. What's it like, anyway?"

"Posh. All kinds of jacuzzis and toning treatments and what-have-you. In the middle of the Wicklow mountains, about a hundred miles from anywhere you might get a drink or a bar of chocolate."

"Oh, goody," Eileen said. "Just what I've always wanted, death by starvation in the middle of nowhere. I can't wait!"

Colette laughed. "Will I book for early January? I promise you'll love it! Oh, and watch the post tomorrow."

"What for?"

"Call it a belated birthday present. Bye."

She went back to her list, quickly wrote

5. *Paris*

6. *Sort out money.*

She'd send cheques for £20,000 each to Eileen and Therese, as well as to her brother Tim and his wife. She'd been leaving it on the long finger since September, trying to get Martin to sit down and plan what they should do.

Which was what she wanted most, she decided, as she wrote *"Talk to Martin"* beside *"Sort out money."*

The problem, of course, was to get Martin to talk to *her* and give over that ridiculous huff he'd been in for the past two weeks, since his mother refused to go "where I'm not wanted" on Wednesdays, or any other day for that matter.

Which should have been all Colette's Christmases coming at once, but Martin's sisters would probably wipe the floor with her when they saw her again.

Which reminded her . . .

She was just writing

7. *Assertiveness classes*

when the front door opened and she heard voices in the hall. Ciara – her half-day – and Declan. What was he doing home at 12.45?

"No school?" she asked him as the two of them came into the kitchen.

"No point," he said, dropping his bag in the corner and sprawling out on a chair.

"What do you mean, no point?" She could feel her blood-pressure rising.

"I mean, no point!" he repeated. "Useless bloody place anyway. Who needs it?"

She took a deep breath, trying to keep calm. They'd been down this road before.

"You do, for starters," she said in what she hoped was a calm and patient voice, the kind the parenting manuals told you to use.

One look at Declan's face made her wonder if the people who wrote them had teenagers themselves.

"I'm not going to college, Ma," he drawled. "I told you that. And I'm not getting into one of those dead-end jobs that pays peanuts. I'm starting my own business."

"You are?" she asked, torn between exasperation

and amusement. "Doing what? And using what for money?"

"Logos on tee-shirts, that's what I'll do. Transfers, that kind of thing. Everyone wants them. I was talking to a guy who can get me started for ten grand. I said I'll let him know by Friday."

"I see." She was pleased with the way she kept her voice an even keel. To the best of her knowledge he had somewhere around £200 in his bank account – and she could guess where he thought he was getting the rest.

"That'll take a lot of earning," she said.

He nearly fell off the chair. "Why would I want to earn it? Could you not give me my share-out early?"

Deep breath again, Colette. Steady. "What share-out would that be, Declan?"

"Our bit of the winnings. What you were going to give us for Christmas."

"You surely don't –" she began.

"But Ciara said –"

"I only said she *might*," Ciara said, flashing him a look before turning back to Colette. "I should have known better. I suppose this means I'm not getting the computer and music centre I need." Her eyes were pure venom, and for the first time Colette realised who her daughter reminded her of.

She was the living spit of her granny.

And Colette was not about to go through that kind of relationship all over again.

If you keep doing what you're doing, you keep getting what you're getting.

Things would have to change around here.

And she couldn't be sure of changing Ciara and Declan. She could try, but she couldn't be sure. If she wanted changes, she'd better start with herself. And start right now.

She looked from one rebellious face to the other.

"The money doesn't belong to you. It belongs to me and to your father. And of course we'll give you some. He's already spent loads on you both. But we'll be investing most of it, for your future as well as for ours. When I can get him to sit down and talk sensibly about it, I'll tell you a bit more."

She looked directly at Declan.

"So my advice is to get yourself back to school and do the best you can, because you'll need *some* kind of results if you're going to be in business for yourself. Get your results, and *then* we might talk about giving you enough to get you started."

They didn't say a word. They were too busy getting their heads around this new Colette.

"Therese is collecting Emer from school," she continued before they could get their voices back, "so I'm going out. You can get your own lunch. See you later."

The dam finally burst, but she ignored their protests, picked up her list and went into the hallway to ring the most expensive hairdresser she could find.

Chapter Twenty-one

Maeve managed to hold herself together until she had left Robert Shaw's office and was on her way downstairs in the lift. She was absolutely *not* going to let herself break down in front of Larry and that toad of a solicitor of his, Morgan Lee.

She was certain that Lee had put him up to this, was getting him to turn the screws on her in the hope of a big fat fee for himself. He must know that there was no possible way she could get the kind of money they were asking for.

Deep breath, she told herself. *Take a deep breath and get into the car and drive yourself home. You'll figure something out.*

You'll have to.

The light was on when she pulled up outside the house, but there was no car there. Which meant Val wasn't home yet, and Orla was.

Maeve felt her heart sinking, followed by an immediate stab of guilt. Imagine feeling like that about your own daughter, she thought. But the encounter with Larry had completely drained her. She was in no fit state now to be cross-examined by their daughter.

And that was why Orla was home early, of course. To find out what had happened at the solicitor's.

Most of the time she acted as if it didn't matter a damn to her, this ongoing feud between her parents and Maeve's anxiety about the house, but Maeve was beginning to suspect, from one or two things Orla had said, that it mattered much more than she would admit.

The trouble was, it was Maeve she was holding responsible for Larry's absence.

She appeared at the top of the stairs as soon as Maeve opened the front door.

"There was nobody here!" The voice was accusing.

"I told you, Orla. Remember?" Maeve said, trying to keep her patience. She didn't need this right now. "The boys are at Maura's, and Val –"

"Shouldn't be here in the first place!"

"We've been through all this, Orla." Maeve no longer tried to hold her patience – she'd had as much as she could take for one day. "She needs a place to live. We need the money. End of story."

"It is *not* the end of the story! Don't you dare say that to me!"

She came quickly down the stairs to stand in front of

Maeve, eyes blazing. "Just how do you think it feels to have that creepy woman treating my house as if she owns the place? She used my hairdryer this morning! How much does she pay you for *that*!"

"She didn't!" Maeve paused in the act of hanging up her coat, horrified. "Orla, you don't mean she went into your room and –"

"I never said she went into my room." Orla was still in fighting form but had the grace to look embarrassed. "I left it in the bathroom, but I could hear her using it later in her bedroom – I wanted to go in there and kill her."

"I'll say something to her." Maeve hung up her coat and turned back to Orla. "I'm going to make some tea before the boys get back. Want some?"

Orla shook her head but followed her to the kitchen nonetheless. She sat down at one corner of the big pine table.

"What happened, anyway?"

Maeve busied herself filling the kettle, wondering how much to say. She had always tried to be fair to Larry where the children were concerned, but this time he had made it nearly impossible.

She sighed and sat down opposite her daughter.

"You know he wants money."

Orla nodded.

"And you know by now, don't you, that he has a real problem with gambling? That no matter how much money he has, he'll never be able to keep a penny of it?"

"That's up to him." Orla said sharply. "He has the right to spend his money on whatever he wants."

Maeve bit her lip. That's what Morgan Lee had said. Not quite in the same words, of course. Oh, no – it was "my client's best interests" and "my client's entitlements" and "equitable distribution of jointly held assets" – but the message had been the same. Larry was entitled to his share, regardless of what he might intend to do with it.

"Fine, Orla. Maybe you're right. Would you like me to make a cheque out to his pals at Ace Racing and save him the trouble?"

"There you go again, criticising him! Do you never think that maybe it's your fault he gambles! Ciara says . . ."

"Go on, Orla! Don't stop now! I'd love to know what *Ciara* has to say about it! And I promise not to laugh at what a spoilt fourteen-year-old child who doesn't know her arse from her elbow has to say about gambling, or about my marriage, or about anything else on God's earth! Because as far as I know she hasn't a brain in her head, and wouldn't know what to do with it even if she had! So, go on, tell me –"

She tried to stop herself, but it was no use. Her voice was rising out of control.

"Pathetic," Orla said, standing up. "That's what she said, that you're pathetic and it's your fault Dad left because why else would he have gone? And she can't believe you were so stupid about the lottery. She feels sorry for me that –"

"That's enough, Orla!" She tried to get her voice under control again, tried to ignore the hand that was itching to slap her daughter. She had never done that before, but she had never been pushed this far before either.

She took a deep breath, realised her heart was racing.

"I wish you'd show me some bit of loyalty and respect. You are not to discuss what goes on in this house with Ciara or with anyone else. It's none of her business! Do you hear me?"

Her daughter faced her with a look of disdain.

"Do you really think everyone doesn't know what's happening? Johnny Griffin said you're the talk of the place in Ace Racing, the way you treated Dad! And –" she saw Maeve's face, knew she was on dangerous ground but kept going – "before you lecture me on loyalty, think how Colette will feel when she hears what you said about your 'best friend's' daughter!"

"You are *not* –" Maeve began, but Orla had turned on her heel and was gone off up the stairs. Probably to do some more packing, Maeve thought. She was leaving for France in four days' time – if Maeve didn't kill her first.

The phone rang and Maeve sighed as she went to answer it. Ciara, probably. She rang three or four times every day. God knows what they found to talk about.

Me, Maeve realised as she reached for the phone. They talk about me. If it's Ciara, I won't be able to be civil to her.

"Hello, is that Maeve?" The voice was familiar, yet she couldn't place it immediately. Sugary-sweet, smug, a bit like –

"Hello, Lorraine," she said as it came to her.

"I hope I'm ringing at a good time," Lorraine said. "There's something I want to talk to you about."

"Yes?" Maeve had no idea what Lorraine might want to talk to her about – and she didn't particularly want to hear, after the way Lorraine had treated her in the run-up to leaving the office.

"I'd come round –"

Over my dead body, Maeve thought.

"– only I've so much to get organised for Christmas. I'm sure you're busy too, so maybe we can do it over the phone. I want to put in an offer for your house."

Maeve nearly dropped the phone.

"I think it could suit the two of us," Lorraine continued blithely. "Of course, I'd expect to get it for a good price because from what you said it needs a bit of work, doesn't it? And I'm only moving so David can be near his mother, and he wants the children to be near the beach. I could take it or leave it myself, I'm perfectly happy where I am, but I *would* like somewhere with a bit more space, and it would save me the hassle of looking. What do you think?"

What Maeve thought wasn't anywhere near polite.

"My house is not for sale, Lorraine," she finally managed in a strangled voice.

"Oh, I know that," Lorraine said. "But it will be,

won't it? And I thought if I got in first with an offer it would benefit us both. You'd sell it to me for a reasonable price because you know I have the money to close the deal, and you wouldn't have the trouble of showing it to dozens of people. It could work out very nicely."

"Lorraine, I don't know if you heard me. I am not selling this house."

There was a slight pause at the other end of the phone.

"From what I've heard, it's only a matter of time."

"Who said –"

"Oh, a little bird. Word gets out about these things! So let me know when you change your mind, Maeve. My number's in the book. Only don't leave it too long or I might start looking somewhere else. I –"

Maeve slammed the phone back down onto the receiver. The cheek of her! The complacent little bitch, thinking she could just ring up out of the blue and Maeve would sell her the house! Where did she get the notion that –

Larry. Larry and his big mouth. He'd probably told half the people he knew that he was going after the house. His friends at work, his drinking buddies, the guys in the golf club, not to mention the crowd at Ace Racing – everyone would know.

Dublin was a small place, it wouldn't take long for word to get around – and trust Lorraine to have found out about it.

Well, she's not getting my house, Maeve thought. I'd burn it to the ground before I'd let her in the front door.

The bell rang, making her jump before she realised it was Maura back with the boys.

They dashed in, said a quick hello and rushed to switch on the soccer on television.

Maura followed them in, laughing.

"I don't know how you keep up with them. I –"

She saw the look on Maeve's face. "Was it that bad?"

"That bad," Maeve said, leading the way to the kitchen where they could talk undisturbed.

"He's out to get me," she said once they were sitting at the kitchen table. "No question about it. And even if he wasn't, that smug gobshite of a solicitor will encourage him to keep after me. And the whole of Dublin knows about it. Lorraine Kearns rang up offering to buy the house."

"She did not!"

"She did! I suppose it shouldn't surprise me – Orla said everyone knows in that betting office he goes to. And she's doing her bit too, telling Ciara Comerford, and God knows who else, everything that's going on here."

"Maybe it's no harm she's going off for a while. It'll let you get the new lodgers settled in. How's she taking that?"

Maeve turned to look out the window, saying nothing.

"Maeve, I said how is she – Maeve! You did tell her they're coming, didn't you?"

"Not yet," Maeve said, turning back towards her

sister. "I was trying to work out the best way of breaking it to her. Senan knows. He helped me paint the rooms and I have him sworn to secrecy. Orla didn't even notice we were painting."

"Well, you can't let them just arrive. That's asking for trouble. You'll have to tell her."

"Tell me what?" Orla's voice, from the kitchen doorway. She was as quiet as a cat when she wanted to be.

Maeve and Maura glanced quickly at each other before turning to her.

"Tell me what?" Orla repeated in a more insistent voice. "This is about me, isn't it? I know by your faces! What are you supposed to tell me?"

Maeve took the bull by the horns. "We have two girls coming to look at the spare rooms tomorrow. One of them is a friend of Val's –"

"They're *what*? You're not thinking of bringing anyone else in here! Isn't it bad enough having that woman creeping around the place and talking to nobody and stealing my hairdryer, without bringing all her friends in. I'll have to lock everything up when I'm gone to France."

"Orla, we –"

"We need the money! Go on. Say it. That's all you can think about, getting more money! For all the good it does. I'm ashamed of the crappy clothes I have to take with me. And if it wasn't for Noeleen, I wouldn't have a penny to spend, or even be going in the first place! If you hadn't been stupid enough to –"

"That's enough, Orla!"

"It's true," Orla said, but the expression on Maeve's face made her change tack. "Do what you like. You will anyway! Why don't you put a dozen people into my room while you're at it, and turn the garage into a crèche, and have a shop in the living-room and someone's granny in the attic! Then you'll have all the money you want, and I might get some of the things I need!"

She turned on her heel and stormed through the door, leaving Maeve feeling as if she'd been chewed up and spat out.

"God!" Maura said finally. "I see what you mean, Maeve – she was never that bad before. How do you put up with it?"

"You mean I have a choice?" Maeve said, attempting a smile. "I don't know what to do with her, short of locking her in the basement for a week! And I'd much rather see her go to France, at least that way –"

"The basement!" Maura said. "Maeve, that's it! How did we forget about the basement?"

"Maura, I wasn't serious. We can't lock her –"

Maura laughed. "No, that's not what I mean, bad and all as she is! You need money, right? So why don't you rent out the basement? You finished off all the work on it, didn't you, before Larry left?"

"Don't remind me," Maeve said. She didn't need anything to remind her of Larry's great scheme of turning the vast basement of the house into an office for himself – to do what, God alone knew. He had never used it and all Maeve knew was that she was still paying through the nose for it.

"So how come you never thought of renting it out?" Maura asked. "There are three or four rooms, aren't there?"

"Four, but it wouldn't be suitable for anything – there's no bathroom, only a toilet, and there's no proper kitchen. It would take a lot of work to make an apartment out of it."

"But it would make a great crèche!" Maura said. "Why didn't I think of it before? There's a separate entrance, and isn't there a patio door out to the side garden?"

"Yes, but – a *crèche*? I wouldn't know the first thing about –"

"Maeve, listen a minute! Mary Doyle up the road from me is looking for new premises for her crèche. Her lease is up after Christmas. And you have four rooms just sitting there! All you'd need to do is clean it up a bit and maybe put on some fresh paint, if she's interested. There could be good money in it."

"I'm not sure, Maura. There could be all kinds of complications."

"Promise you'll think about it, anyway. And if she doesn't want it, someone else will. The location's great, and don't they say that's everything?"

"I'll think about it."

She walked out to the hallway with Maura and was closing the door when she heard the crash from the living-room. She dashed in to find Orla on her knees trying to pick up shattered fragments from all over the floor near the fireplace.

"I didn't mean it. It was an accident. Honestly, I didn't mean it!" She turned a look of pure anguish on Maeve, but it was lost as Maeve's eyes darted to the mantelpiece, then back to the scattered pieces on the floor. The St Nicholas statuette. Her grandmother's heirloom.

She held out her hands, not trusting herself to speak, as her daughter, still tearfully protesting that it was an accident, passed the smashed remains of the statuette carefully to her.

No hope for it, Maeve thought numbly as she stood looking down at the fragments cradled in her hands, oblivious to Orla's tearful apologies.

No hope for it at all, like so much else in her life.

Chapter Twenty-two

The December air was sharp on her face as she came out of the Métro station near Rue Montmartre. It was a bit of a distance from her new apartment, involving a change from one Métro line to the other, but it was well worth it. Chartiers was one of Olivia's favourite places for lunch.

And today she had a particular reason for coming.

Today she was having lunch with Suzanne and Finn.

Briefly she wondered what he was like. From half-remembered, not-really-listened-to-in-the-first-place office gossip she knew that he was an architect, a few years older than Suzanne and apparently besotted with her. Which was more than she was with him. Olivia recalled Suzanne coming in, on more than one occasion, with tearful looks, telling anyone willing to listen that it was "over for good this time – definitely".

Hmm, Olivia thought as she passed the chestnut-seller – taking a deep breath of the rich aroma wafting from his stand – and turned left into the little laneway leading to Chartiers. Some things it didn't do to be too definite about.

She went through the revolving door and into the bright, noisy, crowded interior of the restaurant. She had told them to look out for her along the right-hand side of the room, somewhere towards the back wall. That was where she usually sat, facing out into the room if possible so she could watch the other diners.

It was something she never used to do, but she was fascinated by Chartiers, by the people who frequented it, by the very *Frenchness* of it, so that she found it hard to resist the odd discreet look around from time to time.

She glanced towards her favourite table, hoping it might be free, but it was already taken. She was a few minutes early but she scanned the room anyway while she waited for a table, in case Suzanne and Finn had managed to get there before her. There was no sign –

"Madame Olivia, bonjour!"

She turned as the waiter greeted her. *"Bonjour, François!"*

"Vous êtes seule, madame?"

No, she explained, she wasn't alone today. There were two friends joining her.

"Ah," he said, his face lighting up. *"Madame Ellie?"*

It still amazed her the effect Ellie had on people who, like François, barely knew her. She watched his flicker of disappointment as she told him that it wasn't Ellie today, it was some friends from Ireland, on their way back home from a long holiday abroad.

He nodded, glancing round for a table just as the people at the corner table by the back wall – her favourite – stood up.

He signalled her to wait a moment while he rushed to claim the table for her, then gestured for her to sit down as he began clearing it.

Suzanne and Finn arrived just as he was replacing the paper sheet that covered the table top. Olivia saw them standing near the entrance and waved.

Suzanne glanced in her direction, looked away, turned back again in a classic double-take.

Of course, Olivia thought, amused. She was expecting to see me, but not – me. She arranged to have lunch with Olive of the grey hair, grey clothes, grey life. Whereas *Olivia* –

She smiled and stood up as Suzanne led the way towards the table.

"Olive?" It was half-question, half-exclamation.

Olivia laughed. "Yes and no. It's Olivia now." She turned to smile at Finn. "I've heard about you," she said as they sat down across from her.

He was exactly the type of man she would have chosen for Suzanne. Tall, very attractive, with reddish-brown hair and a look of the outdoors about him.

"I suppose it would be indelicate to ask what you heard," he said, smiling.

Charming, too. She wondered for a second why he and Suzanne had broken up so often.

"Don't ask unless you *really* want to know!' she

teased, while Suzanne stared open-mouthed at this new Olive-Olivia.

"Paris suits you," she said finally, by way of a question.

Olivia laughed. "Now who's being delicate! I've changed, haven't I?"

"I nearly didn't recognise you. Your hair, your clothes – you're like a different person!"

"And that's exactly what I am, a different person," Olivia confirmed. She caught sight of herself in one of the big mirrors that covered the wall of the restaurant. The ash-blonde hair that she still wasn't quite used to, the rich crimson dress that Olive would never have chosen – yes, she was different. The wonder was that Suzanne had managed to recognise her at all.

"But these are only the trappings," she continued as François came towards them with the menu. "The real changes are on the inside, where it counts."

"Olive – Olivia – I'm dying to ask –" Suzanne began, then hesitated, trying to gauge Olivia's possible reaction.

"Food first, then you can ask what you like," Olivia said. "Eating is a serious business in this country."

"I've noticed," Suzanne said as she chose quickly, her head close to Finn's as she got him to translate the menu for her. She settled on chicken, as Olivia did, while Finn opted for steak.

"I'll never eat chicken again after Thailand," he said. "They really know how to cook it there!"

"You're saying the French don't?" Olivia asked, amused.

"I wouldn't dare!" Finn responded. "But they *do* know how to cook steak. Though Suzanne won't touch it here, will you?" he asked, smiling at her.

"Not a chance!" Suzanne replied. "I like my meat to look dead!"

François returned and Finn gave their order in confident French. Suzanne watched as the waiter scribbled it on a corner of the paper tablecloth.

She caught Olivia's eye and smiled.

"How did you find this place?" she asked. "I love it!"

"A friend of mine – Ellie. She brought me here a couple of weeks ago. It's a favourite place of hers for lunch. And of mine, now."

"I can see why. It's amazing!"

It was. The high, high ceilings with their suspended fans, the brass and mahogany coat racks dividing the big room down along the length of the crowded tables, the huge mirrors creating the illusion of space and intimacy all at once in the soft light of the ornate globe light-fittings. And everywhere the chatter of people and clatter of cutlery.

It was a bit like Bewley's, Suzanne thought, and yet it was so much what she expected a French restaurant would be, with its rushing, formidable waiters in black trousers, long white aprons and black bow ties, terrifying in a way as they hurried between the tables, scribbling down the orders on the paper tablecloths, standing impatiently while diners dithered over the menu.

And yet – and this was what amazed Suzanne most –

Olivia seemed completely at home here, chatting easily and fluently – and in French! – to the waiter with the black moustache who bowed, and shrugged, and smiled and called her "Madame Olivia."

"He seems to know you well," Suzanne said as François hurried away with their order.

"He knows me as a friend of Ellie's," Olivia said. "And Ellie seems to know everyone!"

"Is she the reason you came to Paris?" Suzanne asked. "That's what I was dying to know. You amazed us all by leaving the way you did!"

Olivia laughed. "I astonished myself, because I certainly hadn't planned it! And I didn't know a soul here. I met Ellie only four or five weeks ago." That still surprised her, how much Ellie had become a part of her life in such a short space of time.

"And you've become friends?"

Olivia caught the tone in Suzanne's voice. "I know," she said. "That's even more amazing, isn't it, that Olive who hadn't a word to say for herself actually has friends here!"

"I didn't mean –"

"Of course you did!" Olivia said, laughing. "But I know you didn't mean it unkindly."

François arrived with their meals and any potential for embarrassment passed.

"Now," Olivia said as they began eating, "tell me all about Thailand. Or would you rather tell me first why you rang?"

Suzanne paused in the act of spearing an asparagus tip.

"I'm not sure," she said after a moment, looking candidly at Olivia. "I suppose I thought it would be nice to see you again since I was passing through Paris. It was a bit difficult getting hold of your address – Maeve rang your brother and he wasn't sure at first about giving it."

"He rang me to check and I told him it was fine. I must admit, I was intrigued."

"Why intrigued?"

Olivia smiled. "Suzanne, you must realise we were never more than colleagues when we worked together."

Suzanne glanced at Finn for support.

"Maybe I shouldn't have contacted you –"

Olivia reached out to touch Suzanne's hand. "On the contrary, I'm delighted that you did. I was simply surprised, that's all. I wasn't even sure what we would find to talk about! But I always liked you, Suzanne," she added quickly as she saw Suzanne's expression, "and I was pleased when Raymond rang to say you wanted to get in touch."

"Good," Suzanne said, relieved. "I just wanted to see how you were, really, since we were passing through. I wouldn't like to think –" she broke off abruptly, concentrating on her food.

"Yes?" Olivia prompted softly after a few moments.

"Well, you know," Suzanne said, looking directly at her again, "if you were lonely or anything, finding it hard to settle in –" She paused, gave a big smile. "But I obviously got it very wrong! Maeve said you'd changed but she didn't say how much!"

"She has no idea how much! And, far from getting it wrong, you got it very right, Suzanne. It's very good of you to take the time and trouble to contact a woman you knew to be rigid, and stand-offish, and never more than civil to you."

Finn began choking on a mouthful of beef and Suzanne started thumping his back while Olivia passed him some water and François came running to help.

"Went down the wrong way," Finn gasped when he finally managed to get his breath.

"By which I take it that I was repeating Suzanne's very words, or something close?" Olivia said with a smile and a raised eyebrow.

Finn turned to Suzanne and back to Olivia.

"Close," he admitted, laughing.

"So you were expecting some desiccated old woman with not a pleasant word to say for herself."

"Not exactly," Suzanne said, "because Maeve had told us you'd changed."

"But you would have come anyway."

"We would have come anyway."

Olivia said nothing for a long moment. "You have no idea how much that means to me, Suzanne. And Finn," she said, turning to include him.

"It really wasn't a big deal," Suzanne said. "We were just going to meet you for an hour or so, in case you were missing people from home. If it was obvious you didn't really want to see us, we were going to make our excuses and leave."

"And now?" Olivia asked, amused.

Suzanne and Finn looked at each other and laughed.

"We'll have to make our excuses and leave anyway," Finn said ruefully. "You'd want to see the list of things Suzanne intends to do here in two days – we only have an hour or so for lunch. But I'm sorry, I really am, that it's not longer. I'll never believe a word she says about anyone again!"

"It was all true," Suzanne said.

"It clearly wasn't," Finn countered.

"Indeed it was," Olivia said. "Believe me, Finn, I'm a very different person from the woman who worked with Suzanne less than three months ago."

"You said it! But Olivia, what happened? I mean, you're *totally* different! The money has completely changed you."

Olivia made a quick decision. "It wasn't the money, Suzanne. Well, I suppose the money was the catalyst, and it gave me the freedom to do what I needed to, but it went far deeper than that."

Very briefly she outlined what had happened with her mother, her sense of being used and not allowed to be herself for most of her life, her collusion in that until she finally realised what her mother was doing to her.

"So that was it, really. I had to face up to the fact that she didn't love me and that I'd never meet her standards as the perfect daughter, because she didn't

233

want me to. She preferred being able to criticise and complain and bully me – so no matter what I did, I was never going to please her. When I finally realised that, I had no choice but to break free and try to find a life that suited me."

"And you don't regret it?"

"No, not at all. I should have done it years ago, but I couldn't leave her on her own."

They said nothing, waiting.

"I know," she continued after a moment or two. "I *did* leave her. But only when I could provide for her financially – and when I saw what she had done to me. I wasted most of my life; I couldn't let her ruin the rest of it."

"You could have stayed in Dublin," Suzanne said.

"Perhaps. But I wanted to come here."

"Will you go back?" Suzanne asked.

Olivia looked alarmed. "Go back? Why on earth would I go back?"

"I mean, for Christmas," Suzanne said quickly. "You know, just for a few days, to see your family and friends –"

"I hadn't really thought about it," Olivia said quietly. "Would you believe, I don't have a single friend in Dublin? Not one, after spending my whole life there. Whereas here – it's a different world completely, because of Ellie."

"Will you spend Christmas with her?" Finn asked.

"No, she'll be back in Montreal, visiting her own family. She has two grown-up sons there. So I probably will go back to Dublin for a few days. Because that's what people do, isn't it? Spend Christmas with their families?"

For the first time since meeting this new Olive Suzanne felt sorry for her. Imagine looking so sad at the thought of going home to your family. Suzanne couldn't wait to see hers.

"You'd need to book a flight straight away if you decide to go," she said. "It's two weeks exactly to Christmas Day, it'll be impossible to get anything if you leave it much longer."

Olivia nodded but Suzanne wasn't sure if she had taken that in.

"I suppose we should skip dessert?" Suzanne asked, looking at Finn. "There's not really time –"

"Oh, no," Olivia said. "Look what I've done, completely taken over the conversation when I wanted to hear all about Thailand, and what you've been up to, and whether you have any news of the others –"

"At least let me finish my steak," Finn said, laughing. "I don't think we have to rush off this very minute, Suzy. We can always come back after Christmas if we don't manage to empty the shops this time!"

"Now, there's a *great* idea," Suzanne said as Olivia signalled François to bring some coffee and they settled back to talk about the amazing experience of visiting Thailand.

Olivia began to relax over the next hour or so – only then realising how tense she had been while talking about her mother – as they conjured up images of gold temples and countless statues of the Buddha, and saffron-robed monks everywhere, and the most incredible markets in the streets, on the canals . . .

"You should see it, Olivia, really! The weather's amazing, sunshine at this time of year, imagine! And there's loads to do. We travelled up north and met masses of people. We went rafting with some guys from Wexford and rode through the jungle on an elephant. A bit scary, but brilliant fun! Can you imagine trying that?"

Olivia laughed. "I'm doing all sorts of things I never imagined, Suzanne, and I hope to do many more. But I can promise you riding an elephant isn't one of them!"

Finn grinned wickedly at her. "Never say never, Olivia!" He glanced at his watch. "Look, we'd better go, but if we *do* make it back in January –"

"Promise you'll contact me."

"For definite," Suzanne said, standing up. She hesitated for just the briefest moment, then bent to kiss Olivia's cheek. She was rewarded by a warm smile as Olivia took her hand.

"It was wonderful of you to ring me. Have a lovely Christmas."

"We will. I hope you do, too."

Finn reached across to take her hand, then they were gone in a flurry of goodbyes, leaving some money with François on their way out.

Olivia sat watching as they left, envying them a little. They were so at ease together, seemed so right for each other. She wondered what that must be like, to have someone special to be with, to travel with . . .

The one and only time she had had the opportunity, Bridget Grace had put a stop to it immediately.

Regrets? That was the biggest regret of all, Olivia thought, that she had let Bridget come between her and Richard. A long time ago now, thirty years almost, but the bitterness was still there –

"Olivia? May I join you?" The warm voice speaking in softly-accented English broke into her thoughts, so that for a moment she didn't react, and he hesitated. "Or would you perhaps prefer to be alone?"

Alone? Why on earth would she want to be alone, when she had thought of little else but him for the last two weeks?

Heart pounding, she looked up into the intense blue gaze of Thierry de Rochemont.

Chapter Twenty-three

Three days before Christmas, and Maeve was tearing her hair out. Fergus had decided what he really, really, *really* wanted from Santa, as distinct from what he had really, *really* wanted just two weeks ago when the final Santa letter was sent.

She had tried telling him that, Christmas post being what it was, Santa probably wouldn't get the letter on time and he should settle for what he was going to get – which would, of course, be wonderful – and try his luck next year. She had Senan upstairs working on him this very minute, while she gave the kitchen a quick tidy before Colette came, but she had no idea how successful he might be.

Christmas. Peace and goodwill. She hoped, not for the first time, that Larry would get that particular message over the next few days.

She wondered where he would spend Christmas

this year. His sister's again, probably. The woman had the patience of Job but not a bit of cop-on. She was quite likely to send Larry out with £100 to buy the Christmas dinner and whatever else he could think of, and be surprised when he came back empty-handed. You'd think she'd have learned her lesson the time he stole the best of her jewellery and tried to make it look like a burglary.

And she hadn't even pressed charges. She couldn't, she said, not against her "baby brother". And so that particular episode was glossed over, like all the others, and Larry wasn't one step nearer taking responsibility and doing something about what his sister persisted in calling "his little habit".

She's welcome to him, Maeve thought. I've enough on my plate as it is.

Orla had arrived home from France in a huge sulk earlier on, hardly looking at Maeve or the boys when they picked her up from the airport and sitting silently in the car all the way home.

And Fidelma, one of the lodgers, had just announced that she was moving to her boyfriend's flat at the beginning of January so she'd be staying in the house over Christmas to get her money's worth instead of going home as planned. Oh, and Maeve wouldn't mind if the boyfriend stayed too, would she, because they wanted to be together, especially as his cousin and a couple of friends would be around for a few days – in fact, they might stay over as well if Maeve had any spare sleeping bags.

The word "no" didn't seem to be one Fidelma

understood. And Maeve didn't want to seem too harsh about it, so she tried to get the message across gently at first. But when "It really wouldn't be a good idea" and "The room isn't big enough for two" and "I'd really prefer not to have strangers in the house" didn't seem to be getting through and Fidelma was still standing there with a blank look and her mouth hanging open, Maeve finally had to resort to a bald "no".

And then all hell broke loose as Fidelma started telling Maeve loudly, and in no uncertain terms, what she thought of her and her "kip of a room", and the commotion brought Orla down and she dived in to take Maeve's part and put Fidelma back in her box.

Well, at least *that's* something! Maeve thought as Fidelma went storming up the stairs muttering to herself, and Orla, with barely a glance at Maeve, went off to the television room.

I'll sort it out later, Maeve told herself. Young Fidelma is leaving all right, sooner than she thinks.

She checked the oven and took a bottle of wine from the rack. Colette would be here in a few minutes, and dinner was almost ready.

They had started the tradition a few years back, as a cheaper alternative to going out for a meal in the run-up to Christmas. And it had always worked out well, taking it in turns to cook and host the meal, making sure as far as they could that the kids were fed and settled beforehand so they could relax and enjoy themselves.

It had always worked well, that is, until tonight.

Maeve was half-dreading it, with emotions running so high all over the place, and the problem of the Christmas present.

That was another part of the tradition. They always got each other little gifts, nothing over £5 or so, and wrapped them beautifully, and handed them over with great ceremony and had a lot of fun trying to guess by the size and shape and feel of them what the packages might contain.

But this year – what could you buy with £5 for your friend the millionaire? That had been Maeve's dilemma as she trawled the shops looking for ideas.

She had finally found what might be the perfect present in an old bookshop, where she'd picked up a postcard as well for good measure – a reproduction of a card from the 30's showing a thin, elegant woman in a cloche and a daring, backless dress, a silver cigarette-holder in her right hand, leaning nonchalantly against a red sports car with the Eiffel Tower in the background.

Now all she had to hope was that Colette stuck to their agreement and kept within the £5 budget. Maeve would be mortified if she had done anything else.

The doorbell rang and Orla went to answer it. Season of miracles for sure, Maeve thought, listening to the voices in the hall as she lifted the roasting-dish from the oven and placed it on the granite worktop. Even if Orla was only enquiring after Ciara, at least it was *something*. Normally she didn't have two words to say to Colette or anyone else.

"Nice timing!" Maeve said as Colette came through the kitchen door. They hugged briefly and Maeve caught a hint of something subtle, flowery, expensive.

"Just look at you," she said, holding Colette at arm's length, suddenly aware that her own scent was compounded of cooking smells and the whiff of washing-up liquid still clinging to her hands. "Don't you look *gorgeous*!"

She did. Her hair was cut in a sleek new style, and her make-up looked professionally done. And the dress –

"It's fabulous," Maeve said, reaching tentatively to touch it. "For God's sake, mind you don't spill anything on it," she laughed, indicating a chair to Colette. "I'll be afraid to put anything near you!"

"Go on," Colette laughed as she sat down. "It wasn't that dear, anyway. I found it in that posh place in Clontarf that's closing down."

"That place we were always afraid to go into?"

"That's the one! I got courage once I had the hair done. They were a bit sniffy when I told them what size I wanted, but I didn't give a damn. I'd love to swan back in there once I lose a bit of weight, but they'll be closed. Good enough for them!"

"You don't need to lose much, do you?" Maeve asked, bringing plates of smoked salmon and brown bread to the table.

"Plenty!" Colette said. "But I'll forget about it for tonight. Time enough for dieting after Christmas, when I go to that health farm with Eileen."

"You're definitely going?"

"Booked and all. I can tuck into this with a clear conscience!"

They laughed and chatted as they ate the salmon and then Maeve brought the wine and main course to the table. The kids were mercifully occupied watching television – Senan having calmed Fergus down a bit – and Fidelma hadn't reappeared, so Colette and Maeve were able to enjoy the luxury of talking undisturbed.

"What about the other resolutions?" Maeve asked. "How are they coming along?"

Though they hadn't seen each other in about three weeks they had talked regularly on the phone and Maeve was up to date with Colette's plans.

Colette quickly filled her in.

New car, driving lessons, new image – so far so good. And the health farm was booked. Once she'd been there she'd have the courage to join the nearest snazzy health club and keep up the good work.

"So that just leaves Paris, sorting out money, and assertiveness classes," she said, looking pleased. "And I feel I'm making some kind of progress. Martin still won't sit down and work things out, but I've started going through the information I got from the lottery people, and, you know, it's not too hard to understand. So I've transferred most of the money into an old account with about £20 in it that I had in my own name. Martin doesn't even know I've done it, and when I tell him he'll *have* to sit down and talk. I'll break it to him after Christmas."

"Isn't that a bit sneaky?" Maeve asked. "I mean, I think you're dead right, but he'll hit the roof, won't he?"

"Let him! Maeve, I've been asking him for three months to look at what we're spending, but I might as well be talking to the wall. Every time I suggest it he looks hurt and says that surely I don't begrudge his family a few bob. Few bob, my eye! There's nearly half a million gone already."

"You're joking!" Maeve said.

"I'm serious. It wasn't all his doing – I paid off the mortgage, and sent cheques to my sisters and brother, and set up an account for my father's bills because he'd only worry if I gave him a lump sum. That took care of a lot of it, but the rest is flowing out in dribs and drabs, and that's what worries me. Now he's talking about giving up work as well, and I don't think that's on the cards, not at the rate he's spending. I had to do something."

"He still won't like it," Maeve said.

"Tough. He should have listened to me."

Maeve laughed. "Wow! I thought you hadn't done the assertiveness course yet?"

"Maybe I won't need to," Colette said. "God knows, I'm getting enough practice with Declan and Ciara – I could probably *give* classes at this stage!"

"Still putting pressure on you about the money?"

"Still trying to. Declan wants to join a rock band now. I ask you! He hasn't a note in his head, but he wants £1,000 for an electric guitar."

"So you're not thinking of getting him one for Christmas?"

"No, I am not," Colette said firmly, taking a sip of wine. "It was logos on tee-shirts last week, God knows what it'll be next week! He can forget it – unless Martin is stupid enough to give in."

"And what does Ciara want?" Maeve asked with some trepidation. Whatever Ciara wanted, Orla was bound to want two seconds later.

"How much time have you got?" Colette laughed. "But what she wants and what she'll get are two different things. That's where I'm *really* putting my foot down. Martin's giving her far too much as it is. I caught her last night with a fifty-pound note. Pocket money, she said!"

Alarm bells rang for Maeve. "That's a dangerous amount for a fourteen-year-old to have."

"Don't I know? Bad enough spending it on clothes and make-up, but she's just at the age when she might want to start drinking, or worse."

"Does he give her that kind of money often?"

"He says he doesn't, but I'm not convinced. And it worries me that they're getting the habit of money. You know, the feeling that there's plenty more where that came from."

"Once you tighten the belt after Christmas they'll get the message."

"They'd better. They seem to think the money's there for the taking. I've missed twenty- and fifty-pound notes from my purse a few times now."

"And what did they say?" Maeve asked.

"Denied it point-blank, the two of them, and were furious at me for asking."

"And are you sure it was them? It wouldn't have been Martin – or Peter?"

"Martin always tells me if he goes to my purse. And Peter wouldn't dream of it. I'd have no worries at all if the others were like him."

Maeve decided to say what was on her mind. "I'm glad you're putting the brakes on Ciara. To be honest, I was afraid herself and Orla would get themselves into trouble if they had too much money. That's one thing you have to say for Ciara, she's generous."

"I know. And she has other good points. They all have. It's just a question of digging very deep sometimes!"

Maeve laughed. "Okay, enough talk about kids. Time for dessert!"

She stood up, moved the plates from the table and opened the fridge to take out the cheesecake. As she put the coffee on to percolate she saw Colette reach for her bag – dessert was their traditional time to exchange gifts – and take out a very slim package wrapped in gold foil, with a little gold and silver bow in one corner.

An envelope. It wasn't large enough to be anything else. And top of the list of things Maeve had hoped it definitely wouldn't be was an envelope.

There were very few ground rules about the presents: nothing over £5, no potpourri because they both hated the stuff, and no gift vouchers. They both agreed that it was a cop-out to buy a £5 gift voucher, that the real challenge was to find something the other would really like, within the budget. And, this year, Maeve was very sure that a gift voucher – or, worse, a cheque – would be way beyond their agreed limit.

She really didn't want it, and hated being put in the position of having to refuse it.

She brought the cheesecake to the table, took her own present from the top of the dresser, placed it in front of Colette and went back to get the coffee.

When she sat down again they looked at each other, Colette said "go on" and they each picked up their packages, turning them round and round trying to guess what was in them. With sinking heart Maeve decided that it was definitely an envelope. It couldn't be anything else.

"A note promising a lift in your new car when mine conks out?" she joked half-heartedly.

"Close, but not close enough," Colette said. "Something to do with travel all right. And this is a book. Has to be!"

"Got it in one," Maeve said as she opened the envelope, holding her breath, and Colette began unwrapping the book.

Colette looked intrigued when she saw the title. *The Kitten Who Could*. A children's book, old but in good condition. She began skimming through the beautifully-illustrated tale of a kitten who crept around timidly, trodden on and tormented by all and sundry with not a squeak out of her, until the day she finally turned around and faced them and opened her mouth and roared like a lion – and was never tormented again.

"Watch this space," Colette said, laughing. "*And* this one," she added, fingering the postcard and looking from it to Maeve.

"It's the one thing you haven't done anything about yet," Maeve said. "I thought it might encourage you."

"Open your present," Colette said. Maeve caught the twinkle in her eye.

"Colette –" she began.

"Go on. Open it!"

Maeve fumbled at the wrapping, dreading the moment of actually opening it.

An envelope. And inside, some kind of voucher. Not a gift voucher, some kind of sales receipt or something. Her eyes darted to the bottom line and relief flooded through her. £5. Whatever it was, it was for exactly £5. But what was it?

Quickly she glanced down through it, tried to make sense of disjointed words and numbers. Finally realised what it was: a return ticket to Paris, for £5.

A joke.

Smiling to hide her disappointment – why waste money on a joke? – she asked brightly if Colette would like some coffee.

"But what do you think?" Colette asked, looking puzzled. "I mean, I don't want to back you into a corner, but I did only spend £5 on it, you'll have to pay the fees and taxes yourself but they'll only be about £12 or so, that's not too bad, is it? And the hotel wouldn't cost much, I've checked, and I thought, if your sister could mind the kids – Maeve, will you at least think about it?"

"Colette, what are you talking about?"

"Paris. In April, just before my 38th birthday. You know I really want to go, and I want you to come with me. You said you'd love to, remember? Well, here's your chance. I got two return tickets for £5 each, so that's all I'll lose if you won't come. But I'm hoping you will."

"But it's a joke! You can't get tickets to Paris for £5!"

"You can on special offer. It's no joke, Maeve – don't ask me how they do it, but it's for real."

Maeve looked more closely at the voucher this time.

"A week in Paris, in April? For £5?"

Colette nodded.

"In a real aeroplane, with a pilot who knows how to fly?"

Colette nodded again. "It's real, all right. Therese told me about their special offers – she's done it loads of times! Mind you, they usually cost a bit more than that, but it's a special promotion or something."

"I'm not sure I can afford the hotel and spending money," Maeve said slowly.

Colette said nothing.

"But maybe I can work something out. An evening job or something, for a few weeks. Maura would mind the kids . . ."

Colette still said nothing. She was holding her breath.

"April in Paris, Colette. Think of it!" Maeve said.

Colette smiled. "I *am* thinking of it. What's more, I'm going, Maeve. And I hope you'll come with me – but one way or another I'm going to Paris in April."

Chapter Twenty-four

Had it always been like this? Olivia wondered. Had Paris always been full of lovers, in the cafés, on every street corner, engrossed in each other and as careless of passers-by as she had been of them? Everywhere she looked . . .

Even in the Métro as she made her way to the Place du Tertre she saw them. That young couple opposite, for example, looking as if they had just left the bed, or should still be there – she with long blonde hair, a leather jacket and one slim, blue-jeaned leg thrown casually, possessively over his – in the Métro! – and he, long dark hair flowing across his face as he bent to kiss her fingers, one by one, oblivious to everyone but her.

And over there an older couple, elegantly dressed, leaning against each other and whispering as the train swayed in the tunnel.

A week ago Olivia wouldn't even have seen them. Now she could see nothing else – because now she was on her way to meet Thierry.

It had been three days since she saw him last. Three very long days, where everything else in her life was suspended and she counted the minutes.

"A quiet lunch," he had suggested that day in Chartiers. "Somewhere a little less public than this."

And Olivia had known what that meant.

Because even though he had come alone to Ellie's soirée and to the Opéra, Thierry de Rochemont was married. No-one had said so but she was certain of it.

Because why would a man like Thierry de Rochemont be alone?

He could, of course, be separated, or divorced. But something told her that wasn't the case. The suggestion of "somewhere less public", perhaps.

She had wished that Ellie wasn't in Montreal visiting her sons. She had even wondered if she could find an excuse to ring and then ask, very casually, "Oh, by the way –"

But of course she couldn't do it, any more than she could ring that pleasant woman she had met at the Opéra, who seemed to know him very well. And she couldn't ask Thierry. Because, she finally admitted to herself, she didn't want to know.

And there was no need to know. She would meet him for lunch, and that was all. One lunch, which she wouldn't spoil with complications such as enquiring into his marital status, and then she would put Thierry de Rochemont firmly out of her mind and move on.

Unless it turned out that he really *wasn't* married –

Lost in thought, she missed her stop and had to get out at Barbes-Rochechouart, pushing her way through the crowded pavements outside the low-budget shops before she could turn right and begin walking up the hill towards Sacré-Coeur.

When she reached the narrow street at the foot of the Sacré-Coeur steps she changed direction automatically, heading towards the *funiculaire*, the cable-car that would take her to within a few steps of the cathedral. She joined the little queue but as her turn came to get onto the car she suddenly changed her mind and, with a smile and a *"Pardon"*, she made her way back over to the steps and began the long climb. There was plenty of time, and she needed a few minutes more to prepare herself for meeting Thierry.

She wasn't sure what to expect; she only knew she had to see him again. She had never before felt this excitement about any man.

She walked up the final few steps – scarcely out of breath, which pleased her because there were close to a hundred of them – and went around to the left of the church and into the cobbled streets of Montmartre.

She loved it here. It had been one of the first places she visited in Paris, drawn to the colour and clamour of it, intrigued by the artists who sat day after day in front of their easels, their work ranged around them, hoping to sell to the droves of tourists who filled the little square. Everywhere she looked there were paintings. Copies, mostly, as far as she could make out, but some of them were quite wonderful.

She stopped for a moment to watch the artist in the corner, a woman who reminded her of Ellie. She was finishing a portrait with deft strokes, glancing occasionally at her subject – a heavyset man in his sixties whose eyes were almost hidden by folds of flesh – as she concentrated on her task. She had, Olivia noticed, managed to improve subtly on nature. The portrait captured the proud tilt of the jaw, the slight impatience in his bearing, while taking several years off his age. The artist was certain of at least one satisfied customer.

She caught Olivia's eye and smiled, raising an eyebrow in silent invitation.

Olivia returned the smile and shook her head slightly. She turned away, glancing at her watch as she left the square and made her way towards *L'Aventure*. Well named, she thought as she entered the little restaurant half-hidden behind a souvenir shop. One way or another this was an adventure for her, a journey into unknown territory.

She was ten minutes early, but Thierry was already there, sitting at a table near the back. He stood up as she entered and she made her way towards him, her heart thumping.

This is ridiculous, she told herself. I'm a grown

woman, for heaven's sake. She took a deep breath, hoping her anxiety wasn't obvious.

If it was, he showed no sign, looking at her with intense blue eyes as he took her hand in both of his.

"I am happy that you have come, Olivia."

She nodded, suddenly feeling warm and relaxed.

"I'm happy to be here. I haven't been in this restaurant before."

"One of my favourites," he said as a waiter came to take her coat and they both sat down.

They studied the menus, ordered and made small talk as the waiter poured some wine.

Thierry touched his glass against hers in a silent toast and took a sip. "I was not sure that you would be free to come," he said. "But I wanted very much to see you again. I have thought of you every day since the night at the Opéra."

It was a line, and for all her lack of experience Olivia recognised it for that. But what if she was wrong?

She took a chance. "I was hoping we'd meet again, even before that night. I saw you at Ellie's soirée."

She saw from his face that he hadn't seen her there. He smiled, shrugged, a self-deprecating gesture. "Incredible that I did not see you. But I was in a hurry that night, as I was the night at the Opéra. That is why I had to leave early."

"And are you in a hurry now?" she asked, hardly able to believe that she had said that.

His deep-set blue eyes held hers for a long moment.

"No," he said finally. "I am in no hurry at all. Today I have all the time in the world."

He continued to hold her gaze as the waiter brought the food. She began eating, hardly tasting it. She wasn't hungry. All she wanted was to sit and look at him and have him smile at her as he was smiling now.

"I must confess to you that I know little about you, Olivia. I have not seen Ellie alone to ask her, and in any case . . ."

"Yes?" Olivia prompted.

He shrugged again. "Sometimes it is better to – how should I put it? – be private about certain matters. Do you also feel like this?"

Olivia hesitated, then nodded. "I'm usually a very private person."

"That was my impression." He looked at his plate, eased a piece of beef onto his fork.

She watched his hands, the long fingers curving round the fork as he moved it towards his mouth. A beautiful, wide mouth that turned up slightly at the corners. She wondered what it would be like to kiss that mouth, flushed slightly at the thought and hoped he didn't notice.

"And would you like to know what is the rest of my impression of you?" he asked after a few moments.

Olivia felt her heart racing. Slowly, she told herself. Take it slowly. But who could resist a question like that?

"As long as it's good."

He laughed – a rich, mellow sound – throwing back his head.

"If it were bad, do you think I would wish to be sitting here, having lunch with you? No, it is good – of course, it is all good, my impression of you. That is why I have asked you to come today, because I feel that you are somebody I would want to know better. And I know it might not be easy. Because you are – how do you say? – reserved. A woman who is a little bit – mysterious!"

Olivia smiled, uncertain what to say. She could hardly tell him that she wasn't in the least mysterious, that she was really very ordinary if he knew her.

"You see?" he continued. "That is what I mean! Another woman would have said 'oh, yes, or oh, no, or oh – something'. But you, you retain your air of mystery. I know nothing about you, except that you are a reserved, attractive woman."

Attractive? She had never in her life been called attractive.

"And I know nothing at all about you," she said.

They were concentrating on each other now, all thoughts of food forgotten.

"And what would you like to know?" Thierry asked, as the waiter came to remove their half-empty plates.

If you are married, she thought.

"As much as you want to tell me," she said. It was true. She wanted to know everything about him. Including whether or not he was married.

"I can tell you very quickly," he said. "I am fifty-eight years old, born in Paris. I have lived here all my life. I work in the family business – it was my

259

grandfather's, then my father's – but I would much prefer to have been a musician. I play the violin a little. And I paint, a little, but not very well. That is why I have a small apartment here in Montmartre, so I can live my foolish dream and tell myself, from time to time, that I could have been a truly great painter." He laughed. "That is what I do, when I can find the time, when I can make my escape from the business. It does not need me so much now."

"What kind of business is it?" Olivia asked.

"Boring. Very boring. So we will not talk of it. I would much prefer to talk of you."

The waiter came, offering menus again, and they waved them away, ordering coffee.

"Olivia?" he prompted gently.

"I've had a very boring life," she said with a small laugh.

"Oh, I doubt that!"

"No, it's true! I wish I could tell you something interesting, but –"

"Then tell me something interesting! I am interested to hear who you are – but if you do not want to tell me who you are, then tell me perhaps who you would like to be!"

She laughed again. "If only it were that simple!"

"Oh, but it is, Olivia. We are all of us many people. We change a little in every situation. I am a painter sometimes, or a musician, and sometimes a businessman. As the Olivia I see is not exactly the same Olivia that

Ellie sees, or your friends in – where in Ireland do you come from?"

"Dublin," Olivia said. "It seems very far away now. And you're right. My friends there – they were colleagues and neighbours really – would hardly know me. They never did," she added, almost to herself.

"Tell me why," he said softly, as the waiter came with the coffee.

And she did. They talked for hours, until the waiter came just after four o'clock to tell them apologetically that they were closing for the afternoon.

"Would you like to see my apartment?" he asked.

"Thierry –"

"Or some other time, perhaps?" he asked, sensing her hesitation. He signalled the waiter and quickly settled the bill.

They took their coats and opened the door to the chill, darkening December afternoon.

"I will remember this afternoon, Olivia." They stood facing each other in the cobbled street and she knew, somehow, that there would not be another time. It was now, or not at all.

"I'd like to come to your apartment." She said it quickly before she lost courage.

"Are you sure, Olivia?" His voice was warm, compelling, very French.

She wasn't sure. Of course she wasn't sure. She only knew that she was quite incapable of walking away from him.

Chapter Twenty-five

Colette kicked off her shoes and sank into the sofa. It was a relief to be back at home after an evening with the Comerfords.

They had all gathered in Shay's house, as they usually did on Christmas Eve.

Shay was all right. He was Martin's eldest brother and Colette had always got on well with him and his wife Phil, but for once she'd like to have given the Christmas Eve ritual a miss. She'd be seeing plenty of them over Christmas anyway, and she still had things to organise for tomorrow.

And Martin would be no help. He was a bit miffed that she had insisted on leaving early – early, at quarter past ten on Christmas Eve! He hadn't a clue. He thought it was great being surrounded by the whole lot of them, without giving a minute's thought to everything Colette had to get finished.

In a way she couldn't blame him – she had done all the organising every other year without a murmur, and he was never happier than when he was surrounded by his whole family. It just wasn't her idea of the best way to spend Christmas Eve. She'd have preferred to be at home getting sorted, or maybe going out to Mass on her own – for a bit of peace as much as anything – but she'd never have been let do that.

The only acceptable excuse for any member of the family not turning up at Shay's Christmas Eve get-together was if you happened to be away – and even then you'd be expected to come home specially for it.

Michael, Martin's nephew, had come straight to Shay's from the airport last year, and it had been the high point of Alice Comerford's Christmas. She hadn't let any of them forget it all year.

"Couldn't wait to see his granny. Imagine, and him with that big job in London – he couldn't wait to get home to see me. He told me so himself."

Of course he did, Colette had thought. What else could he do, after you backed him into a corner and went on at him for twenty solid minutes? It never occurred to you that he came back to Dublin to see his parents or friends. He was still serious about Sorcha, a girl he'd met just before going away, but of course it would never occur to Granny Comerford that *that* might be who he came home for last year.

The romance had lasted, and Sorcha had been very much in evidence tonight, sporting a discreet little ring on her left hand. Michael had been back and forth all year and they had announced tonight that they were getting married next July.

Alice, of course, had been very sniffy about it, and didn't bother keeping her opinions to herself.

"He's too young," she said, to anyone who would listen. "He's not even twenty-four yet. He's just starting out in life. He shouldn't be tied down so young."

And she had glared at the unfortunate girl who was sitting in the corner beside Martin's sister Anne, her soon-to-be mother-in-law.

"Ah, give over, Granny!" Michael had said finally, laughing. "Sure, weren't you only nineteen yourself when you got married."

"Different times. We didn't have your opportunities. My God, if we'd only had your opportunities. Let me see the ring," she said suddenly, pouncing on Sorcha. "Hmm. I'd want better glasses than these. I can't see any sign of a diamond in it at all – it must be very small."

"There isn't one," Sorcha explained. "I didn't want one because I heard some diamond mining is used to support the arms trade. I'd rather not have one at all than take the chance."

Alice Comerford looked at her as if she had just landed from another planet. For once she was speechless, and Sorcha had gone back to chatting to Anne.

At least she knows what she's letting herself in for,

Colette had thought. Not that that stopped any of us.

It had felt like a very long evening, and it wasn't over yet. Martin was out in the kitchen making her a cup of tea – must be Christmas – and Emer was still awake, high as a kite with the excitement of Santa coming. She'd been good as gold over in Shay's house, keeping them all amused with stories of how Santa worked his magic.

And the others had been on best behaviour as well.

Colette wouldn't have known Ciara and Declan. For once they weren't bickering at each other or snarling at her, and they even made the effort to talk to Martin's brother Des who thought he had "a way with kids", but whose conversation was mainly of the "so what class are you in now?" variety.

And they put up with it this evening without a word. They must be trying hard not to blot their copybooks in one last go at getting what they wanted for Christmas.

A bit late now, she thought. They'll get what they're getting and be grateful for it – or else I'll murder them, Christmas or no Christmas.

She didn't really mean it. She had gone way over budget in spite of herself – she usually did a bit, but this year was different. She had only set a budget in the first place to try and be sensible. Part of her wanted to splash out and get everything they ever wanted, make it a magical Christmas they'd always remember. She had even thought of going to Lapland, talking them all into it, Ciara, Declan, everybody – but Martin had thrown cold water on that, saying it would be freezing and anyway it wasn't worth going all that way just for a couple of days.

So she had settled for making the best Christmas she could at home and getting the kids at least *some* of things they were looking for.

Emer had been the easiest, of course. A baby doll and some clothes, and she wanted a pram as well if Santa could fit it on his sleigh. But the others! It was no surprise that this year their expectations were sky-high.

She didn't even know what a DVD player with surround-sound was, until Peter patiently explained it to her. It was the only thing he'd asked for in years, and finally she gave in, reasoning that it would be in the living-room so the whole family could use it, and that would justify the cost of it. Sort of.

So that wasn't a problem. The problem, as usual, was Ciara. She had spent the past month trying to persuade, nag and cajole Colette into believing that she couldn't live without her own computer. She certainly seemed to believe it herself. And because Colette knew that the next step would be Internet access and dodgy chat rooms she had put the foot down, hard – and then, in an attempt to make it up to her, she bought the very expensive and highly overrated music centre Ciara also wanted.

Which meant that she had to get something very expensive for Declan – and since his list of "must-haves" now included a car, a motorbike and a Gibson guitar – none of which he was getting – she had given in on the drum-kit he asked for on condition that he try to arrange some kind of lessons and set it up outside in the garage.

He had agreed reluctantly, looking amused when she said he couldn't make noise after 9 p.m.

"Sure, Ma," he'd muttered, with a look that said she was off her head.

She'd worry about that *after* tomorrow, Colette decided. For once, she wanted a day with no friction, a day when they could all be happy together. It seemed to happen less and less often these days.

She felt her eyes closing, then roused herself as Martin came in with the cup of tea. He still wasn't looking too thrilled about having to come home early. Really, he hadn't a notion of the work that went into making a Christmas.

He had laughed last night – something else that was happening less and less often – when he saw the huge amount of food she'd bought.

"Whose army is this for?" were his parting words as he left to go to the pub to meet "a few of the lads". He had come back late, a bit the worse for wear, and insisted on going up to the attic to bring down the outdoor Christmas lights he hadn't got around to putting up yet.

And that had been about the height of his contribution to Christmas so far. At least, she supposed, it had got him out of the way and given her a chance to get started on the Christmas wrapping. Still, he could have helped, since most of it was for his family anyway.

It was a tradition Colette had learned to dread years ago – the Christmas morning visit by Martin's whole family. As if Christmas Eve wasn't enough! And then Christmas night in his mother's house . . .

She had stopped asking years ago why they couldn't just exchange presents on Christmas Eve, or even Christmas morning. But no, it had to happen on Christmas night, in his mother's house. No matter where Alice Comerford went for her Christmas dinner – she took careful turns going round all of them – they all had to come to her house on Christmas night. It was tradition, she insisted. So the son or daughter who had the misfortune of having her with them for Christmas dinner – though, in fairness, they didn't see it like that – had to bring her back to her own house at five p.m. "so everyone can come home for Christmas".

Colette was sick of it. It wasn't as if they didn't see enough of each other all year. But just for tomorrow she'd put on a brave face and put up with it. They'd only be here for a short time anyway. Just as well, since Colette's own family – all eleven of them, including her five nieces and nephews – were coming for Christmas dinner. She just hoped she could ease one gang out the door before the next arrived in . . .

It would work out fine, she told herself. She was determined to let nothing spoil this Christmas. For the first time in her life she didn't have to worry about the cost of it, and she was going to enjoy every minute.

"Tired?" Martin asked as he sat down across from her, opening a can of beer.

"Exhausted," she said. "But it'll be worth it to see their faces. Wait'll you see the stuff I bought!"

He looked a bit alarmed. "Did you spend much? When I went to the bank yesterday to take out ten grand they'd only give me seven. They said that's all there was in the account. Idiots. It's a mistake, right? I mean, how much did you spend –"

"Martin, what in God's name did you want ten thousand pounds for?"

He looked a bit uncomfortable. "I only took out seven."

"Seven, then. What do you need that much for?"

"For the family," he said, as if it was obvious. "I wanted them all to have a bit extra – you know, with the cost of Christmas and everything. I meant to say it to you – I need you to ring the bank and sort it out, but it'll do after Christmas. I'll have to give them all a bit less but they won't mind, I can make it up to them afterwards . . ."

"Martin –"

"What? Colette, it *is* a mistake, isn't it? I told the bank people not to be ridiculous –"

I don't believe it, she thought. *No way am I going to have this conversation with him now, on Christmas Eve, after three months of trying to make him sit down and talk.*

"Relax, Martin," she said, trying to keep her voice calm. "The money's all there, in the bank. Well, what's left of it – still over a million. We'll get it sorted after Christmas."

And how, she thought. He won't know what's hit him. He'd better enjoy Christmas, because he's in for a rude awakening the minute it's over.

"Feel like giving me a hand bringing in the presents?" she asked. "They're in the dining-room."

"It's too early to bring them out," he said. "They'll see them."

"No, they won't. Emer should be asleep by now and the lads know better than to go near them. Peter's out anyway. And Ciara won't even notice – she's probably still on her mobile to Orla. She rang her the minute we got back. We should never have –"

She stopped herself in mid-sentence. Christmas Eve, she reminded herself. Shut up and stop complaining.

But it really got to her, the amount of time Ciara spent on that phone. Colette used to feed the whole family for a month on less than the cost of Ciara's last phone bill.

"I'll go and have a look at Emer," Martin said, ignoring any mention of the phone.

"Okay," Colette said. "I'll start sorting the stuff out."

She went to the dining-room, unlocked it and stood in the doorway for a moment, admiring her work.

Forty-two presents, all carefully chosen and beautifully wrapped, were heaped in glittering piles all over the room. A whole month's work, she thought, smiling. No wonder she felt wrecked. But it would be worth it. She couldn't wait to see their faces. Something for everyone, all wrapped and labelled.

All except Emer's presents. They were still hidden upstairs in the wardrobe, with the stocking-presents for the other three.

She'd kept up that tradition all through the years and though Declan and Ciara scoffed she was sure they were secretly pleased to get them. She hoped. She'd hate if that particular magic had gone from Christmas for them. And this year she'd made a special effort. Lots of jewellery and make-up for Ciara, and she'd lost track of all the stuff she'd got the lads.

"My God," Martin said, coming up behind her quietly and putting his arm around her waist. "Hope there's something in this lot for me!"

She turned to him and laughed. "Whoops," she teased. "I knew I forgot someone!"

He smiled. "Doesn't matter. This is all I want for Christmas," he said, leaning forward to kiss her.

The action was warm, spontaneous, and she responded, thinking – if it was always like this I wouldn't care how much time he spent with that family of his. It used to be like this. He used to notice when I was in the room with him. He used to talk to me.

He was talking now. "You got stuff for my crowd as well?"

"Don't I always?" She said it gently. The one thing she knew he hated more than anything was shopping for other people – he never knew what to get. For the past couple of years she'd even had to get her own presents and give them to him to wrap, just to be sure of getting what she wanted.

"You're great, you know that? You've put a lot of work into it."

"Glad you noticed."

"Oh, I did my bit, too. I got loads of things for you, to make sure there's something you like – though you can always change them, I won't mind –"

"Oh, Martin –"

"Ah, come on. Don't go mushy on me. I probably got all the wrong things anyway, and I forgot the wrapping paper. Have you any left? I'll wrap them after we shift this lot."

"Emer's asleep?"

"Sound – but we'd better move. She'll probably be awake in an hour or two!"

They were sitting on the couch half an hour later, looking at the tree surrounded by presents – everything but the Christmas stockings – when Declan wandered in.

"What is it, Christmas or something?" he asked, his eyes wide as he looked around the room. "I'm going out for a while, okay? Just to meet Rob and Alan. Any chance of a few quid for chips?"

Colette was about to protest, then stopped herself. The chipper was only up the road, and it wasn't even midnight yet.

"There's a tenner in my purse, over there. Take that."

"Thanks, Ma."

He went to her handbag and took out the purse. "No, not here."

"What?" She was puzzled. She was sure there was a tenner among the notes in it. "Well, take the twenty, then – but bring me back the change."

"There's no twenty here either. It's empty."

"It can't be!" There had been at least £80 in it earlier that evening, a fifty as well as the ten and twenty. She was certain of it.

He handed the empty purse to her.

She took a deep breath to control the mounting anger.

"Right. This has gone far enough," she said, standing up. "I thought I was imagining it before when money went missing, but this time I know I'm not. And you haven't been taking it, Martin, have you? Twenty and fifty pound notes?"

"Of course not, I'd have told you. But –"

"Then it has to be Ciara or Declan. The money's definitely gone – and I'm sorting it out now once and for all!"

"Well, you needn't look at me!" Declan stood opposite her, his face reddening.

Anger, or guilt? she wondered. "So you're saying it's Ciara? Get her down for me, this minute!"

"I never –"

"I said, go up and get her down!"

He knew she was deadly serious and stopped arguing.

"Look, love," Martin said, standing up and taking her

arm as Declan left the room. "Couldn't we just leave it a few days? There's no real harm done. It's only a few quid–"

"Martin, if I counted up all the money I thought was missing in the last month, it's over £400!"

His eyes widened. "So why didn't you say something?"

"Would you have listened?" Her anger was all over the place now. So much for a happy Christmas.

"What –"

"You're saying I'm a *thief*?" Ciara interrupted as she burst into the room. "As if I'd take your bloody money. Dad gives me whatever I need anyway."

"Maybe that's part of the problem!" Colette's voice was rising but she couldn't stop herself. "You get everything so easy you think it's there for the taking!"

The three of them confronted each other, anger bristling between them, while Martin looked uncertainly from Colette to his children and back again.

"I believe them," he said finally.

She turned quickly round to him. "You do? So would you like to tell me who took it, if you didn't and they didn't? I know the money was there before I went out, and I don't think your family took it, do you? So where did it go? It *has* to be them!"

It was Declan's turn to look uncomfortable.

"Look, Ma. I hate to burst your bubble, 'specially at Christmas, but if none of us took it, I'm pretty sure I know who did." He stopped talking and stood watching her face.

Light dawned.

"You're saying *Peter* took it?"

"That's what I'm saying, Ma. Peter. The Boy Wonder."

"He couldn't have!"

"And Ciara and myself could've? Get real, Ma. He's not as perfect as you think he is. No-one's as perfect as you think he is!"

"And have you any proof? What would he be doing with that kind of money?" Her voice, full of ice-cold anger, didn't sound anything like hers. Declan had gone too far this time.

"Maybe you should ask *him*, Ma. Ask him about that stuff I found in his drawer when I went looking for some socks."

They all turned at the sound of the front door opening. She got to the hall just in time to see Peter's glazed expression and hear his voice slurring "Ppy Chris-mas" before he swayed against the wall and started to slide slowly downwards as Declan and his father rushed to catch him.

Chapter Twenty-six

When Suzanne pulled back the bedroom curtain, snow was falling. Perfect, or what? she thought, grabbing her dressinggown and dashing for the shower. Just what she wanted for Christmas Day – snow, and being back home.

She had woken at the sound of her father's footsteps going downstairs and was easing herself back under the duvet when she realised what day it was.

Her parents were thrilled to have her back home for a while and wouldn't mind how long she stayed in bed, but Suzanne was determined to be up early and make the most of every minute.

Besides, her mother would need a hand.

Maureen Halpin was both capable and hospitable, and at the last count there were only five joining them for dinner – a doddle compared with other years – but Suzanne always enjoyed helping with the preparations. And you could never be sure how many would actually turn up for Christmas dinner in the Halpin household. Mick Halpin and his brother-in-law Brendan were two of a kind, believing in "the more the merrier", and they'd invite the whole world in if they happened to pass them in the street.

Suzanne loved it. She loved all the razzmatazz of Christmas, and opening the door to all and sundry had been part of it for as long as she could remember.

She'd often shared her Christmas dinner with people they barely knew or didn't know at all, and usually it turned out to be great fun. Well, maybe not the year Mick invited the new neighbours from up the road because their cooker had blown up on Christmas Eve, and the pair of them picked fights with everyone and bickered their way through the meal about whose fault it was that they had to have their Christmas dinner "with a crowd of strangers we know nothing about".

Suzanne had nearly choked on her plum pudding trying not to laugh, while Maureen, being Maureen, chose to rise above it and concentrate on keeping the conversation going around them. They eased the couple out the door straight after the plum pudding and it turned into a great party after that.

It said a lot about her parents' relationship, Suzanne thought, that they had still been on speaking terms afterwards. And it hadn't quietened Mick's enthusiasm for bringing people in – if today was anything like other years, there'd be at least a dozen people calling for a Christmas drink.

"Happy Christmas!" she said, coming into the kitchen and giving her mother a hug. "So, what's the story?" she asked, looking at the pile of vegetables Maureen was preparing. "Did Dad get carried away again? Have we dozens of people coming? No, don't tell me!" She grabbed a piece of toast from the toaster and sat down beside her father, who was in the middle of his breakfast. "I can guess!"

"Happy Christmas yourself, Suzy," Mick said, smiling. "That bit of toast is your present, by the way. It was mine. Now it's yours. So enjoy it."

"Oh, good," she said, grinning. "Thanks, just what I wanted for Christmas! Do I get tea as well?" She lifted the teapot to see if there was anything left in it.

"Help yourself," Mick said. "God knows you'll need all your energy – wait till you see the jobs your mother has lined up for us."

"I need *something* to keep you out of mischief, Mick Halpin," Maureen retorted, leaving the water out of the sink and reaching for a towel to dry her hands. "Anything to stop you getting at the punch too early. Now, where did I put my list . . .?"

Suzanne and Mick looked at each other, laughing. Maureen and her lists were legendary.

"Go easy on us, woman!" Mick said, rolling his eyes. "Christmas is meant to be a break from work!"

"It is, of course," Maureen said. "And who d'you think is going to look after all the neighbours when they call?"

"Right," he said, standing up. "I'll get started on the punch –"

"Why did I ever marry him?" Maureen appealed to her daughter.

"As an act of charity," he said, "to spare some other unfortunate woman." He crossed to where she was standing between him and the cooker, put his arms round her waist and said "Now, out of my way, girl. I've work to do."

Suzanne watched the familiar warm look that passed between them. They're so lucky, she thought. Must be great to find someone who's exactly right for you.

They were still standing close together when she left the kitchen to check that the spare bedrooms were ready for the Sullivans.

Maureen's sister Kathleen always came for Christmas with her husband Brendan and their children, Roz and Gerry. And Ursula, Maureen's other sister, who was a nun in the local convent, would be coming as well.

Suzanne loved it when the whole family was together. She'd envy Maureen the closeness with her two sisters if she didn't get on so well herself with Roz and Gerry. Roz was just a year younger than her and Gerry two years.

"Steps of the stairs" the sisters had called them, until Gerry shot up when he was about sixteen, leaving everyone in the family – including his 6'1" father – behind.

The rooms were fine. No surprise, Suzanne thought. There was no-one more organised than Maureen when she put her mind to it.

She just had to fix up the spare bed in her own room, where Roz usually slept. It was a good arrangement. She loved talking late into the night with her cousin, and there was a lot of catching up to do.

She was coming downstairs again when the first of the neighbours arrived and she was caught up in a whirl of taking coats and getting drinks and chatting to people and answering the door again.

Her father had excelled himself, she thought. The room was filled to overflowing.

She worked her way round, with a few words for everyone, and was doing fine until she came face to face with Mrs Doherty. She never did like that woman, but Mick wouldn't have dreamed of excluding anyone from a Christmas morning invitation.

She was looking at Suzanne now with piercing little eyes.

"And aren't you looking great!" she said. "The colour of you, and at this time of year. I heard you're spending all your time out foreign – isn't it well for you, now, that you can afford it! But of course, money isn't everything. Tell me, did I see you at Mass this morning, or was it someone else –"

"Someone else, probably," Suzanne said lightly. "We went to Midnight Mass last night."

"You'll have heard about the appeal, then. The

money they need for the new church. I thought, sure it'd be no bother to someone like you to make a huge contribution and not even miss it –"

"I'll think about it, Mrs Doherty," she said, flashing a smile as she edged away.

"That's right. Think about it. It's not right for a young girl to have that much money. It's only putting temptation –"

"Suzanne!" She turned in relief to Mark, the guy from next door. He was in his mid-twenties and felt exactly as she did about the Mrs Dohertys of the world.

"Carping oul' begrudger!" he said in a half-whisper. "I heard every word. As if she'd give away a penny of her own. So don't listen to her – why give it to the Church, when you can spend it on your pals? I hope you got me something decent for Christmas this year," he teased.

"A Harley-Davidson," she said, deadpan.

"Brilliant. Just what I wanted!" Mark was a motorbike fanatic.

"It's in your garage – I helped Santa sneak it in last night."

"Sure," said Mark, grinning.

"Check it out, if you don't believe me."

Smiling, she turned and went towards the kitchen, stopping a few times to greet people, accepting the warm congratulations of those who hadn't seen her since the win. Once or twice she thought she heard the odd sly remark but she decided to ignore it. She knew by now who her real friends were, and so did her parents.

Mrs Doherty wasn't among them, and nor was Annie Daly, but she was someone else Mick felt he couldn't leave out.

"So I suppose you'll be selling up any day now," Annie was saying to Maureen as Suzanne came into the kitchen.

Startled, Maureen looked up from the plate of smoked salmon she had just finished preparing.

"And why on earth would we do that?"

"Well, with all that money, wouldn't it be foolish not to? You could get a place with a lovely big kitchen." She looked disparaging around the little kitchen. It was, Suzanne knew, a bit on the small side, but that was no business of Annie Daly's. "I'm sure Suzanne wouldn't begrudge you the money, now would you, Suzanne? Not after all they've done for you –"

"Mum and Dad love it here," Suzanne answered in a cool voice. "They wouldn't dream of moving. All their friends are here." As well as a lot who shouldn't be let in the door, she thought.

"All the same –"

"I wouldn't worry about it, Annie, really," Suzanne said. "After all, you manage, don't you? And your house is *much* smaller."

She caught the plate as Maureen nearly dropped it.

"Now, would you like some smoked salmon before you go?"

* * *

"I'm sorry, Mum. I really am. I just couldn't stand it any more."

The last of the neighbours had left and the two of them were in the kitchen putting the finishing touches to the dinner.

"She'll never talk to me again, you know," Maureen said.

"I know," Suzanne said glumly.

"So one good thing came out of it anyway." She laughed at Suzanne's expression. "Now cheer up, girl, and start bringing in this stuff for me – they'll be here any minute."

The doorbell rang just then and they could hear Mick opening it to Sr Ursula and, a minute or two afterwards, the Sullivans.

Dinner was a warm and lovely occasion, as it always was on Christmas Day. Roz, especially, was in great form, teasing her brother.

"Better enjoy it while it lasts," she told him. "By this time next year – !"

"Something we should know?" Suzanne asked.

Gerry looked around the table. "I'm giving you all a day out," he said. "I popped the question –"

"She didn't say yes, did she?" Suzanne teased. "She must be mad!"

"Totally!" Gerry agreed, grinning.

"But *he's* not," his mother said. "Girls like Yvonne don't come along every day. I told him –"

"The very same thing about every girl I ever went

out with. Only this time, Mum, you happened to be right!"

Mick filled all their glasses again to celebrate the announcement, and they left the table to move over to the sofas round the fire. This was their traditional time, and place, for exchanging presents.

Suzanne was thrilled with her gifts. A sweater from her parents, some silver earrings from Roz, a book from Gerry.

"We weren't sure what to get you this year," her aunt Kathleen said.

"So we got you the same as last year," Brendan added. "A voucher for some CDs. We know you don't really need it now," he said, looking a bit uncomfortable. "But –"

"It was a great idea last year, and it's a great idea this year, Brendan." she said, going across to give him a kiss on the cheek.

Ursula, as usual, gave her one of the little carved sandstone figures which were made on her convent's Mission in Africa. Suzanne had quite a collection of them now and loved the colours and the smooth, warm feel of them.

"Gorgeous," she said, running her hands over it before passing it to Maureen to admire.

"They're all lovely. Thanks a million. I wasn't sure what to get everyone –"

There was a flurry of protests that they didn't want anything. And they were genuine, she knew. Not for the first time she thanked God, or Fate, or whoever decided these things, for the family she'd been given.

"So I just got little things, but there are some cheques as well. I know you didn't want them before," she said, looking around. "But this is different. They're a Christmas present. Ursula," she said, turning to her aunt, "yours is for the Mission, so you'll take that, won't you? And Gerry, you'd do the same for me, wouldn't you?"

He laughed. "Course I would. It's Roz who wouldn't."

"That's okay," Suzanne said. "I know she can't be trusted with money –"

Roz protested while the others laughed. It was well known she was even worse than Suzanne where money was concerned.

"– so I spent her share on something I know she needs. It's outside, around the back."

They all stirred themselves and trooped out behind the garage to admire, in the fading light, the little blue van that was sitting there.

"Taxed for the first year," Suzanne said, enjoying the look on Roz's face. "Now we just have to sort out the insurance."

"I can't –"

"You'd better! We can't have you disgracing the family, cycling around Cork with a shovel tied to your bike."

Roz was a struggling landscape gardener of great talent but, so far, limited income.

"I don't –"

"My spies tell me you do."

"Only once!"

"Well, now you won't have to at all," Suzanne said, as Brendan reluctantly got out of the driver's seat to make way for Roz.

They were back inside, sitting round the fire with cups of tea, when they heard frantic knocking on the back door.

Mick went to open it and wasn't surprised to see Mark there – the O'Malleys and the Byrnes, their neighbours on either side, were the only ones who ever came in that way.

"Suzanne," Mick called, and she went to the door. Mark had apparently refused to come in, and his face was a picture.

"It's a joke," he finally managed.

"No joke," she said. "Come in. It's freezing out here." The snow had melted away but there was a chill wind blowing across the garden.

He shook his head. "I can't take it, Suzy."

"You have to," she said. "I don't know anyone else mad enough to ride motorbikes."

"I'll pay you back –" he began.

"Do, by not starting it up too early in the morning. Now, come in or go home, I'm freezing!"

He struggled for words, couldn't find any, grinned, leaned forward to give her a quick kiss on the cheek and sprinted back to his gleaming new Harley-Davidson.

* * *

"You've no idea the difference the van will make, Sooz."

The two of them were sitting cross-legged on the beds in Suzanne's room, facing each other. It was after midnight but neither felt ready for sleep yet.

"Sure I do. No more shovels tied to bikes."

Roz laughed. "More than that – I'll probably end up having to live in it!"

"How come?"

"Didn't Mum tell Maureen? The landlord's selling the place. We'll all have to leave."

Roz lived in a big rambling old house in Audley Place, at the top of Patrick's Hill, with four other women.

"Shame," Suzanne said. "You love that house, don't you?"

Roz nodded. "And the rent's cheap. We'll never get anywhere else as big for that kind of money. I hate the thought of us having to split up –"

Suzanne sat bolt upright.

"We'll buy it!"

"What?"

"We'll buy the place. Why not? Has he had an offer yet?"

"I'm not sure – no, hardly. He always said he'd let us know well in advance before he put it on the market –"

"So what d'you think? It makes sense."

"Sooz, you always said property was a bind. You didn't ever want to buy a house –"

"I know. But I'll have to now – the house I was in

was sold while I was away. And if I'm to be a property-owner I might as well do it big-time!"

"Will you –" Roz left the question hanging between them.

"Move in with Finn?" Suzanne shook her head. "Still just good friends, Roz."

Roz raised her eyebrows. "Even after Thailand? I don't get it, Sooz. You were lovers, right? And now – you're not? That's not how it's supposed to work. You can't go backwards."

"And we can't go forward, Roz. We're stuck."

"But *why*?"

"We had a brilliant time in Thailand," Suzanne said. "The spark was back, the magic."

"You said you weren't sleeping with him any more," Roz said.

"I didn't," Suzanne said. "*You* did."

"So what do you mean, 'good friends'?"

"I mean I don't see a future in it," Suzanne said slowly.

"That's crazy –"

"He wants kids, Roz. Lots of them."

"So?"

"And I'm not sure I do."

"Ah."

At least Roz hadn't said that every woman wants children. That had been Michelle's response.

"So what next?" Roz asked.

"We're kind of playing it by ear," Suzanne said.

"He'll be down in a couple of days to talk to Mum about extending the kitchen – it's a surprise, don't tell her – and then we'll go back to Dublin and see if we can find a run-down house to renovate."

"Why would you want to do that?"

"Because I need somewhere to live. And Finn wants a challenge."

"And he thinks he hasn't found one?" Roz asked, dodging the pillow Suzanne threw, laughing as she reached for the light-switch.

Chapter Twenty-seven

It wasn't fair of the whole family to come to her *every* Christmas night, Lorraine thought as she looked around her tidy kitchen. Now it would be all messed up again and the children would get over-excited and impossible to manage.

She didn't see why someone else couldn't take a turn this year.

"But you always said they had to come here," David reminded her. "You said if they wanted to see you on Christmas Day, they knew where to find you."

"And they do," Lorraine said. "I just don't see why it has to be *every* Christmas."

"We'll change it next year," David promised.

She glanced at him, her eyes sharp.

"We certainly will," she said. "Because next year we'll be in our new house and I don't intend leaving anyone in to mess it up."

"Lorraine –"

"I know, I'll have to let them in so they can see what it looks like. But no more parties. Besides, they cost too much."

David bit his lip and turned away. He knew better than to argue with Lorraine when she was in this kind of mood.

He hoped she'd be in better form by the time they all arrived in an hour or so.

He went into the playroom where Amber and Gavin were sitting surrounded by their new toys.

At least this was one room where Lorraine wasn't too particular and they could all relax. He sat down on the floor beside the children, helping Amber to complete a Postman Pat jigsaw and showing Gavin how to play with the little toy garage that had been his Christmas present.

"Where's your new dolly, Amber?" he asked, looking around as she lost interest in the jigsaw.

Amber's thumb went straight to her mouth, something David had noticed her doing recently when she was upset.

"Where is she?" he asked again, gently. "Come on. I'll help you look for her."

Amber sat solidly on the floor, resisting his attempt to help her up.

"Come on, pet. What's the matter?" he said.

It took a few more minutes of coaxing before she said "Don't want her. Want Milly."

Milly was the rag-doll Lorraine's mother had given Amber for her first birthday. Amber was rarely without her.

"But you can have two dollies," David said. "I'm sure Milly won't mind. Come on. Let's –"

"Milly *lost*!!!" It came out as a long wail.

"I'm sure she's not lost. She's just hiding somewhere. Let's see if we can find her."

But in spite of a thorough search of the playroom and Amber's bedroom, there was no sign of Milly.

He went into the living-room where Lorraine was curled up on the new leather suite, looking very pleased with herself.

"Have you seen Milly, Lorraine? We can't find her anywhere."

"Milly? Oh, that old rag-doll thing!"

"Amber's looking for her."

"Why? Hasn't she a lovely new doll and pram to play with?"

"She wants Milly as well."

"Well, she can't have her. I put her out this morning with the rest of the rubbish."

"You couldn't have!"

"Don't be ridiculous, David. The whole family is coming in a few minutes. I've spent weeks making sure the house looks good – you don't expect me to leave that kind of thing lying around! Besides, she doesn't need it now she has a new one. I never liked it anyway, I'm sure my mother got it from a market stall somewhere –"

"Lorraine," David struggled to keep his voice low, "where did you put the rubbish bags?"

"Out in the shed, of course," she said, looking at him as if he were mad. "David – don't you dare –"

He didn't hear any more as he tore down the dark path to the timber shed at the bottom of the garden. It took ten minutes of groping through stuff he didn't even want to think about, with the aid of a failing torch, before he managed to find Milly – luckily, in a bag of pillows and other things that seemed clean and dry. She'd still need a wash – his hands were filthy – but at least she was in one piece.

He ran back up the path clutching the doll, stopped at the playroom door to tell Amber that Milly would be fine once she'd had a bath, and ran upstairs for a quick shower himself.

His family had already arrived when he came back downstairs ten minutes later. As he came into the living-room Lorraine looked daggers at him. She obviously didn't appreciate being left alone to entertain them.

"Where's Emm and Polly?" David asked, once he had greeted everyone.

His parents, James and Margaret, were sitting uneasily on the new couch with his sister, Helen. Cathal, her partner, sat opposite with eighteen-month-old Cian on his knee. There was no sign of his other sister and her little daughter.

"They're in the playroom with your two," Cathal said. "This fella wouldn't go!"

That accounted for Lorraine's annoyance, David thought. Visitors were supposed to go where they were told, and stay there.

The doorbell was a welcome interruption, and Lorraine's family came flooding in. The younger children – Audrey's three and Paul's ten-year-old – went straight for the playroom while his elder girl Katie followed the adults into the living-room.

Quickly David scanned the room to see if there were enough chairs. Lorraine's brother Stephen had brought Sinéad, his fiancée, which meant nine adults in all, plus Katie. He'd need three more.

"Sit down, folks. Make yourselves at home. Back in a moment."

At least they'll all talk to each other, he thought as he brought the chairs in. It'll cover up Lorraine's silence. God knows what's got into her today.

"Now, who'd like a drink?" he asked as he got them all settled.

"Wouldn't say no!" Paul answered. "Any beer around?"

"Plenty. Fran, some wine?" he asked Paul's wife.

"Lovely. Red, please, if you have it."

"We don't," Lorraine said, her voice icy. "But I think there's a small bottle of white around somewhere."

"White would be fine," Frances said. Her smile was fixed and she was sitting on the edge of her chair. She was obviously here under protest; herself and Lorraine had never seen eye to eye.

"We've loads of red, no problem," David said. "Anybody else? Dad?"

He took the orders and went to the kitchen with Lorraine hot on his heels.

"David, you know I didn't get any red wine," she hissed. "There was no point in buying a bottle – Frances is the only one who drinks it and she only ever has one glass!"

"Relax, Lorraine. I got some yesterday."

And knew better than to mention it to you, he thought. "Now, would you bring in the sandwiches while I sort –"

"Sandwiches?"

"The turkey sandwiches."

"What makes you think there are turkey sandwiches?"

"Lorraine, we always – what have you got instead, then?"

"These," she said, removing the paper napkin covering a tray of cheese and pineapple pieces on cocktail sticks.

"And what else?" he asked, very slowly and very carefully.

He had been banned from the kitchen while Lorraine, with her 'I'll manage better on my own' expression, had prepared the party food. At least, that's what she *said* she was doing.

"They won't need anything else, David. I'm sure they all had a very good dinner."

"Lorraine, you can't just give them these. Where's the turkey?" he asked, bending down to look in the fridge.

"In the freezer," she replied. "I managed to make twenty separate portions out of it. Nobody eats the turkey sandwiches anyway. There's always a lot of waste. This way, we can use it for –"

"Have we any crisps, or peanuts?" David asked, starting to look around frantically. "Or what about the smoked salmon I bought?"

"I thought that was your parents' Christmas present. It's there, wrapped up at the bottom of the fridge."

And it was, in crumpled gold wrapping-paper he was sure he recognised from his own present – a shirt – this morning.

"But I got them that little china clock –"

"I'm sure they'll be delighted with the salmon," Lorraine said. "I can get a refund on the clock after Christmas."

Words failed him. He grabbed the wine and beer and dashed into the living-room.

"Steve, do the honours with these, will you?" he asked. "The whiskey and gin are in the cabinet there."

What next? he thought. Minerals. Ice. Those cheese-and-pineapple things. He dashed back into the kitchen.

Lorraine was nowhere in sight.

He grabbed what he needed, dropped it on the living-room table and ran upstairs in search of her.

She was lying on their bed with the curtains drawn and the light off.

"I feel a headache coming on," she protested as David snapped on the light.

"No, you don't. You've never had a headache in your life, except when it suited you. Now, please get up, go downstairs, and at least try to *act* as if our families are welcome here!"

Without waiting for a response he went back to the kitchen. He had never, in six years together, used that kind of tone to her. There'd be hell to pay later.

And that's when he'd deal with it.

Later.

Right now he had enough on his plate – which was more than he could say for their guests.

He tore the wrapping off the salmon, began slicing it as carefully as he could, grabbed some brown bread and thanked God he'd remembered to buy lemons.

"Not bad," he thought, surveying his handiwork for a second before opening cupboards in search of some crisps. One bag, way at the back. It would have to do.

"Sorry for the delay, folks. Slight technical hitch!" he said breezily as he came back into the living-room. Lorraine, he was pleased to see, was back among them, looking grim but making conversation with her sisters, Denise and Audrey. She never said more than she could help to *his* sisters, but no matter. At least she was there.

The food was finished quickly, the drinks more slowly because David kept replenishing them to try to inject some party spirit into everyone – literally, if he had to. And Steve was well into the role of barman, persuading even Margaret, David's mother, to have a little drop of the sherry he'd found at the back of the cabinet.

David began to relax. The party was starting to perk up. There was a buzz of conversation all around the room. It was safe to leave them while he made some tea and coffee to go with Joan's Christmas cake and the mince pies his mother had brought.

"Need a hand, kiddo?" a voice asked behind him as he reached for the tea and coffee.

"Emm! God, I forgot all about you!"

"Thanks a bunch!"

He laughed, a relief after the tension of the past hour. "Serves you right for skulking in the playroom with the kids."

"Someone had to do it!" his sister retorted. "And the Queen Bee obviously wasn't going to." She ignored his protest. "Did I see you haring up the stairs after her? What was that all about?"

"Emm –"

"I know. Mind my own business. But you *are* my little brother –"

"Only by ten months!"

"And I'd hate to think everything wasn't all right for you. It is, isn't it?" she asked quietly, searching his face.

"Sure!" he said, a bit too quickly. "Come on, I'll get you something to eat."

"A drink would be better."

"Whatever. Help yourself. The stuff's all inside. Oh,

and carry in this, will you?" He handed her the plate of Christmas cake, knowing he hadn't fooled her for a minute. Emma and Helen knew him better than anyone. Including Lorraine.

He banished the thought, concentrated on making the tea and coffee. He had it done just as Joan and Margaret arrived, offering help.

Margaret, he noticed, was wobbling a bit. Must have been more sherry left than he thought, and she wasn't used to it.

He handed her the mince pies – should be safe enough – and gave the coffee-pot to Joan, following them back in with a tray laden with cups.

"Dig in, everyone." He handed round cups, glanced at Lorraine, hoping she'd at least get up and pass the cake around. "Then we can get down to the serious business."

Everyone laughed, maybe a bit too loudly. They always exchanged presents after the tea and coffee. Usually it took about two minutes flat, since Lorraine saw no point in giving anything to most of the adults.

This year, to David's relief, she had bought something for everyone. Though you wouldn't know it from the pitiful little pile –

His parents' present.

"Sorry, Cathal," he said as his brother-in-law started to say something. "Back in a second." He dashed back upstairs to get the china clock.

He knew just where to find it. Lorraine kept a special

shelf for all the things she'd return after Christmas, including anything she was given that she didn't like.

Wrapping paper next. That was on the top shelf of the wardrobe.

Lorraine really was good at organising things, he reminded himself. That was one of the reasons he always left the shopping to her.

That, and the fact that he'd never hear the end of it otherwise.

Paul was coming back in from the car with a pile of presents as David came downstairs.

"Santa's here," Paul said, grinning. "Will you get the kids?"

David rounded up the four big kids and three very tired little ones from the playroom. He thought, not for the first time, that it was crazy giving them presents at this time of night, when they were high as kites and strung out, and hardly knew who was giving them what, and could barely keep their eyes open anyway.

But Lorraine insisted. This was what Christmas was all about, everyone coming with presents for her children.

She was sitting forward in her chair, eyes bright, looking at the presents in Paul's arms. "The one on top's for you, Lorraine. Can you take it?"

"Oh, goody," she said, looking thrilled. Paul hadn't bothered getting her anything last year. Well, he'd given her a little cheque to buy something for the new bathroom, but that wasn't the same at all . . .

The others followed, producing boxes from beside

chairs or from where they had left them in the hall, and soon she was surrounded by half-a-dozen or so colourful packages.

She began unwrapping the paper carefully – some of it was quite nice, she could use it again next year. She kept an eye on what the children were getting as well, to see if David's sisters had been as stingy as they were last year.

The presents, she was pleased to see, all looked very nice. She began unwrapping her own, a little surprised that everyone seemed to have got her something this year. It was only fair, of course, when she was hosting the party, but some of them had taken it a bit badly last year when she explained that funds were tight and she wouldn't have anything for them.

"This is lovely," she said finally when she had everything out of its wrapping. And it was. They were obviously getting the message, and, for once, everything was well-chosen and looked gratifyingly expensive. She mightn't need to bother going into town to exchange things this year.

"Our turn now!" she said brightly. "David, give me a hand, will you?" and she went to the tree and lifted the pile of presents from under it. She put them on the table and began passing them ceremoniously to him.

"This is for Paul and Frances," she said, "and this one's for Katie and Ruth. I'm sure they won't mind sharing it."

She continued calling out names, a big smile of

largesse all over her face, as David went around handing them out, bending to kiss his mother's cheek as he gave her the little clock. He was regretting that he hadn't, just this once, overruled Lorraine and splashed out on something really lavish for Margaret. It wasn't as if they couldn't –

"Well, that's it!" Lorraine said brightly. "Happy Christmas, everyone!"

David glanced around the packages that were being opened, noticing that Sinéad, Stephen's fiancée, was sitting empty-handed. Quickly he glanced back under the tree. Lorraine must have –

There was nothing there.

She couldn't have done that – got something for everyone else and nothing for Sinéad.

But obviously she had.

David was mortified.

He knew Lorraine was careful. He knew she counted every penny twice over. And when they'd needed to, when money had been really, really tight, he had appreciated her thrift.

And then, as things got easier and any money saved went towards curtains and new furniture and other "essentials" he'd been happy to see their home growing comfortably around them.

But even if it meant not having a chair to sit on, and eating with his fingers, he wouldn't dream of leaving someone empty-handed on Christmas Day while everyone else had presents to unwrap.

This wasn't 'careful'. With £1.6 million in the bank, this was mean, nasty and – he searched for a word – *despicable*.

He looked at Lorraine as if he had never seen her before.

And then he looked at the present Helen had just opened, and felt sick.

A bar of soap.

Okay, it was that fancy *l'Occitane* stuff from that French shop near Grafton Street. But *one bar*?

And Emma was opening her present to reveal exactly the same.

"No diamond earrings, Dave?" she joked.

"Well, if you don't like it –" Lorraine said sharply.

"Oh, it's gorgeous," Emma said. "I love it – the little girl next door got me one just like it. With her pocket-money –"

"If *that's* your attitude – !"

"Another drink, anyone?" David said quickly. "Dad?"

"I think I've had enough, thanks." Was it his imagination, David thought, or did the words sound loaded? "We'd better get on the road in case it gets icy –"

"You're probably right," Lorraine said. The bright smile was back as she stood up. "I'll get your coats. Thanks for coming, everyone, and for the lovely presents."

Nobody moved.

There wasn't a sound.

"You mean, that's it?" Audrey asked finally.

Lorraine looked puzzled. "Well, yes. We've had a lovely evening but I wouldn't want to keep you too late –"

"But what about –" Frances began. She was slurring her words, and David glanced at the bottle of red wine. Nearly empty. *God*, he thought. It was his fault, plying them all with drink. He'd never known her to go past one glass before.

"Tell her. Tell her she has to –" She was staring fixedly at Lorraine as she spoke. Paul quickly tried to hush her but she turned on him. "You have to tell her. I won't – I won't go . . . until you tell her –"

"Leave it, Fran. Come on, time for home," Paul said. David had never seen him look tense, but he was making up for it now as he stood up and tried to coax Frances to stand with him. "We can't – I won't – not until – until she gives us –"

She swayed slightly and lapsed into silence.

Lorraine brought in the coats, but still nobody moved.

"Would somebody like to tell me what's going on?" Lorraine asked. "Because I'm really tired, I'd like to clean up and get to bed."

"*I'll* tell you what's going on!" Audrey said, standing up to face Lorraine, her voice barely controlled. "We thought that, for once, you might get us something decent for Christmas. I suppose we should be glad to get anything, the way you've behaved other years, but we always put that down to you being sensible. Mean, but sensible." She was struggling to stay calm. "And then, when you won the lottery, we thought –"

"I only got a *small* share, I told you that!"

"Come off it, Lorraine! I *know* what you told us, and I know the truth as well. Did you really think we wouldn't find out, in a place the size of Dublin? So spare me, please! God, if I'd known you were going to turn into such a mean, grabby little bitch –!"

She stopped, her blood pressure obviously getting the better of her.

Lorraine was standing, mouth open. None of her family had ever in her life spoken to her like that.

And they weren't finished.

"Audrey's right," Denise said. "I'm disgusted with you, and I bet everyone else is, with these piddling little presents." She glanced scathingly at the tiny wooden photo-frame she was holding.

"That cost –"

"I don't give a *shite* what it cost!"

She stood up, swaying a bit, and David wondered how much wine *she'd* had. Enough, anyway. She was normally quiet and ladylike, but this was a whole new Denise.

And she was in full spate now. "I'll give you the bloody money for it, or you can have it back – I don't want your lousy little present! After everything I've done for you, everything we've *all* done, I thought you might think about *us* for a change! I thought *this* –" she held the picture frame with the tips of her fingers, waving it around " – was a gold chain or something, or that maybe you had cheques for everyone as well –"

"Are you *mad*?"

"Obviously!" Denise said loudly. "I'm *obviously* mad to have done everything I did for you all your life, everything we all did! We have only ourselves to blame. We spoiled you rotten just because you were the youngest –"

"Well, I certainly don't think you did!" Lorraine was spitting fire now. "And anyway, what's that got to do with –"

"Learning to grow up and start giving, as well as taking?" Stephen said. He sat holding Sinéad's hand, hurt expressions on their faces. "Nothing, if you're anything to go by! I don't mind so much for us, I've learned my lesson. I'll never be a fool for you again! But what about Mam? How could you do that to her, a set of *saucepans*, for God's sake?"

"She said she needed some –"

"Not crummy little half-price ones! And not for her bloody CHRISTMAS PRESENT!" he roared, standing up. "Come on, Sinéad. Let's get out of here. I've had enough."

James Kearns stood up, taking Margaret's hand. "We should go too," he said to David.

He looked – David searched for the word – sad, that was it. Sad, and disappointed.

"Dad –"

"I'll ring you tomorrow."

"Wait, Dad. Do you think –"

"Look, son, I don't want to get into this, not at Christmas. But I think your chickens are coming home to roost."

"What do you mean?" David asked urgently, but James shook his head.

"He means," Margaret said over her shoulder as James led her from the room, "he means –" her sherry-soaked words dropped into the sudden silence " – that I was right. I was right. You never should have married her. You could have done much better than her. She's nothing but a little –"

The rest was mercifully lost as James, helped by Cathal, half-dragged and half-carried her out to the car.

Emma bent to lift Polly, then said, with a bright smile, "Families!"

She and Helen left, carrying their children and followed by Lorraine's family.

David thought he heard Frances muttering 'rich bitch' as he closed the door behind them.

"Say something!" Lorraine demanded as he came back into the room, slumped down on the couch and sat there with his head in his hands.

But he couldn't, because there was too much he wanted to say, and too much he needed to think about.

Like what the hell had gone wrong.

And what he'd ever seen in her.

And what in God's name had possessed him to marry her in the first place.

Chapter Twenty-eight

Maeve and her sisters always got together for lunch on the 6th January, Little Christmas.

It was a tradition, dating back to their grandmother's time, that all the women in the family would gather together then for their own celebration.

Maeve's first memory of it was when she was five or six and there were twenty or so of her relatives all squashed happily round the big kitchen table, aunts and grandaunts and cousins and her mother and the four little girls themselves, with her grandmother sitting at the head of the table like the matriarch she was, delighted to be surrounded by so many of her "girls".

"*Nollaig na mBan*," she had reminded them. "Women's Christmas, our own day for celebrating, before it all finishes for another year."

Maeve and her sisters used to love it. They made

sure to carry on the tradition even after their mother died, and they always had a sense of her presence then, even more than on Christmas Day itself.

Occasionally one of their female cousins would join them, and Maisie, their aunt, would come if she felt up to it, but usually it was just themselves. And even if they had managed to see a lot of each other over Christmas, it was a day they could all be sure of being together, one they all looked forward to as a time for catching up.

And this year, for the first time ever, Maeve wasn't looking forward to it. This new year was one which seemed to hold no promises at all of anything good.

Snap out of it, she told herself firmly. Her sisters would be here in a few minutes and she'd better make a determined effort to enjoy herself. It might be the last –

There I go again! she thought, furious with herself. She had resolved not to let thoughts of Larry spoil Christmas for her, not to let herself dwell on anything to do with him or the house until Christmas was over.

And she'd been doing fine – until he turned up, unannounced, on St Stephen's Day. In the late afternoon, of course, once the racing at Leopardstown was finished for the day. And in great humour, which probably meant he had done well.

Maeve and the children had spent most of the day at Brenda's and she was trying to get them settled after all the excitement when there was a loud rap on the door. Senan had opened it to find Larry on the doorstep, half-concealed behind the stack of presents he was holding.

"There's a few more in the car, Sen. Here, take these," he had said, handing them over.

Senan had glanced at Maeve, who nodded, feeling she had no choice. He took the packages from his father and went into the living-room while Maeve stood by the front door, watching as Larry brought in a big box with several more brightly wrapped packages balanced on top of it.

He gave her a big smile before walking in the door as if he owned the place.

Which was exactly what he thought, she realised bitterly. He was acting as if he still lived there, as if the confrontation in the solicitor's office had never happened, as if he'd never dream of looking for more money from her, let alone expect her to sell the house.

The cheek of him!

She was speechless with rage, which was the only thing that stopped her telling him exactly what she thought of him. That, and a reluctance to spoil it for the kids.

Fergus, of course, had been thrilled. To have his daddy there was brilliant, as far as he was concerned. And the PlayStation 2 Larry brought had been the icing on the cake, the very thing Fergus had put on his Santa list , without much hope, at the last minute.

God knows how he got hold of it, Maeve had thought. Either he's had a few good sessions at the races, or his sister is giving him a dig-out again. And then he has the gall to say he's short of money . . .

It had been a difficult couple of hours for her.

Senan had kept his distance from Larry, torn between his obvious desire to talk to him and cuddle up against him like the vulnerable child he still was, and his equally obvious desire not to upset Maeve.

And Orla had been moodier than ever – unusual when her father was around – giving him a long, cool stare and barely saying 'thanks' when she opened the box he'd given her to reveal a chunky and clearly expensive gold chain.

Larry had been thrown by her reaction. He was more used to her hanging on his every word.

"You don't like it?" he'd asked, perplexed. "I can change it. You can have whatever you want."

"It's okay."

"If there's something else you want instead –"

"I said, it's okay." And she had turned on her heel and left the room.

Larry had looked at Maeve for a second, had been about to say something and thought better of it. Instead he had gone into the playroom with the two boys and stayed there, setting up the PlayStation with them and playing games until it was time to leave.

Orla hadn't bothered coming down to say goodbye, leaving Maeve with a sense of quiet satisfaction mixed with irritation at her daughter's bad manners.

Larry had hesitated for a second on the doorstep. He and Maeve hadn't said a word to each other in the time he'd been there.

"Maeve –" he began, one hand on the door handle.

She had cut him short with a brief "Goodbye, Larry." If he had something to say, he could do it through Robert Shaw and that creep, Morgan Lee. She'd heard it all before, whatever it was. There was nothing she wanted to hear from Larry now except that he'd come to his senses and was going to leave her alone.

No time to think about it now, anyway, she told herself as she set the table for lunch.

She was stirring the soup when Orla answered the door and she heard her sisters' voices in the hall.

"Only three, Mam. Anna didn't come," Orla said, ushering her aunts into the kitchen. Maeve wasn't sure, but she thought Orla sounded a bit disappointed. But probably not, since Orla usually found Anna, three years younger, a nuisance.

"She's gone off with her dad and the lads," Brenda explained. "We were surprised you didn't come with them." Eighteen-year-old Shane, Brenda's son, had called to collect his young cousins an hour or so earlier. Thrilled with his brand-new driver's licence and very old banger, he was happy to bring anyone anywhere, and Orla was usually happy to go. But this time she had given it a miss, offering no explanation, and Maeve had assumed she had plans to go out with Ciara instead.

"Everything okay?" Brenda added lightly.

Orla looked uncomfortable. "Fine. I thought I'd stay here instead."

They tried not to look surprised. It was years since

Orla had come to the *Nollaig na mBan* party. She usually went willingly enough to Brenda's house, where John, Brenda's husband, did childminding duty for the duration of the party.

"My *real* Christmas present to my sisters-in-law!" he called it.

"You're joining us?" Maeve asked her, carefully.

"I could go to Ciara's if you want," Orla said quickly.

"Now, why would you do that?" Noeleen asked, going over and giving her a hug. "You can't just abandon us. We need you here. You're the next generation of the McGoverns, don't forget, even if your last name is Redmond."

She laughed, and Orla smiled – a rare sight these days – and that set the tone for the afternoon.

It meant they couldn't talk about Larry, but that was a blessing. Today was a day for celebrating, not for going over old ground. Besides, Maeve had already filled the others in by phone straight after he left on Stephen's Day, and the last thing they needed was a re-hash that would spoil their party.

She began to relax as they finished eating, still talking, while the cinnamon-scent of the mulled wine Noeleen had made floated, warm and Christmassy, round the kitchen.

In many ways this was the very best part of Christmas for Maeve. She loved being surrounded by them all, wondered briefly what it would be like not to have sisters.

She'd never have survived Christmas Day without them.

She had gone to Maura's with Orla and the boys, as usual, and by the time Noeleen joined them for dinner Maeve was feeling miserable, caught up in thinking how different the day would have been if only she'd stayed in the damned lottery syndicate.

Her sisters were having none of it.

There were 364 days of the year to be in bad humour and this wasn't one of them.

They played with the kids, and got everybody out on the beach for a walk, and put on some dance music in the evening, and finally their infectious good humour had lifted her spirits and she started to enjoy herself.

Noeleen, of course, had been in her element. She tended to take over at family occasions, making herself a sort of master of ceremonies, to the amusement of her older sisters.

And she was doing it now.

"Has everyone a full glass? Good. Okay, girls, resolutions!" she said.

There were exaggerated groans all round.

This was part of their tradition, leaving the making of New Year resolutions until they were all together on the 6th.

"You first, then!" Maura suggested.

"The usual," Noeleen said. "No ciggies, and lose a stone. Starting tomorrow."

They laughed. She made the same resolution every year. Her record so far was two weeks.

They went round the table, still laughing, teasing each other as all the usual resolutions, and a few weird and wonderful ones, were trotted out.

Orla resolved not to murder any of the lodgers, but at least she said it lightly and they all laughed.

"Maeve?" Brenda prompted then, when she didn't respond to her turn.

"You remember last year?" Maeve said, finally. "I was going to win the lottery, give up work, do something with my life. Remember?"

Too late, they remembered. All except Orla, who hadn't been there.

"That wasn't a real resolution, Maeve," Maura said. "That was –"

"Something that could have happened, that would have made a huge difference to us all," Maeve said, powerless to stop the sudden tears. "And I blew it."

"You did no such thing," Brenda said. "You made a decision that was right at the time. It was just bad luck –"

"We make our own luck, Bren. No-one forced me to leave the syndicate."

"Well, if that's true, then make your own luck now," Noeleen said, knowing that Maeve would respond best to a cheerful, no-nonsense approach. "What would you change, if you could?"

"How long have you got?" Maeve said, laughing as she began to reel off her list. "I'd give up the job and stay at home with the kids. I'd have a bit more money. I'd think about going back to college. Most of all, I'd get Larry off my back." She looked at her daughter. "Sorry, Orla."

Orla shrugged.

"So what would it take to do all that?" Noeleen asked, trying her best to be business-like in spite of several glasses of mulled wine.

"Only a few hundred thousand pounds. Any ideas?"

"Maybe," Noeleen answered, looking thoughtful. "Say Larry's out of the picture. The court could find against him, or he might decide to back off – whatever."

"In my dreams!"

"Go with it, Maeve, just for a minute. If you didn't have to pay him off, what would you want most?"

Maeve thought for a second. "To be at home with the kids. That's the one thing I really envy Colette."

"You'd go mad here all day," Brenda said. "You know you would. Besides, the kids would be at school –"

"I'm going mad as it is, Bren. Anyway, I'd find something to do with myself."

"And something to do with that basement of yours," Maura said. "Have you thought any more about renting it to –"

"Never mind the basement a second, Maura. Let's concentrate on Maeve –"

"God, Noeleen, you're bossy," Maura laughed. "Anyone ever tell you?"

"All the time! Go on, Maeve. You were saying,

before you were rudely interrupted" – a grin in Maura's direction – "that you'd find something to do with yourself. Like what?"

"I'd give anything a go. Something with kids, maybe. Or office work, if I could do it locally and I found something I enjoyed. Whatever. I'd go out and clean houses if I could earn enough . . ."

Brenda laughed. "God knows there's a market for it. I hear all my neighbours saying they can't get anyone to mind the kids or clean the house or do any of the other things they'd be doing themselves if they weren't out at work all day. You could charge anything you liked as a back-up service for overworked women with kids!"

"She's right, you know," Noeleen said thoughtfully.

"You could take in more lodgers," Maura said. "Especially now that Orla's promised not to murder them," she said, with a quick smile in her niece's direction. "And there's nothing to stop you renting the basement if you got planning permission – it has everything you'd want for a crèche . . ."

"A *crèche*?" Noeleen said. "Where did you get *that* notion?"

"My neighbour Mary Doyle is looking for a place. Her lease is up –"

"And you really think it would suit?" Noeleen asked.

"Suit?" Brenda said. "It's perfect! Look at the location – up the road from the school, hundreds of kids living nearby –"

"Location, location, location?" Noeleen said,

laughing. Brenda had been working part-time in an estate agent's for the past year.

"Well, it's true!" Brenda insisted. "It would make a great crèche."

"She's right, Noeleen. It would," Maeve said.

"If it would, then maybe you should think about running it yourself." Noeleen said. "Well, why not?" she asked as Maeve's expression changed. "You want to be at home, and you're good with kids, aren't you?"

Maeve laughed. "Not good enough to mind hundreds of them on my own, thanks very much!"

Maura and Brenda looked at each other, and back at Maeve.

"Who said you'd be on your own?" Maura asked.

They meant it. She could see that from their faces.

She took a deep breath.

"There's still Larry. I could end up with no house, no job –"

"It won't happen," Brenda said.

"Let him just try it," Noeleen said. "You heard Maura. You're not on your own."

Maeve blinked back tears. It might work. Maybe.

What was it she'd said to Colette after the lottery win?

When I find out what I want, I'll go after it. And if it takes money, then I'll get that too.

Okay, she thought. So she didn't have money.

But she had something better than any amount of money.

Her sisters.

Chapter Twenty-nine

Olivia eased herself quietly from the bed so she wouldn't disturb him. She took his dressinggown from the hook at the back of the door and slipped into it as she went through to the little bathroom. She was already late. A quick shower, and then she'd have to leave.

The slight creak of the door woke him as she came back into the room.

"Chérie?" He stretched, smiled, watching her as she gathered her clothes. "You are sure you must go?"

She went to sit on the edge of the bed, stroking his cheek slowly, loving the slightly abrasive feel of it.

"You know I have to. Ellie will be there."

"She will not have left her apartment yet. You could telephone her, say you will be a little late."

His hand, which had begun caressing her face, followed the curve of her neck on down to trace the bare warmth of her shoulder beneath the dressing-gown. He reached to untie the dressinggown, slipping it back from her shoulders as she pulled away gently.

"Thierry, I –"

"Shhh!" he murmured, drawing her down towards him, holding her with her face close to his. "Say you will stay," he whispered. "Just a little longer, *chère* Olivia. I want nothing more than to be with you at this moment."

"You could come with me," she suggested. "Join us for dinner, maybe stay –"

"I cannot, tonight," he said, his voice regretful. "And tomorrow I go to Lyon, I will not be back until after the weekend –"

"Only a few minutes –" The rest of her words were lost as he kissed her.

* * *

She was almost an hour late.

"So, don't cook dinner!" Ellie had said, when Olivia phoned from Thierry's apartment. "We'll get some take-out pasta from the restaurant on the corner. No problem."

"Ellie, I –"

"If you're going to apologise, don't. No need. Ring me when you get home."

Olivia had the fire lighting and the food on the table when Ellie arrived.

"I'd almost believe you did it all yourself!" Ellie said, laughing as she came into the room.

"I'm trying to convince myself I did," Olivia said as they sat down. "I feel so guilty –"

Ellie raised one eyebrow, a grin spreading across her face.

"About not cooking, when I invited you to dinner," Olivia said firmly. "But this is much better than anything I could produce."

"So, what delayed you?" Ellie asked, still grinning. "Let me guess . . ."

She didn't have to, of course. She'd noticed the change in Olivia as soon as she saw her after Christmas. Subtle, but unmistakable. Olivia was a woman in love.

It hadn't taken long, either, to guess with whom.

Within a few days of her return Ellie held a dinner party, inviting Thierry and Olivia along with some other friends – and it was obvious to everyone there that they were more than mere acquaintances. They were careful not to do more than exchange polite conversation, but it was there in the way his eyes followed her as she moved around the room, the way she listened with a slight smile as he spoke.

"You're lovers, aren't you?" Ellie had asked in her direct way when she called round for coffee a few days later.

Olivia had been stunned into silence.

"It's okay. You don't have to answer. None of my business, anyway," Ellie had said cheerfully.

"Is it so obvious?" Olivia had asked finally, relieved and surprised that Ellie was taking it so casually.

"Only if you watch closely," Ellie said.

"And the others –" The other guests were friends of Thierry's as well as Ellie's.

"Will be very discreet."

Which meant that he was married, Olivia thought, her heart sinking. Otherwise, why the need for discretion?

She knew already, of course, at one level. The flat in Montmartre, comfortable but sparsely furnished. No photographs, nothing much of a personal nature other than a few of his own paintings on the wall – competent but unexciting scenes of Montmartre which she loved simply because they were his – and some art materials in the tiny spare room. He obviously had another home as well, with a wife – and presumably a family – there.

He had started to tell her, that first afternoon they went to his apartment, but she hadn't wanted to know, had silenced him by leaning forward to kiss him, stilling the voice in her head that called her brazen.

This was like something in a different world. Time out of time. Somewhere *Olive* had never existed, a place where Olivia could be who she wanted to be, do what she wanted to do.

And she wanted him, more than she had ever wanted anyone or anything in her life.

He had responded with eagerness and passion, then surprise when he realised that this was the first time for her.

"You are sure?" he had asked quietly, and for an

answer she had kissed him again and he had begun caressing her slowly, his skilled gentleness smoothing away any lingering trace of doubt until her whole world was urgency and insistent longing and a sensation, entirely new to her, that every nerve-ending in her body was awakened and clamouring, hungry for him.

Afterwards the guilt had crept in, but by then it was too late. She was committed, alive, in love. She didn't want to know about his other life, didn't ask questions when she stayed in Paris for Christmas and he wasn't free to see her. And when she saw him afterwards and gave him the gold watch she had chosen and he left it carefully on the bedroom locker when he left the apartment with her, she opted to ignore what that must mean.

"Olivia?"

Her mind had wandered, only half-concentrating as Ellie served the pasta and salad and talked about her plans for the next six months which would see the end of her stay in Paris.

"You're miles away. I'd say, at a guess, somewhere near Sacré-Coeur."

"Sorry," Olivia said, filling their wine glasses.

"Never say sorry." She laughed. "Life's much too short for 'sorry'. And for guilt, Olivia."

"You don't really mean that."

"Actually, I do," Ellie said, taking a mouthful of pasta. "Mmm, great. Anyone ever tell you you're good at ordering pasta?"

Olivia tasted it. Not bad. And a major improvement on her own cooking.

"I don't –"

"Order good pasta?" Ellie raised her eyebrows again. "Or feel guilty?" This time she looked serious.

Olivia sighed. "Feel guilty. I started to say I don't, but of course I do. He's a married man. It goes against everything I grew up believing in."

"So do a lot of other things."

"This is different."

"How? Only tell me if you want, but I'd be interested."

"Because – I suppose because it involves somebody else. I know she's there, somewhere in his other life. I don't want her to be, but she is. And I have no right to hurt her."

"Olivia, let me tell you this. Nadine doesn't –"

"Nadine?"

"You didn't know her name?"

Olivia shook her head. *Nadine.* An elegant name. What does Nadine look like? she wondered. How old is she? What does she do while Thierry is with me in Montmartre?

She brought her attention back to Ellie. "No. I wouldn't let him tell me. I haven't even let him tell me he's married."

"That makes you feel better?" Ellie asked.

"I don't know. I suppose so. It lets me not think about her."

"And that makes it easier?" Ellie prompted.

"It makes it possible." That was true, Olivia thought. She hadn't realised it until she said it.

"Olivia? I really don't know the best way of saying this, but – how serious are you about Thierry? Is it, you know, something fun, that makes you feel great while it lasts but you know it'll pass – or is it more than that?"

Olivia didn't have to think of the answer. "More than that. Much more than that."

She hesitated for a moment, took a sip of water, and when she began again the words came tumbling one over the other.

"It's as if – Ellie, have you ever felt as if you only come alive, *really* alive, when you're with a particular person? As if everything you've been, and felt, and done in your whole life, has been leading up to that first moment of meeting him, and your life would have been a waste if you'd never met him? Have you ever felt like that?"

Oh, God, Ellie thought. She's got it bad.

"Not since I was about seventeen," she said softly.

"And what happened?"

"I married him. It was fine for the first year. After that, it was all downhill."

"What went wrong?"

"You remember I said don't feel sorry and don't feel guilty? With Jeff, I got plenty of practice at both. What I got from that marriage was two great sons and the belief that everything – from the cost of home heating to the Canucks losing at ice hockey – was my fault. Two years ago I'd had enough. The boys were old enough and I was forty-three. I decided it was time to take back my life."

"So you left."

"I had to, before I went under. For a year or so I went wild, had several affairs. It was like discovering myself all over again, growing up, but at the age of forty-three, not seventeen. I was making up for all the time I'd missed."

"Can you ever really do that?" Olivia asked, half to herself.

"I believe so. I believe I did. And I believe –" she paused, gauging Olivia's reaction. "I believe it's what you're doing now. Olivia –" she reached across to touch her hand, "forgive me, but I get the sense that, well, that you don't have much experience with men. And I don't want to see you hurt. If you can enjoy it for what it is, fine, great. Thierry's an amazing man. I just wouldn't want to see him hurt you."

"Thierry wouldn't –"

"Wouldn't mean to hurt you. And I can see how you've changed, how you're – sparkling, more at ease with yourself. I know he's done that for you. But it can't last, Olivia. You can't depend on him – because he'll never leave her. I'm sure of that."

"I don't expect him to. I don't let myself think about her, so it's not an issue, but – how do you know?" she asked, watching Ellie's face closely. Realisation hit her. "He's done this before, hasn't he? Ellie?"

Finally Ellie nodded. "I guess that's why I wanted to talk to you about him. I'm not worried about Nadine, Olivia. Nadine will take care of herself. She and Thierry have been married a long time, they have an understanding of some kind and it works for them. And if it works for you, great. I'm all for taking your chances where you find them. Just as long as you know the score. As long as you know it can't last and don't let yourself fall in love with him."

It was already too late, Olivia thought. Already, she loved Thierry de Rochemont far more than she had imagined it was possible to love anyone.

Chapter Thirty

She was going to kill the lot of them. Strangle them all with her bare hands.

Well, not Emer, of course. But the rest of them. Starting with Peter.

If anyone deserved it, he did.

It had been a fiasco of a Christmas. Everything she'd planned so carefully, every ounce of effort she'd put into it, all gone to waste. The atmosphere had been desperate all day, with Martin tiptoeing around as if someone was dead, and whispering to his relations, and all of them giving her knowing glances, and Declan not even bothering to hide his delight that for once he wasn't the one getting into trouble.

Her sisters rallied round once they arrived, trying to liven things up, Eileen telling her to be sure to cram in every mouthful of food she could before they had to go to that hell-farm in Wicklow.

"I think you mean health farm, Eileen," Ciara had said coolly. She was enjoying this too, needling Colette about Peter whenever she got the chance.

"It was supposed to be a joke, Ciara."

Ciara didn't answer – she just rolled her eyes to heaven.

Somehow Colette had got through the meal, her mind in turmoil. Peter was still skulking in his bedroom, so she'd had no chance to ask him what in God's name he'd taken. Nothing very much, more than likely. He'd come round very quickly the night before once Declan and his father got him upstairs to the bed.

Colette, of course, had been all for calling the doctor or bringing him straight to the hospital, but Declan had tried to reassure her by saying he'd be fine, he'd been like this a few times before, he'd snap out of it. Which, however well-meant, had put the wind up her completely.

"Before?" she'd asked, trying not to shriek, and Declan had muttered, "Just leave it, Ma," and between himself and Martin they had encouraged her to go to bed.

She hadn't slept a wink, of course, getting up every ten minutes to check on him.

* * *

And now, ten days later, she was still raging with him for ruining what could have been a great Christmas.

He hadn't done it all on his own, of course.

No, he'd had a lot of help. And from an unexpected source.

Martin's brothers and sisters didn't surprise her – they were relishing every minute of her discomfort. She was furious with Martin for telling them. But then, if he hadn't, Declan or Ciara were bound to – and anyway they'd have to explain Peter's absence on Christmas, of all days.

He'd had a lot of explaining to do.

He was in the middle of it on St Stephen's Day, swearing blind that he was only trying things out, that of course he wasn't a drug addict, that he knew he shouldn't have been helping himself to money but there was so much around he didn't really think she'd miss it, and that of *course* he hadn't spent it all on stuff for himself – his friends were all keen to have a try as well –

The doorbell had rung just as she was wondering if that meant he was *supplying* the bloody stuff as well as taking it, and her brother Tim was standing there with his wife, Barbara.

And that was when all hell broke loose.

"I know we're probably calling at a bad time," Barbara said, glancing in Peter's direction as she sat down on the sofa across from him. "We heard all about your little problem but don't worry. Your secret's safe with us. I got the name of a good clinic for you. My next-door-neighbour's friend's son went there. She said it did wonders for him. And my neighbour said it was no trouble getting the address for me, even on Christmas Day, once I explained it was an emergency . . ."

Colette couldn't believe what she was hearing. She looked across at her brother, who was looking more uncomfortable by the minute.

"Barbara, I really don't think –" she began.

"You're right. We won't talk about it, because that's not why we're here. I'll just give you the name –" she was extracting a slip of paper from her handbag as she spoke. "No, the reason we're here – now, I know you've had a difficult time –" another glance in Peter's direction "– but it's always better to say what's on your mind, isn't it? Before things get out of all proportion?"

Tim shuffled on the couch beside her, avoiding Colette's eyes.

"It's about our Christmas present," Barbara went on. "I know you've probably been a bit distracted, but –"

"Did you not like it, Barbara? There's no problem changing it."

"What?"

"The silverware. I can easily change it."

"Who said anything about the silverware? That's fine. It's exactly what I was looking for."

"I know," Colette said, puzzled. "That's why I –"

"I'm talking about the cheque," Barbara said.

Tim looked as if he wanted to dig a hole and crawl into it. Colette watched as a flush spread along the back of his bent neck.

"Well, we naturally expected one," Barbara went on when Colette didn't answer. "I mean, it *is* Christmas, and we *are* your family . . . Tim didn't want to ask you, of course, but he finally saw my point. It's always better to have these things out in the open, isn't it?"

She flashed her husband a look, demanding support. In response he settled deeper into the couch, his eyes fixed firmly on the pattern of the carpet.

God, just what I need, Colette thought. *When she finds out I gave Tim a cheque a month ago there'll be murder. But they can leave me out of it.*

"Of course, it was very good of you to give us that little cheque for £20,000," Barbara went on, as if she had read Colette's mind. "Don't think we're not grateful. But –"

"Barbara, I think we should leave this now," Tim said, looking absolutely miserable.

"But why? It's better to get it all sorted out. That's why we're here, isn't it?"

"I don't think –" he began.

"No, leave her alone, Tim," Colette interrupted. "I'd like to hear what Barbara has to say. What exactly do you want to sort out, Barbara?"

Martin and Peter tensed, glancing at each other. They'd never before heard Colette use that particular tone.

Nor had Tim, and he flashed Barbara a warning – but she didn't see it, or else chose to ignore it. Either way, there was no stopping her.

"You *are* going to share the money out a bit more, aren't you? I mean, I know you don't intend keeping it all for yourselves . . ."

"But we haven't," Colette said calmly. "£20,000 isn't exactly small change, Barbara. And we'll probably give everyone a bit more when we've sorted ourselves out."

"How much?"

"I beg your pardon?" Colette asked.

"How much will you be giving us?" Barbara said. "I need to know now, before I get the new car. There's no point in buying a cheaper one and then finding –"

"That I would have stumped up enough for a bigger, better, snazzier one?" Colette suggested.

Barbara nodded eagerly.

"Well, I can put your mind at rest right now. I have no *intention* of buying you a car if you come here acting like you've a right to it –"

"Now, Colette –" Tim began.

"Now Colette *nothing*!" Colette said, turning on him. "Did you put her up to this? No, okay, I know you didn't, but why did you go along with her? Stupid question, she only has to say jump and you do – look at you, you used to have *some* bit of backbone. If you wanted money you only had to ask, but not like *this* –"

"We'd better go. Sorry, Colette." He stood up, looking worse than ever.

"Sorry for *what*?" Barbara demanded, her voice rising out of control. "I'm not sorry at all. Don't think *I'm* sorry for asking for a measly few thousand pounds when the dogs in the street know it's all going to the Comerfords –"

"That's enough, Barbara. We're going. We shouldn't have come in the first place." Tim had grasped her firmly by the arm, looking apologetically at Colette as he steered his wife towards the door.

She turned to throw one last filthy look at Colette. "That money changed you, Colette. I'd never have believed it, but it changed you."

Colette's voice was icy. "Indeed it did, Barbara. And not one single minute too soon."

Peter was no match for her after that. Nor was Martin, for that matter. She had laid into the two of them, telling them in no uncertain terms how she felt about Peter and his stupid drug-taking, and Martin and his stupid spending and his stupid family . . .

"What about *your* stupid –" Martin began, but one look at her face warned him to leave it.

There had been an uneasy truce of sorts since then while they gave her space to calm down. Of course Declan and Ciara had heard everything. The four of them spent the next couple of days reassuring each other that it wasn't like her and she was bound to come to her senses.

Colette felt as if she had done just that.

She'd done everything she possibly could for them and it still wasn't enough. Well, from now on things were going to be done her way – and they could like it, or lump it.

She'd had enough of cheeky, ungrateful brats, and Ciara and Declan could cop on to themselves, and fast. And Martin was back to his old self after that lovely, unexpected few minutes when he put his arms around her on Christmas Eve – and as for Peter . . .

She couldn't even *think* about Peter without wanting to scream.

And it had been like that every day of the past nine days since St Stephen's Day.

Two more days – and counting – until her week in the health farm.

"We need to talk, love," Martin said, coming into the room as she sorted out her packing. "I thought you might have had a chance to get on to the bank by now – you know, they said before Christmas the account was empty –"

"It is," Colette said crisply, reaching into the wardrobe and taking out two of her new blouses.

"It can't be – how –"

"I moved it," she said, barely glancing at him as she began folding the blouses into the suitcase on the bed.

"Oh, right. But you should've told me –"

She turned to face him, arms folded. "And when would I have done that, Martin? If you weren't with your family every night before Christmas, you were in the pub, coming home at all hours –"

"That's not fair, Colette. You know I don't drink much –"

"I never said you did. I just said you were out spending our money, when you should have been here talking about *how* to spend it –"

"Not that again, Colette. Mam and Carmel will be here any minute."

"Why?"

"What?"

"Why are they coming?" she asked slowly. "I didn't know we were expecting them."

It was Wednesday, but Mrs Comerford was still refusing to come for tea since the night Colette had forgotten to cook for her.

"They're coming to pick up the cheque – you know, for the new extension. The builders will be getting round to it any day now –"

"Martin, I'll only say this once, so listen carefully. We are not paying for your mother's extension. We're not paying for a single thing more for your family – do you hear me? – until you sit down with me and plan how we'll spend the rest of the money. Starting with *my* new extension that I've been trying to talk about since last September, but of course you're not interested in *that* –"

"You never said –"

"I bloody well did, but you wouldn't listen!" Her voice was rising. Vaguely she was aware of the others crowding the bedroom doorway, drawn by the noise. Good job Emer's with Therese, she thought. I don't need her seeing me like this.

Declan was stupid enough to butt in. "Chill, Ma. I can't hear the TV."

"*Chill yourselves*, the lot of you! No-one takes a blind bit of notice of me around here and I'm sick of it! The only time any of you bother to come near me is when you're looking for more money – and, my God, do you know how to do that! Well, I'm telling you here and now, it's finished. Things are going to be very different. Starting right this minute!"

Martin glanced uneasily towards the doorway, saw the mutinous expressions there and turned back to Colette just as the doorbell rang downstairs.

"My mother. Come on, Colette. Let me have the chequebook for the new account. Please. I can't tell her . . ."

"It wouldn't be any good to you, Martin. It's in my name."

She smiled a satisfied smile as his expression changed. "But don't worry, you won't have to tell her," she added in a sweet voice that was scarier than the raging anger of a few minutes ago. "I'll be happy to do that myself."

She went down the stairs, the four of them trailing behind, and opened the door to face her mother-in-law.

Chapter Thirty-one

Maeve was exhausted. She kept going by telling herself that it would be worth it, but, God, it was taking it out of her. She hadn't had a minute to call her own for the past six weeks.

But it *would* be worth it. The basement was looking great – Maura was right, some fresh paint had made all the difference – and they'd applied for planning permission for the crèche nearly two months ago, just after their *Nollaig na mBan* party, so they should have a decision fairly soon now, one way or the other.

She hoped it would work. Because it *could* work. The idea was brilliant – the three of them running it between them, providing a "home management" service as well as childcare. Maura was free all day, Brenda worked part-time and as soon as Maeve's job-sharing was approved they could really go all out to make it work.

One of them would stay in the crèche – or two,

depending – leaving the other free for the "home management" end of things. They had put notices up all over the place, offering to clean, or house-sit, or be available to pick up dry cleaning or shopping – all the things working women spent their lives trying to juggle. The things Maeve and her sisters were willing to do for them instead – for a price.

It was Maura who'd come up with the name, Maura who was showing most enthusiasm for the project. And the more they talked about it, the more Maeve believed *Jugglers* could be a great success.

If she didn't die of exhaustion first.

The supermarket job had been Brenda's idea.

"You'll need money for Paris," Brenda had said. "And you won't take it from us so you'll have to go out and earn it. It won't take long, a couple of months should do it, and I'll mind the boys in the evenings and at weekends."

And it *hadn't* taken long. Maeve had found a part-time job in the local supermarket and was into her sixth week now, and in spite of giving some of her earnings to the taxman and some to the kids she'd managed to put away over £350. Another four weeks and she'd have enough saved, in plenty of time before they were due to go to Paris in late April.

She couldn't wait to see Colette's face at lunch today when she heard that Maeve was really going. In fact, she couldn't wait to see Colette. They didn't get much of a chance to meet these days, especially since Maeve had started working at weekends, and talking on the phone just wasn't the same.

And Suzanne was joining them for lunch, which would have been the icing on the cake except that Maeve needed to talk to Colette about Ciara, and it really couldn't wait. She'd just have to try and get Colette on her own for a few minutes.

It still troubled Maeve that Ciara had so much money, that she was sharing it with Orla and that they could get into God-knows-what kind of trouble.

Their two guilty faces said it all five minutes before. Maeve had gone into Orla's bedroom with clean clothes, not realising Ciara was in there with her – they both had a day off school – and found the two of them sitting on the bed counting a pile of notes scattered between them on the duvet.

Orla had gathered them up quickly, cramming them into her pocket, and Maeve had bitten back the questions she wanted to ask. Orla would have a lot of explaining to do the minute Ciara left.

She cornered her as soon as she heard the door closing behind Ciara.

"So? What's going on?"

"Nothing," Orla muttered, not meeting Maeve's eyes.

"Don't give me that! I saw you, there must have been a hundred pounds there."

"It's okay. It's mine." She's changed, Maeve thought. A month or two ago she'd have been screaming that it was none of my business. But it is.

"Where did you get it?"

Orla hesitated, looking straight at Maeve.

"I don't want to say, okay? It's a secret."

"No, it is NOT a secret! Orla, tell me what it's for, or I'll –"

"You'll what?" The defiant look was back in her eyes, and Maeve sighed. She had felt, she really had, that she and Orla were getting along better since around Christmas. Not anywhere close to what she hoped, but at least they weren't at each other's throats these days.

"Orla," she said quietly, "I can't have you taking money from Ciara. You know that."

"It's not Ciara's – it's mine."

"But how? Orla, you didn't take out your savings, did you?" She had over £500 in the Post Office, but she also had an agreement with Maeve that it wasn't to be touched until she was sixteen.

"No, it's not my savings."

"So, how –"

"I sold a few things."

"What things?" Maeve asked slowly.

"My stereo. Leanne in my class wanted one. Her parents said she could buy it –"

"Go on."

"And my chain."

"What chain?"

"My gold chain. The one my father bought me. I went to a second-hand jewellers with Ciara –"

You ungrateful little bitch. The words she had often

been tempted to use, but never had, sprang to her mind and she forced herself to take a deep breath.

"I can't believe you did that, Orla. You *couldn't* have. It cost him a fortune, and if you didn't like it you should have said so –"

"And let *him* sell it and put the money on a horse? Sure."

She's changed her tune, Maeve thought. *It's no time since she was screaming at me that he had a right to spend his own money on whatever he wanted.*

"Orla, he's your father. You are *not* to talk about him like that."

"Why not? You do!"

The little madam. Maeve wanted to grab her and shake the living daylights out of her, but that was something else she'd never done.

She tried to put words on her anger. "*You* are the most ungrateful, selfish little –"

To her horror Orla burst into tears. She hadn't cried for years. Not in front of her mother, anyway.

"Orla? Love –" Maeve felt helpless standing there, wanting to gather Orla into her arms but afraid that might make matters worse.

"It was a surprise," Orla said finally, her voice straining past tears. "I wanted to surprise you. I was going to change it into francs tomorrow –"

"What –"

"For your holiday. So you'd have enough money for Paris."

Orla was still crying, and Maeve felt her own eyes flooding with tears.

"You didn't have to –"

"Yes, I did!" She rubbed savagely at her eyes, struggling to stop the tears. "It's the only thing I can do to make it all right!"

"Make what all right?" Maeve asked, her stomach knotting.

"Your St Nicholas ornament. The one I broke. I saw one just like it, in a little shop in Paris on our way back, but I hadn't enough money –"

"Orla –"

"I know." She was calmer now. "I know it's not the same, but I thought you'd want it anyway, only I couldn't buy it – that's why I was furious when I got back – and then you told me you had a ticket to Paris and I got Noeleen to ring. I had the name of the shop, they're keeping it, she put a deposit on it with her credit card –"

She paused, out of breath, and Maeve finally found words.

"Orla, you didn't have to –"

"I did! I never meant to break it. Besides –" She paused to look at Maeve, trying to gauge her reaction. "I didn't want the chain. It's lovely, but I didn't want it. Not from him."

"He's your father, Orla," Maeve reminded her again, but more quietly this time. "Will you tell me what's wrong, love? Did something happen?"

This provoked a fresh outburst of tears, and Maeve was nearly sorry she'd asked.

"He brought you nothing for Christmas, that's what happened –" Orla said as soon as she could speak again.

"But –" Maeve began, then stopped herself. This wasn't the time to tell Orla that it had been years since Larry got her anything for Christmas.

"And I wanted it to be special for you, to make up for the statuette, and the lottery and everything –" she paused, rummaging in her pocket for a tissue and blowing her nose – "and then he came with loads of stuff for everyone else and nothing for you and I wanted to kill him! He treats you like dirt, Mam. I hate him. You'll take the money, won't you?" she asked anxiously, changing tack.

Maeve went and put her arms around her. "I can't, love. I can't take your money from you."

Orla moved back, her face mutinous, but this time Maeve realised it was pretence.

"You have to." Her expression changed. "Please. It's the only thing that'll make me feel better about your granny's statuette. Please, Mam. Tell Colette you can go, and when you get there, buy the statuette –"

"Colette – oh God, what time is it?"

"Please, Mam."

Maeve reached to touch her daughter's face. "God, I feel awful about the things I said –"

Orla's face broke into a big smile. "I know. You're a desperate mother. Will you take the money?"

Maeve kissed her on the cheek. "I'll take it, love. Thanks. Look, we'll talk later. I have to fly, okay? I'll be home by four."

She ran downstairs, grabbing her coat and purse, and reached the bus stop outside just as the No. 30 pulled in. With luck, she'd only be a few minutes late.

She arrived, out-of-breath from running up the quays to the restaurant, but more-or-less on time, to find Colette and Suzanne already there, deep in conversation.

"Training for the mini-marathon?" Suzanne laughed as Maeve sat down beside them and caught her breath.

"In my dreams! I don't even have time for my walks any more. I'll have to go to that fancy health club of Colette's to get back into shape."

"Forget it," Colette said. "Nothing's worth that kind of torture."

But it clearly was. True to her word, she had joined the new health club straight after she got back from the health farm, was working out at least four times a week, and it showed. She looked relaxed and toned and fitter than Maeve had ever seen her.

"I'm filling Suzanne in on the latest," Colette said.

They spent the next hour in animated conversation, bringing each other up to date.

Colette's mother-in-law still hadn't recovered from the news that Colette now controlled the purse-strings. Martin had been furious once he got over his shock, and had lapsed into a long, raging sulk. But for once Colette was standing firm. Even Declan and Ciara were beginning to realise, finally, that Colette meant business. And Peter, after several long sessions with Colette and one with his local doctor about the utter stupidity of experimenting with drugs, wasn't putting a foot wrong.

"It's only the beginning," Colette declared. "I've had it with trying to please everyone. From now on I call the shots. Martin didn't know what hit him when the builder called about the extension. He probably thought he could put me off the idea until the kids had left home and we didn't need it any more."

"You managed to get a builder?" Suzanne asked, perking up. "He doesn't happen to have any friends who aren't busy, does he?"

They laughed at the improbability of that as Suzanne quickly outlined her plans. Her offer for the house Roz was living in had been accepted and the paperwork was almost complete. Spurred on by the excitement of it, she had started, with Finn, to look for a suitable house in Dublin that she could renovate – preferably into flats so Val and some of her other friends could share with her.

"That's if you don't mind, Maeve?" Val was still living in Maeve's house, along with two new lodgers, and it was all working out well.

"I'd miss her, of course. But they're beating down the door looking for rooms so I wouldn't be stuck. As long as she keeps in touch!"

Suzanne laughed. "She'll do that all right. She's always saying how good you are and how much she feels at home there. I'm probably kidding myself to think she'll ever leave!"

"Even if she doesn't, you'll have no trouble getting people," Colette said. "What size house are you looking for?"

"Actually, it's houses," Suzanne said. "Once we get the first one up and running we're thinking of buying a few more in bad condition, doing them up and renting them out."

That's what the lottery does for you, Maeve thought. *You can talk as casually as that about buying a few houses while the rest of the country is hard pushed to buy one.*

"We're going into partnership and doing it properly," Suzanne went on. "That way, if it works out, we'll never have to worry about money again –"

"Like you worried before?" Colette laughed. "And tell us about this partnership –"

"Strictly business," Suzanne said firmly.

Colette and Maeve nodded solemnly.

"Sure," they said together.

"I mean it."

"You're mad, Suzanne," Colette said.

Suzanne waited, surprised. Colette usually tried to say things diplomatically. At least, the old Colette did.

"He's a lovely man. You're together – what? Two years now?"

"If you're going to say why don't we get married, Colette –"

"I wasn't going to say it. But of course I'm thinking it."

"Well, don't," Suzanne laughed, making a joke of it. "The only thing I'm thinking about now is how to be sensible for once in my life. The money won't last forever. We'll find the houses we want, go to the Canaries for a couple of weeks, and then afterwards –"

"That's being sensible?" Maeve asked.

"Sure. Life's too short for skipping holidays!"

Maeve laughed, letting go of the last of the tension from her talk with Orla.

"You're right. And that's why Colette and I are going to Paris."

She looked at Colette and was rewarded by an expression of pure delight.

They were going to Paris together. And they'd have the time of their lives.

Chapter Thirty-Two

There was a bitter chill in the air and rain was beginning to fall in big, drenching drops as Olivia made her way along the cobbled streets to Thierry's apartment.

She knew the route blindfold now, had lost track of how often she'd been here. Twenty times? More?

Sometimes it felt as if her whole life had been lived in these last nine weeks.

It was a fantasy, of course. In her saner moments she knew that.

And it was wrong.

There was no getting away from that, no matter how hard she might try.

But, God, it was wonderful.

She had never known she could feel like this.

Once, for a brief interlude when she was seventeen, she had felt this sort of passion, this sense that the whole world was hers, that anything was possible. Of course, it had lasted no more than the blink of an eye once her mother found out.

Olivia wouldn't allow herself to dwell on that, to think of how different her life might have been if she had said 'yes' to Richard, and 'no' to her mother, rather than the other way round.

She wouldn't allow herself to think of it because her life, from now on, was the present and the future. The past, apart from cherished memories of her father, stretched back precisely twenty-two weeks, to the day she had decided to leave Dublin and come to Paris.

Her present was here, and now, and Thierry de Rochemont.

And the future . . .

The future was full of promise and possibility.

The light was on in the front window of the apartment as she slipped down the side alley and rapped quietly on the front door. Thierry, smiling, led her inside to the large, lamp-lit room where soft music was playing.

She loved it here.

Occasionally they met in her apartment, but usually in his. She suspected – but had never asked him to confirm – that he was concerned about being recognised, in an area where she now knew several of his friends lived.

Here it was different. In the bustle of Montmartre there was more freedom to come and go, and though Thierry seemed to know several people locally – the staff of the nearby restaurant, his elderly next-door neighbour who called one evening while Olivia was there, enquiring about her lost cat – mostly he kept to himself, and Olivia had a sense that this was a place which would value his privacy.

He took her hands, holding her at arm's length.

"You look wonderful, *chérie*."

She *felt* wonderful.

Her long woollen coat was new. She was wearing a new cashmere sweater and linen trousers underneath. Her first ever pair of trousers. So many firsts, so many things she had never thought to do.

She had gone shopping with Ellie, the two of them giggling like schoolgirls as Ellie persuaded her to look at lingerie she'd never have dreamed of herself. And then, still giggling, she had bought it, protesting that she'd never wear it. And of course once she got home and slipped it on her first thoughts had been of Thierry, and how much he would love it.

Lovemaking wasn't all they did together, but it seemed so. Everything else was an interruption, something that must be endured until they could be together again like this. Even when they went for a meal together, or to the cinema or the Opéra with Ellie and some friends – all of them carefully colluding in the illusion that Olivia and Thierry were simply two other individuals in the group – even at those times Olivia lived in a state of heightened awareness where every small movement of his spoke to her, and she could think of nothing but the sheer pleasure of knowing that soon, soon they would be together again, alone.

Two or three times each week they met, usually at his apartment. Sometimes she stayed overnight, slipping out early into the already-busy streets as he got ready for his other life.

And, carefully, she asked nothing about that other life, sidetracked him skilfully if he seemed about to divulge something. Because, as she had told Ellie, what she was doing was only possible if she denied to herself that he had any other life at all but this.

She never let herself think about how he explained his absences, was content in her assumption that he told his family he was alone in the apartment, painting.

Olivia didn't want to know what he told them.

She quoted to him once some half-remembered lines from a poem about making 'one small room an everywhere', and he smiled, saying this was everywhere to him, and she was everyone. And she had smiled too, not needing any more than that.

"You would like a coffee?" he asked now, taking her coat, bending to kiss her lightly on the cheek, prolonging the anticipatory pleasure of taking her in his arms. "Or something to drink, perhaps?"

He brought some *absinthe*, something else that was new to her, and they sat on the sofa, curled up together, talking quietly. He had booked the restaurant for 8.30, he told her. There was no hurry. It was just around the corner.

"You are hungry?" he asked.

"Not much," she admitted. She never seemed to be hungry these days. Excitement and passion for him eclipsed her every other need.

"Are you?" she asked.

He laughed. "I am hungry for you, *chérie*. As always."

He kissed her then, lingeringly, and she returned the kiss urgently as he began caressing her. Finally, she pulled back, her breath coming fast.

"Thierry, we had better –"

"Cancel the reservation, *non*?" he laughed as he lifted the phone, dialled and spoke quickly, apologetically, before taking her hand and leading her into the little bedroom.

This is all I need in the world, she thought as he closed the door softly behind them. And then she stopped thinking at all as he began again to kiss her and there was nothing else, nothing else in the world but his arms around her, his warm mouth on hers and the urgency of her need for him.

Afterwards, exhausted, exhilarated, she lay against him, loving the scent of him, the feel of his arm around her as her fingertips traced a pattern in the hair on his chest and moved down along his side, lingering at his hip, finally coming to rest on the warm firmness of his thigh.

"You are happy, *chérie*?"

"Very happy," she said, moving slightly to lean over him, bringing her hand back up to touch his cheekbone, his lips. "And you?"

He looked deep into her eyes.

"I am happy. Yes, of course. But sometimes I worry –"

She reached down to kiss him on the lips. "Life is too short for worrying."

"I do not want to hurt you, Olivia. You are so beautiful a woman –"

Fear gripped her.

She gave a little laugh, reassuring herself. He'd never hurt her.

"Beautiful? No. Whatever else I am –"

"To me, you are beautiful. You are so alive, so – what is the word? – trusting. I have seen how you look at me when I enter a room. I would never want to hurt you, Olivia."

She couldn't ignore it this time – the word, or the panic in the pit of her stomach.

"You won't hurt me, Thierry."

"I would not mean to, certainly. But sometimes people hurt each other, not meaning to. That is part of love."

"It doesn't have to be! If people love each other –"

He touched his fingers gently to her lips, silencing her.

"Perhaps you are right. I hope you are right, *chère* Olivia."

His hands moved slowly, caressing her warm skin, and she was beginning to relax, his lips on hers, the last traces of fear leaving her, when the telephone rang.

For a moment she thought he wasn't going to answer but then he muttered something and left the bed, going quickly to the phone in the living-room.

She could hear, but not understand, his rapid French. And then he came back into the room, his face strained.

"You must leave," he said. "I have to go. My little granddaughter –"

He has a granddaughter? Olivia thought as they dressed quickly. *I didn't know he had a granddaughter.*

He was still talking. She caught the words 'car accident' and 'hospital' and then Thierry was getting her coat, hurrying her down the stairs.

He said a distracted goodbye, closed the door behind them and rushed off into the night in the direction of the nearest taxi rank.

Chapter Thirty-three

Nothing was going right for Lorraine today. In fact, nothing had gone right so far this year, she thought angrily as she put the children sitting at the table with beans and toast in front of them.

She was furious. The estate agent had just rung to say that the house she had put an offer on – a large red-bricked house in Terenure village – had been taken off the market. "They can't do that," she had protested. "It cost me £200 to get a surveyor –"

"Sorry," the estate agent had said, sounding as if she didn't care less. "I'm sure we'll come up with something else –"

Lorraine had slammed down the phone. She didn't want something else. She wanted the house in Eaton Square. It wasn't fair that people were allowed do that. After all her trouble and expense they should be *forced* to sell it.

Just wait until she told David –

But David wouldn't care either, she realised. David didn't seem to care about anything these days.

Really, it was ridiculous. He should grow up a bit. He couldn't continue like this. She wouldn't let him. It wasn't fair.

And it wasn't just David. The rest of the family – both families – had hardly spoken to her since Christmas. Three whole months! In fact, the only one she had any real contact with now was her mother.

Joan was still minding the children every day. Well, it made sense, as Lorraine had told her, because she was so busy herself these days looking for the perfect house.

Of course, she used to think the one they were in now was perfect, but that was before the lottery win. She couldn't be expected to stay here now, especially with the neighbours being so snotty since she refused to contribute to their silly "Best-kept Estate" fund.

She really didn't belong with people like that, and the sooner she moved, the better.

As long as it was close to her mother. That was important. Lorraine didn't intend to spend half her day trekking to and fro with the children when she had so much else to do. That would be a total waste of time. And they had to go *every* day, whether or not Lorraine was at home herself.

Because otherwise – though she'd never admit it – they would drive her completely mad.

Lorraine was a superb organiser.

Everyone said that, no matter what else they might say about her.

But she couldn't organise her children if her life depended on it.

She could organise their clothes and food and toys. She could dress them and get them into the car and get them to her mother's in the most organised way imaginable.

But what she absolutely could not do was organise their day when they were with her so that they played when she wanted them to and ate what she gave them and slept when she needed them to, leaving her free to get on with other things.

Instead, they complained and whined and followed her around so she hadn't a second to call her own and, really, she couldn't live her life like that. She just couldn't.

It was all Joan's fault, of course. She spoiled them rotten, and so did David. Amber and Gavin expected undivided attention every minute of the day, thanks to them.

And Lorraine had far more important things to do than watch Postman Pat or play with dolls and toy cars. Joan had all the time in the world for those things, and besides, she *liked* doing them, so really it worked well all round.

Lorraine was congratulating herself on getting the children to bed early with – for once – the minimum of fuss on their part when she heard David's car in the drive.

"Go to sleep!" she said sharply to Amber as the little

girl lifted her head from the pillow and excitedly called her father.

Great, Lorraine thought as she slammed their bedroom door and went downstairs. Just when I had them settled.

David stepped into the hallway to be greeted by the noise of the children from upstairs and a look of fury from Lorraine.

"You've upset them," she said coldly, "so you can just go up now and get them back to sleep."

She was curled up on the couch with some tea when he came down half an hour later looking exhausted.

"Your dinner's in the kitchen," she said. "Just put it in the microwave for a –"

"I'm not hungry."

"Suit yourself. It will keep for –"

"We have to talk, Lorraine."

"I know. The estate agent rang. The house in Terenure is –"

"I don't give a *damn* about the house in Terenure, Lorraine."

She scowled at him. "Do you think I don't know that? It's all left to me and –"

"I'm not moving."

She paused, stunned into silence.

"You'll have to," she said finally. "Because I'm not staying here."

"Suit yourself. But I'm staying, and so are the children. You can do whatever you like."

"Just what exactly is that supposed to mean?" she asked, her voice like ice-water.

"It means I've had it, Lorraine. I've done the best I can, and it's not enough. I don't think moving's the answer. And I don't think I can go on living with you."

He said it so quietly it frightened her. He nearly sounded as if he meant it.

"I don't know what's wrong with you tonight," she said sharply. "Actually, I don't know what's been wrong since Christmas. You walk around with a sour face, barely talking to me, sleeping in the spare room. Well, I've had enough of it, David!"

"So have I, Lorraine." His voice grew louder now. "You don't know what's wrong since Christmas? I'll tell you what's wrong! I spend every waking minute wondering how in God's name you've changed so much. I know you were always tight with money. We had to be, so I didn't mind – well, I did a bit, I hated always being on the receiving end – and when we got the lottery money I thought this is it, this is pay-back time for our families. But you don't see it that way, do you, Lorraine? You don't see anything except yourself, and –"

"That's a lie!"

"No, Lorraine. You're spoilt and used to getting your own way, and I'm through making excuses for your meanness. I did enough of that, because I loved you, but –"

"What do you mean, 'loved'?"

He sighed, ran a hand through his hair.

"I don't know what I mean any more. I don't even know what I *feel* any more. I just know it's not fair on anyone, especially Amber and Gavin –"

"What about *me*?"

He sighed again. "It's always about you, Lorraine, isn't it? Everything has to be about you. Well, it's about time you realised you're not the centre of the universe –"

"This is ridiculous," she said, standing up. "I've heard enough. I'm going to bed. Maybe in the morning –"

He stood up to face her. "In the morning I'd be gone, if it wasn't for the children."

"You don't mean that!"

"I've never meant anything more in my life. You've changed, Lorraine. You were always mean, you always thought of yourself first, but –"

"I did not! My children –"

"Would be miserable if it wasn't for your mother. Admit it, Lorraine. You can't wait to get them over to her in the mornings. I thought when you won that bloody money and decided to stay at home all day that you'd learn to handle them, maybe even enjoy being with them. But I should have known better. I should have –"

"You don't even realise how much time and effort I'm putting into trying to find a home for us –"

"Instead of thanking God for the home we've got, and spending the money where it's needed."

"And what's that supposed to mean?"

"Did Joan tell you Audrey's house is being re-possessed? I'm sure she did, but do you even care? She could do with that money, Lorraine. There was a time when you might even have given her some. I don't know. All I know is that ever since the lottery win you can think of nothing but spending every penny on yourself. You don't care about upsetting our families or embarrassing me –"

"But I'm doing this for us, David. The new house will be much nicer for the children –"

"Will it? You mean you'll let them put their toys on the floor without complaining about the mess? You'll let them stay at home sometimes instead of carting them off to Joan's? You'll –"

"They like it there!" Her voice was shrill now.

He took a deep breath. "They do. But it's about time you asked yourself why they don't like it *here*."

"That's why we're moving –"

"I told you, Lorraine. I'm not moving. At least, I'm not moving with you. If you want a fancy big house then go and get it. Nobody's stopping you. But the kids and I are staying here –"

"You don't expect me to move out on my own! That's the most *stupid* – you're my *family*!"

"Well, then, if you want to stay here, I'll go," David said reluctantly. "I'll call every day to see the kids, of course –"

"You can't leave me on my own with them! I won't manage –"

"You won't be on your own. Your mother will have them every day, and I'll call and put them to bed –"

"And what am I supposed to do?"

He sighed, moving towards the living-room door. "Whatever you want, Lorraine. You could start by taking a good, hard look at the kind of person you're turning into –"

"I'm the same as I always was! I said the money wouldn't change me, and it hasn't. I don't know what you're –"

"Maybe you're right, Lorraine. Maybe I was just too dumb to see it. But I'll tell you something. If you were always like this, if you really *haven't* changed –"

He had her full attention now.

"Then maybe it's time you did."

Chapter Thirty-four

Suzanne had just spent a great weekend with Roz in Cork.

The house in Audley Place was hers, and she couldn't believe how good that made her feel.

Roz, of course, was thrilled. No worries now about doing the rounds of grotty bedsits with landlords who charged an arm and a leg and expected undying gratitude along with exorbitant rents. Her four friends had been equally pleased, especially when Suzanne said they could have a free hand with the decorating and she'd foot the bill. The house was basically in good condition but the decor was definitely on the dodgy side.

Nothing his pals couldn't sort out, Gerry promised, saying he'd arranged for a couple of them to start work in a week or two.

Suzanne wasn't holding her breath. She knew every painter or decorator worth his salt – and a lot who weren't – was booked solid for the next six months or more.

But there was no rush. The house was comfortable and sound, just a bit shabby, and Roz and her friends had lived there happily for years and were only too delighted to stay there, re-decorated or not.

The main thing was that it was a great house for parties, Roz said as she rang round all their friends on the Saturday to invite them to a big celebration bash.

"Good job we only have scraggy old carpets and beat-up furniture," she said to Suzanne in the middle of the party. "No need to worry about beer spills. But wait 'til we get the new stuff, I won't let anyone in the door."

"I doubt it, somehow," Suzanne laughed. "Leopards don't change their spots."

"You don't think so?" Roz said. "What about you? I thought you'd be halfway to China by now instead of up to your eyes in buying houses. But fair play to you, girl. It's a good job one of us has sense!"

"Sense? I think we're mad myself – you'd want to see the houses, two of them are in bits! But I haven't changed – we're off to Lanzarote next month."

"When it's Beijing let me know. *Then* I'll believe you haven't changed!"

* * *

Suzanne was singing as she left the outskirts of Cork. With luck she'd be in Dublin by lunch time and Finn would be free.

She was in really good form. Nothing like a little retail therapy for lifting the spirits and she'd spent all day Monday shopping with Roz.

Definitely her favourite occupation, next to travelling.

And she'd get all the retail therapy she needed – and then some – with the three houses in Dublin to sort out.

She hoped they were doing the right thing. At first she hadn't been sure, but Finn had used all his powers of persuasion.

"Can't go wrong," he'd said. "The house in Ranelagh's in great shape, structurally sound, re-roofed, new damp-proof course, the works. Maybe a bit expensive, but it's in walk-in condition. You want a house of your own, and you love that one, right?"

"Sure. It's exactly what I want. But the others –"

"Are the best investment we'll ever make. I can raise enough for my share of the two of them against my own place, and once we've got them done up and rented out they'll pay for themselves. But if you're not sure –"

"I'm sure. They just need a lot of work, that's all."

"We'll get it sorted," he'd promised.

And she believed him.

But that didn't mean they weren't mad, she thought. She'd never worked so hard in her life as in the last three months.

Three houses in Dublin, as well as the one in Cork. Crazy!

She'd looked at houses until her head was spinning. She'd gone over and over figures with Finn because he was determined to put up his fair share of the deposits. She'd even found a little shop in Harold's Cross that just might work for the idea she was still toying with – an interiors shop with her name, in red and gold, above the doorway.

And preferably somebody else to look after the hard graft of actually running it, because right now there just wasn't time for all the things she had to do –

And she was loving every second.

She phoned Finn on the mobile as she neared Dublin.

"Good timing, Suzy! Look, I've just been to the house in Fortfield Gardens again with the auctioneer, and I think we should up the offer if they push it. It's definitely worth another 10k. If you agree, I'll ring him now. Meet me at the office, okay? I should know by then."

He did. There was a bottle of champagne sitting on his desk to prove it.

"Sorted!" he said, with a big grin, leaning back against the desk, arms folded, looking dead pleased with himself. "And for our first offer. Didn't want to tell you, but there was another guy looking when I got there. He seemed serious –"

"Must be as crazy as we are! I hope the champagne's chilled?" She went over and kissed him on the cheek.

"Chilling," he said, putting his arms around her and kissing her properly. "It's for later."

"Oh?"

"Yeah. I've got a great idea –"

"Really!" she smiled. "So when's Karl back?" Karl was Finn's partner in Brogan McNamara.

"Ten minutes."

"And you think –"

"I think an afternoon off would be a great idea. To celebrate. I thought we'd go to Powerscourt, the three of us –"

"*Three*?" she said, raising an eyebrow.

"Three. You, me and the champagne."

They were still kissing, oblivious to all else, when Karl came back.

* * *

Two hours later they were sitting on the hillside above Powerscourt Waterfall, sipping champagne. The gorse was coming into bloom, lighting up the hillside, and the sky was a deep blue that reflected in the glint of sea far in the distance.

A perfect day, warm for late March. Just perfect.

"Brilliant idea!" she said. "This is exactly how I want to spend my life, drinking champagne in the sun – what more could I want?"

"All my ideas are brilliant," he said with a big smile. "It's why you love me."

"It is *not*!" she laughed.

"Oh? So why do you love me, then?" He said it lightly, but the question was there in his eyes.

"Because –" She wasn't laughing now. "Finn, who said I loved you?"

"You know you do, Suzy. Go on, admit it!"

"Sure of yourself, aren't you?" she teased, matching his tone.

"Most of the time," he said. "Wish I could be as sure of you . . ."

"You mean you're not?" She laughed again. "Tell me, who else would –"

He touched her hand, interrupting her, his face suddenly serious. "Marry me, Suzanne?"

The perfect day shattered for her.

"I can't."

"Suzy –"

"Don't, Finn. Please. You know how I feel –"

"That's just it, Suzanne." He looked upset now. "I really *don't* know how you feel. I know I love you, I think you love me, everything's been great since Thailand and I thought –" He broke off, watching her. "Tell me you don't love me and I'll –"

"It's not that."

"Then *what*?" he asked. "Suzanne, this is crazy! If you love me, where's the problem?"

"There's no problem, it's just – Finn, we're doing fine. Let's not spoil it."

"That's what you think marriage would do? Spoil it?"

He was still watching her, searching her eyes for an answer. He sat at one side of the tartan rug, she at the other, the remains of their picnic filling the space between them.

A small space, a couple of feet, but suddenly it felt like a continent as she looked across at him, trying to find a reply.

Finally she nodded, shifting her gaze from his.

"But *why*?" he asked, his voice rising in frustration. "That just doesn't make sense, Suzy. Look at your parents, look at my brother – marriage doesn't have to wreck a relationship. That's not what it's supposed to do, for God's sake!"

He shifted on the rug, moving slightly nearer as if that could bridge the gap between them. "This *works* for us, Suzy. Finally, it's working for us. Marriage can only make it better!"

"I'm just not sure, Finn. I'm happy as things are. Why can't we –"

"Go on like this, for the next ten or twenty years, you living in one place, me in another, never making any real plans for the future? No, Suzy. I don't think so. I –"

"What kind of plans?" she asked, alarmed.

"Just –" he shrugged "– plans. For some kind of future together, in one of the houses, maybe a couple of kids –"

"No way! No, I'm sorry, Finn, really I am. I'm just not ready for that. Even the *thought* of that scares me. Can you see me with kids? I mean, can you? I wouldn't have the first clue what to do with them! Besides, I see Michelle and what's happened her – she was great until she got married and had the kids. Now she's got to ask Keith's permission to go outside the door –"

"You know that's not true!"

"He made a real song and dance about her going to Crete –"

"Hardly the same thing. And besides, you know I'm not like that –"

"But marriage is! You've got to think about somebody else first all the time –"

"So? That's what people *do*, Suzy, when they're with someone. Whether they're married or not. And marriage doesn't mean you stop doing things –"

"It changes you, Finn. And kids change you. Look at the big production it is for Michelle and Keith to go anywhere. You stop *wanting* to go, it's so much hassle. I mean it. Marriage changes you, and kids change you more than anything, and I really don't want to change –"

"It's a bit late for that, Suzanne! Look how you've changed in the last six months. And you'd probably have changed even without the lottery. *Life* changes you, not the lottery, not marriage and kids –"

"Finn, I don't want children. I really don't. It's too much responsibility."

He sat quietly for a minute or two, looking into the distance, before turning to her again.

"We don't have to have them, Suzy."

"But you want them. I've seen you with your nephews. You know you love kids –"

"I could live without them."

"But you shouldn't have to, if you really want them."

"And if I really want you?"

He looked so hurt she almost gave in. But she couldn't do that to him. She really couldn't. He wanted children. He should be able to have them. And it would have to be with someone else, because –

The thought of Finn with someone else was like a sudden sharp pain. But there was nothing she could do. The thought of children and all that responsibility terrified her. She just wasn't used to kids. And she was happy the way things were. Or, at least, she had been.

"Finn –"

"Leave it, Suzy, okay?" he said, reaching for her hand. "We'll go on as we are, if that's what you really want."

It wasn't what he wanted. She could see it from the set of his shoulders, the hurt in his eyes. She wanted to put her arms around him, tell him she would marry him and have his children, tell him anything at all that would take the stricken look from his face.

But she just couldn't do it, because she couldn't change how she felt.

Together, and in silence, they gathered the remains of their picnic and walked back down the hill to the car.

Chapter Thirty-five

It was over.

Neither of them had actually said it.

But both of them knew it.

Five weeks had passed since the night he hurried from his apartment to the hospital. Five weeks with no contact, not a single telephone call. Five weeks in which Olivia had all the time in the world for thinking about him, and about herself.

Finally, when she couldn't stand the uncertainty any longer, she had dropped a note into his apartment suggesting they meet the following Saturday evening at a *bistro* they had often gone to in the Place du Tertre, near Sacré-Coeur.

She waited twenty minutes, toying with a glass of Badoit, before he came rushing in.

"I would have telephoned –" he began as he sat down.

"How is your granddaughter?" she asked, cutting across him.

"Better. Much better now. For a long time it was not certain."

She believed it. His eyes were tired. There were new lines in his face.

He looked intently at her, reaching across the table to touch her hand.

"I am sorry, *chère* Olivia. So terribly sorry."

He meant more than not having contacted her, and she nodded, understanding.

"You know what I am saying?"

Again she nodded.

"I never wanted to hurt you –"

She attempted a smile. "You did try to warn me. Last time. Remember?"

"I did?" he asked, a slight frown on his forehead. "No, *chérie*, I do not remember –"

"Don't call me *chérie*," she said sharply, and he looked at her, contrite.

"I thought of you every day, Olivia. But it was just not possible –"

"Don't say it unless you mean it, Thierry. Please, don't."

He gave a slight shrug, then sighed. "I am not sure what to say."

She took a sip of water, watching him steadily.

"Then don't say anything. I think we both know it's over," she said softly.

"You must believe that I wish it were otherwise."

"Otherwise, how?" she asked, her voice still soft. "Do you wish you weren't married? I don't think that's what you mean, is it?"

"Olivia –"

She raised a hand, silencing him.

"Thierry, I've had a long time to think about this. Five weeks can be a lifetime, sometimes."

Again he began to speak, and again she stopped him.

"I couldn't contact you. I didn't know what was happening. You didn't return Ellie's calls –"

"I tried. It was difficult, Sophie was in hospital until just three days ago –"

"I know it was difficult. Impossible. That's how it's been for me, Thierry. Impossible. I didn't realise until you were – gone."

"I wasn't gone –"

"You were, Thierry. In every way that matters, you were gone. When my brother Raymond and his wife were here last week –"

"I did not know –" He winced. "Foolish of me. How could I have known?"

"It brought home to me that this – what's between us – isn't real. It's not – lasting."

"I never said –"

"I know. How could you? But I realised how difficult it would have been if we were together. You couldn't have met them. You're not part of my life, nor I of yours, in any way that matters."

"How can you say that? After what we have been to each other?"

"And what *have* we been to each other, Thierry?" she asked sharply. "A fling? A bit of excitement, something to pass the time pleasurably –"

"More than that, Olivia. Believe me, much more than that."

"But not enough. I need more, or nothing at all."

"I can offer no more, Olivia," he said quietly.

"I know, Thierry. And that's why it must be over."

The words almost stuck in her throat. There were tears in her eyes.

Seeing them, he reached for her hand again.

"I did not mean this to happen. I cannot bear to see you sad, and that it is my fault."

"It's nobody's fault, Thierry. It happened. And for the rest of my life I'll thank God it happened. You opened up the whole world to me, you made me feel cherished, attractive –"

"And so you are. I have told you many times how beautiful you are, Olivia." His smile was wistful. "But you have never believed me, have you?"

"No. No, I suppose not. Because I look in the mirror and that's not what I see. But I see something else now. A woman who is sure of herself, a woman who values herself. I never had that before, Thierry, and it's thanks to you that I do now."

"And so – must it be over?"

"You know it is, Thierry," she said gently. "Your

priorities are with your wife and family – that's how it has to be, and I believe that's how you want it."

It was true. She could see it in his eyes.

"And my priority must be me, and how I feel about myself. For a long time I pretended your wife didn't exist, though I knew she did, and that's how I could love you, and sleep with you. Then I had to stop pretending and it didn't make me particularly proud of myself."

"Nadine does not mind –" He had never said her name before.

"Perhaps not," Olivia interrupted quickly. "And maybe she should, though that's up to her. But I mind, Thierry. I mind very much. Because it was wonderful, it was more than I could ever have imagined – I never loved anyone as I've loved you. But it's wrong, and there's no getting away from that."

"Wrong, how can it be wrong?" he asked. "Something so wonderful –"

"Can still be wrong. And for me it's wrong. I can't speak for anyone else. I came to my senses when Raymond and Dell were here. Because I couldn't have introduced you, even if we'd been together. You'd never have met them –"

"Most certainly I would. Ellie would no doubt have arranged something, a soirée, a concert –"

"Probably. And we'd have met in a group. You'd have been introduced as a friend. Pretence, nothing more –"

"And that matters?" he asked, raising his eyebrows.

"I found it did. I found it mattered very much. I wanted them to see me as I am. I wanted to be, in their eyes, a woman who is loved, who finally –"

"As you are, Olivia. I have never said it, but –"

She touched his hand.

"Don't, Thierry. Not just for the sake of it, not when it's not true –"

"It is true, you must believe that."

She saw from his eyes that it was probably true, at least at that moment.

"Don't make it harder, Thierry. Please. It's hard enough already. I want to say goodbye, and then go."

He looked at her a long time, saying nothing. Then he reached for her hand again and brought it to his lips, his eyes never leaving hers.

"I will never forget you, *chère* Olivia." Then he stood up and walked to the door, not looking back.

A minute or two later she gathered her coat and handbag and made her way to the Métro.

She had done the only thing possible, she knew that. But knowing didn't make it one bit easier.

Chapter Thirty-six

"I feel guilty that I ever introduced you to him," Ellie said.

They were sitting at one of the outside tables in the Rodin garden tearooms. Nearby, groups of people strolled round the gardens in the April sunshine, but at this hour the tearooms weren't busy yet.

"You told me never to feel guilty, remember?" Olivia replied. "And there's absolutely no need."

"He hurt you, Olivia. I should have seen it coming."

Olivia said nothing for a moment as she sat looking into the distance. "So should I." She turned back to look at Ellie. "He never meant to hurt me. It happened, but he didn't mean it. That makes it easier. And I'll always be glad I met him."

"Even though –?" Ellie said.

"Even though he hurt me," Olivia said firmly. "The hurt doesn't matter in the long run, because something more important happened, Ellie. He changed me. He changed the way I look at life and the way I see myself. So don't dream of feeling guilty. I wouldn't have missed being with him for anything."

"And do you miss him now?" Ellie asked. "I guess I thought –" She stopped.

"That I'd be upset."

Ellie nodded. "Well, yes. And angry, probably. Especially at me –"

Olivia laughed. "Ellie! You don't really believe that, do you? The choices were all mine. Nobody forced me to be with him and nobody forced me to end it. And you're right. I thought I'd be far more upset than I am. But instead I feel – liberated. That's the word. It hurt like hell for a week or so after that day in the *bistro*, the day we ended it. But then, gradually, I realised it *had* ended and I put him out of my mind. I've hardly thought of him since. Can you believe that?"

"I'm surprised," Ellie admitted. "But if that's how it is, I'm glad for you. I know you've changed. I've seen it. And I guess I was afraid you'd close down on all that. You know, put men off your agenda completely –"

Olivia laughed again.

"Maybe I have. I don't know. But it doesn't bother me now. That's what he did for me, Ellie. I know I can still love, and be loved. That's enough for the time being. Maybe forever. I don't know. It doesn't matter."

"It's definitely over?"

Olivia didn't hesitate. "Oh, yes. Because I realised something else during that time I didn't see him, while

I waited for him to contact me and he didn't." Her voice was firm, with a determined edge. "I'll never again be second-best to anyone, Ellie. I did that for most of my life, with my mother. The only man who ever put me first finally left because I couldn't put *him* first. She wouldn't allow it and I gave in to keep her happy. But never, never once, did she think of me and *my* happiness."

"There was someone else?" Ellie asked, surprised. "I thought – I'm not sure why, but –"

"Thierry was the first man I was serious about, Ellie. The first man I slept with. You didn't, in Ireland, in those days. Well, certainly I didn't – I can't speak for anyone else. I was very young, barely out of school, Richard was the same age. There was a kind of innocence about us."

"Did you love him?"

"I think so. I wasn't sure then what love was." She laughed quietly. "I'm still not sure. But yes, I think I loved him. I think he loved me."

"What happened?"

"He wanted to travel. It was the end of the sixties, only the sixties hadn't really hit Ireland yet. London was where it was all happening. He wanted to go there and be part of it, and maybe move on across Europe and over to India. He knew someone who had done that. It was all he could talk about. I was scared witless, of course. My mother wouldn't have let me out the door if she knew I was seeing him, let alone talking about India. I hardly even knew where India was. If that's where he was going, he'd have to go without me."

"So, did he go?"

"To India? I never knew. He stayed around for nearly a year, meeting me when I could get away, trying to talk me into sharing his dream. But it was his dream, not mine. Finally he said he had to go, he needed to go, that he'd be back in a year or so. But of course he wasn't. I never knew what happened. I simply never saw him again."

"Do you regret it?" Ellie asked gently.

"I won't let myself regret it. I won't let myself regret anything about my life, for fear of opening the floodgates. I am where I am, and that's enough for me. The one thing I wish –" She stopped, looking into the distance while Ellie waited. "I know I shouldn't let it bother me at all. I'm old enough now to have given up wishing for anything. But I suppose we never do, do we?"

She lapsed into silence again, until finally Ellie said, "What do you wish? Or maybe you don't want to say –"

"A simple thing. It doesn't seem so much to ask. I haven't seen my mother for over six months, Ellie. And of course I've written, but she hasn't replied. She was angry when I left and so was I. I never wanted to see her again. But when Ray and Dell were here I found myself hoping she'd sent some sort of message, anything. Even though I'm a different person and it seems a lifetime since I saw her, she's still my mother. I just wanted something, a word, anything, to say she still cares about me. But there was nothing."

"I don't suppose they just forgot to tell you?"

"They wouldn't do that. It's the first thing they'd have said."

"So she's still angry?"

"Yes. It doesn't surprise me. I'd say she's finding it hard to manage on her own. My brothers are doing what they can, which in Vincent's case is almost nothing. She probably feels she needs me there and that I abandoned her."

"But you didn't –"

"But I did," Olivia said quietly. "And I'd do it all over again, because I've learned now how to value myself. Does that sound harsh? I was dying slowly there, wasting my whole life before you and Thierry gave it back to me. Whatever I might regret, it won't be coming here, or meeting him."

"Well, good for you, Olivia. We only come round once. Better make the most of it!"

Olivia smiled for the first time in the conversation. "I certainly will. Starting now, because my friends are on their way at this very minute."

"Might I get to meet them?"

Olivia laughed. "Meet them? I'm counting on you to arrange all kinds of diversions for them! I'd better go. I'll ring tomorrow, all right?"

She stood up, kissed Ellie's cheek and was smiling as she made her way to the Métro around the corner. Colette and Maeve would be in Paris in less than an hour.

* * *

The French countryside looked almost exotic in the warm April sunshine, with red-roofed farmhouses and quaint little villages dotted everywhere along the route, just visible from the motorway as they sped towards Paris.

Paris itself was everything they had imagined. Chaotic traffic driving on the wrong side of the road, tall grey buildings, impressively ancient, lining the wide Seine – and then, when they least expected it, that first, thrilling sight of the Eiffel Tower.

Maeve had thought she mightn't get here at all, had hesitated at the sight of Fergus's pale, worried little face as she stood in the hallway saying goodbye.

"You'll be back, won't you, Mam?" he'd asked, and even Senan was looking a bit anxious. She'd nearly unpacked the bags there and then, thinking, *damn Larry, damn him*. It wasn't so long since the boys wouldn't let her out of their sight for a single minute for fear that she, too, might leave.

And then Maura was urging her to go and Noeleen was beeping outside and Orla was assuring her that of course they'd manage the crèche on their own, how hard could it be with just six little kids? And Maeve had laughed, saying, "Harder than you think!" and had given them all a quick hug and sped down the path to Noeleen's car before she could change her mind.

The bus dropped them near the centre and within minutes they were on their way to Olivia's by taxi.

"Are we mad?" Colette asked. "I mean, what if it's awful, all tense and polite and no-one knowing what to say?"

"It won't be that bad," Maeve said. "She *did* invite us to stay. She obviously wants us there. And if it's awful we'll make our excuses and go and find a cheap hotel. But it'll be fine."

"I hope," Colette said, not sounding convinced. "I know Suzanne said Olive's completely different now –"

"You mean Olivia!"

"God, I'll never remember to call her that. And she might have changed her name but she can't be *that* different, can she? No-one changes that much!"

"Look who's talking!" Maeve laughed. "Will you relax. Enjoy yourself – we'll never get this chance again!"

"Maybe you're right," Colette said after a minute. "All we have to do is remember to call her Olivia and we'll be fine!"

The taxi pulled in to the kerb and she paid the fare while Maeve got out with the bags and stood staring up at the tall, grey building as if she could tell from the facade which was Olivia's apartment.

"Olivia, Olivia," Maeve practised, grinning at Colette as they pushed the buzzer on the intercom and waited for Olivia to appear.

And then she was standing there and they could see that Suzanne had been right. The woman who was smiling warmly at them, taking their hands in hers, bore only a passing resemblance to the Miss Grace they had known a bare seven months ago.

She brought them to the lift and up to the apartment which was amazing, and yet no surprise at all. It was large and bright and furnished with simple elegance. It was, in fact, just what they might have imagined.

The real surprise was Olivia herself.

Their first impression lasted as she showed them their room, asked about their journey, told them to make themselves entirely at home. She was relaxed, friendly and welcoming, and they began to relax too, stealing a glance at each other as she went to make coffee.

Maeve raised an eyebrow and Colette nodded slightly. Without needing to discuss it they knew they'd be fine here.

"So," Olivia said, coming back in with the coffee and setting it down on the little table in front of them, "was it difficult to arrange everything so you could get away?"

"Easier than I thought," Maeve said, "if I can just get over the guilt! I've left my sisters looking after my kids and the crèche *and* the home back-up service – *Jugglers* is right!"

"*Jugglers?*" Olivia asked, amused. She handed them coffee, passed the milk and sugar.

"The name of the crèche," Maeve explained. "For women who spend their lives trying to juggle everything!"

"And the – what did you say, home back-up service?"

"An idea we had – we still don't know if it'll work,"

Maeve said. "It's a bit of everything, really – we'll do the cleaning or the shopping, or stay in someone's house if they're expecting a delivery –"

"I love the 'we'," Olivia laughed. "Aren't you getting off a bit lightly?"

"I'll make up for it when I get home. And the timing wasn't *too* bad – it's just beginning to get off the ground so they should manage . . ."

She looked a bit concerned, though, and Colette jumped in to reassure her.

"Of course they'll manage. Better than my lot, anyway! I've left enough food in the freezer and clean clothes in their wardrobes to last a month, let alone a week, and they'll still be complaining when I get home!"

"Does it worry you?" Olivia asked.

"Not a bit!" Colette laughed. "Emer's staying with my sister Therese, and as for the others, it's high time they learned to look after themselves and stop seeing me as a skivvy."

"I think that happened when you went to the health farm, Colette!" Maeve said.

"Well, they can see this as a refresher course."

They were still laughing as they finished their coffee and began making plans.

"Seven days seems short," Olivia said. "But I promise we'll try to pack everything in. What would you like to do?"

"Go to the top of the Eiffel Tower," Maeve said

immediately. "And a boat-ride on the Seine – and we have to see the Sacré-Coeur –"

"I might not be able to go everywhere with you." Olivia looked guarded for a moment. "I've one or two things to do this week, though I'm free for most of it. But no matter, I'll give you a map and you'll find your way easily. What about you, Colette? Is there anything in particular you want to do?"

"Go shopping!" Colette said without hesitation. "Now that I'm finally the size I was always meant to be, I'm dying to see these Paris fashions everyone talks about. I'd love to go to a fashion show."

"You're kidding!" Maeve said.

"I'm deadly serious!" Colette answered. "But I don't mind going on my own –"

"We'll all go, for the *craic*," Maeve said. "Have you ever been to one, Olive – Olivia?"

"Actually, no, though it's something I wouldn't mind doing. I believe they hold them in Galeries Lafayette on Tuesdays, so we could go then. That gives us a few days for sightseeing first."

* * *

They were almost too exhausted by Tuesday to even think of shopping, but they had the satisfying sense of having "seen Paris" and at least, as Olivia reassured them, they wouldn't have to move for the duration of the fashion show once they actually got there.

It was a disappointment. It took a while for Colette to

admit it but she felt intimidated by the vast, exclusive department store, by the very thin and very beautiful models, and most of all by the clothes, which didn't look remotely like anything she'd ever dream of wearing. The only part of the whole experience that gave her any satisfaction were the very comfortable chairs which she was reluctant to give up, in spite of the flashing strobes and pounding music that she found hard to take after a while.

She'd like the clothes just as much – or, more to the point, just as little – she decided, if the models paraded in them under fluorescent lights with the tapping of their high heels as the only accompaniment.

One look at Maeve and Olivia told her she wasn't alone in her suffering.

"Let's go," she hissed at Maeve, who turned to whisper to Olivia, and the three of them left as quietly as possible, slipping round the backs of the gilt chairs, trying to ignore the disapproving looks from all around.

"Not my scene at all!" Colette said, with a sigh of relief as they left the building. "And did you see that little wisp of a purple and silver thing? You'd catch your death in that!"

Olivia laughed. "You sound exactly like my mother – only it's decency she'd worry about, not pneumonia!"

"One way or the other, I can't imagine anyone paying good money for stuff like that!"

"So what kind of stuff did you have in mind?" Maeve asked. "I kind of fancied the little purple and silver thing myself, whatever it was –"

"And you can just see me in it, can't you?"

"God, you're no fun at all, Colette." Maeve laughed. "Wouldn't you love to get it, just to see Martin's face?"

Colette grimaced. "Martin wouldn't even notice it – he'd say I was blocking his view of the telly and ask me to shift myself!"

"Typical!" Maeve said. "I suppose it makes it easier, though. You've only yourself to please."

"Too true. That's going to be my motto from now on. I think I'll have it tattooed on my forehead to keep reminding them!"

"Do you think they still need reminding? From what you said –"

"I know, they're beginning to get the message. Forget the tattoo. I'll settle for a few new outfits, the kind the old me would never have bought."

"Do you have anything in particular in mind?" Olivia asked.

"Haven't a clue! Something classy – I haven't a notion what, though. The kind of stuff you get in Arnott's, I suppose. Only a sort of Paris Arnott's."

"Au Printemps," Olivia said decisively. "Just beside us, there. I think you'll like it."

They loved it. Shopping heaven. Colette thought she could probably spend the rest of her life right there and die happy.

"Coffee first," Olivia said, dragging them away from vast displays of scarves and cosmetics.

Not bad, Colette thought as she replaced a long,

shimmering deep-blue scarf on its stand. *550 francs, that's only about £60, I think . . .*

She was laughing as she followed Olivia and Maeve to the escalators.

"So what's funny?" Maeve asked.

"I can't believe I could think £60 is cheap for a scarf."

"That's what money does for you," Maeve said lightly as they stepped off one elevator and on to another which brought them to the *Terrasse* restaurant on the top floor.

God, Colette thought as they went outside to find a seat while Olivia got the coffee. *Me and my big mouth. I'll have to be a bit more careful what I say.*

The view from the roof was great, taking in the Eiffel Tower in the near distance and the hill of Montmartre with the Moulin Rouge clearly visible among the higgledy-piggle of buildings climbing up towards Sacré-Coeur.

Colette gave a quick glance to check that Olivia was still queuing for the coffee.

"Maeve," she began quickly, "I'd like to buy you something –"

"Not all that again," Maeve said, rolling her eyes. But at least she looked amused instead of cross, so Colette took courage and continued.

"Nothing much, a souvenir," she said. "Something for £100, or maybe £200. It'll be no bother to you to buy me something in return once the crèche is up and running, if it makes you feel any better."

It was a done deal by the time Olivia arrived with the coffee.

"Well, you two look very cheerful! This place obviously suits you."

"Nothing like it obviously suits you," Maeve said, grinning as she took the coffee. "I can't believe you're the same person, Olivia. Really, I can't!"

"That's because I'm not," Olivia said. She paused, taking a sip of coffee. "Most of the time I don't recognise myself. Not the old me, anyway. Even when I look in the mirror it's like looking at someone else."

"And is that not a bit – well, frightening?" Colette asked.

"Not at all. It's completely exhilarating. Imagine being able to re-invent yourself and become the person you always wanted to be. That's what I feel I'm doing."

"And it's what we'll do with Colette once we finish the coffee," Maeve said. "I can't wait to get her back down to those make-up counters. We'll get her done up in Estée Lauder stuff, or Nina Ricci –"

"Steady on!" Colette said, looking a bit worried. "I'm not sure I'm ready for that yet –"

"No time like now," Maeve said. "And at worst you can scrub it all off again."

"I suppose . . ." Colette said, still not looking convinced.

"Colette, you've changed everything else about how you look. Your hair is a different colour and – now, don't mind my saying this, but you've lost a fair amount of weight, haven't you?" Olivia said. "So why not go the last half-mile and see how good you can really look? As Maeve said, you can always take it all off again – they'll probably be happy to sell you something very expensive that will do just that!"

"I'll give it a try," Colette said finally.

They almost didn't get there because first they had to pass through the kitchen and soft furnishing departments, and Maeve had to forcibly drag Colette away from at least half a dozen displays of things she fell in love with.

"You're right," she conceded finally. "I've no idea what to do with half these things, much less where to put them. I'd need a whole new kitchen . . ."

"Nothing to stop you buying a whole new house and stocking it from here," Maeve said, amused. "But first the make-up."

It took twenty-five minutes and looked, Colette had to agree, stunning. She felt amazing. Nothing at all like herself. As if she could take on the whole world and win. Even better, she could probably face those snooty sales assistants in the fashion department . . .

A whole new wardrobe was exactly what she needed to go with her whole new look. And when she got home, a whole new kitchen.

Maybe even a whole new house.

She stood up, delighted, hardly able to drag her eyes from the mirror, and bought a huge amount of make-up before leading the way to the nearest fashion area of the shop.

On route she passed through the men's department and stopped, entranced by the clothes – Yves St Laurent, Pierre Cardin, other names she didn't recognise. Gorgeous, wonderful clothes that were a world away from the stuff Martin usually wore.

For a moment she was tempted to buy him something, but only for a moment.

Forget it, she told herself. *For that kind of stuff, what I'd need is a whole new man.*

She couldn't know it, of course, but she was just about to meet him.

Chapter Thirty-seven

The little antique shop was easy to find. Olivia had marked it on the Métro map for them, telephoning first to make sure they still had the St Nicholas statuette.

"He's expecting you," she told Maeve when she came off the phone. "Your sister phoned again, apparently. I've no idea what his prices are like but it may be possible to haggle –"

"With my French?" Maeve laughed. "Forget it. He can charge whatever he likes, and besides, Orla's already paid a deposit. A thousand francs is what they agreed on."

Olivia looked doubtful. "I hope it's a fair price. Perhaps I can change my arrangements and come with you –" They were going on to Sacré-Coeur afterwards, and she had already explained that she wouldn't be free to go with them. She had managed to avoid bumping into Thierry so far and she had no wish to do so now.

"We'll be fine," Maeve said. "It'll be an experience – and I can always walk away if I have to. But if it's the same as the one I had, it should be well worth that."

"And you know how to find your way to Montmartre, and then to the *Galerie Julian*?"

They'd all been invited to an art exhibition which was being hosted that evening by a friend of Ellie's.

"We'll find it," Colette said. "We'll be back here first to change, though. We'll need a shower after traipsing round Paris all day – and there's no way I'm going to a posh do dressed like this!" she added, indicating her jeans and walking shoes.

"It won't be that posh," Olivia said.

"But it's probably the only chance I'll ever get to wear that cream silk dress," Colette said. "I can't exactly see myself doing the shopping or the school run in it, so if it's ever to get an airing it'll have to be tonight!"

* * *

"Here goes," Maeve said, taking a deep breath as they opening the door of *Bertholier et fils – Antiquités.* She approached the young man behind the counter – the *fils*, she presumed – and began, in faltering French, to explain her purpose.

He smiled and answered in excellent English.

"We have been keeping it safe for you, *madame*. A moment, please, and I will get it."

He went into the back of the shop while Maeve waited at the counter. Colette began looking around, moving to the far end of the counter which held several display cases full of jewellery.

There were some really gorgeous rings and bracelets there, as well as a dozen or so expensive-looking gold chains. There was one she loved, an intricate design in red, yellow and white gold. She'd never in her life had anything like that and had always thought of gold jewellery – apart from her wedding ring and simple little engagement ring – as an indulgence.

Well, maybe now was the time to indulge herself, she decided. It would set the silk dress off beautifully.

"Here it is, *madame*," the assistant said to Maeve as he returned, cradling the statuette carefully in his hands. "Shall I wrap it for you – or do you wish to examine it first?"

"I'll have a look at it," Maeve said, taking it from him.

It looked almost exactly the same, and yet of course it was completely different. It was just an ordinary little statuette, she thought, disappointed, wondering what else she had expected. *Memories*, she realised. The other one, *my* one, was part of Christmas as long as I can remember. My mother and grandmother held it, minded it, loved it. This one has someone else's memories.

"It is not what you are looking for?" the young man asked, watching her expression. "The young lady was so certain, so pleased when she discovered it in the window. But it does not matter, *madame*, I will make you a refund –"

"Not the same?" Colette asked sympathetically, coming back to her.

Maeve set the statuette back on the counter, feeling the prickle of tears. "It *looks* the same."

Colette nodded, understanding. "Will you take it anyway?"

"I'll have to. I wouldn't want to upset Orla. But –"

Colette waited.

"It's just not the same," Maeve said, biting her lip. "My mother gave me the other one."

"Well, your daughter gave you this one," Colette said. "And you can give it back to her when the time comes."

Maeve laughed, immediately feeling better. "Let's hope she has a long wait!"

She handed the statuette to the young man, nodded, and he began wrapping it for her.

"Now, have a look at the jewellery with me," Colette said. "Tell me what you think of this chain."

She led Maeve to the display case and indicated the one she had in mind.

"God, it's gorgeous!" Maeve said. "How much does it –" She laughed. "I know, it doesn't matter a damn what it costs. I'm just curious."

"I can't really see," Colette said. "The tag's tiny – but I think there's a good few zeros."

"Try it on, anyway," Maeve suggested.

The young man moved along the counter towards them. "You wish to see something?" he asked, looking at each of them in turn.

"That gold chain, there," Colette said.

"Ah, an excellent choice, *madame*," he said, taking a cluster of keys from his belt and opening the display case to remove the chain. He unfolded a square of black velvet onto the counter beside the case and placed the chain on it, smoothing it deftly with his fingertips to show it to best advantage.

"You wish to try it on, *madame*?" he asked, handing it to her when she nodded, watching for a few moments as she, and then Maeve, fiddled unsuccessfully with the catch.

"May I?" he asked, stepping round the counter. It took him just a second or two to fasten the chain. "There is a little trick to it," he said smiling, as he moved back inside the counter. "It is not complicated – I will show you."

Colette didn't answer. She was examining her reflection in the little mirror on the counter, still distracted by the unfamiliar sensation of his fingers brushing her neck, shocked by her reaction. He surely hadn't even been aware he had touched her, and yet she felt as conscious of it as if it had been a caress.

Grow up, she told herself. *You've been married too long.*

She'd laugh about this with Maeve later. Or maybe she wouldn't. She'd feel too stupid admitting that she found a simple, impersonal touch exciting.

She concentrated on the chain, wondering if it suited her and if she'd ever get a chance to wear it. She'd wear it tonight, of course, but after that –

After that it didn't matter a damn, she decided. She was in Paris, where she'd always wanted to be, so just for these few days she'd do what she wanted and be who she wanted. And it didn't matter what the chain cost – she wanted it so she'd buy it. It would be worth it, even if she never wore it again.

Still exhilarated from the assistant's fleeting touch and hardly able to meet his eyes, she said "Thank you. I'll take it."

He bowed slightly. "Do you wish me to wrap it, *madame*? Or you would perhaps prefer to wear it?"

She was undecided for a moment. She wanted to experience that brief touch again, but –

"I'll leave it on," she said. "How much does it cost?"

He told her and she handed over her credit card, telling herself it was okay that it cost a fortune. She *had* a fortune. And anyway it was so beautiful she wouldn't care if she never bought anything else for the rest of her life.

Still trying to persuade herself that of *course* she didn't feel guilty about the cost, she turned to Maeve.

"Would you like something?" she asked. "You promised you'd let me, remember?"

"You got me the dress, Colette."

"But it was only –"

"It's perfect," Maeve said firmly, just as the assistant returned with the credit-card slip for Colette's signature, and that ended the discussion.

"A pleasure, *mesdames*," he said as they thanked him. "Another time, perhaps."

"He's a fine thing, isn't he?" Maeve said as they left the shop. "What our daughters would call a –"

"Stop!" Colette said, laughing. "I don't think I want to know!"

Maeve laughed with her. "You're right. It's probably better not to worry too much about what our daughters discuss!"

"I'm more worried about what they might get up to –"

"Don't even think about it!" Maeve said. "Not for these few days anyway."

They turned left at the corner and went down the steps into the Métro station.

"We need the *Porte de la Chapelle* direction," Maeve said. "That'll get us to Sacré-Coeur."

"I'll take your word for it."

Maeve had worked out the Métro system in about five minutes flat. Colette couldn't get her head round it at all.

They spent the next few hours wondering happily round Montmartre before going for something to eat and deciding to make their way back early to the apartment.

"I'm exhausted," Colette said. "I'll never be able for tonight."

"You'll be fine," Maeve laughed.

And she was.

"Wish I could look like that," Maeve said when Colette came out of the bedroom, all dressed up, just in time to leave for the art exhibition.

"I think we all look wonderful," Olivia said, looking at them both and glancing at herself in the living-room mirror. "Do you think Mr Malone would recognise us now?"

"Don't remind me!" Maeve said. "I'm back to work on Monday."

"But not for long?" Olivia asked.

"Not if the crèche works out," Maeve said. "We'll see. But forget about that now. Just tell me what you're supposed to do at an art exhibition!"

"Enjoy yourself!" Olivia answered. "Good," she added as the buzzer sounded. "Our taxi."

Galerie Julian was a modern, bright building behind an elegant old facade, and there were already dozens of people there, most of them dressed up, a few very conspicuously dressed down. A bit daunting, Colette thought. There was a buzz of conversation, as if they all knew each other, and for a moment she panicked, wondering what she could find to say about the paintings when she really hadn't a clue about art.

She glanced along the walls as she followed Olivia in search of Ellie. Thank God, she thought. At least I can recognise what's in them. It's not this abstract stuff – I'll surely be able to say *something* if anyone asks me –

But of course no-one would ask her. They wouldn't know a soul except Ellie and they had met her only once, at dinner two nights ago. But she'd been warm and friendly, and in a place like this it would be a relief to see a familiar face.

She was surrounded by a little group of people when they found her, and gave them a great welcome, introducing them round so quickly that Colette lost half the names. But one she heard – Alix Bertholier, the artist.

He didn't fit her image of an artist. He wore a suit, for one thing, and his hair and beard were neatly trimmed. He smiled and nodded at the introduction, then went back to speaking to the woman beside him.

"Scrubs up well, obviously," Maeve whispered. "He looks like a banker or something."

"I thought he looked like that guy in the jeweller's today," Colette said.

No surprise. She'd seen about ten people that afternoon who reminded her of the young man in the jeweller's.

"Maybe," Maeve said. "Same name. But half the people in Paris are probably called Bertholier, like –"

"Jean-Philippe!"

The artist looked animated now as he left the little circle of people to greet someone just arriving. The man from the jeweller's. It really *was* him this time, Colette realised, watching as the artist embraced him, talking rapidly, laughing as he drew him back towards the group.

"You're blushing," Maeve whispered, grinning.

"It's the heat," Colette answered, shifting her gaze slowly, too casually, towards the nearest painting.

Alix began performing introductions in French, then Ellie took over, translating.

"Jean-Philippe, Alix's brother," she explained.

"We have met already," Jean-Philippe said, smiling

as he took Colette's hand. "This morning, *madame*, you remember?"

"It's Colette."

"Colette," he repeated. He was still holding her hand. She was every bit as conscious of him as she had been earlier.

"And Maeve," Ellie added.

"Maeve," he said, turning to her, letting go of Colette's hand to take hers for a moment.

"The name Colette I know, but Maeve I have not heard."

"She was a warrior queen in ancient Ireland."

"*Ah, bon!*" He had a wicked grin that lit up his whole face. "So I should beware, no?"

"Suit yourself!" Maeve said, laughing.

He looked puzzled. "I do not —"

Alix interrupted, apologising, saying he wanted to introduce him to Julian, the gallery owner.

"I've been to a few of these before," Olivia said as Alix led Jean-Philippe away. "Ellie knows Julian well. He invites her to everything. He'll make a little speech now, then Alix will probably say a few words, and after that we're free to start buying the paintings."

"Do we have to?" Colette asked, a bit alarmed. There was nothing here that looked remotely as if it might suit her house. *I can always get a new house*, she thought, panicking slightly as Ellie, who had just turned to talk to them, hastened to reassure her.

"I've been to dozens of these, and I've only got one

410

little oil painting. I tell Julian I don't want the trouble of shipping them home. Really, I don't want the trouble of going without food to pay for them!"

She stopped a passing waiter and handed them each a glass of champagne from his tray. "Now, relax, enjoy. If you want to buy, buy. If not, there's absolutely no pressure."

The speeches began then – short, funny, and totally incomprehensible to Maeve and Colette. They smiled and nodded, laughing when everyone else did, feeling part of it all, content that Olivia would translate in a few minutes.

It didn't matter at all what was being said, of course. The important thing was that they were here in Paris, drinking champagne at an art exhibition and loving every minute of it.

"Better than my childcare class any night," Maeve said quietly. "That's what I'd be doing tonight if I was at home."

Colette held back a laugh. "You could be giving those things by now," she whispered.

"I probably could – but I need the bit of paper if I'm to get the go-ahead for the crèche."

There was a round of applause which they took to mean the end of the speeches and the start of the buying.

"We'll have a look, anyway," Colette said, as people started to move towards the walls to examine the paintings.

They were all very nice, she decided, but nothing

she couldn't live without. Not at those prices, anyway.

And then she saw it.

A small painting in a simple frame, showing a grey house with a sloping roof, pots of red geraniums in the front courtyard and, just at the edge of the painting, a sports car. A red sports car.

She caught her breath, turned to show it to Maeve, and found instead that it was Jean-Philippe who was standing beside her.

"You like it?" he asked. Then he laughed. "It is okay, Colette. You can like it without having to buy it."

"It's the car that caught my eye."

He smiled. "It is my car. My parents' house – and my car."

"You have a red sports car?" she asked.

He caught her tone. "It is so unusual?"

"No. Well, I suppose not. It's just –"

She stopped. How could she explain to this man, ten years or so younger than her, that she'd always wanted to drive through Paris in a sports car, just because of how that song made her feel? And that some part of her secretly hoped it might somehow happen while she was here? Ridiculous.

And yet –

"You like sports cars, Colette?"

"I've never been in one."

She was almost holding her breath. There was something about the way he was asking, the way he was looking at her . . .

"Ah. And what else have you never done?" he asked, raising an eyebrow.

"Lots of things. Loads. But most of them I don't want to do."

"So, what is it you *want* to do?"

"I'd love to drive round Paris in a sports car," she admitted.

"Then later, I will take you for a drive in a sports car. If that is what you would really like to do."

She couldn't. This was mad. What would Martin –?

She answered quickly, to stop herself thinking. This was Paris. She could say what she pleased, do as she pleased and it wouldn't matter. It wasn't her real life.

"It's what I'd really like. More than anything. But I can't ask you –"

He waited.

"Are you sure? I mean, you don't have to . . ." was all she could think of saying.

"I am certain." He smiled at her, went back to join his brother and Colette turned to find Maeve standing beside her.

"Maeve –"

"I heard."

"Am I mad?"

"You're mad. Will you go?"

"Try and stop me!"

* * *

It was warm enough to have the top down. She relaxed,

413

refusing to let herself think of the speed he was doing as they tore along the bank of the Seine and then did some manoeuvres that brought them, finally, to a wide street she thought she recognised.

"*Les Champs Élysées,*" he said, turning to smile at her. "This is what you wanted?"

"This is exactly what I wanted," she said.

And it was. The air was warm. The streets were crowded. They were driving slowly enough now to watch the people sitting outside cafes along the *Champs Élysées*.

Fields of Heaven, Olivia had said the name meant. And that's how it felt. Just for these few minutes she was doing exactly what she wanted. It was a rare, wonderful feeling of freedom – and the young man beside her added to the exhilaration of it.

The music on the CD player – French, unfamiliar, very romantic, gave way to Celine Dion and Colette closed her eyes, living in the moment, letting her mind drift.

"You are happy, Colette?" he asked softly.

"Mmm," she answered just as softly. She opened her eyes. "Oh, yes."

He found her attractive. She knew he did. It was there in the way he looked at her, the way he touched her arm briefly as she sat into the car. Why else would he be doing this, if he didn't find her attractive?

They reached the end of the Avenue, made their way back along the Seine.

"I am sorry it has been short," he said as they neared the gallery. "But Alix has waited a long time for this exhibition and worked hard. I must be there."

They pulled into a parking space just outside the gallery.

"We are fortunate," he said smiling, then quickly hopped out and opened her door for her.

"Jean-Philippe," she began. He took her hand as she got out, and at his touch her breath caught for a moment. "It was . . ." She paused, at a loss for words. He was still holding her hand and she wanted to stay like this with him in the warm Paris night, prolong the moment, say nothing that would end this conversation.

"It was . . ." she began again.

"Too short?" he suggested, smiling at her. "Tomorrow night, if you would like, we will go for a longer drive. And dinner, perhaps?"

"I can't." She thought she saw disappointment in his eyes.

Stop kidding yourself, Colette. He's half your age. Well, young, anyway. And you're married.

"I'm having dinner tomorrow with Maeve and Olivia, for my birthday."

"Ah." He smiled. "Your birthday is tomorrow?"

"Saturday. An early celebration."

"Then Friday, perhaps, another celebration? If you want?"

Oh, yes, she wanted. She definitely wanted. And it was only dinner – where was the harm?

"I'd like that," she said. Quickly she gave him the address, hoping Olivia wouldn't mind, and they arranged a time.

The first thing she noticed when they went back inside was that the little painting was gone, obviously sold.

It didn't matter, though she had been half-thinking of buying it.

All that mattered was that she was seeing him again on Friday night.

* * *

They went by Métro to the restaurant because it was only a few stops away.

"It's one of the things I'll miss most about Paris," Maeve said. "Dublin Bus will never be the same!"

"You'll have the LUAS shortly, won't you?" Olivia said. "A light rail system will make a huge difference to Dublin. And are they still talking about an underground?"

"That's all they're doing, talking," Maeve said. She laughed. "And it's adding insult to injury that they're calling the light rail LUAS – it means speed in Irish, doesn't it? Speed, how are you! They should have looked up the Irish for digging the whole place up because that's exactly what they're doing. You wouldn't recognise it now!"

"Will you ever come back?" Colette asked Olivia.

"I don't think so," Olivia said. "I love Paris, though I'm not sure how I'll feel when Ellie leaves in June. I'll probably stay here, I feel almost part of it now. I certainly won't go back to Dublin to live."

"But maybe for a visit?" Maeve suggested.

"We have a date for June. You haven't forgotten?" Olivia asked, smiling. "Lunch in Peacock Alley on the 14th."

"You're coming for our lunch?" Maeve asked, delighted.

"I certainly intend to," Olivia said. "It will be a chance to see my family."

Colette was debating whether to ask about Olivia's family – she had very delicately side-stepped all previous mention of them – when a man with an accordion boarded the train and began playing, and the opportunity was lost.

The man was middle-aged, moustached, wearing a black suit over a white collarless shirt.

"*Excusez-moi de vous déranger,*" he said, before launching into something fast, complicated and very French.

Most of the passengers avoided his eyes as he finished and withdrew a little cloth sack from his pocket, holding it out as he made his way through the carriage.

The three of them dropped some coins into the little bag, then Maeve turned to Colette. "I wouldn't have missed this for anything," she said.

"The music?" Colette asked, amused.

"Paris. The whole thing."

"I'm very glad we came," Colette said.

"And so am I," Olivia added. "We'd better make the most of what's left. I thought that tomorrow night we might –"

"I've something arranged," Colette said, quickly, watching as the other two exchanged a quick look.

"Anything you want to tell us about?" Maeve asked, raising an eyebrow.

"Just dinner."

"I see."

"Maeve, it's just –"

"I know," Maeve said, smiling. "Just dinner."

Olivia very carefully said nothing.

They reached the restaurant a few minutes later, had a leisurely dinner and then, over coffee, Maeve produced a package from the big shoulder bag she was carrying.

"From both of us," she said. "A kind of thankyou and happy birthday and souvenir of Paris all in one."

Colette opened the wrapping to reveal Alix Bertholier's painting of the grey house with the red sports car outside it. She looked from it to the two of them.

"You shouldn't –"

"Don't say we shouldn't have, because I won't be able to pay this month's ESB bill, and Olivia had to mortgage the apartment. So you might as well enjoy it," Maeve laughed.

"Oh, thanks. Great," Colette said. "You can imagine how good *that* makes me feel. But seriously –"

"Seriously, we thought you'd like it," Olivia said.

"Do you? Because if not, Julian said we could return it."

"I love it," Colette said.

And she did. But nowhere near as much as she had loved being with Jean-Philippe last night.

* * *

It was the most romantic thing she had done in her life.

She hardly noticed what she was eating as the Bateau-mouche cruised slowly down the Seine towards Notre Dame. Jean-Philippe was excellent company – attentive, and with a host of anecdotes about the pieces he bought for the shop and the people to whom he sold them.

But mostly his focus was on her and she found herself responding to his subtle flattery as they left their table and went up on deck to watch Notre Dame come into view.

This evening it was chilly and she could feel the warmth of him beside her as they stood by the rails.

She moved away slightly, trying to stifle her guilt. Right now Martin was at home, trying to cope with cooking and washing –

My eye, she told herself. I bet they're eating at his mother's and sending everything to the launderette. Forget about Martin and enjoy this – it'll never happen again.

And she didn't move away this time when Jean-Philippe put his arm lightly round her shoulder.

It felt strange, exhilarating, scary. She tried to relax, tried to slow down her breathing and concentrate on what he was saying but it was impossible.

Relax, Colette, she told herself. *Enjoy it for what it is, a friendly gesture, that's all.*

And then he drew her nearer and all thoughts of relaxing vanished as his warm breath lingered on her cheek. They stood like that for several minutes, talking quietly, heads close together while her heart raced and her senses danced in awareness of him.

The boat docked and he took her hand to lead her back up the steps to the quays.

Don't let go, she wanted to say as he stopped by the river wall, still holding her hand.

"Would you like to walk for a short while?" he asked. "You are not too cold?"

"No, I'm all right," she said. "I'd love to."

They walked on past his car and he led her towards a wide bridge filled with people, mainly young, all walking slowly, or sitting around to chat.

A young man was playing a guitar while several of his friends sat listening, and over to one side a group of people were actually having a picnic, with everything spread on a rug at their feet while they sat talking on two of the metal benches.

He laughed quietly, indicating them. "Too cold for me!" he said. "Many people do that on this bridge, it is a gathering-point. But not usually so early in the year – or so late at night!"

They reached the far side of the bridge, waited for a break in traffic to cross the road, then walked under an arch on the far side and Colette recognised where they were – the broad courtyard of the Louvre, with the giant glass pyramid at its centre.

It looked impressive and strange as it reflected the light of the full moon.

"You like it?" he asked.

"I'm not sure," she answered. "I think so."

"And do you like Paris?"

She smiled. "I *love* Paris."

"And tomorrow you return home."

She nodded.

"So we must make tonight special for you."

"Jean-Philippe –"

"Yes, Colette?"

He stopped, turning to face her and taking her other hand as well. They were very close, their bodies almost touching now. She could feel his warm breath on her face, smell the unfamiliar, tantalising scent of his aftershave.

"Why are you doing this?"

"Doing what?" he asked softly.

"You know, dinner, going for a drive – you must have dozens of other things to do –"

"But this is what I want to do," he said simply.

"You don't have a girlfriend?"

He shrugged, still holding her hands in both of his. "A few. And you, you have a husband, no? But it does not matter. Just for tonight, it does not matter."

True, she told herself. *It doesn't matter. We're not doing anything.*

"I live not very far from here," he said quietly. "Maybe you would like to come back for coffee?"

She caught her breath. It wasn't only coffee on offer. If she knew anything, she knew that.

He sensed her hesitation.

"Only if you want," he said. "We will do only what you want, nothing more. You have my word."

She laughed a little unsteadily.

"I'm not sure what I want," she said. "But I know I should go home."

"Home is tomorrow, no? For tonight, you are in Paris."

The moon went behind a cloud, plunging the courtyard into darkness, and he heard her intake of breath, tightened his grip reassuringly. "Do not be afraid, Colette. Truly, there is nothing to fear."

Did he only mean the darkness?

"I'm not afraid."

"Good. Because you are free to choose, Colette. And life is short, no?"

He moved slightly and almost before she knew it they were kissing and it was entirely new to her, a wave of sensations that took her by surprise.

She had never in her life kissed anyone but Martin and the few guys she had known before she met him.

And she had never in her life been kissed like this, or even imagined being kissed like this.

You are free to choose, Jean-Philippe had said.

It's true, she thought as they paused for breath. The moon came out again, lighting up the deserted courtyard, and she could see his face clearly, hear his breath coming as quickly as hers.

She reached her hand up to touch his cheek, saying, "Jean-Philippe," and she chose.

* * *

"Nothing happened," she said to Maeve and Olivia, seeing their expressions as she walked through the door, her face still flushed. But that wasn't quite true. Something *had* happened.

Something that changed everything.

Chapter Thirty-eight

"I feel different," she said to Maeve. "I'm not the same person who went to Paris."

The plane had just started its descent and they were peering though the window, straining to catch their first glimpse of Dublin.

"Oh?" Maeve said cautiously.

"Yes. I can't explain it, but –"

"Colette, you didn't fall for him, did you? Don't –"

"God, no, nothing like that."

"You didn't –" Maeve left the question hanging in the air between them.

"What do you think?" Colette said, with a slight smile.

"You didn't!"

"Are you telling me or asking me?" This time the smile was wider.

"I don't know," Maeve said. Colette was different all right and she wasn't sure what to make of it.

"I know. Isn't it great?"

"Great? What's –"

"You never would have asked me that kind of thing before."

"There was never any reason to before!"

"Exactly – and that's what's great about it!"

"Colette, are you all right?"

"Great. Wonderful. Never better!"

Maeve sat looking at her, not sure what to say. Colette *seemed* all right, but –

"I still haven't decided how I'll explain it to Martin. I've been giving him a fairly tough time recently. I mean, he needed a bit of shaking up, but –"

"You can't!" Maeve burst out finally.

"Can't what?"

"Can't leave Martin. He's a decent skin, Colette, even if he is too caught up in that family of his. You could do a lot worse than –" She stopped in mid-sentence, perplexed by Colette's laughter.

"Who said anything about leaving Martin?"

"Didn't *you*?"

"No, I did not! Maeve, nothing happened between Jean-Philippe and myself. I mean, I didn't sleep with him, though I'm sure he wanted me to – he asked me back to his place and – well, it doesn't matter, I didn't go. I was awake nearly all night, thinking. But it was Martin I was thinking about."

"What do you mean?" Maeve asked.

"Jean-Philippe said he wasn't putting pressure on

me. I was free to choose. And that's what's so great, that I had a choice. I've made a lot of choices these past few months. I've changed a lot of things. But I realise now that I don't want to change Martin."

"You don't?" Maeve asked, laughing as she remembered the very long list of things about Martin that Colette had said he'd better change, or else . . .

"I want to change things *about* him all right," Colette said. "And I want him to be the way he was years ago, when he used to notice I was around. But I wouldn't want to change him *for* anyone else. I realise that now."

"Not even for a gorgeous twenty-five-year-old Frenchman in a snazzy red sports car?" Maeve teased.

"Not for anyone in the world, even that gorgeous Frenchman!"

"Last night, I was so sure – you looked so *alive*, thrilled with yourself . . ."

"Because Jean-Philippe changed everything for me!" Colette said, laughing. "Imagine! It's years since anyone but Martin even *looked* at me, let alone anything else. But last night I had a choice. The idea that he could find me attractive, at my age, even if it was only for a fling –"

Maeve laughed, interrupting her. "You're hardly over the hill yet! Thirty-eight today, that's still young –"

"But it's years since I *felt* young. Years since I felt anything but married. It was the best birthday present I could get, to have someone interested in me. It made me feel great about myself. But when it came down to it, there was no contest. It's Martin I want."

"Then good for you, Colette. Now all you have to do is tell him and sort things out."

"And live happily ever after?" Colette laughed. "We'll see. I'm still not going to put up with rubbish from anyone. I've changed too much for that. But things can be a lot better than they were. Like the man said, I have a choice. We both do."

* * *

She was supposed to be going home with Maeve and Noeleen but they were waiting for her in the Arrivals Hall, the whole lot of them – Declan and Ciara as well as Martin and Peter. Emer, Ciara explained, was at home with Therese getting a birthday surprise ready for her.

"Some surprise now, you eejit!" Declan said to her, but at least his tone was good-humoured.

They said goodbye to Maeve and Noeleen at the entrance to the car park.

"How was it?" Martin asked as they made their way to their car, the three teenagers ahead of them.

"Grand. And I got to ride in a sports car, just like I wanted."

"Oh?" he said, looking a bit concerned.

"Yes," she said, smiling at him. "But I've decided the family jalopy suits me fine."

The other three had reached the "jalopy" and stood waiting for them.

"Colette." He stopped walking and she stopped too, turning to look at him.

"What's wrong?" she asked.

"Nothing. Just – I've been doing a lot of thinking," he said. "And we need to talk, don't we?"

She nodded. "I've been saying that for months. There's a lot to talk about, Martin. I'm a different person now."

"I know. But different can be okay. Can't it?"

"Well, yes. But I've changed, you know. Even while I was away, I changed – so other things will have to change, too."

"And other people?" He gave a wry laugh. "I'll do my best. I can't promise miracles."

"I don't want miracles," she said. "I just want you."

He stood for a moment, his eyes searching hers. "I love you, Colette. No matter how much you change, I'll still love you. You know that, don't you?" he asked quietly.

"I think I've always known that," she said.

"Good. Come on. Let's go home."

She didn't have to go anywhere. She was home already.

And it felt great.

Chapter Thirty-nine

Everything was going brilliantly for Suzanne.

She had already moved into the house in Ranelagh – her own house, close to Finn's apartment – and the final documentation on the other two houses was ready for signing. In no time at all – she hoped – they'd have them up and running, with people living in them.

And in the meantime Gilly and another friend, Liss, had moved in with her because Val had decided to stay on in Maeve's.

There were no hard feelings, though. Val had just spent the morning in town with Suzanne, gathering ideas for the shop in Harold's Cross.

Now that Suzanne owned the building she couldn't wait to get started on plans for *Designs On You*.

"You wouldn't think of running it, would you?" she asked Val as they examined the shelving the carpenter was putting in. He had just left, promising that another few days should do it. After that they could get down to the serious business of ordering in stock.

"I'd give you a free hand, more or less. You've an eye for this sort of stuff – you had more of a clue than I did this morning!"

Val laughed. "I'm in great demand these days! Maeve is trying to lure me into running her crèche for her. But I have to say I'd prefer this. I'd be my own boss?"

"Sure. And your own secretary, tea-lady, the works. What do you think?"

"If we can work something out, why not? I've been dying to tell Hegarty where to shove his job for the past ten years. This could be my big chance!"

"Don't do anything stupid," Suzanne said quickly. "Let's sort everything out first and make sure you're happy with it."

"Will you listen to who's giving good advice!" Val said. "You sound like my mother. What happened to you?"

"Nothing."

"*Something* did. Go on, Suzanne, you were never sensible in your whole life!"

Suzanne laughed. "Maybe it's time I started."

"It's the money, isn't it?" Val asked. "That's what changed you."

"I don't know," Suzanne said. "I mean, I don't really feel as if I've changed. I always spent a fortune. I'm still spending a fortune. The only difference now is it's my own money I'm spending, not the bank's."

"That's a hell of a difference! And look what you're spending it on, bricks and mortar. Go on, tell me that's not being sensible!"

"Maybe it is. But it's great fun! I've all sorts of plans –"

"And is Himself any part of them – or should I ask?"

Suzanne hesitated. "Himself" might well be part of them – but she couldn't say anything until after she'd seen him tonight.

She smiled. "Don't ask," she told Val. "Just think about running this place, and let me know, okay?"

"Okay," Val agreed. "And, Suzy, thanks. Your money could end up changing *my* life too, if I play my cards right!"

She left and Suzanne lingered for another few minutes, loving the smell of the fresh wood, imagining small items of furniture dotted around the room and the shelves and counter-tops full of wonderful fabrics, cushions, scented oils, kitchen accessories – the possibilities were endless.

What she wanted was to be able to put together a "look" for her customers, people who lacked the time or confidence to plan their own home decor.

It would, as she had told Val, be fun. And might even make money, but that didn't matter too much. The building was in good nick, in a great area, and hadn't cost an arm and a leg to buy. It had cost plenty to renovate, but that was another story. It'll add to the value, she had told herself, and it was probably true.

She couldn't lose.

And Finn, though he teased her about it, was behind her all the way.

"One thing at a time, okay?" he had protested, amused, as she tried to persuade him that *Designs On You* was exactly what the whole of Dublin was waiting for. "Haven't we enough on our hands?"

"But it's all part of the same thing," she had insisted. "You know I loved doing up my own place, and I'll get cracking on the other two when they're in a fit state, but in the meantime I can practise on other people's houses, with *their* money!"

Finn had laughed, thinking that Suzanne was bound to go way over budget and end up making a loss while her customers got a great deal. But, what the hell, it was only money – and so far she'd been really disciplined about her spending. Well, disciplined for *Suzanne*.

"Go for it!" he had told her, and she did.

Now, fingers crossed that Val would go for it too. She could look after the day-to-day business of running it while Suzanne did all the really boring stuff like purchasing trips to Hong Kong and Singapore . . .

And everyone thought she'd changed?

Well, maybe a bit. She locked up the shop, thinking she'd never have believed just six months ago that this is how she'd spend the money. She'd have bet huge amounts that she'd have blown the lot by now on parties and holidays and presents. And she hadn't done badly on those counts – but her investments meant that now she'd be able to go on doing all those things and still be able to afford it. There was no danger – as long as she was a tiny bit careful – of ever running out of money.

And it was all thanks to Finn.

She'd be lost without his enthusiasm and support.

She'd be lost without him.

They had never mentioned marriage again since the day in Powerscourt. They carried on as before, pouring all their energy into the houses, high on the excitement of seeing everything fall into place, carefully avoiding any discussion of anything too personal.

And yet it was there always, like an undercurrent. She saw it in the occasional flicker of hurt in Finn's eyes as he looked at her, in his reluctance to make plans for the future about the houses, holidays, anything.

She was still thinking about him as she went home, showered and dressed for her date with him. Well, not a date, exactly, because they were staying in to cook dinner in his place. And they were practically living together, staying sometimes at her place and sometimes his, so "date" didn't really come into it.

But it would be a special night. Because, finally, she'd come to a decision.

It had taken a while, because she needed to be absolutely certain. She couldn't risk hurting him all over again.

But now she *was* certain. Tonight, she would tell him that she was ready to talk about marriage.

It was Michelle, really, who had set the ball rolling. Up-to-her-eyes-in-kids-Michelle, who had rung last week and said casually, at the very end of the conversation, "Oh, and by the way, we're off to the States for a year. In a camper van."

"You're *what*???" Suzanne had asked. "You can't do that!"

"Just watch us!" Michelle had said. "My sister's taking over the house while we're away – we've upped the mortgage a bit to pay for the trip and Keith's got a year off work –"

"But the kids?"

Michelle had laughed. "They'll love it. And so will we. It's once-in-a-lifetime, Suzy!"

"You're mad!"

"Thanks for the vote of confidence!" Michelle had sounded amused.

"Sorry. Just, I thought once you had kids you had to kind of stay put, you know?"

"Rubbish! They adapt better than we do. There's life after kids, you know. As you might find out sometime, if you let yourself!"

It had changed everything for Suzanne. More, even, than the lottery.

She'd always seen marriage as the end of everything, not the beginning of something.

But maybe it didn't have to be like that.

Her parents had a great relationship. Maybe not what she'd want, a bit too much staying at home and focusing only on her and on each other, but it worked for them.

And marriage worked for her aunts and uncles; it even seemed to be working again for Colette.

There was no reason in the wide world why it shouldn't work for herself and Finn.

They were living on borrowed time, she knew that. She was thirty-two, Finn thirty-five. If he really wanted marriage and children, then the day would inevitably come when they'd have to go their separate ways.

And that was the last thing she wanted.

What she wanted was Finn.

She loved him, no question, and he still loved her in spite of his hurt.

Over the past months they had built something together that was deeper and stronger than any business arrangement. And she'd spend the rest of her life regretting it if she let him walk away just because she thought marriage was the end of everything.

For days she had turned it over and over in her mind.

Michelle and her gang in a camper van.

Finn, married to someone else.

Panic gripped her every time she thought of that.

And then . . .

Finn, married to her.

Finally, it seemed exactly the right thing to do.

Not marriage-and-four-kids. She really couldn't handle that.

But marriage. Herself and Finn. That just might work.

They loved each other. They'd *make* it work.

He opened the door before she even knocked, and his eyes were anxious.

"We need to talk, Suzy," he said abruptly.

"I know," she said, a little startled, as she followed him to the living-room. "I've loads to tell you. Important stuff. You'll never believe –" She stopped as she looked at him properly. "Finn, what's wrong? You look –"

Worried, that's how he looked. In a cold sweat.

"You'd better sit down."

She sat hesitantly on the edge of the sofa and he stayed standing, his face grim.

"There's no easy way to say this," he said quietly. "I wish to God there was. Marguerite just phoned. You remember –"

"Yes," she said quickly, cutting him off. There was a knot of panic in her stomach. He'd seen Marguerite several times last October, before he and Suzanne got back together. He'd told her about it in Thailand. Nothing too serious, old college friends, just a fling that happened to suit them both at the time.

Now Suzanne wondered if he'd told her the full story.

"I didn't know until now," Finn said, as if answering her. "I swear. She phoned just half-an-hour ago, said she couldn't keep it from me any longer."

Suzanne didn't breathe as Finn sat down slowly across from her, his eyes holding hers.

"I had no idea, Suzy. I swear I didn't. But she's pregnant. The baby's due in June. And it's mine."

Chapter Forty

Lorraine sat in the car, looking at the house across the road. A horrible little house. She couldn't imagine why Audrey had bothered buying it in the first place.

And now she was about to lose it.

Served her right for buying a place she couldn't afford.

But Lorraine could.

The question was whether or not she wanted it. And whether it would make things better if she bought it.

It certainly couldn't make them any worse.

It had been a really horrible month.

She hadn't believed at first that David would leave. He loved the house, she was sure of that. But he'd meant what he said, and when she refused to move without him, he said he couldn't stay.

Which was rubbish. There was nothing to stop him staying but he was being ridiculous about everything, as usual.

And now he said he was missing the children and wanted to move back in – which meant she'd have to leave, he said. Until she "came to her senses", anyway.

It wasn't fair that every single one of them was against her.

They were all jealous of the money, that had to be it. Winning the lottery certainly hadn't made things better for her. They'd been fine before. She'd had a house and a family, and now, when she could have a dozen houses, the family had all turned their backs on her.

And she missed them.

She missed David, she missed her brothers and sisters, she even missed Gavin and Amber for the few hours they were with Joan every morning.

She'd begun taking them to the park herself in the afternoons, first one or two days a week, and then every day as the weather got better.

And to her amazement, she'd even begun to enjoy it. The children were getting used to her because she was with them so much, and most of the time they even did what she wanted them to.

And she'd found a house in Terenure that was even better than the one in Eaton Square. If she wanted to she could be living there by early June.

But she didn't want to.

Without David, there wasn't much point.

There was no pleasure any more in looking at furniture or getting paint charts when she wasn't even sure where she might be living next month.

Which made her, for the first time, feel some kind of sympathy for Audrey and what she must be going through.

Though Lorraine was in a much better position, of course.

At least she could buy herself a house, and Audrey couldn't.

Which was why she was sitting here outside Audrey's house, trying to get up the courage to go in.

Which was ridiculous. It was her sister's house. She should be welcome there. Especially when she was going to offer to buy the house and let Audrey and her family stay living there.

But Audrey hadn't said a word to her since the party on Christmas night. No-one had, except Joan.

And it was Joan who had kept her up to date on the situation and given her the idea in the first place.

"I don't like asking," she had said the other day. "To be honest, I don't even feel I should have to. But there you are with all that money, and Audrey hasn't a hope of finding a place. If they moved in here it would take them all day to get to work. And Rory is sitting his Junior Cert. It's the worst possible time for him to change schools –"

"If Audrey had been working all along, like I had to, I'm sure they could have paid the mortgage," Lorraine had said. "There's no point getting a job when the building society has the house up for sale – it's too late then."

"And there's no point in talking to you either, is

there, Lorraine?" Joan had said. "I really don't know why you turned out like this. All the others would give you half their heart. Maybe they're right and I spoiled you, and God knows I'm sorry if I did because we've nothing to be proud of, either of us, the way you turned out."

Lorraine had been speechless. Joan had no right to talk to her like that, even if she *was* her mother. And yet –

She had dropped the children at Joan's this morning, barely saying a word to her, still annoyed. She certainly wasn't giving her a chance to start lecturing again.

She didn't need to. What Joan had said kept repeating itself in Lorraine's head like a tape set on replay.

And there was no getting away from it. One thing was certain.

Whatever else it had done, the money hadn't brought her happiness.

She used to be happy when she had to save up for stuff. Well, now she was feeling miserable. Just like Audrey must be.

She took a deep breath, got out of the car and crossed the road to talk to her sister.

Chapter Forty-one

If it wasn't for Larry everything would be perfect, Maeve thought.

And even with Larry to deal with, things could be a hell of a lot worse. But she could have done without that particular complication when she needed to put all her energy into *Jugglers*.

The two letters had been waiting for her when she returned from Paris. Two brown envelopes. She had hesitated before opening them, going first to unpack her bags and watching the look of sheer pleasure on Orla's face as she unwrapped the St Nicholas statuette.

There *is* a God, Maeve had thought, looking at her. The change was subtle, but there was no denying it. Orla was showing every sign of turning into the kind of daughter Maeve had nearly given up hoping for.

"Do you like it?" she'd asked, handing the statuette carefully back to Maeve.

"I love it."

Orla didn't even try to hide her delight.

"We missed you," she said. "A bit, anyway!"

"The cheek of you!" Maeve laughed. "I missed you a lot."

And Orla had pulled a face and smiled at her. *Better than a smart answer any day*, Maeve had thought. *Let it last. Please let it last.*

The icing on the cake would be if both the letters had held good news, but of course they hadn't.

One out of two isn't bad, Maeve had decided. She had the go-ahead for the crèche – and a court date for the divorce proceedings.

And now, a month later, it was time to make serious plans, which was why her sisters were coming round this evening.

There were floods of enquiries about places in the crèche.

Just as well she'd finally got approval to job-share, now that they had eighteen children coming on a regular basis and several more on a waiting list. Maura and Brenda were barely managing as it was, with some help from Maura's friend Lil – and with summer coming the demand was bound to soar from working parents whose kids would be off school.

Maeve was just hanging up the phone after yet another enquiry when the doorbell rang and a moment later Orla led her aunts into the kitchen.

They said a quick "hello" and seated themselves round the table. Noeleen obviously had them warned that there was no time for chat – one look at her told Maeve that she was in business mode and wasn't about to waste a single minute.

"Tea or coffee?" Maeve asked as she moved the cups across to the table.

"Orla will get it," Noeleen said. "Won't you, O? And you sit down, Maeve – we need to get going on this." She lifted a notebook as she spoke, smiling at Orla to take the sting out of giving orders, but there was no need. They'd got on really well together while Maeve was away and Orla would stand on her head for Noeleen now without thinking twice about it.

She began making the tea and coffee without a murmur of protest while Maeve sat down with the others.

In fact, she protested about very little these days, apart from the odd outburst which was only to be expected at her age and which reassured Maeve that she was still, essentially, Orla. Life had become unbelievably easy in the Redmond household over the past few weeks, in spite of the pressures of lodgers and the crèche and trying to set up the "home management" service.

Just sort out Larry and start the job-sharing and you won't know yourself –

Noeleen interrupted her thoughts. "Okay everyone, concentrate," she ordered. "Time to work out our battle plan."

"The kids in the crèche aren't *that* bad!" Maeve laughed. "You wouldn't want to let their parents hear you!"

"It's not the kids in the crèche I'm talking about," Noeleen said, fixing her with a look. "It's that soon-to-be-ex-husband of yours!"

"I thought we were meeting to discuss the crèche." Maeve said. She really wasn't in the mood for thinking about Larry, didn't see what could be achieved at this stage by having yet another re-hash of the whole situation.

"Maeve, there won't *be* any crèche if Larry has his way," Noeleen pointed out in a reasonable tone. "The court hearing's the fifth of June, isn't it? Only two weeks away. So we need to be ready for him."

"But I don't see what we can –"

"Trust me," Noeleen said. "Now, quiet, everyone, and listen!"

She launched into her explanation of how they could deal with Larry and the only sound was the soft clatter of cups as Orla passed the tea and coffee round. Her aunts and mother took them, not even glancing at her; Noeleen had every bit of their attention.

"Now, this is important," she said. "Suppose the worse comes to the worst and the court finds in Larry's favour. Don't look like that, Maeve," she added quickly. "I've got it all worked out. Just listen and don't panic." She consulted a page of her notebook. "When you separated he got the shares Aunt Verna left you, right? And they were worth about seventy or eighty thousand?"

"Eighty," Maeve confirmed.

"And the house was valued at £250,000 – but there were the two mortgages on it, the original one and the one for the basement. You're still paying those, right?"

Maeve nodded. Too sure, she was still paying those, and without a penny from Larry.

"And now the house is worth, say, £600,000."

"Not a chance!" Maeve said. "It's not worth anything like that."

"It's worth every penny of it!" Brenda said. "You'd want to see some of the stuff we're selling these days – they're nothing like as big as this. You couldn't swing a cat in the gardens and you wouldn't believe the prices we're getting. Noeleen's right. It has to be worth at least £600,000!"

Maeve was stunned. No wonder Larry was fighting for it.

"He's right," Maeve said after a minute. "I *am* sitting on a goldmine!"

Noeleen laughed. "If you are, it's you three who are mining it! I don't see Larry lifting a finger to help." She took a sip of coffee, then looked serious again. "But unfortunately that doesn't stop him trying to get his hands on some of it."

"I can't see how he'd be entitled to a single penny more!" Brenda said hotly.

"And maybe he won't *get* a single penny more!" Noeleen's voice was firm. "But we need to be prepared, just in case. I talked to my friend Kate – you know, the solicitor – and she said much the same as Robert Shaw, that there are no guarantees of anything. But the court would more than likely take into account that he pays little or no maintenance, that Maeve is still paying a mortgage, and what the value of the shares would be now –"

"Zero," Maeve said bitterly. "The only one who got any benefit from those shares was Tom Griffin who owns Ace Racing."

The expressions round the table said it all. The money had been hard-earned by Maeve's godmother Verna and it had really been intended as an education fund for the children, not for squandering in a bookie's office.

"He got them, though," Orla said. She had been sitting at the table drinking coke, saying nothing but listening to every word. "That should count for something because he *got* them. It's not *our* fault if he was stupid enough to blow them!"

Our fault, Maeve thought. It was the first time Orla had ever given any indication that she saw Maeve's problems as hers too. For that, it was nearly worth the grief Larry was causing them.

"Orla's right," Noeleen continued. "He got them, so they'll be taken into account. So, at worst – I won't bore you with the figures but I've got them all worked out here – the very most he can lay claim to, if my sums are right, is £240,000. That's half the value of the house and shares, less the £80,000 he got already and the amount still owed on the mortgage."

She sat back, looking satisfied with herself.

There was silence for a second, then all hell broke loose.

"But how in God's name would I get that kind of money?" Maeve asked in a stunned voice when she could finally make herself heard.

"You mightn't have to," Noeleen said. "As I said, it's the very worst case scenario. He might even end up with nothing, because it *is* the family home and besides, he doesn't pay any maintenance and if I know Larry he'd prefer not to have to get into that. But you do need to be prepared, and that's why I'm looking at a figure of £240,000, because that's the worst it can possibly be."

Maeve said nothing. *I'm going to lose the house,* was all she could think. Because no way on God's earth could she find that kind of money.

She said it aloud, nearly choking on the words. "If it comes to that, I'll lose the house."

"Of course you won't lose the house," Noeleen said calmly. "You'll get another mortgage."

Maeve gave a wry laugh. "How? I can hardly keep up with the ones I have – they'll never give me any more."

"Of course they will," Noeleen insisted. "The banks and the building societies are falling over themselves to lend money at the minute, and you have a valuable asset to offer them. How much do you owe already? I estimated £40,000."

"Close enough," Maeve said. "Seventeen thousand on the house, and there's still nearly twenty thousand owed on the basement."

"So we can probably write some of that off as a business expense," Noeleen said. "Had you to spend anything else to set up the crèche?"

"Very little, so far. Insurance, heating, wages for Lil. There was very little to do to the place itself – once we had it painted we only had to get play equipment and some extra toilets. Oh, and the mural. That cost a fair bit."

But worth every penny, they had all agreed. It covered one wall of the huge room that was the main playroom and showed three clowns juggling coloured balls and, in the corner, a very harassed-looking mother juggling kids, shopping, briefcase, an iron and ironing board.

"Says it all!" was the usual comment from parents coming to collect their kids, one or two adding acidly that it would, of course, be the *mother* who was doing the juggling.

Noeleen was busy doing sums in her little notebook. Maura, who hadn't said a word since she got there, looked worried as she got up to put the kettle on again and cleared away the half-finished cups of cold tea and coffee.

"It would cost about £1,800 a month for the new mortgage," Noeleen said. "On top of what you're paying already. And I think you'll be able to manage it easily, even after paying wages and tax and your other expenses, once the crèche gets going properly. Just as long as the kids keep coming!"

"They'll keep coming all right," Maeve said. "I had six more enquiries since we said we'd open from 7 in the morning to 8 at night."

"Then you're home and dry! And you could increase the numbers if you got someone else in to help," Noeleen said. "But it's a hell of a long day, isn't it?"

"It'll be worth it. Anything, to keep the house. You're sure about the figures?"

Noeleen nodded. "As sure as I can be. You've no overheads at all except heating, insurance and wages, and you're taking in the best part of £7,000 per month –"

Brenda whistled.

"How much does she pay you?" Noeleen asked, grinning.

Maeve had the grace to look a bit embarrassed. "Nothing so far, it's all in an account. That's what I thought this meeting would be about, sorting out what I owe Maura and Bren. They wouldn't take a penny –"

Brenda laughed. "Only because we didn't know that Larry was right and you're coining it in!"

"Simple arithmetic!" Noeleen said.

"Easy for you to say." Maura was smiling. She was sitting down again, having put fresh tea and coffee and some biscuits in front of everyone, and was looking greatly relieved since she heard how much money the crèche was making. "You try looking after eighteen kids all day – you won't know your own name, let alone how to add up!"

The others were beginning to look relieved, too –

this time, they were relaxed enough to start drinking the tea and coffee instead of just letting it go cold in front of them.

"But it's working okay, isn't it?" Noeleen asked after a minute. "You haven't taken on too much, have you, between the "home management" bit and everything?"

"We're doing fine," Maura said. "The home management isn't bringing in much so far but it'll be grand once we have it up and running. We've a couple of people who pay extra now for us to drop the kids home and have a dinner going when they get there and a bit of shopping done for them –"

"But how do you find time for all that?"

"We don't," Brenda explained. "We've an arrangement with a couple of the Mums who don't go out to work but like to leave their kids at the crèche anyway so they can mix with other kids. They pay us a few quid for looking after their kids, they get paid a good bit more for doing the home back-up stuff and everyone's happy! And then there's Phyllis, she looks after the ironing service –"

"What does that do to my figures?" Noeleen asked, horrified. "How many of the eighteen kids –"

"Only two," Maura said quickly. "We're getting paid full whack for all the others. Phyllis hasn't any kids but she loves ironing and loves the company. She says it's better than staying at home any day. And she's right. There's a great buzz in the place. It's like being at home with all your friends calling in, bringing their kids with them –"

"God forbid!" Noeleen said. Not for the first time she resolved not to have any kids, ever. "And whose is the ironing – or should I ask?"

"People leave in their laundry when they drop the kids in the morning, and pick it up in the evening. Phyllis spends all day doing it and swears she loves every minute, and we get half and she gets half of what they pay."

"A bit unfair on Phyllis, isn't it?" Noeleen asked.

"She wants the company," Maura reminded her. "And we give her a place to iron and people to do it for. She says she wouldn't dream of doing it in her own home."

"Well, if it works –"

"It works," Maeve said firmly. "And it brings in a few bob, and there are four people paying us to hold keys for them in case the alarm goes off while they're at work, or the plumber needs to get in or something."

"And people pay you for that?" Noeleen asked, surprised.

"Sure," Maeve said. "A lot of people don't have anyone to do those kinds of things for them any more. Neighbours and families used to but everyone's out at work these days. So they're delighted to have our back-up service – it makes their lives easier and they're willing to pay for it. Not much, but it all adds up –"

"Well, keep it adding up!" Noeleen said, laughing. "You'll manage the mortgage, Maeve. Even when you're job-sharing and down to half your salary and paying Bren and Maura –"

The two of them interrupted immediately, saying they didn't expect to be paid, they were happy to do it to help Maeve keep the house.

Noeleen raised a hand, silencing them. "Fair's fair. You'll be happier in the long run if you get something out of it too, and I'm certain there'll be enough money to cover everything – especially if you don't have to pay Larry that much," she said, turning to Maeve. "But even if you do, you'll manage. You still have the lodgers, that's another six hundred a month, isn't it? You'll be fine."

"I'll be fine," Maeve said. "Just as long as the bank agrees with your figures. I really couldn't bear to lose the house. I don't know what I'd do."

"You'll keep the house," Maura said firmly. "If you can't get a mortgage I'll sell up my own place, give you the money and move in here. The lads would love it."

"Maura, you couldn't do that!"

"Course I could," Maura said, leaning back in the chair and folding her arms, a big smile on her face. "I was thinking about it as a possibility and I decided for definite a few minutes ago, when Noeleen was running rings around us with figures and I was beginning to get into a panic. My house must be worth well over two hundred thousand, and I'd sell up tomorrow if it meant you could keep this one. That's if we could put up with living with each other!" she said, laughing. "I'd sleep in the attic if I had to, or double up in your room – whatever it took, just as long as you could pay off that fella and be rid of him!"

There were tears in Maeve's eyes as she reached for Maura's hand. "You'd give up your house? You'd do that?"

"I love it here," Maura said. "And so do the kids – and I'm having the time of my life since the crèche got going."

"I still wouldn't dream of letting you sell your house –"

Maura gave Maeve's hand a squeeze. "You know I'd do that and more, if I had to," she said softly. "We all would."

Noeleen and Brenda nodded. Not for the first time Maeve thanked God for her sisters.

"The trouble is, I still wouldn't be rid of him, would I?" she asked quietly. "He's still the kids' father. He'll have to be some part of our lives."

"No, you'll never be rid of him entirely," Noeleen agreed. "But the sooner you get this divorce and get the money sorted out, the better. Then maybe you can start getting on with the rest of your life."

Chapter Forty-two

There was a slight breeze blowing in the graveyard, stirring the leaves of the horse chestnut that stood in the shadow of the wall.

The priest recited a prayer, bent to take a handful of earth and sprinkled it on the coffin. Then the gravediggers took up their spades to finish the task.

Olivia left the graveside and began making her way down the narrow path with her brothers, their wives and children, and the rest of the mourners.

"You'll come back to the house?" Raymond asked anxiously.

"For a short while," Olivia agreed. "My flight is at five."

He nodded, turning to accept condolences from someone who tapped him on the arm.

For a moment she was alone in the crowd, and then someone approached her. Mrs Madigan, a woman

Olivia had never liked, who lived on her mother's road.

"You killed your poor mother. You know that, don't you?" she hissed, her eyes close to Olivia's, her stale breath on Olivia's face. "Leaving her alone like that, you should be ashamed of yourself!"

Olivia turned quickly from her, taking a deep breath. She had heard the same thing muttered several times in the church by some of the women who clustered there, scowling their disapproval at her.

They would just have to disapprove. Her mother's death had been a huge shock, but she would *not* let herself feel guilty. She had done the best she could. Letting herself feel guilty now, or upset by what those women were implying, would destroy everything she had worked hard to create for herself.

She moved quickly along the path, hoping to avoid further confrontations.

"Olive," a voice said quietly as someone fell into step beside her.

She turned to look into the unfamiliar, familiar face and the eyes she would have known anywhere.

He was older, of course. Fifty-five now, she calculated. Tall and spare, dressed in a dark suit, his hair greying but still full and curling on his forehead as it used to.

Her fingers moved, wanting to reach out and brush it back.

Instead she smiled, offering him her hand. "Richard."

"I'm sorry about your mother," he said, shaking her hand firmly, briefly.

"Thank you."

He stood, seeming uncertain what to say. He had aged well, she thought, then stopped herself. She should be thinking of nothing but her mother now – as she had thought of nothing but her mother since Raymond phoned two days ago to say she had passed away. "Peacefully," he kept repeating. "She passed away peacefully."

It hadn't been peaceful for Olivia. All day and all night she had cried her eyes out, raging at the waste of it, the loss, the unfairness of it all. A little girl, crying for the mother who had never loved or appreciated her.

And then, just as suddenly, it was over, and with dry eyes she made her way to the airport, and through the funeral, and stood here now with Richard as calmly as if she had met him by chance.

"How did you hear?" she asked.

"My sister. She saw it in the paper and rang me. I'm living in London. Did you know?"

"No. I asked, a long time ago, but she wouldn't tell me."

He grimaced.

"I told her not to give out my address. I didn't mean –"

"Did you ever get to India?"

He laughed quietly. "No. Not then, anyway. I finally went two years ago."

"Why didn't you go before?"

"I got as far as London and lost my nerve. I ended up getting a job in an import-export business there."

461

"You could have come back."

"After all my talk? No, I couldn't come back. So I stayed on, worked my way up and ended up owning the place. Maybe it worked out for the best, I don't know. Besides –" He looked away, concentrating on the gravel on the path. "There was nothing to come back for. Was there?"

They walked in silence down the path. Several people came over to sympathise with her, some of them glancing at Richard, one or two looking a second time as if they recognised him.

"I should have gone with you."

He didn't answer. She wondered if he'd even heard her over the quiet hum of voices round them.

"Are you married?" she asked finally, as they neared the gate.

"Divorced. A long time ago."

People were beginning to get into cars. She could hear someone calling her name.

"Look, I know it's not the time or place," Richard said quickly. "But, well, I get to Dublin often. Maybe –"

"I live in Paris now."

His eyes widened. "Paris? Why Paris? I mean, are you –"

She shook her head.

"I do a lot of travelling," he said. "I'm in Paris at least once a month. Do you think –"

"I'll give you my number." Quickly she took a pen and some paper from her bag and scribbled something.

"Olive, we're going."

Vincent's voice, sounding annoyed.

"Go ahead. I'll catch up." She handed Richard the scrap of paper.

"Olivia?" he asked, looking at it.

"That's my name now," she said simply.

"Olivia," he repeated, smiling. "I like it. It suits you."

Her heart lifted and she turned to go through the gate to where the cars were parked.

Vincent and Raymond had both left. She glanced round. There were plenty of others she knew here. She'd easily get a lift.

"Olivia!"

Maeve's voice.

She turned, searching. Maeve was standing by a small red car, waving.

"Do you need a lift?" she asked as Olivia reached the car.

"Please," Olivia said. "I'm really not up to making small talk with relatives I haven't seen in years. I'd much prefer to go with you, if that's all right."

"Sure." Maeve opened the back door and Olivia sat in. Colette, in the driver's seat, turned to her.

"I'm sorry –"

"Don't be." She saw Colette's face. "I know. That sounds awful, doesn't it? I didn't mean it like that. But she wasn't a very happy woman."

"Where do you want to go?"

"Sundrive Road. I'll give you directions."

"Sundrive Road". Not *"home"*. Not even *"my mother's house"*. It hadn't been her mother's house for a very long time. And home was Paris now.

"You're sure you don't mind?" Olivia asked. "It's miles out of your way – unless you'll come in?"

"Maybe for a few minutes," Colette said. "I'm afraid we didn't make the funeral itself."

"We came straight from the court," Maeve added. "Colette came with myself and Brenda, for moral support."

"And?" Olivia wasn't quite sure she should ask, but Maeve looked happy enough.

"Adjourned," Maeve answered. "Wouldn't you know? Seems he's gone into some kind of treatment programme."

"And will it work, do you think?" Olivia asked.

Maeve shrugged. "Who knows? I mean, people don't really change, do they?"

And then they all realised what she'd said.

They were still laughing when they pulled up outside the house on Sundrive Road.

Chapter Forty-three

"Looks like we could be celebrating on our own!" Colette said, glancing towards the door. It was the twentieth of June, just after 12.30, and they were sitting in Peacock Alley, a bottle of champagne on ice beside them, waiting to see who would come.

"At least I've something to celebrate this time!" Maeve said.

"I know, it's amazing, isn't it?" Colette said. "Even without the money, you've changed more than anyone."

Maeve laughed. "I wouldn't exactly say that. But the lottery did something for me as well, didn't it? A kind of wake-up call. If you hadn't all left, I wouldn't have been feeling so sorry for myself last Christmas and I'd never have got the idea for the crèche, or anything else!"

"You're definitely doing the course?"

Maeve nodded. "Three whole years. I must be mad.

But I love working with kids. It's what I should have been doing all along. I just didn't know it!"

"And you think you'll stick it? Thirty-five little tinies in a classroom, day after day?"

"I'll give it a go, anyway. If I can handle them in the crèche, I can surely do it in the classroom."

"You'll manage the money? I mean, not working for three years?" They could talk about money, finally, with no embarrassment.

"Think so. The numbers in the crèche are going up all the time."

"So who'll look after them? You'll need someone else to replace you."

"Maura has someone lined up. I won't be in college all the time, anyway. I'll be off for all the holidays and that's when I'll really be needed. And we'll manage the money somehow – it's just a question of choices."

Colette smiled. "That's what it's all about, isn't it? Not money at all. Choices."

"Money helps," Maeve said. "But you're right. We all make choices. We just don't realise it sometimes."

"Any word of Larry?"

"Still on that programme. At least he's sticking it. We'll see."

"Do you think you'd ever –"

"Not a chance. I want things to work out for him, Colette, and I want the divorce sorted so I'll know where I stand. And maybe we can even be friends sometime, for the kids. But that's as far as it goes." She smiled. "Just because you're doing the happy-ever-after bit –"

"Oh, it's not all sweetness and light, let me tell you –" Colette laughed.

"But it's okay?"

"Better than okay. Martin and I are talking. I mean, really talking. He told me the other night that he's fed up in work, he has been for years, and it's only when I gave it up myself that he realised how hard he was finding it. He envied me being able to stay at home and all that kept him going was the excitement of the money and the buzz he got from being able to splash out on things."

"God, that sounds fairly awful! And can he do something about it?" Maeve asked. "I mean, get another job or something?"

"I'm not sure. Maybe. There's still plenty of money left. He could re-train if he finds something he's interested in."

"What are the chances? Is there anything –"

"He's looked at about twenty different things so far," Colette said, laughing, "and he has sound reasons for not picking any of them. We'll see. The main thing is, we're happy again, we're talking, we've started going out a bit in the evenings. And the kids are acting like civilised human beings and even my mother-in-law is finally showing a bit of cop-on. She complimented my cooking the other night and I nearly choked with the shock!"

Maeve laughed. "Sounds like you're getting places!"

"Private party, or can anyone join in?"

"Suzanne!" Colette said, turning.

"Brilliant!" Maeve said. "We weren't sure you'd make it – Val said you were away."

Suzanne nodded. "That's why I wasn't at the funeral. But I wouldn't have missed this for the world." She sat down. She looked great, with a big smile and a glowing tan. "Even if I *did* have to drag myself back from Morocco!"

"Lucky you."

The smile wavered a bit. "Not so lucky. I had to get away for a while."

"Everything okay?" Maeve asked cautiously.

"It is now," Suzanne said. She picked up the menu, playing for time.

"I might as well tell you," she said after a minute. "Val will probably let it slip, anyway. You remember Finn and I split up around the time we won the lottery?"

They nodded.

"Well, he met somebody. Met her again, really – he knew her from college. They went out a few times. And – well –" she took a deep breath, "she's just had his baby. A little girl."

The glass Colette was holding slipped, sloshing water onto the tablecloth. "Oh, Suzanne!"

There was a pause as they all sat looking at each other.

"And – what happens now?" Maeve asked finally.

Suzanne gave a little sigh. "I'll have to see. We're still together. I just had to get away so he could be with her and I wouldn't have to think about it."

"Easier said than done," Colette said.

"Tell me about it! The irony is that the night he told me, I'd gone there to tell him I'd marry him. Finally, I made up my mind – and look what happens! Good enough for me."

"So how come you're still together, if –" Maeve began.

"Because neither of them wants anything permanent. They were just good friends. Finn said it shouldn't have happened. It just – did. They'll have a lot of contact because of the baby, but that's it. They don't want to be together – and I want to be with him."

"And can you handle that?" Colette asked. "That he'll be in contact with her?"

Suzanne shrugged, then smiled slightly. "I'll have to, won't I?"

"Complicated," Maeve said.

"Sure. But life's complicated. I thought it would be plain sailing when we won the money but it's not, is it?"

"No, it's not," Colette said.

"Because it's not about money at all, is it?" Suzanne said. "It's about choices."

"We've just said that!" Colette exclaimed.

"Choices – let's drink to that!" Maeve said. "Looks like Olivia won't be here, so we might as well go ahead –"

"There she is!" Colette said, as the door opened.

They waved, and she came across and took the one remaining chair.

"So we're not expecting Lorraine?" she asked.

The others grimaced.

"What do you think?" Maeve asked.

"I know, silly question. I'm delighted the rest of you are here."

She turned to Suzanne, took her hand. "Thank you for your card."

"I would have been there, but –"

"Don't worry."

"Are you okay?" Suzanne asked quietly.

Olivia nodded. "I am, now. The floodgates opened for a few days but now it's over. You know how things were between us, so I think I was crying more for what might have been."

"We weren't sure you'd make it," Colette said. "I mean, you've only just gone back, and with Ellie leaving –"

"She doesn't go until the end of the month. I've already made plans to visit her in Montreal, probably in September."

"You were still very good to come back," Maeve said.

"You think I'd have missed this?" Olivia smiled. "Besides, I wouldn't have been in Paris anyway. I'm due in London tonight."

"Anything exciting?" Colette asked.

"I'm meeting a friend."

Suzanne was looking at her closely. There was something about her expression –

470

"Olivia, this friend wouldn't by any chance be a man, would he?" Suzanne's eyes were sparkling and her smile had more than a touch of her usual exuberance.

"What makes you think that?" Olivia asked. But she was struggling to keep a straight face, and they started bombarding her with questions.

"Wait! Stop, this definitely calls for champagne!" Suzanne said, signalling the waiter, who opened the chilled bottle and began to pour.

"It's only for dinner –" Olivia protested.

"That's good enough! Any excuse!" Suzanne said, laughing.

And then they're all talking together, watching the fizzy liquid dance into the glasses, lifting the glasses, toasting each other, still talking, laughing, and nobody notices as the door opens again.

"You could at least have kept a place for me."

They look up at her, startled, pleased, as the waiter quickly brings another chair.

She's still Lorraine.

She'll probably count out the pennies for her share of the bill.

But she's there. And she's smiling.

It's a start.

THE END